NAVEGATOR

NAV*e*GATOR

Geoffrey Iley

For Eileen with best wishes from Geoffrey Iley

Book Guild Publishing

Sussex, England

First published in Great Britain in 2012 by
The Book Guild Ltd
Pavilion View
19 New Road
Brighton, BN1 1UF

Typesetting in Baskerville by
Norman Tilley Graphics Ltd, Northampton

Printed in Great Britain by
CPI Group (UK) Ltd, Croydon, CR0 4YY

A catalogue record for this book is available from
The British Library

ISBN 978 1 84624 663 0

... there was some special spirit abroad in the late fourteenth and fifteenth centuries ... in the mentalities of navigators ... the modest heroes who conquered the only new frontier ... a zone of navigation ... in previously uncharted waters, bound by the Azores in the north, the Canaries in the south and the Iberian and African coasts in the east. Most were 'unknown pilots'. Many known by name are recorded only or chiefly on maps ... They came, to begin with, mainly from Majorca and Genoa, homes of the art of the 'conners of the sea', and – later and increasingly – from Portugal and Andalusia ... In the map of the Atlantic made by Gabriel Vallseca in 1439, the ... treatment of the Azores ... (shows the islands) strung out in clusters from the south-east to the north-west, just as they would (appear) to a conscious explorer unequipped with means of verifying his position on the open sea but determined to rough out bearings that would help find them again.

Extract from *Millennium,* by Felipe Fernández-Armesto

To Loïs, with love and thanks

Author's note

The largest of the Spanish Balearic Islands, Mallorca, has a strategic position in the western Mediterranean. The local language, Mallorquin, is still widely spoken and is related to Catalan; it is quite different from Castilian, which is now the official language of Spain.

A Mallorcan navigator made the first map of the Azores in 1439; his name was Gabriel Valseca. He would have learned his craft at the world's earliest school of navigation in the capital, Palma. The idea that his genius could be inherited by future generations has inspired this fictional story. However, the people and events portrayed are not based on any real-life persons or happenings. Many of the places described really do (or did) exist; a few have had their names changed; others are figments of the imagination.

Acknowledgements

I offer sincere thanks to so many people who have helped with corrections, suggestions and local or expert knowledge. Special mention must be made of the assistance given by Anna Skidmore of Foment del Turisme de Mallorca, also by former Moscow resident Ekkehard Schirrmacher and Professor Joan-Miquel Fiol of the Universitat de les Illes Baleares, Palma. The staff of the Institute of Catalan Studies at the University of Sheffield and Humphrey Carter of the *Majorca Daily Bulletin* were also particularly helpful.

A huge debt of gratitude is also richly deserved by my wife Loïs – not least for introducing me to Mallorca – and by other family members, especially my daughter Paula for diligent proofreading, perceptive insights and constructive criticism; also my stepson Simon Parkes and his wife Rosaura, not forgetting my cousin Jill Teltscher and her husband Werner. All of them urged me to stop hanging about and get on with it. Their support was immensely encouraging.

Geoffrey Iley
Towcester
January 2011

Prologue

Sunday, 15 June 1969 – Mallorca

Doctor Carbonell heard the distant roar of the Land Rover's engine. He called softly to the housekeeper, Antonia, and together they tiptoed from the darkened bedroom. There, two small cots were set side by side near the window, away from the motionless shape beneath a white sheet on the big oak bed in the centre of the room.

At the main door of the long stone house the doctor and the housekeeper stood together as the Land Rover tore up the drive and skidded to a standstill in a hail of gravel.

Vasco Valseca jumped out, followed more slowly by Guillem, Antonia's husband. Vasco rushed up to the silent couple in the archway. The doctor, a little older than Vasco, thin, pale and serious alongside Antonia, who had tears running down her rosy cheeks. Bonnie and Clyde, the golden Labrador retrievers who would normally have given their master a noisy greeting, came towards him with their tails drooping and slumped to the ground at his feet.

Vasco gripped the doctor's hand.

'Guillem met me at the port but I can get no sense out of him. For God's sake, Carles, tell me what's happened.'

'This is dreadful news, Vasco, I hardly know how to tell you.'

He took a deep breath and went on.

'It was an accident. Just after four o'clock, after her siesta, Joana came downstairs for tea on a tray in the drawing room. She must have climbed on a chair to reach a book

1

from a high shelf, then overbalanced and couldn't save herself. It was a very bad fall. She hit her head on the corner of the table beside her chair. Antonia heard the crash and called me at once. I came immediately, but there was nothing I could do. By the time the ambulance arrived it was too late.'

Vasco started to speak, but the doctor held up his hand and clasped his friend's shoulder.

'You must hear the rest. As you know, Joana had been wonderfully healthy during her pregnancy. A normal delivery was expected soon. Just before she died she gave birth to twins. At least you will have two fine children to remind you of her, a boy and a girl.'

Vasco froze. He opened his mouth, but no words came. The housekeeper looked up at him, her eyes brimming.

'We did everything we could, Senyor, but it was hopeless. It's very hard, but you must think about the babies. Please let me look after them for you.'

Without a word, Vasco strode past them into the house and ran up the staircase. He strode along the gallery to the master bedroom, only pausing to shut the door carefully behind him. There was a long silence, except for some faint whimpering noises from the twins. Guillem, who had followed the others into the house, looked up anxiously towards the bedroom. Then he turned to the doctor, but he raised his hand and shook his head. After ten minutes or so, which seemed like an eternity, Vasco opened the door and came slowly down the staircase, clinging onto the handrail like a man exhausted by a long journey. Finally, he looked up at the silent group.

'I've lost Joana.'

He lowered his head, paused and swallowed before looking up again.

'If I hadn't gone off on this sailing trip then I'd have been here to reach that book for her. It's all my fault.

2

She's dead and I'm the one to blame.'

He took a deep, shuddering breath.

'I just can't deal with this situation tonight. It's too much to bear so suddenly.'

He paused and swallowed again.

'Yes, Antonia, please look after the babies. We'll talk again in the morning when I've had time to think. For now, please leave me. I must have some time completely alone.'

He stumbled into his study and slammed the door. The doctor spoke softly to Antonia. Together they went up to the bedroom. Gently they collected the twins and took them to Guillem and Antonia's apartment at the end of the house. Guillem stood at the foot of the stairs twisting his cap in his hands, tears running down his weather-beaten face.

About two hours later, Antonia tiptoed to the bedroom to place flowers at the feet of Joana Valseca, but just before her hand reached the door handle, Antonia heard a faint sound and stopped. Through the heavy panelling she could make out despairing words and broken sobs. She stood stock still and, after a moment, moved away silently to keep her vigil with the twins.

Next morning, after a disturbed night, Guillem went out early to see to the horses. When he came back to the house he found Vasco sitting on the terrace looking out across the fields towards the mountains. He hadn't shaved and looked as though he had spent the night in his clothes. His sunken eyes emphasised the misery etched on his face.

'Senyor, can I ask Antonia to bring you something?'

'Thank you, just some coffee – and I'd like to talk to you both.'

Guillem went to the kitchen, leaving Vasco staring into the distance.

A few minutes later, they returned with a tray: coffee, rolls and local honey. They stood awkwardly as Vasco sipped his coffee. Finally he turned to face them. It was obvious that he'd spent the night making hard decisions. Normally he was very relaxed with Antonia and Guillem, but now it was difficult for him to control his emotions, so that he seemed unnaturally stiff and formal.

'I've had a few hours to think about this tragedy. First I must thank you both for your help and for your loyalty, which means a great deal to me. Thank you again, Antonia, for looking after the babies. Please go on giving them your love and care.

'Last night I said that Joana's fall was all my fault and now, this morning, I'm even more sure that I'm the guilty one. My selfish pursuit of my own interests has blinded me to the really important things in life. So, I must do penance, rubbing salt in the wound to remind me of my obsession with navigation and my pride in my seafaring ancestors. I'm going to do this through the names I've chosen for the twins. That way, they'll be a constant reminder of this terrible day. The boy will be called after my ancestor Gabriel Valseca, the navigator who first charted the Azores. The girl will be named Isabel, after the Queen of Castile who sent out Columbus on his fateful expedition.

He paused and took a deep breath.

'I'm very grateful to both of you for all the support you're giving me. But you must excuse me if I shut myself away for a while. I've lots of things to do and arrangements to make. I expect to be on the phone for several hours, so don't bother about meals or anything else till I call you.'

Vasco turned, picked up his coffee cup and drained it. Although he tried to be careful, it rattled against the saucer as he set it down. He called softly to the dogs curled up at his feet and they followed him, tails drooping, as he moved along the terrace like a sleepwalker and went back into the house. Antonia shook her head sadly at Guillem as they heard the distant slam of the study door.

4

1

It was a dark, grey, miserable morning. A biting wind swirled around the Pentagon building, carrying a penetrating drizzle which drenched the roadway. A charcoal-grey limousine with dipped headlights slowed, stopping at the entrance gate. Security was rigorous and it took a while to get clearance for the Cadillac to move forward. Finally it pulled up beside the southern entrance. A lean, grizzled officer in a US Navy greatcoat limped as he was helped from his seat by a smartly dressed black driver, who handed him a battered briefcase. Admiral Jethro Hobring, known to everyone as Hobnails, nodded his thanks.

'Don't wait around, Moreton. This feels like it's going to be a helluva long day. I'll have Charlene call you when it looks like the meeting is going to break – and I'll be needing you to take me to the White House directly afterwards. The President wants a personal briefing, dammit!'

'Yessir. Are you still going on vacation tomorrow, Admiral? I'll be on standby for that early flight you mentioned.'

'The way things are looking, son, I just don't know when I'll be getting any vacation at all. But I guess tomorrow's trip is definitely off.'

The admiral turned and headed for the armoured doors, his jaw clenched as he forced his twisted leg to hurry him to the conference room. He needed this assignment like a hole in the head. A long-serving veteran with a lifetime in communications and surveillance, he had been seriously injured in a helicopter crash in Vietnam and was looking forward to retirement. Why couldn't they get one of their young hotshots to come up with the answers on this one? When he swung open the door to the spacious, walnut-panelled conference room with its long oval table, he had the answer to his own question.

There were almost thirty people standing up and talking loudly. Most were younger than twenty-five, with not one older than thirty. Many were women, and under half the group wore uniform, with the civilians dressed in anything from Armani suits to bib and brace coveralls and fatigues. The veteran paused in the doorway almost deafened by the noise. Then somewhere a voice called out:

'Jesus, it's Hobnails!'

The chatter quickly subsided into silence.

'My name is Admiral Jethro Hobring,' he barked. 'You will have the courtesy to address me as Admiral. Kindly take your seats and speak when spoken to. Is that clear?'

There was a hubbub as the crowd found places, mainly close to colleagues and acquaintances. Hobnails handed his greatcoat and cap to an orderly, who hung it on a rack at the side of the room and left quietly, gently closing the door behind him.

The admiral frowned sternly at the motley group before taking the chair at the centre of one of the long sides of the large oval conference table. At last there was quiet. He opened his briefcase, sliding out a slim grey folder. Running his fingers through his close-cropped white hair, he cleared his throat, looked sourly at the array of faces and adjusted his glasses.

'We are here because of what happened almost a week ago. I hardly need to remind you of what took place last Friday, February 26 1993. That will be a historic date, for sure. Thank God, the terrorist attack on the World Trade

Center didn't cause major damage and failed to bring down the twin towers. But it was a miracle that we didn't have a terrible catastrophe on our hands.'

'Our security services are moving quickly to prevent anything like that happening again. All of us around this table are to be a vital part of building a stronger, more effective defence against another terrorist attack. All of our intelligence techniques are under review right now as a matter of extreme urgency. Naturally, long-standing activities for monitoring hostile groups are being strengthened, but emerging technologies dictate that we must be particularly vigilant in two areas.'

'First, consider the cell phone. That's becoming a lot more commonplace now ... two years ago, they were just beginning to come into widespread use. Now, I guess almost all of you in this room have one. Our people have to get a lot smarter in figuring out ways to monitor and disrupt cell phone conversations between people who wish our country harm. We know about other ways to misuse this developing communication technology – for example, a cell phone can be used for remote detonation of an explosive device. And we've just heard that some guys in Finland have succeeded in sending a text message between two cell phones. That may sound a stupid thing to do and it's hard to see how anyone could make any money out of such an oddball idea – but if there is any possibility of terrorists finding a way to use that capability, then our people have to understand it.'

Admiral Hobring paused and consulted his notes. His eager listeners were looking forward to having some fun with cell phones. He looked up and went on.

'Unfortunately, people, we didn't get the chance to play with cell phones. We were assigned the second task and it seems we've drawn the short straw – our assignment is the World Wide Web. We have to find a way to operate globally so we can identify potential threats to our security. There's

7

just been a near disaster at the World Trade Center. If only there had been a greater ability to intercept and monitor all kinds of internet activity, then this plot might have been nipped in the bud. The terrorists behind this cowardly attack would have been arrested before they could strike.'

He paused and cleared his throat. A young man in fatigues stifled a sneeze.

'So, now you'll begin to understand the nature of our special task which is so vital to the security of the United States. I didn't want this assignment, but I shall run it to the best of my ability. My job, God help me, is to lead you bunch of misfits in an exercise which is going to tax the intellect and stamina of every one of us. Although I may have given you a hint just now, none of you has been told exactly what our mission is. I'm about to do that, and I must remind each one of you that our operation is subject to the highest level of security classification.'

There was a subdued murmur as he opened the folder and began to read.

'"By direction of the President of the United States of America, the Supreme Command, acting in partnership with the Central Intelligence Agency, is required to set up a Task Force with responsibility for tackling electronic terrorism. Specifically it will be mandated to develop, commission and implement a secure electronic system."

"The first objective of this system will be to provide, instantly, the precise geographical location of the source of any email with links to electronic terrorism and, additionally, the origin of any virus or hacking activity, at the moment it is initiated."

"The secondary objective is to permit the immediate targeting of any such source, so that it can be eliminated should National Security so dictate. This project will be codenamed Operation Sniper and the initial financial allocation will be twenty million dollars."'

There was a sharp intake of breath from the eager young people at the table. Quelling the excited buzz, Hobnails held up his hand for silence and looked around at the expectant faces.

'Which of you is Gabriel Valseca?'

A slim, dark young man in fatigues raised his hand. A ghost of a smile creased the craggy features.

'Son, you just got lucky,' he growled. 'You're going to be my Personal Assistant.'

Gabriel Valseca looked startled and raised his eyes to meet the admiral's.

'Your CIA bosses at Langley give you very high praise,' the admiral went on, 'and that's something that doesn't happen every day of the week. So, in addition to being my personal aide you've got Communications. That means knowing where everyone in this room is at any and every hour of the day and night. You'll need to arrange secure means of contact between all of us at all times – and you get to take minutes of meetings and prepare draft interim and final reports. Your deputy will be Rachel Jefferson. Put your hand up please, Rachel. Any questions?'

Rachel, an attractive African-American woman in Air Force uniform raised her hand. She exchanged an enquiring glance with Gabriel Valseca, then they both shook their heads. The admiral cleared his throat and continued.

'Now here's a little more background information relating to Sniper. Theoretically, it should be possible to monitor a huge amount of email traffic. Programs are in place – or under development – to do just that. But, even if suspicious messages are detected, there's no knowing where they come from. We all know about the damage hackers can do to electronic communications. The banks and the savings and loan corporations have been a tad secretive about the extent of losses they've suffered through electronic fraud. The US government has suffered too, and it has gotten to the point where National Security could be compromised, especially by electronic terrorist activity launched by al-Qaeda or other radical groups.'

'Fact is,' he chuckled grimly, 'we've already had a few heavyweight incidents that I'm not allowed to tell you about. Computer viruses are a potentially deadly problem too, despite the sophisticated anti-virus programs available commercially – and some even more exotic ones which are classified. Some of you may have heard about the costly havoc resulting from the "Satanbug" virus. Well, that was only one of many and it was just the tip of the iceberg. There's a whole raft of new ones out there and we have to do something to get to them – or, to be more precise, to get to the guys who create them – before we have a real live disaster on our hands. And it could be a big one. Clear so far?'

There was a sharp intake of breath around the table and heads nodded. An Army captain looked as though he was about to speak, but thought better of it. It was better to wait for Hobnails to invite comments. Everyone knew that.

Drawing out a bulky green folder, the admiral went on.

'Now to administration. Gabriel and Rachel have another immediate task, which is to assign accommodation to individuals and working space for the specialist teams. You should all know that you were hand-picked for this job. Or, to be more precise,' he chuckled, 'the computer picked you and I second-guessed it. The reason all of you are here is because of particular skills or experience which might be helpful for this task. A complete floor at the Watergate Complex is held permanently available for special assignments like this one. Today it's been requisitioned exclusively for our group to work, sleep, eat and relax – if there's ever any time for that. The bad news is that this activity will be going on seven days a week.'

He looked up at the glum expressions on the faces

around the table. He adjusted his glasses and frowned as he consulted his notes.

'A security team has already secured the whole facility following an inch by inch electronic scan of our floor. You were all asked to come here with your overnight gear, so there's no need to leave our own secure facilities. We've got ways to obtain anything that individuals may require. But if anyone has a particular need to go out, then they must clear it with Gabriel or Rachel. And the reason would definitely have to be compassionate. I'm asking them to keep a register of who goes in and out, and why. And don't forget to check in again when you return.

'All of you will move into your quarters tonight, so don't leave this room without getting your room assignments from Gabriel and Rachel. There will be a computer bureau for monitored use – he consulted a list – and Constance Ginsberg will be in charge; naturally, any private emails will be routed via the departments who assigned you here. There will be no outgoing emails at all, unless previously cleared by Gabriel or Rachel here and countersigned by me personally. Internet access is denied, but there will be super-vised links to powerful computing facilities at NASA and some universities.

'Those of you who have brought cell phones will naturally be required to hand them over for the duration of this assignment. Telephones are installed throughout our facility, but these are for internal calls only within this team, plus a direct link to my office here in the Pentagon. There is one phone – and only one – which you can use for external calls, next to our security checkpoint over at Watergate. It's strictly for essential use only and all conver-sations will be monitored and recorded. Is that clear? Do you all accept what I've been saying?'

Heads nodded around the table.

'That's understood then,' he said, passing the folder

across the table to Gabriel. He paused and consulted his notes.

'Financial control will be with Gina Zito. She will issue you all with the necessary documentation to track the costs on this operation.'

A brunette with fierce horn-rimmed glasses raised her chin and smiled at nobody in particular.

And so it went on and on, with individuals – or small teams and team leaders – assigned to Strategy, Computer Science, Computer Development, Mathematics, Navigation, Lateral Thinking and Administration. Finally, Hobnails came to the end of the list.

'Now we're going to take a little time out for coffee and cookies. Move around if you wish and get acquainted. I'm going to leave you for a short while, but when I come back in around thirty minutes, I want to hear some first thoughts about how we might take this thing forward.'

He pressed a buzzer under the table and almost at once two women in immaculate uniforms wheeled in a trolley with refreshments. They turned and left as the admiral struggled to his feet and limped from the room, pursued by a babble of excited conversation. He instructed Security to find him an empty office nearby. He slumped in a chair by the desk and picked up the phone. Within a couple of moments he was speaking to his own secretary in the Naval Section.

'Morning, Charlene. Any interesting messages or mail?'

He grunted a few times.

'Well, I guess all of those can wait – for a day or two anyway. Now, I've got a tough one for you.'

He cleared his throat, thought for a moment and gave a brief outline of the task which the President had assigned to the Sniper team. He paused for a moment.

'Now here's the tricky part. Although she can't be allowed to know what's happening here, Andrea thinks we're going on vacation tomorrow. She'll be getting home early this afternoon after a few days with her sister in Boston. So, there's a thorny problem. Can you please let her know that I've been given some secret orders, the trip's off and I'll most likely be home late tonight. And for God's sake break it to her gently. Thanks, hon.'

He hung up and stared gloomily at the blotter on the desk for a few moments before pulling himself up and going to see if he could find any of his friends from his time in Vietnam. He spent a few minutes trading reminiscences with a former destroyer captain who produced strong black coffee. Then he limped painfully back to the conference room after calling in at a washroom to give himself his second painkilling injection of the day.

As Hobnails re-entered the room, the buzz of conversation gradually subsided, the coffee cups were cleared and the members of Operation Sniper took their places. After settling himself in his chair, he cleared his throat and called for questions. Lieutenant Amos Stringer, a stocky man in Naval uniform and the leader of the Navigation Team, raised his hand.

'Admiral, at the risk of stating the obvious, this is not going to be easy. As I see it, there are at least two keys needed to unlock this problem – possibly more. The first, I guess, is penetrating the shield; getting past the anonymous remailer or any other electronic smoke screen that the bad guys are hiding behind. Only when that's been done is it possible to try to locate our enemy. So, would it make sense, Sir, to start with groups concentrating on those separate aspects of the problem?'

'Yes, son, I believe it does. Let's do that as a first step and see where it takes us. Now, has anyone else got any suggestions?'

Other ideas, covering a whole spectrum of possibilities and impossibilities were tossed back and forth. Hobnails was

13

getting tired despite a break for a frugal lunch, a later break for coffee, more cookies – and his third painkilling injection. It was getting towards seven o'clock and it was time to send the individual teams away to move into their accommodation at Watergate and get on with their assignments. But, just before closing the meeting he realised that the head of Strategy, Irena Constantinescu from Stanford University, had said very little for the last two hours.

'Irena, is something bothering you? You've been very quiet.'

She raised her eyes reluctantly and met his.

'Yes, Admiral, I do have some concerns. First, we speak of identifying "targets". If that means what I think it means, how is the seriousness of the threat going to be measured – and who gives the order to press the trigger, so to speak? Second, are we going to make the system we are developing available to our allies? Third, just supposing some genius in Silicon Valley or someplace developed an equivalent system first, or one that worked better than ours, then would we buy it from him or what?'

'You may think that questions like that are relevant to our mission,' growled the admiral, 'but it's for other people to grapple with those issues. It's just not our business, OK?'

He frowned and went on quickly before anyone else could speak.

'This meeting is now closed. We'll reconvene over at Watergate at two o'clock tomorrow afternoon.'

He looked at his watch.

'I have to get across to the Oval Office in about half an hour to give a personal undertaking that this show is on the road – and that success is in prospect in, say, a couple of weeks at the most. Good evening and good luck.'

With that, he shrugged on his greatcoat and hat with Gabriel's help. Then he hefted his briefcase and limped to the elevator. A few minutes later he was in the car with

Moreton, summoned by Charlene in response to another phone call made at the afternoon coffee break. Now, he had to go and brief the President, who would not enjoy being told that this job would take more than a couple of days. Then he would return home to a disappointed Andrea and a very late supper.

As the Cadillac headed towards the highway, Hobnails swore softly under his breath. It was still drizzling and the cold, damp weather always made his leg hurt even more, dammit …!

Rachel Jefferson yawned, stretched and leaned back in her chair. It was late evening and she sat alongside Gabriel Valseca at a chrome and metal desk set across the corner of the conference room where they had spent the whole day. It had taken almost an hour to hand out room allocations for the different working groups and accommodation details for every individual on the Sniper Team. There had been bickering and argument but finally everyone had been dealt with and now they were both exhausted. Gathering up their bags, they took an elevator and found a car waiting to take them to their quarters in the Watergate Complex.

When they arrived at the Sniper Team's floor at Watergate, they checked with security before heading for their own quarters to unpack.

'Why don't we meet up in twenty minutes for a drink and something to eat?' asked Gabriel as they were about to separate. 'We could get something from the commissary and take it along to our own office to relax away from these other guys'.

Rachel looked at him; a cool appraisal. After a brief pause she said:

'OK. That's no problem. I'll see you in the commissary at nine.'

Rachel arrived a few moments before Gabriel. She

nodded acknowledgement before choosing a Waldorf salad and a baked apple with yoghurt. He decided to have the southern fried chicken and fries with blueberry ice cream for dessert. They carried their trays out to the room set aside for Administration and ate hungrily.

When he had finished, Gabriel pushed his plate away.

'So, what brings you here on this assignment, Rachel?'

She wiped her mouth delicately with a paper tissue.

'Let's get one thing straight, shall we? My private life is my own business and we won't be doing ourselves any favours if we get our personal histories involved in this mission.'

Gabriel held his hands up.

'OK, OK. I'm not trying to pry. Let's finish off the rest of our jobs before we call it a day.'

They pushed their plates aside and got out the few papers needing attention, then talked about the project for a few more minutes. Eventually, after some good natured bargaining, they agreed how they would share out their individual responsibilities. Gabriel got up to fetch another cup of coffee from the machine in the lobby and a glass of water for Rachel. Then he cleared away the crockery and leaned his elbows on the table.

'Look, Rachel, I know you don't want to get personal. I accept that. But I honestly believe it would help us both to do a better job if we had some idea of each other's backgrounds. What do you say?'

Rachel gave him a hard, calculating look and frowned, thinking for a moment.

'OK, if you put it that way, I suppose there's no harm. I'll tell you my story – but I need to hear yours too – that's only fair.'

Gabriel nodded agreement. She took a sip of water, frowned again and looked down at the table, long black hair framing her oval face.

'Well it's quite a long story. I was raised near Macon, Georgia and at that time my daddy was a schoolteacher there. He had majored in math and I guess I got interested in science and mathematics because of him. Now he's principal of a big school in Atlanta. Anyway, when I graduated, the Air Force was looking for specialists to train as code breakers and communications specialists. They seemed to like my qualifications and I worked on a lot of different projects. After a few years on different assignments I fell in love with my married boss. The affair went horribly wrong and he had a messy divorce. After that I was put forward for special duties.'

She looked solemn for a moment, then threw back her head and laughed – a warm throaty chuckle.

'So here we are! What's your story?'

Gabriel stretched and yawned.

'I'm way too tired to tell you all of my life history tonight, but here's a short version. I come from Mallorca, that's a Spanish island in the Mediterranean. I have a twin sister, Isabel, and our mother died when we were born. It was all very tragic. Vasco, my father, was away on a sailing trip at the time, working on some new navigation theory and he blamed himself for not being there. He was never quite the same after that. For a while he went nearly crazy and took to drink. In the end, though, he got over that and threw himself into his work. I guess he was trying to bury his guilt by working long hours as a very young professor of mathematics at the university back home. He was already obsessed with our ancestors. Then, on top of everything he got involved in local history, culture and a small political party. It's not surprising that my twin Isabel and I got no attention and we grew up completely wild on the family *possessió* – that's a big country estate. My family must have been there hundreds of years, so the property's always been called C'an Valseca – the House of

Valseca. But this must be very boring for you.'

'No, no, it's an amazing story,' said Rachel, 'I'd like to hear a lot more.'

'Fine, but not tonight. I'm almost asleep and tomorrow will be a busy day. Let's talk again another time. It's better we should get some rest now. Thanks for your company. See you back here at eight tomorrow morning.'

Rachel nodded, smiled and gathered up her tray. Gabriel smiled back and followed her out of the office, thinking that some things about this assignment might not be so bad after all.

At the port, beside the Bar Nàutic in the little square close to the harbour, Guillem parked the battered Land Rover. As he got out, a small boy and girl scrambled out from under a pile of sacks in the back and ran along the quayside, laughing. They seemed to be twins, for they were dressed identically in shirts, shorts and sandals and each had a small bag slung around the neck. He called after them, but they took no notice, dark hair catching the sunlight as they played leapfrog over the mooring posts until they reached the end of the jetty. Then, opening their bags they took out fishing gear and, in less than a minute, baited hooks were in the water.

Guillem grumbled to his friend Francisco, sitting at a table outside the bar with a *rebentat* – coffee laced with brandy – and the local paper, *Diari de Balears*.

'I can do nothing with these kids. They should be doing their lessons, but they run off almost every day. Yesterday they took horses. The day before that, they went swimming in the lake. This morning they hid in the back of the Land Rover when I came down here to get prawns for lunch. It's the twins' birthday and the Senyor's spinster sister Teresa is coming, so everything must be done properly. The boss doesn't seem to mind much when Gabriel and Isabel play truant, but Antonia will blame me. It always seems to be my fault. For God's sake, man, buy me a drink!'

Back at the *possessió*, Guillem's wife Antonia stood at the door of the big house where she had been housekeeper to the Valseca family for twelve years. She shaded her eyes with her hands as she gazed across the grassland towards the trees and the mountains beyond, muttering to herself.

'Mother of God, those children will be the death of me! It's long past the time for their morning lessons and they've run off again.'

She turned back into the old stone house, shaking her head as she went along the cool passageway with its ancient flagstones to the lofty kitchen. With the Senyor's elder sister coming for lunch on the twins' eighth birthday, everything had to be absolutely perfect to satisfy her. Looking at the old clock on the wall, she frowned. There really wasn't much time to get everything done. Guillem needed to be back quickly with those prawns for the first course. She peeled potatoes at the sink and then started to prepare a traditional dish, leg of lamb cooked in the red wine of Binissalem with almonds and her own special blend of herbs.

Antonia went back to the spacious dining room once again to check the place settings at the long oak table. It was cool, but the open log fire was only needed in the winter. Silver candlesticks gleamed under the sombre gaze of old portraits of the Valseca family, most of them evidently sea captains or landowners. She adjusted the flower arrangement in the large bowl at the centre of the table then, with a final look round, went into the entrance hall, knocked on the door of Vasco Valseca's study and went in.

In contrast to the rest of the house, the study was furnished like a modern office, with filing cabinets, floor to ceiling shelves filled with books on science, mathematics, astronomy, navigation and history. On the walls hung modern prints by Miró, a brass ship's chronometer and an astronomical map of the northern sky. The only concession to tradition was an antique oak desk under the window, which stood at right angles to a brand new computer, one of the first on the island. Bonnie and Clyde were dozing, but looked up briefly and wagged their tails. Vasco turned away from the monitor.

'Good morning, Antonia, what is it?'

'I thought that I should remind you, Senyor, that it is the twins' birthday today and your sister Teresa is coming for lunch. Would you like me to serve sherry on the terrace at twelve o'clock? I think it will be warm enough.'

Vasco's face clouded, remembering that his children's birthday was also the anniversary of his wife's death. He was silent for a moment, then smashed his fist on the desk and put a hand over his eyes. There was a long pause before he sighed deeply and cleared his throat.

'Yes, that would be fine thank you, Antonia. Oh, and bring me some coffee please.'

As she turned to leave the room, he looked up from the keyboard again.

'By the way, where are Gabriel and Isabel? Perhaps they should finish their lessons a little early this morning and get cleaned up ready for their aunt's visit.'

Antonia looked guilty.

'I don't know where they are, Senyor. They ran off after breakfast and I haven't seen them since.'

Vasco frowned for a moment and shrugged.

'Let's hope they come home in time for lunch, otherwise my sister is going to be even more difficult than usual.'

He returned to his keyboard and Antonia went back to the kitchen to prepare coffee.

Just before twelve o'clock a well-preserved and immaculate white Citroën DS 21 swept to a standstill in front of the house. Out stepped a tall woman in her late forties dressed in a beautifully tailored grey skirt with a cool white blouse. She picked up a slim lizardskin handbag from the passenger seat and then slammed the car door. She stood for a moment, peeling off chamois leather driving gloves before smoothing her skirt and striding to the big door which she flung open without knocking.

'Hello, there! Is anybody about?'

Her voice echoed around the entrance hall, up the stone staircase and along the passageway to the kitchen. In a few moments Antonia appeared, wiping her hands on her apron.

'Good day, Senyora Teresa. Please come through to the terrace. I will tell Senyor Valseca that you have arrived.'

At that moment, Vasco emerged from his study and embraced his sister.

'Wonderful to see you, Teresa. It's good of you to drive up from Palma to see us. Yes, put a tray with sherry and glasses on the table on the terrace, please, Antonia.'

Following a long-standing family ritual, they soon had schooner glasses of fino and toasted each other. Brother and sister sat together on antique iron chairs looking across the paddock towards the plain in the centre of the island.

'I have brought birthday presents for the twins,' said Teresa, 'but I left them in the car. I'll bring them in after lunch. Why don't you let Gabriel and Isabel finish their studies early today, so that they can see their aunt?'

Vasco looked uncomfortable.

'The fact is, Teresa, that they've gone off somewhere this morning and we are not quite sure where they are.'

Then, seeing his sister's expression, he added quickly:

'But they are sure to be here quite soon. They do know that you are coming and they always look forward to your visits. We all do.'

During the half hour that followed, Vasco ran out of

21

small talk and Teresa's mouth set in a grim line. Eventually she could contain her annoyance no longer.

'This is impossible,' she snapped, 'I don't believe that the twins are doing any work at all. Something must be done, and I shall make it my business to ensure that decisive action is taken. You are absolutely useless as a father, Vasco, and you cannot allow these children to run around like wild things and neglect their learning. They'll pay for your lack of discipline all their lives unless they are set on the right path quickly. They simply must get away from this place.'

She held up a hand as Vasco tried to interrupt.

'I've much to thank you for my dear. You know I'll always be so very grateful for your help with my own problems. However, as the twins' godmother and head of the Valseca family I insist that they must leave here very soon. It would have been a very different story if only you had married again. Heaven knows, you would have had no problem ...'

Angrily, Vasco started to get to his feet, but Teresa laid a restraining hand on his shoulder.

'I'm so sorry dear brother, I know that this subject is taboo. I shouldn't have mentioned it. Please let me apologise.'

Vasco sat down again, his face turned to the wall. There was a long silence between them before Teresa continued.

'I really would love to do something for Gabriel and Isabel myself. But it's quite out of the question for them to come to live with me in Palma. Running the secretarial college takes all of my time and energy. And the rest of the family here is not going to be any help. They are all quite useless for one reason or another. And you know very well that there is nobody else here in Mallorca we could trust to bring them up properly.'

She paused and drew a deep breath.

'Hard though it is, I also believe they must be completely separated. It would be unhealthy for them to grow up so

22

closely together as adolescents. So, I will arrange for Isabel to go to live near to London with our sister Margalida in Guildford, where there are some excellent girls' schools. As for Gabriel, he will be educated in America and will go to stay with cousin Rafael in Boston.'

She stood up and laid a hand on Vasco's shoulder.

'Believe me, my dear brother, it will be for the best.'

Vasco sat with his head bowed.

'How long have you been planning this? And why choose today of all days to tell me that I should send my children away?' Teresa smiled thinly.

'Trust me, Vasco, if there was another way, I would suggest it. And, now that Joana is no longer with us I really do believe that this is what she would have wished.'

At this, Vasco's shoulders started to heave silently and he rose quickly, striding into the house without a word.

As Teresa stood uncertainly, one hand on the table, two grubby children burst onto the terrace, shouting excitedly.

'Aunt Teresa, we've caught some fish,' yelled Gabriel.

'And two crabs,' cried Isabel.

'Darlings, it is lovely to see you again,' said their aunt, carefully holding them at arms' length as she kissed their tousled heads. 'This is a special occasion and I think you'll both remember your eighth birthday all your lives.'

She gave a wry smile.

'There are presents in the car. But first we must have lunch, and a special family meeting. Now off you go and find your papa – and don't forget to wash properly!'

Teresa Valseca poured herself another glass of sherry, drained it and muttered something to herself. Then she picked up her handbag, straightened her back and followed the children into the house.

At Watergate, on the second morning of the Sniper Project, there were individual meetings of the specialist groups.

Then, after a break for lunch, Gabriel and Rachel found themselves with a little time to spare. They took cups of coffee and relaxed for a while. Rachel broke the companionable silence.

'We've got a few minutes to ourselves. Why don't you tell me the rest of the story you began last night?'

'Well, do you really want to hear it?'

Rachel nodded.

'OK. I'll try to make it short. There was a big family row because me and my twin sister were running wild. Just after our eighth birthday we were separated and packed off to be raised by relations far away from Mallorca. I was sent to the States, lived in Boston with my father's cousin, went to school and then to MIT. All this time Isabel was getting educated in England, but we wrote a lot and managed to see each other once or twice a year back at home.

'Meanwhile my father got deeper and deeper into his obsession with the glorious past of Mallorca and with our ancestor, Gabriel, a brilliant navigator who made maps back in the middle ages. That's why I was named after him. Actually, Papa's something of a genius – he seems to be able to conjure computer programs out of thin air. I guess another part of the reason he's hooked on astronomy and navigation is because his own name, Vasco, comes from the famous Portuguese seafaring explorer, Vasco da Gama. Even Isabel didn't escape – she was named after the Spanish Queen of Castile who sent Columbus off on his voyage to America.

'Anyway, that's enough about my eccentric father. My own story should have been quite normal, because I did just the same as most of my buddies from MIT when I chose a post-graduate course in computer science. That was great, but it only led to a series of dull jobs. Then one day I saw this harmless-sounding recruiting ad which turned out to be from the CIA. I was actually hired by an amazing woman,

Lynne Kowalski. She was really tough and after training me for a while, she moved to covert operations in southeast Asia. I got to stay behind doing IT stuff and codebreaking.'

He grinned.

'The rest is history.'

Rachel sat back, wide-eyed.

'That is totally amazing. I'd really like to meet Isabel one day. It sounds like she's got an interesting story to tell, too.'

'Well, yes, perhaps she'll come over on a trip sometime soon. But that's enough personal stuff for now. Aren't there some technical issues we should be thinking about before the meeting? For instance, can we push the backroom people for more information about the new higher-speed processors? I know the computer science group is looking at that, but they haven't come up with anything so far.'

'No, that's right. But they didn't submit a report yet. I guess the old man will be getting impatient. And that reminds me. It's time we were getting along to the conference room. We need to be there ahead of the others.'

Rachel got up, gathered papers into her folder and made for the door, with Gabriel close behind. Soon everyone was assembled. At two o'clock Admiral Hobring took his place at the middle of the long table. After calling for order, he asked for initial suggestions from the team leaders. After an hour or so it was clear that his patience was wearing thin. When he could stand it no longer, he slammed his folder shut and threw it down.

'Hasn't anyone here got a single constructive idea? All I'm hearing is platitudes. Somebody even said that we needed more resources. Can you believe that? We've already been allocated twenty million for Chrissakes, so let's not be hearing any more lame excuses like that! Who's next?'

Amos Stringer, in charge of the Navigation group, cleared his throat.

'Well, Admiral, we've been brainstorming for hours on our part of the project. I surely don't need to tell you that this is totally new territory for our people. We all feel we need more computer science knowledge to be able to come up with some useful answers.'

Hobnails looked up, his face flushed.

'Look, Stringer, we don't have the time to run an academy here. None of you are amateurs. It's your job to get on with the task you've been set and not play for time. You're professionals, so get on with it and let's have no more bullshit.'

Amos was about to reply, but Rachel spoke first.

'Admiral Hobring sir, don't you think there might be some advantage gained by mixing up the membership of the teams just a little? There could be an individual who might be spared to contribute some specialist knowledge to the Navigation group.'

The Admiral's face was like thunder.

'Goddammit, when I want your advice young lady, I'll ask for it. Don't you presume to tell me how to run this project.'

Gabriel cut in quickly, before Hobnails could draw breath.

'With respect, Admiral, we all know this is a tense and difficult time with the President putting everyone under such pressure. But I personally believe that Rachel's suggestion is worth considering. It surely could do no harm.'

The old man glowered at him and the room went very still. Nobody dared to breathe. Eventually the rasping voice rang out.

'OK, let me think about that, Valseca. But don't you cross me again boy, or you might live to regret it.' He paused. 'Now I'm going to call time out. We'll break for a while. Just be back in this room in exactly thirty minutes.'

The Admiral got painfully to his feet and limped to the

door. It was time for another painkilling injection.

There was confusion as, intent on finding coffee, people gathered up papers and moved towards the door, chattering animatedly as they shot covert glances at Amos, Rachel and Gabriel.

'Thanks, Rachel,' said Amos. 'That was brave – and constructive too. I'll remember what you did today.'

She turned and gave Gabriel a shy smile, walking out of the room as he was detained by one of the others. The rest of the day was fully taken up with more meetings. After his earlier outburst, Admiral Hobring seemed to have mellowed a little. He even adopted Rachel's suggestion, putting it forward as if it had been his own. Gabriel looked across the table at her and winked, so that she had to suppress a giggle.

Much later, after their evening meal, the two of them left the commissary together. As she said goodnight to Gabriel, Rachel turned to him outside her door.

'Thank you so much for supporting me in the meeting Gabriel,' she breathed, 'I won't forget it.'

Before he could answer, she touched his arm and was gone.

The alarm shrilled on Gabriel's bedside table. It was six a.m. and he groaned as he silenced the beeping and rolled out of bed. Almost a whole unbroken week of constant meet-ings had left his mind feeling scrambled and his nerves on edge. He stumbled to the shower and gradually felt better as the sharp jets of water bored into his scalp. Later, as he finished dressing, he checked his watch and figured he had time to check his emails before going to the commissary for a hasty breakfast.

He called in at the computer bureau on his way to the commissary. He checked in with Connie Ginsberg and was assigned a computer terminal. Several members of the team were already there, checking their incoming emails too. Turning on his monitor, Gabriel grinned when he saw that among the others on the list of incoming emails was a message from Isabel. He hadn't heard from his twin sister for a few days and decided to open that file first. It would be in plain English, because Isabel knew his bosses at Langley had forbidden the use of their native Mallorquin. The department routinely monitored everyone's personal email and phones using the latest software, but they had nobody on staff who could translate the more unusual Spanish dialects. There it was, in plain English text, but very brief.

Where have you been? I can't reach you by phone. Please, please read my letter Biel my dearest bro and phone your sister soonest.
Much much love, Bel xxxxx

Gabriel grinned and then frowned. What was going on? Of course, he had been away from his apartment for five days now, and like everyone else on the Sniper team he had handed over his cell phone to Security. But he just had to know what was getting his twin so excited. Somehow he would find a way to get back to his own place at Georgetown during the day and see if there was a letter from Isabel in his mailbox.

Later, across the table from Rachel at breakfast in the commissary, Gabriel told her about the mysterious message from his sister.

'Oh my,' smiled Rachel. 'Do you two tell each other everything?'

He grinned back.

'Well, almost everything. But, as I told you before, we grew up together and, yes, we are very close. Ever since we were parted we have usually been able to see each other at least twice a year, usually around Christmas and our birthday in June. I guess that's because we're Gemini, after all.'

They had to finish their meal hurriedly to go to their first meeting of the day, but later in the morning the Strategy Group needed time to gather some information and Rachel and Gabriel were able to take an extended coffee break. While they sat together he drifted into a reverie.

'Snap out of it, Gabriel! Where are you?' asked Rachel with her head on one side. 'What's wrong? Still worried about your sister's letter?'

Gabriel sighed.

'Well, yes, but curious more than worried. I really do have to get to my apartment and see that letter from Bel.'

'I know how you must feel,' said Rachel, 'but you know we're not allowed out without good reason – and I guess this would be bending the rules wouldn't it?'

Gabriel snapped his fingers.

'Why am I being so stupid? Charlie Spencer lives on the floor above mine and has copies of all my keys. I guess I could get him to pick up all of my mail and then deliver it here to Watergate for me.'

Rachel smiled.

'Great idea! You go and set up a phone call to Charlie Spencer with that blonde on the security desk who's been fluttering her eyelashes at you. He might even get your mail to you before the end of the day. See you back in the conference room in ten minutes.'

She jumped up, smoothed down her skirt and walked from the commissary. Gabriel was not the only one to turn and watch the sway of her hips as she disappeared into the corridor.

Half an hour after the day's meetings had finally ended Gabriel was back in his own room. He had just returned from a trip down to Security, where the bright-eyed blonde had handed over a bulky envelope full of mail. Earlier, when he had phoned Charlie Spencer at work he had readily agreed to collect Gabriel's letters and drop them off at Watergate.

'What's going on, Gabe? Sounds like they're keeping you in after school – and at Watergate of all places! You must have been a bad, bad boy.'

Gabriel had made some lame reply and Charlie had roared with laughter, but he had been as good as his word.

Gabriel tipped all the envelopes onto the bed. Bills and junk mail mostly. But there, peeking out from underneath, was the slender airmail envelope with a British stamp and the distinctive handwriting he knew so well. Carrying it over to the desk, he switched on the lamp. Then he opened a can of cola, added a slice of lemon and some ice, slit the edge of the envelope and drew out the flimsy sheets. The letter was dated six days previously. Gabriel took a pull at his drink and began to read.

His face showed conflicting emotions as he absorbed Isabel's news. Just as he reached the end his door buzzer sounded. Gabriel sighed, went to the door and opened it, to find Rachel looking at him quizzically. He stepped back in surprise.

'Well, hello, won't you come in? I thought you were going to be writing up some notes before we met up for dinner.'

Rachel eased past him into the room.

'You really don't understand women too well, Gabriel. Did you really think I wasn't just dying to know about the big deal your twin sister is writing to you about? Now you've gotten your mail I badly want to know what's going on. Call it feminine curiosity, if you like.'

'Here,' said Gabriel, 'take a good look.'

He passed the letter to Rachel, who leaned against the desk and peered at the unfamiliar handwriting.

'I can't make any sense of this,' she grumbled after a moment. 'What is this garbage? I can't understand a word.'

Gabriel smiled knowingly.

'Well, Rachel, that's Mallorquin, our own private language. We spoke it at home when we were kids and it's still the best way for the two of us to communicate thoughts and feelings. What Isabel is telling me now makes me very happy for her. And, since you're taking such an interest, I'm glad to tell you about it.'

He stood beside Rachel and took the pages from her, skimming the flowing script for the passage he wanted.

'Yes, there's a lot of brother and sister stuff. And then she tells me her big news. You see, Isabel nearly went off the rails when she was doing math at Cambridge. She fell madly in love with a researcher there and nearly went to pieces when he dumped her for someone else. Then, after a while she came to her senses and picked up her studies just in time to graduate with first-class honours. Directly after that she got a job working for an up-and-coming computer systems company in London, creating new programs. The company's founder, Martin Weston, seems to be an interesting guy. He was an IT specialist with British Intelligence and worked at GCHQ. Then he had a breakdown and that's why he was released to start his own company. And it was an amazing break for Isabel . She helped them develop several suites of highly innovative software and wound up as a partner. I guess that was around a year ago. Then Martin had a tragedy when his wife was killed in a train crash and Isabel practically had to carry the company for a couple of months. You can probably guess what came next. She finished up helping Martin to put his life back together and now she tells me that he's proposed to her – and right here is where she says she's asking for my blessing.'

Rachel turned to him, her eyes shining.

'I think that is so romantic,' she cried. 'Have you met this Martin? What's he like? How old is he? Are there any kids? You will say you approve, won't you?'

Gabriel held up a hand to get a word in.

'Hold on there. From what Isabel tells me he sounds like a very nice guy. But then, I suppose she would say that. I haven't met him yet, but as soon as I can find a way to get to London I intend to do just that. She tells me that she's written to Father in Mallorca too. Although he had so little to do with raising us, he's got very old-fashioned ideas about family and duty. There's absolutely no way Isabel would get married without asking him first.'

Rachel looked up quickly.

'I understand all about the family tradition bit. But you know you can't possibly get to London just now. We're virtually prisoners here. There's no way you could get time off just to meet your sister's fiancé.'

She put her hand on Gabriel's arm and smiled gently.

'I'm sorry, but you'll just have to wait till this job's over.'

Gabriel looked as if he was about to speak, then tried to take Rachel in his arms. She pushed him away.

'Steady there, big boy, don't get ahead of yourself.'

At that moment the phone shrilled insistently. Rachel stepped away and sank into the only armchair, picking up a copy of *Esquire*.

'Shit!' snapped Gabriel.

He crossed the room and lifted the handset.

'Valseca, Sniper Team.' He straightened up.

'Good evening, Admiral.'

A pause.

'Well, yes, I'll do that right away, sir.'

He hung up and turned to face Rachel, stony faced.

'I think you can figure what that was about. Hobnails has just had another roasting from the President. He has to report to the White House first thing tomorrow morning. I'm needed at the Old Man's office in the Naval Section right now. He wants me to help him draft a formal statement about progress and prospects. I could be working all night. This job really sucks!'

He kicked savagely at a waste bin. It bounced off the wall, spilling discarded papers onto the carpet.

Rachel grinned ruefully and stood up.

'Don't worry about it Gabriel. And, if you can take time out from the Pentagon and bring some of the paperwork back here, I'm ready to help you with drafting that report. Give me a call if you figure that's a possibility. I'm not going anywhere and I don't mind putting extra hours in. Then perhaps tomorrow we can find a way to spend some leisure time together. I'd like that. Now don't you keep Hobnails waiting.'

She patted him lightly on the arm, then sidestepped when he reached for her hand. Opening the door, she gave him a dazzling smile.

'It'll be lonely without you in the commissary tonight. Make sure those guys on the Naval Section get you something to eat while you're working. I don't want you wasting away. And please try to get back here if you can, so that I can help out.'

Then, suddenly, she was gone.

Gabriel snatched up folders and loose papers from the desk under the window, ripping open his briefcase to throw them in. Then, grabbing his top coat from the bed and hefting the heavy bag with his free hand, he tore the door open, slamming it behind him. He fumed all the way to Security, where, after taking one look, the bored corporal on duty decided that small talk would be a bad idea. Disappointed, he shook his head and muttered as Gabriel strode grimly towards the elevator.

2

The extensive facilities of the Universitat de les Illes Balears, UIB, are situated a few kilometres northwest of the city of Palma, Mallorca. Close by is the historic old town of Valdemossa. The campus is home to a number of faculties and the university buildings display a mixture of modern architectural styles, reflecting several periods of expansion. The Mathematics Department is housed in a building like a concrete office block, near to a tree-fringed parking area.

It was the morning after Gabriel's meeting with Admiral Hobring. A well-maintained dark-blue Jaguar XJ6 saloon reversed into one of the scarce spaces in the crowded parking lot. Vasco Valseca patted the car affectionately as he got out, carrying an airline bag. A man in his late fifties, he was slim and elegant. His silver hair was a little long, perhaps, but well groomed. He wore bottle-green corduroy trousers, suede shoes and an open-necked brown and cream checked shirt under a tan-coloured linen jacket.

Whistling jauntily, he strode into the building, crossed the hallway, nodded to the middle-aged blonde at the reception desk and trotted up the wide stairway towards the office of Professor Miquel Santiago. Close friends since their time together at Trinity College Cambridge, they both retained some old-fashioned English mannerisms. It came as no surprise when Vasco found his colleague puffing at an ancient pipe as he worked at his computer. Dandruff dusted the shoulders of his old tweed sports jacket and he barely looked up from the monitor as Vasco came in and swept aside some of the dirty coffee cups and papers littering the desk. Having cleared a space, he set down the bag and sank into the only chair not covered with files, papers and text-books. As usual, Vasco spoke to his friend in English.

'Miquel, for God's sake stop playing with that bloody thing for a minute and pay attention. We need to talk.'

A deep sigh and a gurgle from the stained pipe was the only immediate answer, but in a few moments the computer was shut down and Miquel turned to face his visitor.

'What the hell do you want now, Vasco? I thought you were off to London and I wouldn't be seeing you back here until next week. I'm trying to organise myself to deal with your students as well as my own. Why don't you leave me in peace? Can't you see I'm busy?'

Vasco grinned broadly and produced a bottle of Gran Duque d'Alba and two glasses from his bag.

'Yes, yes, I know all about that, you grumpy old bachelor. You can't think about much except work when you sit here puffing that horrible pipe of yours, but this is a very special occasion. My daughter is going to be married and we're going to drink her health.'

'What, little Bel? I don't believe it – but any excuse for a drink in the middle of the morning. My congratulations!'

Miquel's chubby features creased into a surprisingly radiant smile as the two men touched glasses and enthusiastically toasted Isabel with the mellow brandy.

Vasco set down his glass and leaned forward.

'I'm afraid I must call on you for another favour. Now that Isabel has found herself a husband, I need a little time to get to know him – and arrange a special dinner to celebrate their engagement. So I may stay on in London for another day or two. Can you cover for me?'

Miquel frowned for a moment and then clasped Vasco's hand.

'Give me the rest of that bottle and it's a deal.'

Vasco nodded agreement and poured for them both again before handing over the brandy.

'There's just one more problem. We have a meeting of the Partit per l'Independència de les Illes Balears on Friday evening. It's the finance committee and I expect to be still in London.'

'That's OK,' said Miquel, 'I can easily make your apologies. But I'm getting fed up with this Treasurer's job, Vasco. At the moment the PIIB hasn't a chance of getting anything like enough funds to run a proper campaign. At this rate we'll never have the clout to win us greater autonomy from Spain. I know it makes both of us crazy – and a lot more people too. Those bastards in Madrid still pull too many strings here. And did you know that some snot-nosed little bastard of a hacker has managed to raid our bank account? He's damn nearly cleaned us out. The bank says that everything is secure now, but I have my doubts – and they don't seem to have any idea about tracking the source of the problem.'

Vasco frowned.

'My God! Really? No, I didn't know. How much has the little shit left in our account?'

'Less than 20,000 pesetas – hardly enough for a decent meal. He's managed to take just over a million and that's a huge hole in our finances. The Bank isn't exactly being helpful about replacing the missing funds – not yet, anyway. They're talking about an internal investigation, whatever that means. I guess we'll be short of cash for quite a while.'

'Well, they ought to pay the money back to us immediately, but these bureaucratic bastards always seem to take for ever to do anything. All the same, I can see their difficulty in tracking this security breach to its source.'

He paused, frowning.

'On the other hand, though …'

His voice trailed away as he gazed out of the window. There was a silence as Miquel quietly sipped his brandy, knowing that this was no time to interrupt. Suddenly, Vasco slapped the top of the desk, rattling the dirty coffee cups.

'Hang on a minute. I've just had one of my "magical insights". There just might be a way to tackle this. I need time for some thinking and a little bit of software development. Then if it all works out I could practically write the program in my sleep. But all that'll have to wait till I get back from London. Sorry about the PIIB meeting, though. It's about time one of us came up with an idea to produce a lot of cash. We certainly need it badly, especially now.'

Vasco got up and noticed *The Times* on the corner of the desk, with the crossword almost completed. As students at Cambridge they had both become addicted to these cryptic puzzles.

'I see you're having problems with that one,' he chuckled. 'It gave me a hard time too, but I got there in the end. Fourteen down is particularly tricky.'

The two men embraced warmly before he headed for the door.

'Keep in touch,' said Miquel, 'I can't go on doing your bloody tutorials for ever, you know. And give Bel a kiss from Uncle Miquel. She doesn't think of me as a grumpy old bachelor even if you do.'

After a quick look at the crossword and a deep sigh, he turned back to his computer. Relighting his pipe, clouds of smoke had already begun to build up again in the office as Vasco drove out of the car park.

Admiral Hobring stumped painfully into his office in the Pentagon and sat down heavily, throwing a thick folder onto his desk. Papers spilled out onto the blotter and a few pages fluttered to the floor. He scowled and left them where they lay. Another meeting of the Task Force for Operation Sniper had lasted all morning and they didn't seem to be getting anyplace at all. There had been two or three good ideas – one of them really promising – but even the massive computers of NASA didn't have the power to process the complex algorithms involved. Now he was feeling exhausted after another tough meeting with the President, who was getting as mean as a bear with a sore head. Hobnails massaged his aching leg, then sighed and pressed a button on the intercom.

'Charlene, bring me some black coffee please, hon.'

Meanwhile, some distance away at Watergate, Gabriel Valseca sat at his desk looking at a wall chart and making notes. He was working through his lunch break and was starting to feel the pressure. The job of Communications Officer for Project Sniper was wearing him down, even though his deputy, Rachel, was putting in just as many hours as he was. He found himself thinking about her more and more, when he should have had his mind totally focused on the project.

To add to the stress, his bosses at Langley were pressuring him to report directly to them on the details of Sniper, even though he had been expressly forbidden to do so. On top of everything he hadn't had time to write to Isabel. For the time being a brief email sending congratulations on her engagement had been the best he could do. Somehow, he just couldn't get his mind round the sort of letter she would be expecting. If only the pressure would ease up, just for a couple of days.

His telephone shrilled and he grabbed the receiver. A voice growled:

'Admiral Hobring here. Get yourself over to my office just as fast as you can, son. We need to talk.' Then the line went dead.

Later, in the anteroom to Hobnails' office, Charlene

fussed over him like a mother hen, offering him cookies made to her mother's recipe.

'The admiral's on the phone right now, but he won't be more than a minute.'

Then she hummed to herself while she rattled the drawers of the filing cabinets, packing away a mass of papers and reports. After a few minutes, while Gabriel pretended to be absorbed in the *Wall Street Journal*, the buzzer on Charlene's intercom sounded twice and she ushered him into the admiral's office.

'Come on in, son, and sit down a moment.'

Gabriel sat opposite the old man, noticing how his shoulders drooped with fatigue as he continued to read from a report in a crisp yellow folder. He took in the pictures on the walls, mostly of ships and of officers and men the admiral had served with. On a bookcase was a photograph of the previous President shaking his hand and a collection of souvenirs from a long career in the Navy. The American flag was draped along the wall behind the desk, which was bare except for a telephone and two photographs. One showed the head and shoulders of a handsome woman in her sixties. The other was a family group; a fair, good-looking man of around thirty in naval lieutenant's uniform stood alongside a lovely young woman in a cream trouser suit. Between them, holding a doll, was a pretty girl about seven years old with long blonde pigtails.

Hobnails snapped the folder shut and tossed it into a filing tray on a side table. Taking off his reading glasses, he pinched the bridge of his nose and stretched wearily.

'I've just read this report from the Computer Science Group, Gabriel, and they don't seem to have any new inspiration just now. Fact is, the whole damn project seems to be running out of steam and the President keeps biting my ass. We could do with some fresh brains from someplace to give us all a lift. Got any ideas?'

'Well, Admiral, I hadn't thought there was any chance we could go outside the Sniper Group on account of security. Are you saying that we might be able to relax that, Sir?'

'You let me worry about security, son. All I know is, we need a result and we have to have it soon, so somehow we have to get a shot in the arm. But we can't let a whole load of new guys come into this thing. On the other hand, if you just happened to know anyone specially bright from other assignments you've been on, then I'd be ready to think about it. I've been watching you since this project started and now I guess I can trust your judgment and your instinct. But see here, Gabriel, this has got to be strictly between you and me. Do you have any ideas? Take your time, son. Don't give me a snap answer.'

He clutched his painful leg, his mouth set in a hard line.

Gabriel frowned and thought for a while.

'There were a couple of really bright guys I trained with at Langley, Admiral, and we're still in touch. They both got top grades in different branches. Dick Slade was a brilliant mathematician and an inspired codebreaker. Then there was my roommate Joe Karlsen. He came top of the class by a mile in computer science and surveillance techniques.'

Hobnails smiled and relaxed the grip on his thigh, noting the names on a writing pad.

'Well, their background sounds just what we need. And if you say they're good I guess I must take that on trust. So how soon can you contact them – unofficially, of course? Nobody, but nobody, not even Rachel Jefferson or your CIA bosses, can know about this.'

'That's the hard part, Admiral, they're both in London right now. Slade is with the CIA unit at Apex House and Karlsen works at the embassy.'

Hobnails slammed his hand on the desk.

'Shit, that's all I need! Don't you know anyone closer home?'

'You asked for the best, sir, and those two are by far the best I've met.'

The old man swivelled his chair angrily and stabbed the call button on the intercom.

'Charlene – get in here right away with some coffee, hon. And put some rum in it.'

He released the button and turned back to Gabriel.

'Dammit, I can't go pulling guys over here from England on your say-so! Hell, they're right outside my jurisdiction too! And there is no way you could just call them up for a friendly chat about Sniper. So, how can we handle this?'

He glowered at the map of the world spread out on the wall alongside his desk and barely looked up as Charlene came in with a silver tray and two fine china mugs of strong black coffee, generously laced with rum. When she had left the room, Gabriel cleared his throat nervously.

'I have a twin sister in London, Admiral, and we're very close. Ben Jorgensen, my boss at Langley, already knows that. Perhaps I could invent a story that she's very sick and in intensive care – or maybe very badly hurt in a car accident? I might get leave to see her on compassionate grounds. Then, while I was over there …'

'OK son, you don't have to spell it out. That might just work. Tell you what, I can get a very old friend to send a signal which will seem to come from a London hospital. Just give me your sister's name and address, then we'll get the show on the road. But see here now, Gabriel, you can only stay in London a few hours – let's say two days away from here at the most.'

Gabriel smiled and nodded as he wrote briefly on his notepad, tore off the slip of paper and handed it to the Admiral who glanced at it briefly.

'Isabel. That's a nice old-fashioned name. OK, Gabriel, I'll have Rachel Jefferson cover for you while you're away.'

He took a mouthful of coffee and closed his eyes for a moment.

'And don't you worry about your bosses at Langley. They're going to be sick as dogs when they find out that your compassionate leave was a charade. They aren't going to enjoy it either, when they find out that you've been talking off the record with CIA men on other assignments. Never mind that, though, I'll say it was my idea and you were acting in secret on my direct orders. Besides,' he grinned, 'if your CIA buddies in London do come up with an idea that will crack this thing, you can bet your boots that Langley won't be slow to claim a share of the credit.'

Hobnails glanced again at Isabel's name and address.

'OK, Gabriel, I'll fix up this phoney signal from London. I guess it's going to take me a few hours to get that organised, so you should think about leaving on tomorrow night's flight for London. We'll need to talk about your cover story – and exactly what you tell Karlsen and Slade, so come back and see me in three hours' time. On your way, son. Get back to your desk and look busy.'

Gabriel got up, leaving his coffee untouched. He was opening the door as Hobnails lifted the phone. The smell of the coffee and the sweet aroma of rum followed him into Charlene's office. She called after him 'You take care now, Mr Valseca, and come back soon,' as he walked out into the corridor, his mind churning. He would be able to see Isabel again much sooner than expected. There would be so much to tell his twin sister. He was humming as he pressed the button for the elevator.

3

Soon after takeoff from Dulles International Airport the aircraft levelled out. A few minutes later the 'fasten seatbelt' sign was turned off and Gabriel called a flight attendant. He ordered a light snack and, after a chicken sandwich and a diet cola, quickly settled down, trying to sleep. But his mind would not be still and kept taking him back to his last hours at Watergate before he said goodbye to Rachel.

Soon after Hobnails had told him to go on the secret mission to meet Karlsen and Slade, he realised that even a brief parting from his deputy would be hard to bear. At the end of yesterday afternoon's meeting he had announced to the whole team that he was being granted compassionate leave because of his sister's 'serious accident'. Rachel, even more than the others, was touchingly sympathetic as he told the story. Afterwards he felt like some sort of traitor and agonised for a long time. Eventually he realised that he couldn't bear to be dishonest – not with her of all people. So, after a late evening meal evening he sat down with her when the commissary was almost empty.

After solemnly swearing her to secrecy he revealed the real reason for his visit and stammered out his reason for taking her into his confidence. Rachel said nothing at all for a moment then took his hands in hers and looked away. After a long pause she turned back to face him, her eyes brimming. She spoke quietly but very seriously. She hadn't told him before just how badly she'd been emotionally scarred by her affair with a married man. Afterwards, she'd promised herself never to trust another man again. But now Gabriel had put his entire trust in her. That changed everything. She would be thinking about him all the while during his trip and perhaps, when he came back, she would have a new way of looking at things.

Rachel sat up slowly, looked around the commissary and saw that it was empty now. Suddenly she leaned across the table and kissed Gabriel full on the lips. It was a moment he would never forget. As he reached towards her, she jumped to her feet and ran to the door. Turning, she blew him a kiss before disappearing.

He didn't see Rachel on her own again that night. He couldn't find a way to speak to her at the end of the meeting. There were too many others close by when Gabriel went over to her place at the conference table to hand over his work folder. As he was passing it across, she squeezed his hand and looked into his eyes and he almost dropped the folder. Reluctantly he dragged himself away to say his goodbyes to the rest of the team in the conference room.

At last, after running those happy images though his mind many times, Gabriel had drifted into a light sleep. It seemed no time at all before the cabin lights came on again and it was time for a rapid breakfast and the descent into Heathrow. He was travelling light, wearing a raincoat and carrying only a briefcase and a suit bag as he disembarked.

It was now Friday morning. The plane touched down a little early and although it took an age to clear immigration and customs, it was only just after seven o'clock when he came out of Terminal 3 and took the shuttle bus to the car rental parking area. He wanted to use his cell phone – retrieved from the security point when he left Watergate – to contact his former colleagues in London, but it was too early for that. He couldn't call Isobel either, as it was very possible that the CIA would monitor the call. He would just have to wait until he could use a conventional phone. It would have been even more risky to make a call before leaving the USA, because CIA surveillance would have been much more thorough. It would have been obvious to Langley that his 'compassionate' visit to London was a fake. Gabriel gave a deep sigh, then smiled. He would turn up at Bel's apartment and surprise her, just as soon as he had set up his meeting with Slade and Karlsen.

The grey London morning had the usual traffic bottle-necks but Gabriel reached the Cavendish Hotel in Jermyn Street without serious delay. Even so, by the time he had checked into the room that Rachel had reserved for him in advance and arranged parking for his rented Ford Mondeo, it was just after 8.30.

Figuring that the American Embassy's switchboard wouldn't be open at so early an hour, he decided not to attempt a call to Joe Karlsen. He wasn't too sure about Dick Slade's hours either, but tried his cell number. As it was ringing he reminded himself that the conversation would be monitored; he would have to be careful. Then the familiar voice came down the line.

'Slade here.'

'Dick, it's me, Gabriel Valseca.'

'Gabriel! What a great surprise! It's good to hear from you. Are you here in London? Why didn't you warn me you were coming? We could have fixed something – and had Joe Karlsen and some of the other guys along too.'

'Sorry, Dick, it was all very sudden. It's compassionate leave, and I'm on my way to see my twin sister Isabel in hospital right now. She got badly hurt in a car crash here and I've been allowed a couple of days to come and see her.'

Before Dick could say anything, Gabriel hurried on.

'Right now I have to run, but I guess I could be free to meet you – and Joe Karlsen too – for lunch. Any suggestions?'

'I'm real sorry to hear about Isabel. I hope she'll be OK. That's tough for you, I know. Now, coming back to Joe, I'm pretty sure he's available. He's always moaning that he doesn't have enough to do. Let's meet at the Occidental & Alpine Club in St James' Square at around 12.45. Just ask for me at the front desk.'

'That's fine. Thanks Dick – and I'll give you all my news when we meet. Got to dash. Bye now.'

The room was large and square, with long black and white striped curtains along one wall concealing French doors to the balcony of the second-floor apartment. A feeble ray of early morning sunshine lit up a jumble of brightly coloured cushions on a chaise longue. An antique oak wardrobe stood next to a huge wall mirror with an ornate gilt frame. Along another wall a low dressing table leaned against an old bookcase. Posters, prints, watercolours and oils glowed dimly. The door to a white and bronze marble bathroom stood ajar. In a corner, next to another door festooned with gaudy tasselled silk ropes, were a filing cabinet, a desk and a fully equipped computer workstation. On the bed, in a jumble of satin sheets and a bright yellow duvet, lay a slim young woman.

Isabel Valseca smiled in her sleep, her tangle of dark hair with hints of chestnut spread over the pillow. The telephone rang insistently and she reached lazily for the handset.

'Hello,' she said sleepily, 'Oh, it's you, my darling … my God, is that really the time? Yes, yes … OK, I'll see you in the office at 9.30. Love you too.'

Isabel dragged herself from her bed and stumbled sleepily to the bathroom, emerging a few minutes later showered and with her long hair tamed into a French pleat. She put on a pair of camel-coloured slacks, a cream cashmere sweater and calfskin Gucci pumps, applied dark lipstick to complement her almond-shaped brown eyes and her warm complexion, then checked the results in the big mirror.

Going through to the kitchen area of the large adjoining living room, she snatched orange juice from the fridge and switched on an electric jug for coffee. While she waited for it to boil, Isabel returned to the bedroom to switch on the computer and drew the curtains to look across Regent's Park, revealing a grey London morning. It looked cold and she shivered as she turned back to check her emails. There, amongst the others, was a long message from her father and she smiled as she read the familiar Mallorquin words. Her heart jumped as she read the words in the language which she, Papa and her twin brother Gabriel had always used.

My darling Bel,

Your long letter, following such a strange, excited telephone call, has warmed my heart. I always promised myself a return visit to London one day and now God has given me two reasons.

The first is pure chance, as I have been invited to take part in a panel to oversee a debate at the Royal Society in a few day's time – on Monday 15 March, which is a great honour. I hope my English will be equal to the task.

The second reason is fate, bringing an opportunity to meet a man who is beloved by my darling daughter. I hope and expect that he will be a worthy sire for my grandchildren. I had intended to keep this visit as a surprise, but now it is only right that I should give you a little warning.

I shall arrive at Heathrow tomorrow at 16.45 on British Midlands Flight BD 164 from Palma. Please meet a very proud and happy Mallorcan father.

With my fondest love.

Papa

She frowned for a moment, then clapped her hands like a child, as she realised that her father would arrive that same afternoon. Kissing the sheet of text as it came from the printer, Isabel folded it and put it into her handbag, then skipped around the apartment straightening the debris left by last night's passionate evening with Martin. Her mind was in turmoil as she made coffee, ate a banana and sipped the orange juice.

If only she could have an answer from Gabriel too. Every time she phoned his apartment the answerphone was connected and the news about her whirlwind love affair with Martin was something that had to be told heart to heart; no emails, no recorded messages. She had posted him a letter full of love and joy at the same time as the one to their father. But it would probably take longer to reach Washington than Mallorca. For all her volatile Mediterranean temperament, this time Isabel would just have to be patient. Gulping the last of the coffee she grabbed her handbag, briefcase and a black Armani jacket before flying out of the door to catch the tube from Regent's Park to Oxford Circus, just three minutes' walk from Martin's office in Conduit Street.

Behind the clinical reception area was an extensive open-plan working space, filled with bustling young men, women and computers. Beyond the team of programmers, Martin Weston's private office was a warm and welcoming oasis. A handsome mahogany pedestal desk picked up at a country auction in Wiltshire stood on a large Persian rug in muted tones of deep red and gold laid over a plain gold carpet. Gold- and cream-striped velvet curtains flanked Georgian sash windows. One wall was covered with shelving containing books on business topics, military history, astronomy and sailing. Sporting prints and Hogarth cartoons lined the other walls. In one corner a discreet mahogany console concealed a computer workstation and filing cabinets. A bowl of dried flowers and a tray with a coffee pot and two cups stood on a low table beside two club chairs. In one of them, Martin Weston sat munching a piece of toast as he leafed through *The Financial Times*. He was tall and fair-haired, with unusually piercing blue eyes. His clothes were casual: a lightweight pale blue sweater over a dark blue shirt and fawn slacks. He jumped up as Isabel came in and grinned broadly as he gathered her into his arms.

'Good morning my darling Bel,' he breathed, as their lips met. Eventually she pushed him away reluctantly.

'Not now, Martin, there's some exciting news. Papa is so pleased with my letter about our engagement – I think I babbled a bit when I rang him up to tell him last week. And now he's sent an email late last night to say he's coming to London for a few days. He's arriving this afternoon and can't wait to meet you. Here's the printout.'

Martin took the paper, scanned the message and grinned broadly.

'I'm sure it's a lovely message, but I can't understand a word of your weird dialect. But if you say he's pleased, then I'm only too happy to believe you. That's really wonderful. We must have a special party for him – and for us.'

Reaching for a desk diary, Martin flipped over the pages and then looked up.

'This couldn't be better. Stephen Blackwood called to cancel dinner for this evening because he's taking Sue to a company bash in Stockholm, so let's have our party tonight. We'll talk about it over lunch and afterwards …'

The phone rang and Martin picked it up, frowning.

'No, Harvey you idiot, of course I hadn't forgotten that we're selling the company today. I was just on the point of phoning you myself. It will be such a relief to be obscenely rich and a man of leisure at last.'

He grinned at a radiant Isabel.

'I've checked every line of the documents you sent round and everything looks fine. So let's say we'll meet in your office at ten-thirty, as we suggested originally. This time, for once, it shouldn't take long – unless I've forgotten something. All we have to do is sign the contract and take the cheque from Agrippa's lawyers. I'll have to dash though – got an important lunch date. Yes, I had thought about that. We'll organise the celebration later, when the whole team can be there. See you in a few minutes.'

By the time Gabriel had unpacked, showered and shaved it was almost nine o'clock. He knew the address of Isabel's apartment by heart and hoped to arrive in time to surprise her, but after he had bought roses from a stall and eventually found a taxi, almost fifteen minutes had passed. It was raining and the traffic was just as heavy as he remembered. It took another ten minutes to reach his destination. Ringing the doorbell persistently, he cursed his luck. Why hadn't he phoned first? He knew the number by heart, of course, but he didn't remember her work number. She would probably be at her desk by now and he'd left the address and phone number of her office in his personal organiser – and that was still in his briefcase at the hotel.

Gabriel thought of trying find the phone number by using directory assistance on his cell, only to realise bitterly that he couldn't remember the name of Martin Weston's company, not exactly. There was something like 'Icon' or 'Micron', or perhaps 'Diacon' in it. What a fool he was! There was nothing for it, he would have to go back to the Cavendish and start over. Cursing aloud, he tried to find a taxi, but the street where Isabel had her apartment was quiet. He had to walk two blocks before he was able to hail a cab. It took longer than he had expected to regain his hotel room, throw the roses on the bed, check his personal organiser and find the phone number of Martin's company – of course, there it was: Viacon-Weston. He looked at his watch; it was now 10.35.

After he had introduced himself, the switchboard operator was helpful and friendly.

'I'm afraid you've missed Miss Valseca, sir. Your sister and Mr Weston went out just fifteen minutes ago. I know they've gone to a special meeting with the company's lawyers. That would have started already and I know that they can't be disturbed. Then they are out to lunch, but I have no idea where; Mr Weston wanted it to be a surprise.'

Gabriel groaned inwardly.

'Look,' he said, 'if by any chance either one of them phones in, could you please ask Isabel to call me at the Cavendish Hotel just as soon as possible. I'll give you the room number in a moment. Oh, and please tell her not to call my cell phone on any account. But it really is desperately urgent.'

'Yes, of course I'll do that, sir, if you would just give me your room number at the hotel.'

Gabriel sat on the bed, fuming, after he had hung up. He had about two hours to kill before his lunch date with Joe and Dick at the O & A. So, what to do? He shrugged, flexed his aching shoulders and started to relax. No point in fretting; coffee at Fortnum and Mason on the corner across the street from the Cavendish, then a little window-shopping in Jermyn Street. Afterwards, perhaps, a haircut at Truefitt and Hill in Bond Street. Finally he might visit Hatchard's book shop in Piccadilly. That should fill the time nicely. He slipped on his raincoat and decided to come back for his briefcase later, before the short stroll to the Club. By the time he stepped outside, Gabriel was in a much better mood. London had a lot going for it after all – the sun had broken through at last and the sky was blue. Perhaps he might get to bring Rachel here one day. He checked the cell phone in his pocket and smiled as he crossed the street to Fortnum & Mason.

Inside the semi-fortress which housed the American Embassy in Grosvenor Square, the Attaché in charge of internal security had his feet on his handsome mahogany desk and was filing his nails while absently reading *The Spectator*. Joe Karlsen was terminally bored. Although it was less than a month after the botched attack on the twin towers of the World Trade Center, the situation was eerily calm. Outside the building, extra police and barriers provided a very visible deterrent to any would-be terrorist. Inside, additional electronic screening and bullet-resistant glass combined to make the embassy virtually impregnable.

That's why it was all so dull. Nothing had happened for days. Nobody was even stealing blank floppy disks or CD-ROMs any more, let alone smuggling out any that might have been carrying sensitive information. The last anti-surveillance sweep had come up clean once again. Even the CIA infiltration team's penetration exercise last week hadn't broken the system. Very satisfying, but very boring; the internal audits were boring; the interdepartmental emails were boring; even the reports on the not-so-private lives of the embassy staff were boring. And his in-tray was empty.

It would be so much better than this desk job to be involved in some work in the field again, even if that some-times went wrong. But, come to think of it, only yesterday he'd bumped into an old buddy at the American Club. He had passed on some grisly details of an operation that had really gone sour. The CIA had planned to ambush an arms-drop somewhere in south-east Asia. Anyway, the word was that the Russians got wind of it by way of a tip-off, followed by some high-tech torture. Then they warned the locals and there was a firefight. The arms shipment got through and the CIA team got badly mauled.

On reflection, the quieter life here was better – and the natives were friendly. Joe sighed, stretched and strolled to the window, immaculate in a suit from 'a little guy in Saville Row', a shirt and a discreetly flamboyant tie from Pink's in Jermyn Street. He looked out at the trees in the square, still leafless and not yet showing any signs of spring growth. Even with such a dismal outlook though, London was definitely a good posting. Two years into his tour of duty he had a lot to be grateful for. A few strings had been pulled when he first arrived, allowing him to get into the exclusive Wentworth Golf Club. And, in around three hours time, it would be good to have lunch at his club, the legendary Occidental and Alpine with its atmosphere recalling faraway places and another, grander age; another place where he had sidestepped the waiting list.

The phone rang, interrupting his reverie. His secretary had gone to get a cup of coffee and he took the call himself. The gravel-voiced switchboard operator drawled:

'It's your friend Captain Slade, Mr Karlsen,' and the familiar voice of his old colleague was on the line.

'How's the paper chase going, Joe?'

'The excitement's killing me. How are things with you?'

'Oh, nothing special. But if you feel like lunch, why don't we meet at the O & A around 12.45?'

After the briefest hesitation, Joe replied:

'Fine, see you in the bar.'

He then hung up, frowning. This was out of character and distinctly strange. Dick Slade never, but never, had lunch at the Club. Evenings were a different matter and, on occasion, a very different matter indeed. And they had only spoken two or three words on the phone. That was unusual too. There just had to be something brewing.

London's North Circular Road cuts through a sprawling mess of unsightly residential areas and industrial estates, much of it built before World War II. On one of these run-down developments of semi-detached houses was an un-remarkable property with a crooked, amateurish sign, *DAYJAR VIEW*, suggesting that the owner had a weird sense of humour. The house had stained net curtains at the windows, peeling paintwork, discoloured stucco rendering and a neglected front garden. A cracked, weed-grown con-crete pathway led behind the house to an old ramshackle railway guard's van, converted for use as a workshop. Inside, a man in a grubby windcheater sat facing a battery of moni-tors. An old loudspeaker played jazz from a Dutch radio station.

Under a cluttered workbench was a shredding machine and within arm's reach were three telephones, a mobile phone, a fax machine, a photocopier, two powerful com-puters and their printers. A digital clock was fixed to the faded green wall panelling next to a calendar showing a young woman, wearing nothing but a sunny smile. On another wall, the décor was completed by two faded portraits of Stalin and Lenin; between them was a cartoon drawing which seemed to show a younger, slimmer version of the man in the windcheater. He wore a Russian soldier's cap with the red star at the front; underneath was a crudely written caption on a piece of cardboard:

'FOXTROT'
HAEMOGLOBIN UNIT
[Red Cell – geddit?]

The man looked up at the clock for the second time in a minute and dragged a crumpled packet of Marlboro cigarettes out of the pocket of his cheap shiny suit. He lit one, using an old fashioned zippo lighter with a Harley-Davidson badge, muttered 'first today' and had a violent coughing spasm. As his breathing came back to normal the blue phone rang. He lifted it and spoke immediately.

'Foxtrot,' he said, in a surprisingly cultured voice.

His caller talked for nearly a minute and he hung up without replying. Picking up the white handset, he pressed two buttons and spoke almost at once.

'Foxtrot here. The Listeners have intercepted a phone message from Slade to Karlsen ... yes, of course it was encrypted, but with the new software we got from St Petersburg the Breakers decrypted it online. We know they're meeting for lunch and that gives us almost two hours, but we can't take any chances. Karlsen could move at any moment and they rendezvous at Club OA, so get a Watcher to Fort Knox right now. Make sure he follows and reports what happens afterwards. ... Yes, get on with it. And make sure he gets good pictures too. Oh, and have a back-up team in the van with recording gear on standby. You never know, we might get a chance to pick up some conversation.'

Foxtrot hung up and turned his attention to a simulated battle game on one of the computers. Napoleon seemed to be having a bad time at Waterloo – again.

The rain had stopped and the sun was trying to shine by the time Joe Karlsen, wearing a lightweight Burberry raincoat, slipped out of the side door of the Embassy. He decided to walk the few blocks to the discreet portals of the Occidental and Alpine Club. A few yards away a man wearing a crumpled suit and a brown anorak stopped reading *The Racing Gazette*. Leaving the shelter of a doorway on the north side of Grosvenor Square, the Watcher tucked the paper under his arm and followed his quarry at a discreet distance. Finally, the man took a serious interest in the window of a staff recruitment agency, just as Joe bounded up the steps of his Club.

Polished brass fittings and members' personal pewter tankards gleamed in the comfortable gloom of the oak-panelled bar. Dick Slade was already sitting in a leather-buttoned armchair in the far corner, facing the door. It was still early for the usual lunchtime crowd and there were only two others, sitting at the bar and talking about the stock market. Joe strolled across to his friend and noted the empty Martini glass.

'Hi, Dick. So, it's Martinis at lunchtime? And you look like you could use another. I think I'll join you – just this once.'

'It's all very well for you, Joe. Your life is orderly and at least you can plan your diary. Mine, it's coming apart at the seams. This morning I was even planning on taking a vacation, but twenty minutes ago they told me that I'm posted to some god-forsaken hole in central Africa. And I have to fly out tomorrow. But that's not why I'm here. Get the drinks and I'll tell you.'

Over the Martinis, Dick explained about the phone call from Gabriel and the terrible accident to his sister which had brought him to London. Both knew how deeply the twins were attached, but neither had ever met Isabel. They used to joke that Gabriel thought she was too good for any goon from the CIA.

Dick checked his watch.

'I'd better go to the front hall and sign in Gabriel when he arrives.'

He left the bar, found his guest just entering the building and they greeted each other warmly. Gabriel gazed at the panelling, the sweeping staircase and the ancient elevator as Dick wrote in the Visitor's Book. Then he laid a sympathetic hand on Gabriel's shoulder and asked about Isabel's injuries as he steered him to the bar.

Once he had said hello to Joe, and had had been given his obligatory Martini, Gabriel looked discreetly around the bar. He noted the three businessmen who had just come in, then cleared his throat and spoke quite loudly.

'It's really so good of you guys to be concerned about

Isabel. I really appreciate that. Actually she seems to be holding her own.'

Then he slipped across a small card with a handwritten message, which read: *'Isabel's "accident" is cover for my trip to London. Will explain later in secure area.'*

Dick looked up and nodded almost imperceptibly as Joe passed the card back to Gabriel and looked at his watch.

'Well, I guess that has to be good news, Gabriel. Why don't we go in for lunch? Then we should have time for a walk. It would be good to get some air, now that the sun's come out.'

They downed their drinks and made for the dining room, where they all had salads from the buffet. Then after talking about Isabel's imaginary accident and the extent of her fictional injuries, they gossiped about mutual acquaintances, life in the CIA, and finally, with real passion, about American football and the performance of the Washington Redskins.

Outside it was pleasantly sunny and there was a hint of early spring in the air as the trio emerged from the O & A Club and strolled across to the small park in the middle of the square. They found a bench in a sunny spot, sheltered from the light breeze. Gabriel sat in the middle and produced two envelopes, individually addressed to each of his friends.

'This is a personal letter to each of you asking for help. It's from Admiral Hobring – Hobnails – I'm sure you know his reputation. I suggest you read it before we talk. And there's a data disk for each of you too. I'm going to assume that you'll help us on this – if only for old times' sake. When you've had time to think about the details, feel free to work together, so nothing gets duplicated.'

On the other side of the square the Watchers' back-up surveillance team, alerted to the Americans' departure from the Club, reversed their shabby blue Ford Transit van into a parking space. The sides of the ageing vehicle carried a faded sign, *'Aardvark Central Heating Services'*, and on its roof were four plastic tubes, each large enough to carry ten lengths of copper water piping. But this van was different; each of the large tubes was open at the rear and in deep shadow inside was a different type of steerable video camera or laser microphone. The interior held three men seated at a console with a bank of CCTV monitors for normal and infrared reception, audio amplifiers, recording gear and joysticks to control the aim of the cameras and microphones.

A man in a dark blue sweater appeared to be in charge. His bushy red beard gleamed in the dim lighting as he hissed instructions to the other two.

'Pull your finger out, Bravo and get the camera lined up now. You can do better than that for God's sake!'

The image on one of the monitors flickered and swooped as Bravo worked the joystick. Then, suddenly they had a clear view of the Americans. The one in the middle was evidently talking and the two on either side each held a sheet of paper as they listened attentively.

'Is that OK now, Delta?'

'Yes, but zoom in as much as you can to get a better close-up. And get that laser mike lined up quick smart, India. We've not got all bloody day.'

The video and audio recording machines sprang to life and all three listened attentively to the broken fragments of conversation.

'… so the Sniper team is out of ideas? Yes, but … software to pinpoint the exact source … no further forward. How would you suggest … tracking emails and targeting hackers and virus producers … only 24 hours to come up with suggestions … Yes, it's vital. There's a huge budget for this … OK, Gabriel, I'll work all night … my plane to Tanzania

… same time here tomorrow.'

The Watchers looked at each other as the Americans stood up, shook hands and moved away out of sight. Delta spoke into a mobile.

'Yes, Foxtrot, we've definitely got something interesting. But we should get more from a second meeting planned for tomorrow. Yes, we'll be here … OK, I'll type up a report and send it with the encrypted tapes … Understood. I'll send an email attachment. Give me an hour or so.'

He rang off and climbed through into the driver's seat as Bravo and India started to pack up their equipment.

Gabriel walked back to the Cavendish Hotel after parting with Joe and Dick. They had both agreed to help and were prepared to work all night before their meeting tomorrow. It might turn out to have been an impossible assignment but, if they could only come up with a promising line of development, then his trip to London would have been well worthwhile. Others on the Sniper team could work with any useful ideas he brought back to Washington.

Meanwhile, he was fretting because he had received no call back from Isabel. He called the office of Viacon-Weston, only to be told that neither Isabel nor Martin had called in. Frustrated, Gabriel kicked off his shoes and lay on the bed. Before long, he had drifted into an uneasy sleep with strange snatches of dreams. A conference table which stretched into the distance; people jostling his elbows as he tried to help Rachel operate a computer with a weird keyboard; racing with Isabel on horseback along a sandy beach.

The shrilling of his bedside phone woke him abruptly.

'Biel, darling, are you really here in London? How soon can we meet?' said his sister's voice in Mallorquin.

'I'm at the Cavendish,' he mumbled sleepily, 'but I have to leave on Sunday. We've got to talk.'

'Yes, yes! My darling brother, there's so much to tell you about Martin and me. And the other exciting news is that Papa is coming to London and he's arriving later this afternoon. I'm going to Heathrow right now to collect him. Why don't I pick you up at the hotel in ten minutes? Then we can talk on the way to the airport.'

In a daze, Gabriel rang off, changed his shirt and went to the bathroom to freshen up. His father would expect an immaculate appearance, even if it was a surprise visit. Grabbing his jacket, he hurried down to the hotel lobby to wait for Isabel. He walked up and down for a few minutes, which seemed like hours. Finally, just as he checked his watch once again, Isabel sprang from nowhere and hugged him fiercely.

'Come on Biel, we'll be late! The car's right outside.'

Dragging her brother after her, she jumped into her silver Peugeot 206 as he scrambled anxiously into the passenger's seat. Then, charging into the traffic at high speed, she jousted for position in front of Clarence House, along The Mall, past Buckingham Palace, up Constitution Hill to Hyde Park Corner and then through a bewildering succession of traffic lights and intersections. All the while, oblivious to Gabriel's white knuckles, Isabel chattered incessantly about her love affair with Martin and their plans to marry in September. At last her twin managed to get a word in, telling Isabel about her 'accident' and the fact that he was on a mission – but without any details. It was important that neither Martin nor their father should have any hint about the urgency of his visit. They would simply be told that he had managed to visit Isabel in the course of an unscheduled trip to meet with colleagues in London.

Before they knew it, they were turning off the M4 motorway, following the convoy of traffic through the Heathrow access tunnel and finding a space in the multi-storey car park. Running neck and neck, they sprinted into the arrivals hall at Terminal 2, just as passengers from the Palma flight started to emerge. It was Gabriel who saw their father first, his silver-grey hair and distinguished features easily recognised at a distance. By the time he reached the barrier, Isabel was jumping up and down with excitement. Vasco embraced them both warmly, kissing away his daughter's tears of happiness.

'What a wonderful surprise! It's wonderful to see you so radiant, Bel, my darling. But to have Biel here too! That really is amazing – for once I'm speechless.'

With Gabriel carrying his father's bags and Isabel hanging onto Vasco's arm, they were soon back at the car park and then hurtled back into London's traffic, heading for the offices of Viacon-Weston. They all talked incessantly and by the time they arrived in Conduit Street almost all of the news had been exchanged. Meeting Martin for the first time, Vasco and Gabriel were soon at ease with him; all three men had much in common. Martin produced a bottle of Dom Perignon in his office to celebrate their meeting. After a relaxed conversation and a lot of laughter Gabriel went with his father to the room already reserved for him at the Westbury Hotel nearby.

While Vasco unpacked, Gabriel told him that he liked Martin very much at their first meeting and was happy to find that his father also approved of Isabel's future husband. After freshening up, they took a taxi to the Mirabelle Restaurant, where Martin and Isabel were already waiting for them at the cocktail bar. The evening was a great success; memorable food, fine wines and animated talk about the past, present and, of course, the future. Martin was already aware of Vasco's formidable intellect and range of interests, but it came as a delightful surprise to the Mallorcan to find that his future son-in-law shared his own enthusiasms. Apart from his evident skill in computer

61

technology, Martin was also very knowledgeable in the fields of mathematics and astronomy.

As the desserts were being served, Gabriel became very quiet.

'What's the matter, Biel?' asked Isabel, 'you haven't spoken for ages.'

'I guess it's jet lag.' Gabriel answered, stifling a yawn. 'If I don't get to bed now, I'll probably collapse right here.'

They hurried through coffee while quickly making plans for the next day. Gabriel had his own meetings to attend to, but promised to join up with Martin and the family again in the evening. Drooping with fatigue, he was bundled into the taxi which had been called to take him back to his hotel.

The others stayed on for a while, savouring an aged Armagnac. There was talk of a wedding date – in September, perhaps – but first Martin would have to meet the formidable Aunt Teresa, who still relished her position as head of the Valseca family.

'I promise that you will like her very much,' said Vasco, 'her bark is much worse than her bite and she really does have a heart of gold.'

Before Martin could say anything, Vasco went on quickly.

'It's settled. I've just had a great idea. We have a three-day International Mathematics Symposium in Mallorca, starting next weekend. You could register on the Saturday as my honoured guest. While you're with us I can arrange for you to meet with Teresa and we can get to know each other better – perhaps over dinner on the Tuesday evening after the Symposium finishes. You could fly home on Wednesday. That way, we shall be able to kill two birds with one stone. What do you say?'

'How can I refuse?' said Martin. 'That sounds wonderful. I should be able to get away for a day or two. But what about Bel?'

'I was wondering when somebody was going to think about me,' pouted Isabel. Then she suddenly brightened.

'Just a moment,' she cried, rummaging in her handbag and producing her personal organiser. 'I thought so. The Monday, that's March 22, just happens to be Aunt Margalida's sixtieth birthday – we all call her Margo. She invited me a while ago to a celebration lunch with some of her friends in Guildford. Then, on Tuesday there's a hen night for my best friend, Catherine.'

She smiled at Martin and squeezed his hand.

'Don't worry darling, I promise to be good. She's getting married two weeks after that and you're invited to the wedding. You will come, won't you darling? I've already put it in your diary and I want to show you off to everybody.'

'Of course I'll come,' Martin grinned, 'And by that time there should be good news from my trip to Mallorca – always assuming I can impress Aunt Teresa.'

Vasco had put his head in his hands, but now he looked up.

'My God!' he groaned, 'I'd completely forgotten it's Margo's big birthday. Thanks for reminding me.'

He drew his diary out of his pocket.

'Yes, of course. March 22 how could I not remember?' He scribbled a few words. 'I've made a note to do something special about it as soon as I get home.'

Vasco, still shaking his head at his memory lapse, put away his diary. Then they chatted for a while before agreeing to meet at Fortnum & Mason's coffee shop at 10.30 next morning. Soon afterwards, talking and laughing, they stood up to leave. Vasco took a taxi to the Westbury Hotel, leaving Martin and Isabel to take a romantic stroll through the fine cold air. Walking arm in arm to Piccadilly, they finally hailed a taxi. Soon they were in Isabel's apartment, embracing with a new-found tenderness. Their happiness seemed complete, now that Vasco and Gabriel had shown their liking for

Martin so clearly. As he turned over to put out the bedside light, Isabel reached out to him hungrily and gathered him into her arms.

4

The next day was cold but bright and sunny. The battered blue van from Aardvark Central Heating Services was parked at the same vantage point in St James' Square well before the time for the Americans' rendezvous. It was well hidden from the park bench, with only the tubes carrying the surveillance equipment peeping above a high hedge.

Gabriel arrived early to wait for his colleagues. He had spent a happy, animated morning with Isabel, Martin and his father after checking out of his hotel room. Coffee at Fortnum's and a stroll along Piccadilly had been followed by lunch at an Italian restaurant in Jermyn Street. There had been an emotional farewell before he left for his meeting. Afterwards he would have just enough time to collect his bags from the Cavendish Hotel and get out to Heathrow.

The other two CIA men arrived separately, just before the appointed time of 2 p.m. By then the watchers in the van had their video cameras and microphones accurately lined up and they were able to monitor the conversation on the bench better than before. Delta shot a watchful look at his well-trained eavesdropping team. His red beard wagged as he chewed gum in anticipation of a productive session. He grinned as speech and images began to come through loud and clear. He turned off the speakers as he donned headphones. There were the usual greetings, then the talk began in earnest. The reels of the recording units turned hypnotically; there would be time to re-check details of the conversations later. But now the priority was to get the main points logged. That's what Foxtrot had asked for at the briefing. He opened a spiral bound notebook and started to write rapidly as the three Americans started talking.

For ten minutes Delta scribbled furiously at his notes, then the monitor screen showed that one of the trio, Dick Slade, was standing up to shake hands and leave. The other two talked a while longer before they also stood and walked slowly away in the direction of the park gate. Delta finished writing, shut down the monitors, took off his headphones and rubbed his hands. He stroked his beard as he quickly read through the notes he had made. He murmured, 'Well, how about that?' under his breath, slapped his thigh and snapped the notebook shut.

'I think that's a very profitable day's work, lads. Get the kit stowed while I write a note for Comrade Foxtrot. I think he's going to be a very happy bunny. Then we'll park the van at the brickworks yard and spend an hour or two at the Cross Keys. A few drinks are called for – and the first round's on me.'

With the collapse of Russian Communism, many revolutionary groups around the world had lost motivation and members. Some tried to carry on as political extremists but others were disillusioned and turned to halfway-criminal activities. Foxtrot was one of these, converting his group into a small freelance military-style surveillance business, the 'Haemoglobin Unit'. In addition to quite respectable routine work, such as security at factories and offices, hand-picked members of his team undertook all forms of clandestine intelligence gathering.

Naturally, a lot of their activity was sub-contract work for the big security companies and strictly legitimate. But there were other jobs which were definitely not, including industrial espionage and illegal phone tapping. But the most profitable payments came from a Russian group – predictably, Foxtrot called it the 'Blood Bank'. For a regular monthly retainer, Foxtrot's team filed weekly reports on staff at the American Embassy and at other US and British security establishments in the London area. Anything particularly interesting earned a bonus.

Foxtrot's Russian patron was Viktor Dankovitch, a former intelligence officer. He was a huge man, with the physique and strength of an Olympic weightlifter. But he was much more than that, with a subtle, ruthless and formidable intellect which had earned him a meteoric career in the KGB, later to be renamed the FSB. During an 18-month posting at the Russian Embassy in London he had become fluent in English. This was followed by two years in Paris. There he had learned French and also an appreciation of good food and fine wine. He had continued to cultivate his taste for refined cuisine after his return to headquarters at Dzerzhinsky Square in Moscow. Colleagues and acquaintances eagerly sought invitations to his private dinner parties and wine tastings.

Then the end of the Cold War changed his world for ever. Viktor Dankovitch left the service, moved to the city of his birth, Leningrad – which had now become St Petersburg once again – and set up his own criminal business. Of course, he had begun with the usual illegal activities of drugs, protection, gambling and prostitution. His venture made him a fortune in a very short time.

Then he began to employ his special talents, plus knowledge from his time in the FSB to set up a freelance intelligence agency, using his global contacts to collect information. He quickly earned an international reputation and became known throughout the criminal world as Big Viktor. The buying and selling of national, industrial and commercial secrets had grown into a vast business. Through his contacts around the world he traded and brokered information and, occasionally, secured very big payments for military intelligence.

Rich pickings also came from the sale of commercial secrets, with international companies willing to pay large sums to discover the marketing and technical strategies of their competitors. Sometimes they could be blackmailed into buying back their own confidential material. Big Viktor found this the best joke of all. So, in a relatively short time, he had become the undisputed market leader among the independent operators. He continued to stay at the top through the use of sophisticated technology and ruthless information gathering techniques, backed up when necessary by kidnap, torture and assassination.

On this day in March 1993 events seemed to be moving towards a particularly spectacular coup for the Dankovitch organisation. In Foxtrot's 'Command Module', the old guard's van behind his rundown semi, he had just received an envelope from a lanky youth on a Yamaha. He ripped it open and licked his lips as he read Delta's report. He frowned with concentration as he composed a brief email to convey the essential information to his Russian master:

Watchers team confirms meeting this afternoon between CIA operatives Slade, Karlsen and third man from USA (?Langley) – first name Gabriel. Discussion shows Americans desperate to develop program (codename Sniper) to immediately track precise, repeat precise, source of email/hacking/ virus activity with view to targeting/elimination by any means. Large initial budget, believed $20M.

So far, results poor/useless. Hence visit by Gabriel to seek help from CIA experts in London. Responses not encouraging (for the Yanks!).

Slade handed over material (?disk) suggesting possible way to find true identity of source by getting through/around anonymous remailer or other host/alias system. He did not hold out much hope of success.

Karlsen also handed over material (?another disk) proposing method to discover geographical location of source, following penetration of anonymity provided by remote remailer/host/alias (see Slade's proposal above). He was also very pessimistic of useful results from his work.

Before the meeting broke up, Gabriel emphasised that any further ideas were to be passed to him personally on a special unlisted number in Washington (we were unable to capture this: it was written on cards handed to Slade and Karlsen).

He also said that his bosses were getting desperate. They would even be prepared to purchase, repeat purchase, successful program from independent outside software developer. Could this be an opportunity for experts in your organisation?

Foxtrot signed off, then encrypted his text using the built-in program, before sending the message. He grinned as he imagined the Russian's reaction to the information he was just going to send to St Petersburg. After his previous signal it would be no surprise to his paymaster to learn that the Americans were in a flat spin about the electronic threat to their national security.

Their natural response to the abortive attack on the World Trade Center would be bureaucratic panic. The next reflex reaction would be to set up a big, expensive task force generating a lot of frenzied activity. But they were evidently getting nowhere fast and now they were clutching at straws. They had finally reached the point where they were prepared to pay an outside agency big money for a system to pinpoint computer terrorists. That was really rich, quite unique in fact. Foxtrot's 'Blood Brother' would roar with laughter at the news. It could be a golden opportunity to settle old scores and make money at the same time. Big Viktor should come through with a handsome bonus this time.

Soon Foxtrot would shut down his Command Module and join his team of Watchers to collect their detailed electronic intelligence and celebrate over drinks at the Cross Keys. Afterwards he would send the audio/visual recordings to St Petersburg. Transmitting data like this was painfully slow and would take many hours. One day perhaps there would be a much faster method. Meanwhile, he deserved a little relaxation. So, whistling 'When The Saints Go Marching In', Foxtrot booted up one of the computers to run the battle of Waterloo again. Some hand-to-hand fighting at La Haye Saint would put him in the right mood for the night ahead.

5

Even for St Petersburg it was an unusually cold night. Winter had been slow to relax its icy grip and here in a ramshackle industrial jungle the temperature was twelve degrees below zero. In this part of the sprawling city it was not easy to appreciate the vision which had inspired the creation of Peter the Great's wonderful metropolis. Far from the centre, where the lighting was poor or non-existent, ice lingered on the potholed tracks which ran between old warehouses and tumbledown workshops.

In the early hours of the morning there was little movement on these rutted streets. The only signs of life were in the brightly lit areas in the distance, near to the main hotels and along the Nevsky Prospekt, where police cars cruised to secure the safety of any late-night tourists foolish enough to stay out drinking.

In the gloom there was just enough light to reveal a man in dark winter clothing heaving open the rusted gates of a scrap yard. A small covered truck with no lights drove out and stopped. The man closed the gates again and crossed the frozen ruts to the other side of the lane and knocked twice on the door of a semi-derelict office building. Two men came out, dragging a third who struggled violently as he was half dragged, half carried to the waiting truck. Suddenly he broke free and started to run with a zigzag limping gait towards the feeble lights at the end of the lane. Before he could take more than ten steps the gatekeeper

71

had drawn a pistol, aimed and fired a single shot. The fugitive let out a cry, jerked convulsively and fell face down in the frozen roadway. Quickly walking to the fallen man, the gunman fired a second shot into the victim's head at point-blank range. Then he put the gun back in the pocket of his padded jacket.

'That was quick thinking, Ygor,' said one of the other two as they came over to look at the body, now oozing a dark stain onto the icy surface.

'You stupid bastards!' snapped Ygor. 'He could easily have got away. Now take this piece of meat and dump it in the forest where we planned. Let's hope the cops don't find blood here on the ground and start sniffing around. But we'd better make sure. You, Oleg, stay behind and clean up this mess right now. And don't expect Comrade Viktor to give you a loving smile when I tell him about this cock-up.'

Staggering with their burden on the frozen surface, the two men heaved the body into the back of the truck. One got into the passenger's seat as it drove off. Ygor watched it turn the corner then turned and aimed a kick at Oleg as he stumbled across the frozen track towards the crumbling office building. A few moments later he came out with a steaming bucket of hot water and a broom, grumbling and cursing as he worked away at the bloodstained ice.

In another part of the city the singing in the vaulted cellars of the Senat Bar was deafening. It was long after midnight and outside in the bitter cold the lusty Russian choruses sounded surprisingly beautiful. This place had serious history. Here in Galernaya Street, it was the favourite watering hole for members of the nearby Senate. It was a traditional Russian restaurant too and its prime location, within a stone's throw of the magnificent statue of the bronze horseman, made it a magnet for tourists.

Its reputation would later make it the perfect setting for a meal in honour of President Clinton in 1996. If only he could have foreseen that, Viktor Dankovitch would have loved the irony, having just pulled off a major coup at the expense of the CIA. Tonight he had taken over the whole restaurant to celebrate that. By a coincidence, it also happened to be his son Kyril's twenty-first birthday. So, as far as the management of the restaurant were concerned, that was the reason for the party. The atmosphere was thick with cigarette smoke, and premium vodka flowed like water. The evening had begun with style and elegance. Formal toasts had been proposed and drunk in Crimean champagne. Then huge steaks had been washed down with bottle upon bottle of red and white wines from Moldova. Naturally, there were speeches, when formidable aunts congratulated Anya, Kyril's mother, on her son's coming of age. At a certain point Viktor beat the table with his huge fist and called for silence.

'My family and my friends,' he boomed, 'this is a happy day for me and for Anya. It is no coincidence that we are celebrating here this evening, for it was in this Senat Bar that young Kyril began his love affair with computers and information technology. Yes, it was less than two years ago that his imagination was caught by this establishment's unique system for creating customer's bills. Not rocket science, of course, but stimulating for the imagination of a young man. Now, Kyril, my son, you are well on your way to a brilliant future after such excellent results at graduation. Let us drink to Kyril, to his coming of age and to a bright and rewarding future. To Kyril! *Na zdrov 'ye!'*

Chairs scraped as the guests rose with shouts of 'Kyril! *Na zdrov 'ye!'* Then Viktor Dankovitch hammered on the table again.

'Comrades, we are here for another reason too. Please make sure that you all have full glasses.'

There was a commotion as the women of the party

topped up their glasses just as eagerly as the men. Now it was time for the party to begin in earnest.

'My talented son Kyril recently succeeded in breaking one of the Americans' encryption systems. As a direct result, our group was been able to warn a certain government that the CIA planned to intercept a shipment of military hardware. The interception was a failure and we were rewarded with a very big fee for providing the vital information which wrecked the Americans' plans. I'm pleased to say that they suffered a number of casualties in an ambush, including a senior woman officer. They lost significant amounts of hardware too. So, this celebration is also a bonus for everyone in our successful team. This is definitely a proper reward for a difficult job well done. Now let us stand and drink again to all of us. So – *Na zdrov 'ye!* Comrades for ever!' Chairs scraped back and there was a roar of '*Na zdrov 'ye!* Comrades for ever!' Soon the singing started and Viktor Dankovitch began to conduct his drunken choir with a soup ladle.

He was in a particularly good mood tonight. The group run by that crazy Englishman Foxtrot was one of Viktor's most productive listening posts and had often provided useful material. The two of them had worked together for many years and he enjoyed the Londoner's quirky sense of humour. Tonight's party was partly the result of the early tip-off from Foxtrot's people about the arms shipment intercept. Precise details of the CIA ambush were finally extracted by not-so-gentle persuasion carried out by one of Big Viktor's associates in Indonesia.

The chorus ended and Viktor pounded the table with the soup ladle to call for silence.

'Refill your glasses, my friends,' he shouted, 'and drink another toast to my son Kyril and to our colleagues across the world. Everyone will receive a bonus of five hundred American dollars – now isn't that a joke?' His booming laugh bellowed across the vaulted room. 'And one of you, the lucky one, will get the chance to go on an overseas mission quite soon. So, let's drink! *Na zdrov 'ye!'*

There were cheers and an answering roar of *'Na zdrov 'ye!'* as a river of vodka flowed down eager throats. Someone produced a balalaika and started to play an old folk tune and Viktor's sister Natalya joined in with a rich contralto. The party started to break up into small groups – each with a bottle of vodka and another of Georgian brandy. Waiters started clearing the remains of the meal as Viktor sat alone with Kyril savouring a Montecristo cigar.

'A good party, Kyril, and my congratulations again on your outstanding work.'

At that moment a big fellow with oriental features stumbled against their table as he passed. Viktor's glass tipped over, spilling brandy into his lap. With a roar like an enraged elephant Viktor picked up the man like a toy and hurled him against the wall. There was an immediate silence, then three men came over and picked up their fallen colleague. A broken left arm dangled limply as they carried him out. Viktor beamed.

'Well, that's one less with a chance to go on that overseas trip.' He laughed expansively. 'And one less bonus to pay, so we can all have another round of drinks. *Na zdrov 'ye!'* There was an answering chorus of *'Na zdrov 'ye!'* and the balalaika player started up again.

At the other end of the room a figure in a dark padded jacket appeared, carrying a small envelope. He blinked at the brightly lit room, thick with tobacco smoke and alcohol fumes. He shook the hand of one of the revellers at the bar, getting a bear-hug in return. They spoke together for a moment, then the newcomer was taken across to the table where Viktor and Kyril were sitting. Big Viktor looked up and grinned.

'Sorry you had to miss the beginning of the party, Ygor, but we hadn't forgotten you. You will be getting the five hundred dollar bonus like the others – and the chance to go on an overseas trip. Sit down and have a drink.'

Ygor Krasnov eagerly accepted a glass and helped himself to the brandy.

'Tell me,' said Viktor, 'how did it go tonight? Everything OK?'

The glass trembled and paused half-way to Ygor's lips.

'Well, we did have a bit of a problem, comrade Viktor, but it's all been sorted out now.'

'WHAT?' roared Viktor, pounding the table with his fist. 'Can't anyone around here arrange a simple disappearance any more? Tell me what happened, you bungling moron – and there had better be a happy ending.'

He glowered as Ygor admitted the near-escape of their captive, but gave a reluctant grin when he heard about the shooting.

'OK, you're in the clear, Ygor, but I'll give that stupid bastard Oleg something to remember the next time I see him.' He raised his glass, drank deeply and smacked his lips. 'Now what's that envelope you're holding? Give it here, man.'

The typewritten address read *'Viktor Dankovitch – Strictly Confidential'*. Viktor raised one bushy eyebrow at Ygor.

'I met your driver at the door, comrade Viktor. He said that Irena had just had an interesting signal from London and she wanted you to see this as soon as possible.'

Viktor tore open the envelope and drew out the single sheet of paper with the printout of email from Foxtrot. He read it twice, clapped his hands like a child and roared with laughter.

'Oh, this is really wonderful!' he shouted, as soon as he could catch his breath. 'Just read this, Kyril, while I organise another bottle. Find a quiet corner my boy. You may struggle a bit with some of the English words, but I promise you it's worth the effort.'

He thumped his son on the back and signalled to a waiter. Kyril slipped away as Ygor also left the table to join the crowd at the bar.

A few minutes later, Viktor looked up from a light snack of pickled herrings as Kyril returned. He smiled shyly as he sat down and handed back the message.

'That's really great news, Father! The Americans are in the shit again and they are almost ready to pay for outside help to complete this special project.'

'Absolutely! Kyril my boy, it's time for another of your brainwaves. Do you think you could possibly write a program we can sell to the Yanks?'

The young man scratched his chin for a moment and looked intently into his brandy glass before taking a long pull. Then he leaned back with his eyes closed, deep in thought.

'Yes,' he said dreamily, 'there might be a way. Give me a couple of days or so, Father. I might be able to come up with an interesting solution to the Americans' problems. And there's a brilliant young boy, about twelve years old, who's been hanging around. He just might be helpful on this. His name is Konrad and he has a special knack with viruses. How would you like to sell the Yanks a software package with a nasty virus hidden inside it?'

Viktor nearly choked.

'My God, that would be the icing on the cake! But can you really do that when the Americans have failed?'

'Trust me, father, I've built up a team of specialist programmers who are world class. You already know what we can do – and we can do it again. It won't be easy, but we have a few tricks of our very own. With any luck, we can turn this Sniper into a Trojan Horse.'

The two men embraced and toasted each other. Then Kyril gathered his fur coat and made for the door. Big Viktor poured himself another large brandy, smiling broadly as he sat beating time to the music of the balalaika.

After his meeting in St James' Square, Gabriel had dashed to Heathrow just in time to catch the Saturday afternoon flight. He hadn't been able to rest on the plane. He had spent most of the journey preparing an analysis of Karlsen and Slade's ideas so that he could report back to Hobnails. Arrving at Washington's Dulles International Airport, he fretted at the inevitable delays through Immigration and Customs. He was lucky to find a cab quickly and reached Watergate around nine o'clock. He waited impatiently for the elevator to take him to the floor occupied by the Sniper team. Naturally, he was very tired after the family party in London and an exhausting journey. But his fatigue vanished when he hurried through the security checkpoint and almost collided with Rachel. She looked startled for a moment, then gave him a radiant smile.

'Oh, you're back. That's wonderful!' she cried.

Then, for the benefit of the security staff nearby she added: 'I really hope your twin sister's showing some improvement after that terrible car crash.' She gave an almost invisible wink and said loudly, 'I guess you'll be needing a coffee. Why don't I bring you a cup from the commissary? Then you can tell me your news while you unpack.'

She headed off to fetch the coffee. As Gabriel went to his room he overheard someone say that Hobnails had gone home a couple of hours earlier, complaining that his leg was giving him hell. He had only just set down his bag and started to unpack when Rachel burst in with two cups of coffee. Before Gabriel could speak, she had put down the tray and taken him into her arms.

'I've missed you so much,' she whispered. 'It seems like you've been gone for ever and I guess the coffee can wait.' She tilted her face up to his and kissed him gently on the cheek. 'I've thought a lot while you were away and I haven't forgotten how you trusted me with the secret behind your visit to London.' She held herself away from him for a moment and looked straight into his eyes. 'If you really, really want to commit, Gabriel, then so do I.'

Gabriel couldn't speak. He was trembling as he crushed Rachel into a long, life changing embrace. Afterwards, his memory was hazy. All he knew for certain was that he woke in the morning in a wonderful frame of mind. Rachel was gone, but her perfume lingered and she had a radiant smile when he saw her later in the commissary at breakfast.

A little later Gabriel was smiling, lost in his own private reverie, as he waited to see Admiral Hobring on Sunday morning. He looked up as Charlene broke off from her filing to find him some cookies and chattered away, asking about his trip to London. Charlene interrupted his reverie.

'So, did you get to see the Changing of the Guard, Mr Valseca?'

Before Gabriel could answer, the door was flung open and a gruff voice called out, 'Come in, son, and tell me your news.'

As he stumped back to his desk the admiral hesitated, clutched his right thigh and swore under his breath.

'Are you OK, sir?' asked Gabriel as the old man slumped into his chair.

'I guess I'll live,' growled Hobnails, 'but the President is like a bear with a sore butt and he's giving me hell. I have to be at a meeting in the Oval Office in half an hour, so I just hope your trip has produced some answers.'

He looked expectantly at Gabriel, who handed over a slim green folder from his briefcase.

A few tense moments passed, while the admiral skimmed the suggestions from London and Gabriel's critical analysis. Then he sighed and leaned back in his chair before tossing the folder back.

'OK son, I believe these guys have given it their best shot at a moment's notice. But tell me honestly, Gabriel, what's your gut feeling here? What are the chances that either of these ideas might give a result after some additional work? Let's have some odds on this. Take your time.'

The younger man thought seriously for a few moments.

'That's a tough one, Admiral, but I would rate the chances no higher than twenty-five per cent with Slade's suggestion. Karlsen's idea might be slightly better – but still no more than thirty per cent.'

Hobnails threw his reading glasses angrily into the filing tray.

'Shit! I need better odds than that to commit more time and funds. The President is going to hang us all out to dry.'

He paused and pinched the bridge of his nose before hauling himself to his feet.

'Get the Sniper Task Force into the conference room pronto, Gabriel. Give them a detailed briefing, then have some small groups look at Slade and Karlsen's stuff. We're going to need a full meeting at ten o'clock tomorrow morning. Then let's repeat that every twenty-four hours until we know whether or not we have something worth pursuing. I just hope for all our sakes that the team can come up with anything that'll get the President off my back. Right now I'm off to the White House to take another whipping.'

He limped to his secretary's office and out into the corridor, pausing to give her a twisted smile as he picked up his greatcoat. Charlene watched him go sadly, knowing he would be giving himself another painkilling injection on his way to the waiting limousine. She smiled at Gabriel as she came back into the old man's office.

'The Admiral's having a very bad time right now, Mr Valseca, but I guess you're doing everything you can. Now you go and get some rest. You must be very tired after your trip to London.'

Gabriel smiled a weak goodbye as he got to his feet, gathered his folder and briefcase. Charlene was right. Hobring's evident disappointment had brought his jet lag back to the surface. He stumbled a little as he bent down to pick up his coat before heading off to the elevator. Charlene sighed and shook her head as she watched him go.

6

After Hitler's 900-day siege the port, like most of the city of Leningrad, had been left in ruins. Now, with its original name of St Petersburg restored it was a hive of activity once again, even when shipping was at a standstill because of the winter's icy grip. Beside one of the dockside roadways stood a large square building with a faded signboard '*VIKTOR DANKOVITCH SHIPPING*'. It looked like any other warehouse, anonymous, grey and ugly. It had been built hurriedly of concrete during a frantic period of reconstruction after World War II. Inside were fork trucks stacking crates of machinery and office equipment, providing cover for another of Big Viktor's sidelines – a lucrative business in the import and export of arms and surveillance equipment.

Upstairs on a mezzanine floor, the stark interior of the warehouse had been transformed into discreet luxury. Arriving by a battered service elevator, a visitor would enter, as if by magic, a reception area with deep pile carpeting, handsome wood-panelled walls and modern furniture in chrome and glass. In dark-red recesses with concealed lighting, richly coloured icons and Russian oil paintings gleamed expensively. Spotlights picked out a spectacular flower arrangement standing at one end of the vast reception desk, which appeared to have been carved from a single block of red and grey marble. It was designed to impress and even now, after so many visits, it still had an awe-inspiring effect on the younger Dankovitch.

It seemed like an eternity since the big party at the Senat Bar. Kyril was waiting to see his father and he was not looking forward to the interview. He and his software development team had been working continuously round the clock in shifts. Unfortunately, the Russians' attempt to create their own version of Sniper had achieved nothing useful and Kyril would get the blame. Despite the sound-proofing built into the door of his father's office he could hear him shouting angrily into the phone. The colour drained from the young man's face. After a while the shouting stopped and a moment later the door was flung open.

'Come in, Kyril, my boy. I hope you have good news for me,' growled his father. 'It would be a tonic after the lies and excuses they've been giving me from Odessa. All of them are bungling idiots. These days it's not even possible to find anyone who can organise anything as straight-forward as a cigarette smuggling operation. No wonder I'm going grey!'

He slumped into an enormous leather swivel chair and reached into a cupboard for a bottle of vodka and two glasses. Pouring a generous slug into each, he raised his glass.

'To the Russian Sniper – our very own electronic addition to a line of heroes! *Na zdrov 'ye!*'

He downed his drink in one gulp and looked expectantly at Kyril, who had left his drink untouched.

'Well, father, it's proving a more difficult assignment than we thought and …'

The glasses danced as Big Viktor's fist crashed onto the desk.

'What?' he shouted. 'Are you telling me that this so-called genius who I have the misfortune to have fathered can't even write a simple computer program?'

He glowered and poured himself another vodka, then yelled into the intercom.

'Irena, bring us some strong coffee and get a move on!'
Then, scowling at Kyril, 'You've had all the time you asked
for haven't you? Why have you failed to achieve anything at
all, you and your team of simpletons?'

'Well, father, we thought we were on a promising line of
development, but the calculations got so complex that the
system kept crashing. So that's why, so far ...'

Viktor raised an enormous hand to silence the stammered apology.

'I don't want to hear any more lame excuses. I want
results, d'you hear? You'd better come up with some better
news inside a week, or you can forget all about that Harley-
Davidson I promised you. Get back to your bunch of
dimwits and don't come near me again until you have the
answers I want. Now get out of my sight and let me do
something useful.'

Kyril scrambled to his feet without a word and hurried to
the door, almost colliding with Irena as she came in with a
tray of coffee.

It was the day after Kyril's stormy meeting with his father in
St Petersburg. Here in Mallorca the sun was shining, but
there were high clouds in a blue sky although the wind was
cold up in the hills. In this sparsely inhabited rural part
of the island, Vasco's dark blue Jaguar turned out of the
gates of the Valseca family's *possessió* and headed towards
Palma. This was the car he loved to drive, especially in good
weather; the Volvo Estate was reserved for the winter, or the
occasional stormy day. This morning he was in a particularly
good mood and sang along happily with the car radio.
Earlier he had phoned his old friend Miquel Santiago and
arranged to meet for a morning coffee at their favourite
café bar, L'Olivera Vella, near the covered market on the
east side of the city.

He had arrived home from London to a warm welcome

from Guillem and Antonia, who had kept everything in the house and estate running like clockwork in his absence. Drinking coffee together on the terrace, with the dogs at his feet, he told them how the celebration of his beloved daughter's engagement had developed into the happiest family party he could remember. Biel's chance visit had been an unexpected bonus. Above all, he had been delighted with Bel's future husband. He seemed like a younger version of himself, sharing so many of Vasco's own interests and having a generous, outgoing personality.

Privately, Vasco realised that it was a happy accident that his successful visit to the Royal Society's debate in London and his discussions with Martin had started him thinking again about the problem of the hacker who had given the PIIB so much trouble with their bank account. Something had been said which unlocked some new avenues in his mind. He had made mental notes on the flight home to Palma. It wouldn't be easy to crack the problem, but he started to attack it as soon as he had finished sharing his happy news with Guillem and Antonia.

Over the next day or so he spent many hours on the computer, with some riding on the estate to clear his mind when his efforts reached an apparent dead end. Eventually, though, it all fell into place when he had one of his sudden revelations. The previous night he hadn't slept much. After tossing and turning for a few hours Vasco got up and went back to his study to fine-tune the program. By breakfast time, when Antonia scolded him into the dining room and fussed over him with coffee, scrambled eggs and toast, he had completed the job.

The problem was that all hackers and virus developers used a variety of methods to cloak their identity. The key had been finding a way to get inside that system and then insert his own specially designed virus, a trojan, to extract all the information about the originator of the illegal activity. In the end it had been almost unbelievably simple – a matter of patching together ideas discussed at the Royal Society's meeting onto elements drawn from his own research into some specific areas of astronomy and navigation. The trick had been to identify those links and then add some 'special effects'. These had come to Vasco in a flash of insight, triggered by a chance remark made by Martin when they rode out to Heathrow with Isabel to put him on the plane to Mallorca.

Wolfing down his breakfast, he grabbed another cup of coffee and went back to the computer. Now was the time for the all-important test. Vasco frowned. Who could he call without revealing his discovery? Then he realised that it could be much easier than he thought; his incoming emails could easily be checked for their geographical origins. His personal and business emails would be easy to identify, since he could pinpoint the source in every case. If there was unsolicited 'spam' offering cheap mortgages and pornographic rubbish, so much the better.

After twenty minutes or so he sat back in his chair to admire the first printout. There they were; the precise co-ordinates of latitude and longitude, accurate down to a few metres. First, there was the location of Martin Weston's office, then a slightly different set of co-ordinates for Isabel's apartment. There were a few more from friends and colleagues in America and Europe – and all of them seemed to check out. As expected, there were also several 'spam' messages coming from sources all over the world including Kiev, Manila, Florida, Illinois and Sao Paulo. He had immediately telephoned Miquel to arrange their rendezvous; he could hardly wait to tell him the good news. As soon as they could get access to the records at the bank, the PIIB would be able to pinpoint the location of the mystery hacker who had sabotaged the Party's account.

After negotiating the morning traffic on the edge of the

city, Vasco headed into the smaller side streets near El Corte Inglés department store on the Avenguidas. He was lucky to find a space for his car near the market beside the Placa de l'Olivar. Looking at his watch, he found that he was a little early for his 10.30 rendezvous with his friend, so went into the nearby branch of the Banco de Catalunya y de les Illes Balears – the BCIB – which held the account for his struggling political party, the PIIB.

Walking a few paces to the bar he found that his friend was already in his favourite widow seat, smoking his old pipe and frowning as he tackled *The Times* crossword. He looked up.

'Hey, Vasco, how was London? And how is the lovely Bel? You told me nothing on the phone, you dog, so let's have a full report.'

Clapping his friend on the shoulder, Vasco slipped into a chair. Grimacing as he flapped his hand at the clouds of smoke, he called for coffee. A lawyer friend from one of the offices in the Carrer de Sant Miquel looked up, smiled, nodded and continued reading some papers beside him. For the next half hour, Miquel heard all the news from Vasco's trip. By the end of the account, both men were in great good humour and called for a couple of Fundadors to toast Isabel and her fiancé.

'They haven't set a date yet,' said Vasco, 'but it could be September. Martin will be coming over in a few days and I've invited him to come to our Symposium. Then he'll be able to meet Teresa – she's sure to demand that the wedding takes place here in Mallorca. The poor chap doesn't know what's going to hit him!'

They laughed, then Miquel changed the subject and frowned as he explained that the meeting of the PIIB finance committee had been depressing. They didn't take kindly to the news that a hacker had damaged the party's funding very seriously, and there was a desperate need for additional cash.

Meanwhile, neither of them had noticed the quiet man who sat alone in the corner. Paulo Acappella was a regular visitor to L'Olivera Vella. He arrived almost every morning around 10 am, drank two or three cups of strong black coffee and read *Ultima Hora* in depth. Afterwards he would walk back to his nearby apartment, calling into the market a few steps away to pick up vegetables, cheese and fish, lamb or chicken. He rarely spoke to anybody in the café. This was not surprising, for his manner was aloof and superior, the natural result of a lifetime spent as a waiter. And, for the last twenty-five of his sixty years he had had top jobs at some of the most prestigious hotels and restaurants across the world.

During that time he had acquired particular skills; a retentive photographic memory, mastery of three languages – English, French and Spanish, plus some knowledge of German and Portuguese – and a keen eye and ear. Added to that was an awareness that information overheard or secretly observed could be extremely valuable. He had also developed another valuable skill: a unique capability to change his outward personality and bearing at will. One moment he could appear insignificant, virtually invisible. The next he would seem to be a commanding presence, exuding power and authority.

Paulo was able to capitalise on his special talents as an eavesdropper through his own family. His brother Enrico, was four years younger and headed up a major Mafia operation in Genoa. Among his other activities, he had excellent connections to generate profit from information supplied by Paulo.

Years before, when the two of them were in their teens, both their parents had died within a few months of each other and the brothers had run wild. Soon they had joined one of the biggest criminal groups which controlled the waterfront at Genoa. Before long they had become involved in crime and in violent turf wars with other gangs. There had been stabbings, beatings and revenge killings. Enrico was utterly ruthless and, although the younger of the two, fought his way to the top and stayed there.

Then there was a street fight; Paulo was cut with a broken bottle and got blood poisoning from the infected gash. While he was sick his uncle Luigi persuaded him to give it all up, with the promise of a good job. He was manager of a small luxury hotel near the business district and had set his nephew to work in his exclusive restaurant. Paulo took to his new life like a duck to water and never looked back, moving onwards and upwards in the world of hotels and fine dining. In the course of his career he was headhunted by hotels and restaurants in three continents, working his way up to senior waiter, sommelier and, finally, maître d'hôtel. In Rome, Paris, London, Sydney and New York he achieved eminence in his profession with lucrative appointments in the most luxurious hotels.

Meanwhile, Enrico had prospered too, with his fast-growing income flowing from drugs, protection, forgery, prostitution and other traditional criminal activities. However, he had taken every opportunity to cash in on indiscretions overheard by Paulo in the course of his unobtrusive attentions to well-connected clients. Many of these had potential for massive personal blackmail involving the rich and famous. He had also listened in on clandestine business meetings with anti-trust implications, or had become witness to the transfer of information resulting from industrial espionage. Occasionally, vital state secrets would be picked up by Paulo's acute hearing. All of these, and more, had potential for lucrative rewards from Enrico's network of contacts. The two brothers kept in touch regularly and had recently perfected their IT skills to help with the transfer of information. Paulo was often able to scan valuable material contained in documents 'borrowed' from an unguarded briefcase and email it to Enrico for evaluation.

Much of this was in the past, for Paulo had finally given up his career as a formidable maître d' when his Spanish wife – met, wooed and married during a whirlwind court-ship in New York – inherited valuable family property in Mallorca. He retired almost at once and they had moved to Palma, only for her to die suddenly from a massive heart attack. He had quickly come to terms with his solitary life, with four major passions to give him purpose.

He had been a powerful athlete in his youth and had always kept fit and active through regular visits to the gym; secondly, he maintained regular contact with his brother, feeding him scraps of information and scanned documents as before. These came mainly from lawyers with offices in the nearby Carrer de Sant Miquel, who he could overhear discussing their clients' affairs in L'Olivera Vella. The secrets he discovered this way were sometimes surprisingly important, so that in a few cases the resulting 'bonuses' were quite large, sufficient to finance his third interest, a lifelong fascination with philately. As a result, he had been able to build up the world's largest privately owned collection of early Spanish stamps in a remarkably short time. Finally, he had recently revived an early passion for motorcycles and had explored every corner of Mallorca on a fearsome black Ducati 900.

Paulo appeared to pay no attention to the two men who had been talking so excitedly, but as their conversation switched to a discussion about computer software, his nostrils twitched instinctively as he sensed a valuable oppor-tunity. Hidden behind his newspaper, his acute hearing picked up every word.

Vasco was extremely animated as he spoke rapidly to his friend, putting a Compaq laptop on their table and calling for more coffee.

'How do you like this, Miquel? You know, you should really get one of these. I know they're expensive, but the University would pay. Mark my words, in a few years' time the price will come down and even the students will have them. And now, with my new toy, I can show you what my latest program can do right here. This program I've just developed could give us an accurate geographical fix on that hacker who got into the PIIB bank account. All we need is the electronic details surrounding those illegal transactions and I can nail the little creep.'

As coffee arrived Miquel looked sceptical.

'Trust you to have the latest gadget, Vasco!' He held up his hand. 'Even if your program can do what you say, how are we going to get our hands on the details of the phoney transactions on the PIIB account?'

'I'd already thought of that. We could get Ramón Vila over from the Bank. I checked with his Secretary and he should be free about now. He would certainly come if we offer him a brandy to make it more interesting. Why don't you go next door and ask him while I run a final check?'

Miquel sighed deeply and frowned.

'Oh well, as I'm the bloody treasurer, I suppose it's my job to go and ask him. I'll ask him about getting access to the bank's computer records too, but they won't be giving permission easily. Anyway, you would only frighten him off. He thinks you're a bit mad – and sometimes I don't blame him.'

Picking up his aged pipe, Miquel left the café in a cloud of smoke. Vasco took the list of email addresses from his pocket and started to re-check the co-ordinates. After a moment or two he looked startled and examined his list again. The computer was now producing slightly changed co-ordinates, sufficiently different to be significant. He ran his fingers through his hair and drained his coffee cup at a gulp. As he sat gazing out of the window at the sunlight on the olive trees in the square, Vasco went into a reverie, trying to understand why his system was now giving a slightly different set of readings.

He was still lost in his own thoughts when Miquel bustled in with the bank manager and pulled up a chair for him, ordering more coffee and brandy for them all. Nobody paid any attention to Paulo Acappella as he sat in the far corner, apparently completely absorbed in *Ultima Hora*.

'Professor Santiago was telling me about your remarkable development,' said Ramón Vila as he shook Vasco by the hand, 'and my congratulations on your daughter's engagement. You must be very happy.'

Vasco stammered thanks and a greeting before pressing the keys of his computer nervously.

'I can show you the results, Ramón.' He hesitated as Miquel registered his friend's uncertainty and raised an eyebrow. 'But I have to admit that there has been a small alteration in the co-ordinates since I made the first detections yesterday. At the moment I can't account for this, but I'm certain the system can be perfected very quickly. Trust me.'

Vila looked doubtful.

'Sorry, Vasco. I don't see that "trust" is quite good enough. Miquel has told me that you want me to approach Head Office to request authority for direct access to our electronic records. I simply can't do that until you can guarantee absolute accuracy. I'm sure our directors would be ready to agree to that as part of a negotiation to acquire a system which does everything you claim. But I really must have a completely convincing demonstration. Give me a call when you've got something that actually works. Show me guaranteed performance and, if you can really do that, I'll be delighted to buy the drinks. And I'll gladly put forward your request.'

Ramón Vila stood up quickly and drained his brandy,

nodded and left the café, leaving Vasco and Miquel sitting dejectedly at their table.

As Vasco stared moodily out of the window, Miquel shrugged and picked up *The Times*, wrestling with the cryptic crossword to take his mind off their brush-off from Ramón Vila. Vasco gazed across the open space, lost in his own thoughts. Gradually his frown relaxed. After a moment he suddenly grabbed his friend's arm.

'My God, I've just realised what the problem is. Look, Miquel, can you see the shadow from that olive tree in the square? A few minutes ago it was touching that bench, but now it's moved on! Don't you see what that means?'

Miquel sighed, laid down *The Times* and reached for his pipe.

'No, but you're probably going to tell me anyway.'

Vasco grinned.

'Looking at the shadow from that olive tree made me remember an astronomical formula called the Equation of Time. The details are in my study at home, but the principle is simple. Sundials are only precisely accurate four times a year. That's because the movement of the earth goes in a cycle, relative to the sun. So, if you want to get your time really accurately from a big sundial, it's almost always necessary to make a correction according to the day of the year.'

Miquel scratched his chin.

'But what has all that got to do with the errors in the system you've been developing?'

'Don't you see? My program relies partly on astronomical data, but I didn't think to incorporate the Equation of Time. So there is no built-in adjustment for the locations where emails are originating. That's why I've been getting these variations from one day to the next. When I get back home later it should be child's play to amend the program and get the accuracy we need.'

Vasco beamed.

'This has put me in a wonderful mood, Miquel, so now I feel ready for anything. Let's just see if we can polish off this crossword of yours before we celebrate.'

He grabbed *The Times* and frowned for a moment. 'This shouldn't be too difficult. You've done most of it already, but let's have a look at eight across ... "Fermenting grain vat with nothing in it, but a cartographer, perhaps." Hmm. Nine letters. You already have "i" as the fourth letter and "r" at the end and, of course, it's an anagram.' He paused. 'I've got it – the answer's "navigator".'

As Vasco wrote in the answer, Miquel looked quizzically at his friend.

'That's a happy coincidence. You'll be needing a name for this program of yours, so why don't you take the word "Navigator", and substitute an "e" for the "i"? Then it becomes "Navegator", which brings out the electronic element.'

'That's a brilliant suggestion, Miquel. I think I'll do just that.'

'Glad you approve. Now, shouldn't we celebrate – just as if we were launching a ship?'

Vasco beamed and stood up.

'You are absolutely right, Miquel. So I'm going to buy us both a seriously stylish lunch. This place is a great watering hole, but the food isn't the best. I know, let's walk down to the Parlament Restaurant. This is a really special occasion. We definitely deserve to reward ourselves properly for finding a way to get back at that bloody hacker. Once I've done a little fine tuning of Navegator we'll have even more reason to congratulate ourselves. In the morning I'll call Ramón Vila and set up a demonstration at the bank. Then we can come here for drinks – and this time he will be doing the buying.'

Vasco paid the bill, added a generous tip and picked up

his laptop. Then the two professors walked out into the sunshine together. Back in the café Paulo Acappella was trying to put a value on what he had overheard. Was it seriously possible that Vasco Valseca had written a program, Navegator, or whatever he chose to call it, which could pinpoint the source of any email or Web-based signal? If so, what might this be worth? Deep in thought, he folded up his newspaper and paid for his coffee. Then he hurried back to his apartment nearby. It was time to telephone his brother Enrico in Monaco for some advice. With any luck, his reward for this information might be enough to complete the purchase of that amazing hoard of Spanish stamps. What a prize! The rare Queen Isabella issue from 1850 which had just been found in an attic in Saragossa would be the crowning glory of his collection. Just think of it, two complete sets and three more single stamps too! As soon as he had spoken to Enrico he would go round to the stamp dealer and put in a provisional bid.

The eastern end of the Boulevard des Moulins is a soberly expensive part of Monte Carlo, where the rich and famous can live without too much attention from the paparazzi and the gossip columnists. The Swiss-Astoria apartment building stands close to the public underground car park at the Place des Moulins. Those who like to have access to their own Ferrari, Aston-Martin or Maserati close to their luxurious suites in the Principality of Monaco can rent reserved garages inside this multi-storey cavern – not cheap, but chic. It is all very convenient for a quick dash to nearby Italy, or to Nice and the other delights of the French Riviera.

All the Swiss-Astoria apartments have balconies. The most prestigious, on the upper floors, have bedrooms with stunning views of the harbour and the Mediterranean beyond. In one of these exclusive eyries a mobile phone on a bedside table rang insistently for some time. Eventually it was answered a little breathlessly by Enrico Acappella.

'Pronto, what is it this time Paulo? I'm in an important meeting. Can't it wait? … OK. I'll call you back in an hour or so.'

Enrico switched off the phone and returned to the business of the meeting – another storming climax involving the owner of the apartment. She was a wealthy and curvaceous American widow he had met less than two hours ago at the Café de Paris on Casino Square, the location of choice for elegant daytime pickups. On this particular morning it had taken no time at all for flirtation over cappuccinos to lead to insistent fondling during a short taxi ride. Then there was urgent groping in the high-speed lift to the widow's apartment, quickly followed by instant coupling on her satin sheets. This routine was a regular activity for Enrico Acappella, who spent much of his time in Monaco. Here he could make the most of abundant opportunities to indulge in his expensive tastes. Chief of these were fine clothes, food, wine and, of course, passionate and stylish women.

It was easy for him to talk to ladies from most of the European countries. He shared a natural ability for languages with his older brother, learning passable German and Spanish over the years. His English was excellent too, partly thanks to a year-long affair with a gorgeous young English woman who gave private tuition to wealthy Monegasques eager to perfect their vocabulary and grammar.

A little over half an hour after Paulo's call, Enrico emerged from the Swiss-Astoria. Having showered and shaved, he looked immaculate in a suit from Savile Row in London. His patrician looks and confident bearing proclaimed him to be a man of taste and elegance, so that more than one lady watched with interest as this handsome man strolled across the road. True to his deprived background, he rarely took a taxi in Monaco – unless romance was on the menu. Usually he preferred to use the spotless, fast and inexpensive bus service which covered the whole of the tiny Principality. So, taking the public lift from the South side of the Place des Moulins down to the Avenue Princesse Grace, he boarded a No. 6 Bus to Fontvielle. This was the part of Monaco he favoured, less flashy than the area near the casino. Like many of the apartment owners up at the Place des Moulins, he had private garaging nearby for his pride and joy, an immaculately restored classic – a Lamborghini Espada. He had another rich man's toy too; a keen flier, he had invested in a twin-engined Beech Baron 58 which was kept in a private hangar at Nice airport. He alighted from the bus at the stop nearest to the discreet marina – not so ostentatious as the main harbour – and strolled the short distance to the private berth for his yacht, *Angelina.*

The 35-metre ketch was maintained immaculately by his two South African crew; a skipper and bodyguard, helped by his younger brother who worked as deckhand, but also cooked and acted as steward. A few minutes after coming aboard he was sitting in his chart room, which was equipped with all the luxurious refinements of a top chief executive's office. Enrico sipped a glass of sparkling prosecco. Then, picking up a radio phone from a clip above his brass-bound teak desk, he spun round in the leather upholstered swivel chair and called the familiar number in Palma on an encrypted channel.

Paulo answered after only two rings but Enrico cut short the greeting from Mallorca.

'Pronto, brother of mine. What's so urgent?'

Listening intently as Paulo explained what had been overheard in L'Olivera Vella, he pulled thoughtfully at his lower lip while making detailed notes in a slim, leather-bound pocket book. After almost thirty minutes of detailed question and answer, Enrico frowned with concentration and closed the book.

'That could be very interesting, very interesting indeed. And exceptionally valuable. Who knows what this program might be worth – if it really does work. Yes, we must move very fast, but very carefully on this one. Like a nudist climbing through a barbed wire fence to escape from a bull, if you follow me. Now look: it's really urgent that we get after this. We must get hold of this software before the news leaks out. Normally, I'd want to wait until there's been a totally successful demonstration. But there's no time to lose. Just how confident are you that this Professor Valseca can make the adjustments?'

'Trust me, Enrico. I'd bet my stamp collection on the bank manager being convinced by this time tomorrow.'

'OK Paulo. Let's go for it. I must think this over and make some calls. Give me an hour or two and I'll contact you later. Stay near the phone and work on your precious stamps, or look at some motorbike catalogues. Ciao, ciao.'

He hung up and called for the steward to refill his empty glass and bring him a chicken sandwich for a working lunch while he developed his plan. Who would pay the best price for a piece of software with such potential value? The world's intelligence agencies could be very interested indeed, but they were tricky to deal with and it might be better to keep them at arm's length. Looking through his pages of notes, a ghost of a smile crossed his face as he ringed the word 'Navegator,' which Paulo had spelled out for him. Enrico sipped his prosecco and turned on the hi-fi system. Listening to Callas singing was always an inspiration. Closing his eyes, he relaxed, the chicken sandwich forgotten as that glorious voice filled the air.

As the aria from *Madam Butterfly* ended, Enrico suddenly opened his eyes and turned off the sound system before the next track could begin. He had just had an idea. His activities had often involved business with Viktor Dankovitch, Big Viktor, in St Petersburg – and even though he had left the FSB some years ago he would still have high-level contacts in the Russian Security Service. Yes, Big Viktor could be the best channel for selling this Navegator system, if only Paulo could secure it for him. Enrico chuckled as he recalled his more spectacular deals with the Russian. They both had a taste for practical jokes, each of them trying to outdo the other in finding more complicated tricks.

It had all started a few years back when both men were already seriously wealthy. Making a handsome profit was still worthwhile, but between these two this was no longer the main incentive. Some added spice was needed – and both of them scented the other's competitive nature. So, little by little, the tricks had begun, with each trying to outdo the other. It had actually got to the point where the contest of minds behind the practical joke had become more important than the deal itself.

The last occasion was only two months ago, when the Russian had scored with a consignment of stolen diamonds. The handover had involved a complicated journey across Northern Italy, with checkpoints and passwords in Genoa, Turin and Modena. At last, a briefcase was picked up by Enrico's courier from a luggage locker at Milan railway station – but on examination the gems turned out to be paste imitations. Violent retaliation was only averted when, a few hours later, a parcel of chocolate Easter eggs was delivered personally to Enrico by DHL. The genuine diamonds were inside the eggs, the largest containing a personal note from Viktor and a luxury Breitling wrist-watch.

If Enrico could get a good price for Navegator from the

Russian, it would be his own turn to come up with an even more interesting handover scenario. It would be a real bonus to get even. But while he was listening to Callas just now he had had an idea. His knowledge of Mallorca had been built up over the years, thanks to frequent sailing trips aboard *Angelina* to visit Paulo. He had also called in occasionally in his private plane for an overnight stop – or just for lunch – en route to Madrid, Lisbon, Morocco or Gibraltar. Viktor's courier could be made to visit the island to collect the software package and, as icing on the cake, he had just thought of a particularly tricky challenge to be completed before the Navegator software was handed over. But it would all depend on Paulo. Was he still a killer at heart? Thinking of their teenage years together with the dockland gangs in Genoa, Enrico was sure he could persuade his brother to do what was needed. After all, there would be a large cash incentive and Paulo was eager to add some very expensive specimens to his precious stamp collection.

Yes, it could all fall into place. Perhaps it was not too much to ask $5 million from Big Viktor, who perhaps could sell the package on to his old friends in Russian Intelligence, the Americans, the Chinese or even the Israelis for as much as $10 million. But it would be a gamble until he had final confirmation from Paulo that this amazing program would actually work as it should.

He frowned and thought hard for a moment. What the hell, it would do no harm to test the temperature of the water. After a few calls to St Petersburg, Enrico found that Viktor had gone on a 'business trip'. After some persuasion, Viktor's secretary Irena sulkily admitted that this was a two-night visit to his dacha, near Volkhov, about two hours' drive east of Russia's second city. She added that he had gone there with a big fat girl and slammed the phone down. Enrico chuckled. He had visited the dacha himself as

Viktor's guest after a successful venture. The pair of them had shared a weekend of relaxed debauchery which, even now, brought back vivid memories. Finding that he still had the number, he called the dacha. The phone rang for a very long time before Viktor Dankovitch answered angrily. He was not in a good mood – hardly surprising, as the phone had interrupted his activity with 'the big fat girl'. Actually, she was a compliant and muscular blonde physiotherapist and she was using her formidable talents to give him a truly unforgettable erotic experience. Even when Enrico had introduced himself Viktor remained sullen and unfriendly. However, when the purpose of the call had been explained, the Russian was soon paying very serious attention. He was still furious with his son Kyril for his lack of progress in finding a system to match the Americans' ambitions for 'Sniper'. But now his long-term associate was offering him an opportunity to humiliate the team in Washington. It was almost too good to be true. Even if there was no certainty of a deal with the CIA, or whoever was running the American project, it was a gamble well worth taking. With his worldwide contacts he should have no difficulty in finding another buyer; no problem.

So, they began a marathon telephone conversation, arguing and haggling for over an hour. Viktor doubted the performance and value of software developed by some academic – and in Mallorca, of all places. And, even if it was able to achieve what Enrico claimed, it would be very difficult to locate a buyer at all. A potential purchaser with enough cash to provide an interesting deal would be even harder to find. Naturally, he was not about to reveal his knowledge of the Americans' desperate search for an identical system.

Enrico insisted that he had more than one eager customer waiting for the chance to bid for Navegator. He had only given Viktor first refusal for old times' sake. It seemed unnecessary to mention that he had not actually got his hands on the software – or that its capabilities had not yet been fully demonstrated.

In the end, though, a deal was struck at $4.5 million. Enrico would personally underwrite the performance of the Navegator system. Viktor's representative would take delivery in Mallorca, but before passing over the software, $2.5 million would be deposited in Enrico's private account in a Swiss bank. The Russians would also require an absolute assurance that they would be buying the one and only version of the Navegator program, with an ironclad guarantee that no other copy existed. It would be the Italians' job to ensure the continued silence of the software's author, by whatever means. The balance of $2 million would be payable immediately following a successful evaluation and trial of the system by Kyril's team in St Petersburg.

Both men agreed that speed was essential and the rendezvous was fixed for the earliest possible date. It was now Wednesday 17 March; they finally agreed on Wednesday 24 March, only six clear days away, which would give both parties just enough time to set up their own logistics. The Russian courier would find an envelope containing a map and full details of the handover arrangements in the glove compartment of a car to be collected at Palma airport.

At last the call ended and Enrico hung up with a smile. He had renewed his association with Viktor and they had agreed on a weekend of celebration in Paris when the whole business was over. Now it was time to make sure that Paulo would organise the operation in Mallorca. He intended to give Viktor's courier a complicated set of tasks and everything must be exactly right. Enrico laughed aloud as he imagined the Russian attempting his tricky assignments with little knowledge of Spanish.

He thought for a while and finished his chicken sandwich while he made notes to brief his brother. Then, after pouring himself another glass of prosecco, he picked up the phone again and called Paulo's number in Palma. First, it was absolutely vital to ensure that Navegator really would work. Second, he must work out a scheme to capture the software without leaving any traces behind. An ordinary theft was out of the question. The creator of the software would have to be permanently silenced to ensure security of the information. That might be messy, so a surgically clean method had to be found; there must be no incriminating evidence to suggest foul play. Suddenly he smiled. He had just thought of a way to achieve this. His tricky challenge for the Russians would be his best scheme by far.

Paulo, with his detailed local knowledge, would surely be able to make it work. He was going to need his brother's special talents in any case. He would play a key role in the scenario he had in mind; it also promised to leave no evidence – only a false trail. But now it was necessary to find some special items to provide authentic 'window dressing'. He would also need legal advice and some inside knowledge about a major Spanish bank. Perhaps he could even find a mole inside the BCIB itself, which would be a big help. He would need to call in a few favours and make a lot of phone calls. But what a glorious opportunity! He was really going to enjoy every moment of this exercise. It would definitely be the toughest challenge yet for his Russian rival.

7

The day after their unsuccessful attempt to impress Ramón Vila, Vasco and Miquel had been grudgingly granted a 10 o'clock appointment by the sceptical manager. However, the presentation of the revised version of Navegator had gone like clockwork. The banker, normally dour and unemotional, had been positively enthusiastic about this new demonstration. After being sworn to secrecy, his second in command was invited into his small but elegant office to observe the presentation of Navegator's capabilities. The young trainee manager was an IT specialist and pronounced the system's potential 'awesome'. Vasco's overnight adjustments had worked perfectly and the geographical origins of several emails provided by the bank had been swiftly pinpointed, including the Head Office of BCIB in Barcelona.

Vila had been as good as his word and bought Vasco and Miquel two rounds of drinks at L'Olivera Vella. Mutual congratulations took place as he promised to email immediately to his head office in Barcelona, with a full report and an urgent request to allow Vasco and Miquel access to the bank's electronic records.

None of them noticed the quiet man who sat in the corner reading *Ultima Hora*. He sat with his back to the good-humoured group with something to celebrate, but his acute hearing picked up every word.

*

Paulo Acappella was a little breathless as he walked into the expensively furnished study of his apartment. He always jogged up the stairs to keep himself in shape and had been hurrying to get home as quickly as possible so that he could telephone Enrico with the good news. He had slipped out of L'Olivera Vella as soon as possible. His brother would be delighted to have confirmation that their eavesdropping exercise was about to pay off with another sure-fire winner. Quickly drinking a glass of Pellegrino mineral water, he immediately poured himself another before sitting at his desk. Perhaps this development would give his brother's fertile mind another idea for a deal. He crossed over to the desk, sat down at the workstation and picked up the phone next to the computer keyboard for his encrypted call to Monaco.

Aboard his luxurious ketch *Angelina* Enrico set down his coffee cup and picked up his phone as it rang insistently. Apart from 'Pronto' and 'Si' at intervals he said little as his brother gave an excited report on the successful demonstration of Navegator which he had just overheard taking place at L'Olivera Vella. At the end of Paulo's blow-by-blow commentary, he threw back his head, laughed loudly and slapped the top of his handsome desk.

'Brother of mine, that is absolutely wonderful news. You promised me those adjustments were going to work – and they have. It's good to know that your instincts were right as usual. I'm going to have a drink to celebrate our good fortune. I've got most things planned, but there are still some details to be worked out. By tomorrow I'll be able to brief you about your part in the scheme, but right now there are some urgent calls I must make, so let's talk again. I'll phone you in the morning. Si … Ciao, Ciao.'

Enrico picked up his notes. The first call of many would be to a shady lawyer in Barcelona. He had already asked him to research the internal arrangements at the BCIB. By now, with any luck, he should have set up a reliable contact inside the bank's senior administration. Then, in turn, he would phone his team of forgers in Paris, Rome and Amsterdam who had already been put on standby.

The lawyer would provide the key to the whole enterprise. During a lengthy encrypted phone conversation he agreed to help with a lot of detailed work. This was partly for old times' sake – Enrico had got him out of a very nasty problem with a Spanish drug dealer, whose 'disappearance' had mysteriously taken place while on a boat trip from the marina at Barcelona down the coast to Denia. However, he also needed payment for bribes, expenses and, naturally, a service charge. After some amiable haggling, they agreed on a price in US dollars, rather than pesetas; a sum of $200,000, with half to be handed over immediately – and the other half to be paid on successful completion of the project.

The details were vital and there was a critical timetable. Enrico needed to have a quantity of totally genuine BCIB headed notepaper, a great many continuation sheets and some large envelopes. The letter headings would need to show the Head Office address and a small batch would need to be delivered to Paulo in Palma no later than the next day, Friday. A larger consignment of the special stationery would be needed by Enrico immediately after the week end, plus a number of other important items.

The lawyer made light of the task. Getting the stationery was no problem at all. He had what he called 'special access' to the heart of BCIB and it also happened that his brother Pedro was flying to Mallorca tomorrow for a golfing weekend at Son Vida. Nothing would be easier for him than to leave a small package at the hotel next to the golf course for collection by Paulo Acappella. As for the rest of the stuff, that could all be obtained and sent directly to Enrico by a trusted courier to meet the timetable. He would now get to work on obtaining the various items and preparing some extensive legal text for this 'very entertaining project'. He, personally, could send a draft by encrypted email before midday tomorrow.

Enrico was delighted and said so. He promised the lawyer a bonus if everything went to plan and assured him of further business in the future. He rang off and rubbed his hands. All he had to do now was to alert his brother immediately about the collection from the hotel at Son Vida. He also had to be briefed on the other urgent part of the Palma end of the operation; documents had to be printed there by Paulo in good time to be checked and delivered personally on Monday morning. A phone call to Palma established that Paulo was well prepared to carry out those tasks. Using a false name, his brother had even found out from the university where he would need to take that very special letter. It would take no time at all to ride out to Son Antoni to make the delivery – and he could dress up like a regular motor-cycle courier to complete the charade.

Enrico ended the call and smiled broadly. The rest of the telephone session could wait awhile. The key elements of his master plan were now in place. The details would be relatively easy to put together. It was time to celebrate. He called out to the steward to fetch the prosecco. Within a few moments he had brought a foaming glass and grinned broadly when invited to fetch his brother and take a glass for himself. Waiting until the bubbles had subsided, Enrico laughed aloud and stood to face his crew.

'To Navegator!' he cried and, lifting his glass to the South Africans, drained it in a single draught before smashing it against the base of the oil burning stove.

'Now,' he said thoughtfully, 'it's time to arrange some interesting tasks for our friends in St Petersburg!'

*

107

Viktor Dankovitch strode into his palatial office later the same day, threw down his briefcase and smiled to himself. He had come straight to his headquarters after his invigorating stay at the dacha. Memories from those few hours and the news from Enrico Acappella had put him in a particularly good mood. He had already asked Irena to find Kyril as quickly as possible. He reached into his desk for the bottle of Georgian brandy which he always kept handy. As luck would have it, Kyril was in the building already, checking some data disks carrying counterfeit programs. Bill Gates would not have been pleased with Kyril's latest copies of the world's most successful software. Within a few moments he was knocking fearfully at his father's door.

'Come in, dear boy, come in and take a seat.'

Viktor beamed. Kyril sat down, grateful that his father seemed to be so amiable. The bottle was uncorked and the big man poured two generous glasses of the amber spirit.

'*Na zdrov 'ye!*' They clinked glasses and drank together – Kyril less greedily than his father.

'You may be wondering why I'm in a good mood today, eh? Well, it's no thanks to you and your bunch of idiots. However, fate has given me a chance to score another victory over the bloody Americans. My friend Enrico Acappella – you know, that Italian – has stumbled across the very piece of software we have been looking for. And he can get the unique, one and only copy for us.'

Kyril's jaw dropped as his father continued.

'Don't trouble yourself about how this has all happened, I can fill you in on the details later. Of course, you will need to check over the program but, if it's as good as he claims, we can sell it on to the Yanks for millions of dollars. How about that?'

Kyril looked puzzled.

'I don't see how the Italians could have done that. But the main thing as you say, Father, is that it gives us a golden opportunity. How do we get hold of the software and how do we get the Americans to buy it?'

'Leave all that to me. I'm already working on handover details with Enrico. The pickup will be in Mallorca next Wednesday. That's March 24th, which is going to be a very unlucky day for those bastards in Washington. They're really going to hate this. Now, I'd thought of sending you, but you're too valuable to me here. What do you think about Ygor Krasnov? Would he make a reliable courier?'

'He's certainly tough and he showed quick thinking the other night, when that scum we were interrogating down at the freight yard nearly escaped.'

'Right. Krasnov it is then. Tell him to get ready for the trip and stay in this building around the clock until I'm ready to brief him about his mission.'

Kyril nodded.

'As for the contact with the Americans – well, you remember that weird British guy who calls himself Foxtrot? He sent us the original information about the "Sniper" team in Washington. He was eavesdropping on a conversation that included a senior CIA man from the American Embassy in London. He could be our entrance ticket to a very profitable negotiation. Which reminds me – get the office to have two and a half million US dollars available to make an immediate transfer to a Swiss Bank on Tuesday night or Wednesday morning. When you've done that, you can get back to your counterfeit software. Now I'm going to call Foxtrot.'

Kyril got to his feet. Viktor raised his glass again.

'Another toast, dear boy. *'Na zdrov 'ye!'* And success to our enterprise!'

He paused and said with a smile:

'You know, this has put me in particularly high spirits. Perhaps, if this all goes well, I might even buy you that Harley-Davidson after all.'

Kyril quickly left his father's office before he could change his mind.

Meanwhile, in the conference room, another wretched meeting of the Sniper Team had ended. They all sat in gloomy silence after a fresh-faced youngster from Army Intelligence had made a particularly stupid suggestion. Admiral Hobring threw his glasses onto the table in front of him. They bounced and knocked over a not-quite-empty plastic coffee cup. The cold dregs splashed onto a disorderly heap of papers which had spilled out of a manila folder. He winced and clutched his leg.

'Shit!' He roared, 'that's all I need. You're a hopeless bunch of deadbeats. Here in this room we're supposed to have some of the best brains in the USA and we've come up with nothing! This is the nineteenth day since we started this thing – and the fifth since we tried to get some new leads by getting outside help. Those suggestions weren't any good either – and this hopeless crew I've been saddled with is fresh out of ideas too. Now, see here. The President is going ape over this thing and he's got a meeting of security heads at the end of next week. He's going to have us all barbecued if we don't come up with something by then. Hasn't anybody got a glimmer of an idea? For Chrissake, somebody say something!'

There was a stony silence. Nobody wanted to meet his eyes as the admiral's piercing gaze raked the miserable group. Finally he slammed his hands on the table and they all jumped.

'OK, so we are at our wits' end, are we? Well, I guess if we're that desperate there's one last roll of the dice we can try. I'm taking a big gamble here, but as you all seem to be burned out, you're going to get a break from this treadmill. Let's see if a vacation from the daily routine can give us a breakthrough just in time, so that our brains can save our asses. I'm getting Gabriel and Rachel to take all of your contact details. When that's been done you'll be allowed out of quarantine here until next Thursday – that's March 25th. Remember the need for total security – and I do mean *total*. Everyone is to be back around this table at 10am that day with some new ideas that might actually work. Do you read me? Any questions?'

There were murmurs of 'No, Admiral', followed by a relieved but uncomfortable silence. People shifted uneasily in their chairs and started to gather their papers. Admiral Hobring had a final look around the table, stood up unsteadily, hefted his briefcase and limped to the door.

As soon as Hobnails had left, conversations broke out all around the room. Gabriel and Rachel had trouble getting firm contact details, but they all knew that until those had been provided there would be no way out past the security checkpoint. At last they were done. Gabriel picked up an internal phone and punched in the familiar number.

'Hi Charlene. Does the Admiral want a copy of the contact list before Rachel and I finish up here?'

After a pause he smiled wearily and hung up.

'I guess we're off the hook,' he said. 'It seems Hobnails is going to take a break too and doesn't want to be disturbed until we all get back from our R and R.' He paused and said thoughtfully.

'So, Rachel my darling, what are your plans exactly?'

Rachel looked up from her folders. Her shoulders drooped as she sighed.

'I should've liked to go back to Atlanta to see my folks, but they've planned a cruise for more than a year to celebrate their silver wedding anniversary. They were due to leave from Miami two days ago, so travelling home's out of the question. And I imagine you'll want to take a quick trip to London to see your twin sister. So, if I need some company, I guess I'll just have to go and see my old maiden aunt in Boca Raton.'

Gabriel gathered her into his arms.

'Don't be sad my darling. I've got a great idea. Why don't I give Isabel a call? We can make a quick trip to London and I just know she's going to love meeting you in person – especially after I told her so much about you during that flying visit just a few days ago. We don't need to take much with us. You're around the same size and I know she'd be more than happy to lend you any clothes you might need. We could get to the airport in time to make the overnight flight to London. All it needs is a phone call to Isabel. So, what do you say?'

Rachel frowned and was silent for a few moments. Then she looked straight into Gabriel's eyes.

'Are you really sure you want to do this? I think I know what it must mean to you. But, if you're serious, it would be just wonderful – I've never been to Europe and I'd just love to meet the other half of you. Anyway, my passport won't be a problem. It just happens to be here along with my other stuff – I had to have one when I went to Argentina on a student exchange from college.'

'That's wonderful! I'll call Isabel right now.'

He picked up the secure phone on the desk in the corner of the conference room. His conscience told him that he really shouldn't be using this line for a private call, but it only took an instant to convince himself that it was an exceptional situation and all in the line of duty. Within a few minutes he was talking to his excited sister in a torrent of Mallorquin while Rachel dashed back to her room to pack. He was hanging up just as she came back, carrying a pull-along tote bag and a smaller carry-on bag. Her eyes were shining.

'Well, what did Isabel say – can we stay at her place?'

Gabriel grinned. 'Yes, of course – she's over the moon

and wants to meet you so much.'

'Darling, that's wonderful!' said Rachel and threw herself into Gabriel's arms. After a few moments he gently disentangled himself from her embrace and smiled happily.

'I can take a lot of that, but right now I really ought to pack. We need to hurry out to the airport. Come and let's talk while I grab some things for London.'

Rachel began to walk towards the door, then paused and turned frowning.

'Oh, no! I've just thought of something.'

She unzipped her purse, pulled out her Filofax, quickly flipped through the pages and pulled a face as she checked the diary section.

'That's so terrible! My parents' ship finishes its trip to the Bahamas and Bermuda in New York, but it's going to call in at Baltimore overnight for a sightseeing tour in Washington – and that's next Wednesday. I really want to see them so very much and tell them about us. And I want you to meet them too – so do you think we could be back from London in time?'

Now it was Gabriel's turn to frown.

'That's a tough call. It's been so long since I visited with Isabel without Martin there, so I've just promised her to stay until late Wednesday afternoon. That way, we'd both get to see Martin too – he's arriving back from Mallorca around lunchtime and I really need to hear how he got on with Aunt Teresa in Palma. There's an evening flight from London to New York, so we could stay overnight at Kennedy airport, catch the first flight down to Washington on Thursday morning and be here to check the Sniper Team back through Security in time for the ten o'clock meeting …'

He tailed off as he realised that Rachel's mouth was set in a grim line. He took her gently in his arms but she pulled away.

'I really want to see my mom,' she said. 'It's been a long time now.'

'Let's not fight over this sweetheart.' He paused, frowning, then his face lit up.

'Look, there's another way we could fix things. How about this? Suppose we both fly to London tonight, then you travel back on a direct flight to arrive in Washington on Tuesday evening? That would get you here in plenty of time to see your folks on Wednesday. Meanwhile I stay on in London, just like I said, then catch the Wednesday afternoon flight – which gets me back here on Thursday morning in time for the meeting. How about that?'

Rachel considered for a moment, then nodded reluctantly.

'Yes, that sounds okay, I guess. I know it's difficult for both of us right now. Things are moving so fast and I just can't get my mind round all that's happening.'

Gabriel kissed her gently on the brow.

'That's understandable – and it's shaking me up too, I can tell you. We'll talk a lot more later, but right now I need to get my stuff if we're going to catch that flight.'

They went to Gabriel's room where Rachel sat on the bed while he packed a blue haversack and a smaller cabin bag. While he was stowing his gear he continued their conversation.

'I guess I should warn you that there's a sort of catch. Isabel's promised to visit Aunt Margalida down at Guildford on Monday. It's her sixtieth birthday on Monday, so she's having a celebration lunch party and we'll definitely have to be there too.'

He carefully folded a pair of dark green pants and packed them.

'She's a great character. Everyone calls her Margo and she's very special because Isabel stayed with her for almost nine years when she was in school in England.'

He held up a fawn-coloured jacket.

'I guess I'll travel in this to make a bit more room in my

bag. Anyway, Margo and her husband Esteban couldn't have kids, so Bel became their surrogate daughter – they totally spoiled her. And he was seriously rich – his family, the Ponsetis, made a fortune over the years from Majolica pearls, with a factory in the east of Mallorca, at Manacor – and he handled exports to the English-speaking world from an office in London.'

He was gathering up shirts and underwear, stowing them into the backpack. He went on talking over his shoulder as he picked up his shaving kit.

'Eventually Bel got to be a very lucky girl indeed. In fact, her great big beautiful apartment near Regents Park used to belong to the Ponseti family too. Isabel inherited it from Uncle Esteban when he died suddenly a few years back – so, she's got masses of room for gypsies like us. Isn't that amazing?'

Rachel clapped her hands.

'That sounds heavenly. And I can't wait to meet Margo either. She sounds like a really wonderful lady.'

Gabriel zipped up his bag, grabbed his parka and opened the door.

'Come on, let's go. We're going to have a great time in London.'

They strolled out of Gabriel's room, linked arms and sauntered to the security point, where they signed the register and retrieved their cell phones. Soon they were out on the street, yelling for a cab. Within minutes they were embracing on the back seat like kids on their first date. The cab driver smiled into his rear view mirror as he drove through the downtown traffic before heading across the bridge over the Potomac towards Dulles International Airport.

8

The overnight flight from Washington disembarked its passengers at Heathrow's Terminal 3. Gabriel and Rachel were lucky to be among the first to reach the Immigration desks. Both of them had been able to sleep for an hour or two on the flight, a natural reaction after days of intense pressure under Hobnails' hard discipline. They had woken refreshed and tried hard to make themselves look presentable before arrival, but their clothes looked just a little creased from the journey. There were no problems with Passport Control and they made good time into the baggage claim area, where a multinational mob of travellers dragged a motley collection of suitcases from the carousels. It took an age before their bags finally appeared but they got barely a glance from the Customs officers in the green channel. It wasn't long before they were confronted by a sea of faces – the usual swarm of waiting family and friends. All of them seemed to be in a happy mood as they greeted loved ones arriving from every corner of the globe.

It didn't take long for Gabriel to spot Isabel. Following their excited phone call she had not had much sleep; a passionate episode with Martin had been followed by hours of tossing and turning as she tried to picture her brother's new girlfriend. Now, though, she was showered and elegantly made up. It was hard to miss that stylish figure waving and jumping up and down, standing out from the crowd in an off-white raincoat. There were excited greetings, introductions and hugs, but Rachel and Isabel embraced warily. They cautiously linked arms and walked ahead of Gabriel as he struggled with one of Heathrow's more wilful baggage trolleys.

After negotiating the complicated walkways and a crowded lift to the third floor in the multi-storey car park, they finally piled into Isabel's silver Peugeot and set off for central London. Gabriel sat in the back and tried not to be scared as Isabel thrust her way through the traffic. All the while she kept up a non-stop commentary for the benefit of her front-seat passenger. The American girl was wide-eyed and fascinated by everything, especially the semi-detached houses and the red double-decker buses. Finally, after some questions and answers with Rachel about the latest royal family gossip, Isabel half turned to her brother in the back seat.

'Relax, Biel,' she said, 'You're in safe hands. I never lost a passenger yet. But I need to remind you about the other travelling that's going on right now. You'll remember that Papa persuaded Martin to fly out to Mallorca to attend his mathematics symposium.'

She swerved to avoid a white van and made a very unladylike gesture to the driver.

'Well, I watched him check in for his flight to Palma about an hour ago. It's such a pity you've just missed my lovely man, but he comes back next Wednesday, so can you both stay till then?'

As Isabel continued to jockey for position, switching lanes and cutting out less aggressive drivers, she went on bombarding both of her passengers with questions and information.

'How are you, Biel? You look a bit tired – you both do. Do you really have to work so hard? You know I'm planning to go to Guildford on Monday for Margo's sixtieth birthday. Can you both come too? I really, really hope so. I've already phoned her and she's just dying to meet you, Rachel – and she hasn't seen you, Biel, for at least two years. Do please say you'll come.'

She went on and on while Rachel's eyelids started to droop and with Gabriel's mumbled answers getting shorter and more difficult to hear, there was finally no response at all. Isabel looked in the driving mirror and saw that her brother was fast asleep, his head lolling against the head-rest. She stopped talking and concentrated on guiding the Peugeot back to Regents Park as smoothly as possible. Driving into her reserved parking bay, she gently woke Gabriel as Rachel stifled a yawn. Then she took them up the stairs and into her second-floor apartment.

Neither of her guests could manage more than a glass of water, before they were yawning again. She showed Gabriel and Rachel into the guest bedroom, where they eased their shoes off and slid gratefully, fully dressed, into the welcoming bed. Isabel looked at them lovingly.

'Just like the babes in the wood,' she murmured.

Then she drew the curtains and went back to the car for their bags.

It was now mid-morning as Foxtrot emerged from his shabby home. He was unshaven and his crumpled khaki anorak hung loosely over baggy brown corduroy trousers. He scratched himself idly and blinked as he struggled to get the key into the padlock on the steel door of his Command Module – the ancient railway guard's van in the neglected garden of his shabby semi. He was still recovering from a severe hangover and looked as bad as he felt. He fumbled for a Marlboro, lit it and inhaled deeply. This was a big mistake. He was racked by a prolonged fit of coughing and had to hold onto the side of the van for support. As he struggled for breath, he began to remember odd scraps of yesterday's visit to Walthamstow Greyhound Stadium. It was all coming back to him. He had scored a spectacular series of wins on his favourite dog, Stalingrad Hero. That was such a good luck sign that a celebration got organised. Much, much later, after many pints of draught bitter with whisky chasers, a taxi had brought him home long after midnight from a celebration shared by Delta, Bravo and India. He seemed to remember fish and chips at a sleazy restaurant somewhere, perhaps East Finchley and, afterwards, there had been this spectacularly busty blonde ...

Another bout of coughing seized him again, his eyes watered and a dull pain throbbed somewhere deep inside his skull. After a moment or two the spasm subsided enough for him to straighten up a little and drag the heavy door open. The gloom was comforting but there was just enough light to show the time, 11.18, on the wall clock. Foxtrot grunted as he forced the door shut. Then he switched on the shaded lamp over the desk and powered up the computer before sinking into a battered old armchair. He held his throbbing temples and tried to think. It was late Saturday morning now and that would mean mid-afternoon in St Petersburg. Perhaps Viktor had tried to contact him in connection with that Sniper information yesterday evening or, worse still, this morning. If he had, and Foxtrot hadn't replied pronto, then Comrade Viktor would be getting impatient. And Foxtrot didn't want his Russian paymaster to be unhappy. Viktor could be open-handed when he got good service. It was important, very important, to keep him in a generous frame of mind.

The computer tinkled and chimed into life. Foxtrot lit another Marlboro while he waited impatiently for his internet connection. This time he inhaled deeply without coughing and exhaled slowly with a satisfied sigh. Checking the list of emails received showed a lot of the usual garbage and a clutch of routine messages. But there were three from St Petersburg and all were encrypted, using the Russians' own cybercypher system; it was the work of a moment for the computer to translate them into plain text. The most recent, sent at 08:14 UK time, was brutally short.

If you don't answer by return, you cretin, I will personally feed your liver to the wolves.
Dankovitch

Foxtrot winced. Big Viktor didn't issue idle threats and he quickly opened the previous email. It had been sent at 19:38 UK time the previous day and the tone was not so quite so angry.

Where the hell are you? Read my previous message and reply immediately.
Dankovitch

The original signal, sent at 15:49 UK time the previous day, was businesslike and to the point, but not unfriendly. Foxtrot blinked and printed out the text.

IMPORTANT AND IMMEDIATE.
Your information about urgent need of Americans for software assistance was valuable and will be rewarded on usual basis. We are in possession of unique, only, repeat, only, copy of a program which can meet all, repeat, all, of their requirements. Imperative you approach Americans soonest to invite commercial negotiation.
You recently carried out surveillance of CIA operative Karlsen working at US Embassy in London. You are instructed to contact him at once in order to set up discussions with his superiors in Washington.
Acknowledge immediately, repeat, immediately.
Viktor Dankovitch

Foxtrot stared at the printed message and read it again. He lit another Marlboro and coughed briefly as he looked at the clock. It was Saturday morning, almost noon, and the American Embassy would have nobody on duty, except for the US Marines who guarded the building. How could he find Joe Karlsen quickly? If only his head wasn't throbbing so much, he would be able to think.

After a few minutes, helped by two cups of strong black coffee, he had an idea. After sending an apologetic email acknowledgement to Viktor in St Petersburg, he pulled out a dog-eared notebook and consulted his desk diary. After a moment or two he found the entries he was looking for. He had arranged for the American Embassy to be put under surveillance about two weeks go. He had also asked that the Americans' Head of Internal Security, a CIA man called Joe Karlsen, should be tailed whenever he left the building in Grosvenor Square.

It was a few days later that Karlsen had his first meeting with the other two Americans in St James's Square. And here in his notebook were the contact details for the Watcher who was given that assignment. Grabbing the phone, he dialled a number. After ringing for a long time, it was answered by a woman with an asthmatic whine. Between bouts of wheezing, she told him that her husband was helping a friend with an indoor market stall at the Nag's Head on Seven Sisters Road, selling sunglasses and mobile phone accessories. Fighting down his own persistent cough, Foxtrot thanked her politely and hung up.

Turning back to his keyboard, Foxtrot thought for a moment. The effort made his head throb, but soon he had typed a short note.

PERSONAL AND PRIVATE FOR JOE KARLSEN
We understand that the American authorities are anxious to acquire a system for locating hackers and pinpointing the

source of computer viruses. We also know that this project, codenamed 'Sniper', is in serious trouble. You have a very short time to find out whether your masters wish to have first refusal to purchase such a system which actually achieves everything, repeat, everything, that you are looking for. Its uniqueness – there is only one, repeat, one, copy and that is guaranteed absolutely – is coupled with impressive, repeatable performance. If you do not respond before 12 noon tomorrow by phoning 07729 276 159 to set up a meeting, then this priceless system will be offered on the open market.

He left it unsigned and printed two copies, leaving one in an overflowing filing tray. Then he folded the other, slid it into an envelope and stuffed it into an inside pocket of his anorak. A few minutes later he was driving a rusty green Ford Fiesta through the Saturday morning shopping traffic on the North Circular Road, heading for Brent Cross.

The market was not difficult to find. He parked illegally in a Residents Only zone in a side street, then walked among the stalls, looking for the member of his Watchers Team known as X-Ray, though his real name was Freddy Stubbs. Eventually he found the stall he was looking for. His man was immediately recognisable, with large horn-rimmed glasses, a battered pork-pie hat and a grubby sheepskin jacket that was two sizes too large. He was making a half-hearted attempt to sell a pair of fake Armani shades to a pimply youth with green hair. The proprietor of the stall, a greasy fat man with a beard and a dark blue beret was sitting in a deckchair, reading the *Sun* and eating a cheese sandwich the size of a paperback. He didn't look up when Foxtrot approached Freddy. The pimply youth shrugged and walked away without buying the sunglasses.

'Hello, there,' said Foxtrot more brightly than he felt. 'How's business?'

'Bloody slow, if you really want to know,' growled X-Ray,

pulling out a tin and rolling himself an evil-looking cigarette. 'And what brings you here on a Saturday morning looking like death warmed up? Something cropped up, has it?'

He lit up, inhaled deeply and blew out a cloud of acrid smoke. Foxtrot fought back his need to cough and looked round to see if anyone could hear them.

He pushed X-Ray towards an alcove and croaked, 'It's about the guy from the American Embassy you were tailing, Joe Karlsen. The Russians want us to contact him, like yesterday. It's extra urgent and there's a big bonus in it for us. So, where does he go on a Saturday?'

'Well, I just happen to know the answer to that question. But, if I may state the bleedin' obvious, this is a weekend. That means I'm plain Freddy Stubbs at the moment. So, if you're wanting me to be X-Ray on my day off, it's going to cost you. And I do mean up front. I need half a ton to take an interest.'

He drew deeply on his self-rolled cigarette, blew twin streams of smoke from his hairy nostrils and wandered over to a nearby stall selling dodgy videos. Foxtrot coughed briefly, rubbed his throbbing brow and grudgingly pro- duced a crumpled £50 note from a trouser pocket. He followed X-Ray and handed it over without enthusiasm.

'Now look here, comrade,' he said, as X-Ray snatched the money, 'this is in the line of duty, so you need to do it right. All you have to do is find Karlsen as soon as you can and make sure he gets this envelope, like immediately or even sooner. Don't fail on this one or we'll all be in the ess aitch one tee, if you follow me.'

X-Ray pocketed the note and smiled, showing stained uneven teeth as he stowed the envelope in an inside pocket.

'A piece of cake, my comrade. I'll go right now.'

Turning on his heel he spoke briefly to the fat man at the stall selling sunglasses. The greasy beard quivered as he said something angry. Then he shrugged and gave Foxtrot a black look as the man he knew as Freddy Stubbs melted into the crowd and was gone.

His ageing red Vauxhall Astra was parked a block away from the market. It was missing two hubcaps and the front was severely dented, but it started first time. The Saturday lunchtime traffic crawled, but at last Freddy got onto clearer roads as he headed for the western suburbs of the sprawling city. He could bet his shirt that Joe Karlsen would be at Wentworth Golf Club at this hour on a Saturday. While keeping watch previously he had discovered that his man seemed to have a regular partner, a short chubby bloke with the most impressive set of clubs. He had turned up in a left hand drive Cadillac. Karlsen's golfing chum could be an American banker, Freddy thought.

At last he was in a quieter area, with large houses whose entrances were discreetly hidden up private roads. Eventually he saw the sign to the Golf Club and turned up the driveway and into the car park. Some members and visitors gave the old Astra curious looks as he found a place to park at the back, away from the array of shining Porsches, BMWs and Mercedes. Looking around as he got out of the car, X-Ray soon spotted the Cadillac. And there, next to it, was the distinctive pale blue Jaguar sports car with diplomatic plates. Joe Karlsen was here, sure enough.

He tried to look unobtrusive as he strolled across to the sleek Jaguar XJS, but curious eyes followed him as tucked the envelope under the windscreen wipers. It was time to become plain Freddy Stubbs again. He hurried back to his car and breathed a sigh of relief as he drove away and took the road back towards central London.

It was almost four o'clock before Joe Karlsen walked back to his car. He wasn't very happy after being soundly beaten five and four by Charlie Greenbaum. The bastard had taken his fifty dollars without even saying thank you. That man really needed to have his handicap looked at. He frowned when he saw the envelope and tore it open angrily. He looked around and saw that nobody was watching, then read the message and swore angrily. He jumped into his car and set off for the Embassy. He would need his encrypted phone for this one.

Back in Grosvenor Square, Karlsen quickly cleared Security and was soon seated at his desk. Opening a drawer, his black book provided the special 'one and only' number that Gabriel had given him during his flying visit to London. His buddy had been very explicit: nobody, but nobody could know about Sniper and this was the only contact to use in the event that Joe came up with a sudden inspiration. And now this: how could anybody else know about the Americans' search for this 'silver bullet' to take out computer terrorists? He shrugged and dialled the number.

Near the deserted checkpoint in the Watergate Building, a telephone on a side table rang insistently. A janitor in an adjoining office looked up for a moment. Then she got on with her job, replenishing the cups in a dispenser beside a water cooler. After five minutes the phone stopped ringing.

Back in London, Joe Karlsen had just hung up. He checked his options grimly. Because Gabriel had been so insistent about the need for secrecy, even from their own bosses at the CIA, he decided to wait and phone later. Damn! That meant that for the sake of security, he would have to stay here in his own office for the entire weekend. At least he had a camp bed in the closet here. Three hours later, after a round trip to his apartment in Kew, he was back again, armed with books, magazines, sandwiches and a 12-can pack of Pepsi. After another fruitless call, he popped a can of cola, put his feet up and picked up John le Carré's latest novel. It was going to be a long night.

*

Several hours later Gabriel appeared in the sitting room of the apartment. Isabel was getting ready to watch the 10 o'clock news on TV.

'Sorry to be such a wreck' he croaked, rubbing his eyes. 'Rachel's still fast asleep. My mouth feels like I've eaten a very old sock and I'm dying of thirst. Any chance of a drink?'

He sank onto the comfortable sofa.

Isabel turned off the TV and went to the kitchen, returning quickly with a tumbler of iced water.

'I've put the kettle on too, so we can have a cup of tea in a minute.'

She sat beside him and took his hand.

'You're looking rested now, Biel, and I'm sure that Rachel will feel a lot better after her rest. She really is very beautiful – you're a lucky guy. Now please relax as much as you can while you're here. You've both been working too hard. Believe me, I've seen what it did to Martin and I know all the signs. I know you can't say what your assignment is. I do understand that, but you must ease up for a day or two – or one of you is going to have a breakdown.'

Gabriel nodded and took a drink of water.

'As a matter of fact, that's exactly why we're here. Our team's pretty well burned out, which is why the boss has given us a few days off to re-charge our batteries. You get on with your own life, Bel, though naturally we want to spend some time with you – and we'll certainly come along to see Margo on her birthday. Apart from that, I guess the best thing is just to be totally relaxed during our stay. We can be quite happy jogging in the park, reading and watching TV.'

Isabel heard the kettle boiling and went to the kitchen, returning in a few moments with the tea tray. As she poured from a silver teapot into bone china mugs, Gabriel went on.

'I already told you in the car that Rachel has to leave on Tuesday to see her folks.' He froze and turned to face his sister, 'Oh God! I've just remembered – don't you have your best friend's hen night on Tuesday?'

'Don't worry about that, Biel, I can cancel. Trust me, Catherine will understand. There's going to be a big crowd anyway and I won't really be missed.'

She squeezed his hand. 'And the good news is that you don't need to fly back until Wednesday evening. That will give us some time together – just the two of us, like the old days.'

He looked doubtful.

'Yes, it will all work out. And on Wednesday you can catch up with Martin and hear how he got on with Teresa. His flight will get him back here an hour or two before you have to leave. I know you like him and I really want you to grab this chance to see him again.'

'That's great! If he can be here early in the afternoon there should be time for a little celebration. I'll get some champagne and we can hear all the news from Mallorca before I need to head off to Heathrow.'

'That's settled then. I'm going to run you a bath and make a sandwich to go with another cup of tea. Then you need more sleep, Biel. I'll be here when you and Rachel feel like socialising.'

Soon Gabriel was soaking in wonderfully hot water laced with Badedas. He sipped his tea as he lay in the bath. As he relaxed he almost fell asleep in the fragrant water. Shaking himself awake, he climbed out, rubbed himself dry on Isabel's soft cream towels and gratefully climbed back into bed. Rachel, breathing deeply, barely stirred. He only managed to eat half of his ham and tomato sandwich before his eyelids seemed to turn to lead and he sank into a deep dreamless sleep.

The morning sky was bright as the Boeing 737 from London touched down at Palma International Airport. The passengers filing into the bus for the short ride to the terminal were smiling. They could feel the sun's warmth, even though there was still a slight chill in the air.

Vasco was leaning against a pillar near the exit from the baggage-claim area, wearing a dark green rugby shirt, brown slacks and a loosely fitting suede waistcoat. Martin emerged, casually dressed in a long-sleeved navy shirt and pale blue trousers, with a pullover slung across his back. He was carrying a small suitcase and a Singapore Airlines bag. They greeted each other warmly and strolled the short distance to the multi-storey car park building.

Soon they were in Vasco's Jaguar, heading towards C'an Valseca, where an excited Antonia had been preparing a typical Mallorcan lunch for the English visitor. As he drove, Vasco told Martin about the International Mathematics Symposium, which was being held at the newly opened Mansfield Hotel and Vacation Club at Son Antoni.

'I'll take you over there this afternoon to register. And I should have told you, there's a dinner and an opening session tonight,' said Vasco. 'Naturally, I'd have been delighted to give you a bed at the *possessió*, but it felt like a good idea for you to stay at the hotel along with all the other delegates. You'll enjoy socialising with the overseas stars – we've even got a couple of Chinese visitors. And, of course, I'll have to leave you on your own a lot anyway because somebody's got to make sure that the organisation doesn't go off the rails.'

'That's fine with me,' said Martin. 'You must be rushed off your feet and it's wonderful that you've found time for me to have lunch at your place. I'll be just fine left to my own devices. The only important thing is a meeting with Aunt Teresa. I'm under strict instructions to pay my respects while I'm here.'

'That's no problem at all. You're going to meet her over dinner on Tuesday evening. That'll be just after the symposium finishes the same afternoon. I've arranged for us to have drinks and dinner in a private dining room upstairs at Samantha's in Genova, just outside Palma. That way we can talk in private. Oh, and I've asked an old friend and colleague, Miquel Santiago, to join us too. He's a great character and very good company. And don't worry about a thing – I'm sure you're going to make a great impression. Teresa's a shrewd judge of character, you know.'

Martin looked apprehensive at the prospect, but said nothing and looked out of the window at the rolling landscape.

Vasco started to whistle as he drove. He was in a particularly good mood. He was still glowing with the success of Navegator, but he wasn't ready to say anything to Martin about that – not yet, anyway.

As Martin enjoyed the drive through the rural part of the island he passed on the latest news from London. Vasco was delighted to hear that Isabel had received an email from Gabriel to say that he was flying back to London again – and with Rachel this time – so soon after his previous visit.

'It'll be wonderful for the twins to spend some time together while you're over here. I think it's over a year since they had a chance to catch up.'

'Yes, absolutely. I can tell you that Isabel was over the moon when she got Gabriel's phone call. They'll have a great time. There was some idea that all three of them might go to Guildford together and see your sister Margo on her birthday. I know that Gabriel and his girlfriend can only stay a short while. But I'm hoping to have a chance to get to meet him again, and Rachel too, before they have to go back to Washington.'

The Jaguar passed through country roads alongside green meadows and olive groves in the centre of the island. There were almond trees too, and every corner revealed wild flowers in the fields and alongside the stone walls lining the narrow lanes. Soon the terrain became hilly and after another fifteen minutes the dark blue car turned though the gateway into the *possessió* and drove along an avenue of lime trees to the handsome stone house.

Antonia was standing beside the steps outside the front door to welcome Martin and Vasco as they got out of the Jaguar. Beside her stood Guillem, his weather-beaten face creased by a wide grin as he came forward to take the visitor's bags. The golden Labradors, Glove and Mitten, offspring of the original pair, came forward wagging their tails.

'Thank you, Guillem, but don't bring the bags. Senyor Weston won't be staying with us this time. I'm sure he will have many more opportunities to visit us here in future.'

Leaving Martin's luggage in the car, Vasco gave his visitor a guided tour of the house. Then they took chairs beside a table on the terrace, where Antonia had left glasses and a decanter of sherry on a silver tray. After toasting each other and the absent twins, Vasco pointed across the open park-land below them.

'Look over there, Martin. That's one of the trees that Isabel and Gabriel loved to climb when they were kids. And over there, behind the old barn, is a path that leads to the pool with a natural spring where they often went swimming. They still do, when they come to stay.'

His face clouded.

'But that's been difficult for both of them these last few years.'

Antonia came out onto the terrace to tell them that lunch was ready and Vasco led Martin into the dining room, where a log fire blazed in the hearth. Even though the morning had been sunny, it was still cool inside the big old house in early March. They sat down at the oak refectory table, where there were tempting local delicacies and a robust red wine from Benissalem. Olives, home-baked bread and local butter accompanied a rabbit terrine, followed by Frito Mallorquin, a hearty dish of fried meats with vegetables. Cheese from a nearby market and Granissats – crushed ice with intensely flavoured fruit juices – completed Antonia's 'simple meal'. Over their lunch they chatted away like old friends and, as they savoured strong coffee on the terrace, Vasco told Martin more of the island's history.

'You may not realise that Mallorca was once a kingdom in its own right and had a great impact on the whole of the region. That's what drives me – and others – to push for further independence from mainland Spain. Those were the glory days, with our navigators acknowledged as the best anywhere. Our earliest ancestor we know anything about was Gabriel Valseca – of course, Gabriel is named after him – who was trained by a man called Jefuda Cresques. He'd started up a school of navigation, almost certainly the first in the world, here in Palma. It was that first Gabriel Valseca who drew the first detailed map of the Azores in 1439. But I expect Isabel has told you this already.'

'Yes, and it's a fascinating story. But I'm surprised that with your family background and your professional interests in mathematics and astronomy, you haven't worked in the field of navigation too.'

Vasco hesitated, his face darkening momentarily with unhappy memories. He was on the point of telling Martin about his work on Navegator, but decided to steer the conversation in a different direction. Now was not the time to break the news to Martin. Before he spoke to anyone it was important to get concrete endorsement from the BCIB – and he would have to wait a few days for that.

'Well, I really haven't had time. These days, quite apart from my job at the university, I devote myself to studying local history, culture and politics. It's probably not very interesting for other people, but some of us believe strongly that because of our distinctive heritage, Mallorca and the other Balearic islands deserve a greater degree of autonomy from mainland Spain. But that's a matter for us locals, rather than our visitors. It's all pretty boring, I expect. So, let's talk about the Mathematics symposium instead.'

Martin looked at his watch.

'If it's OK with you, perhaps it would be a good idea if I checked in for the conference fairly soon and met up with some of the other delegates. I hate to leave this place. It's so peaceful here and Antonia's cooking is wonderful. Please do thank her for me.'

'Of course I'll do that. She runs the house like clockwork. And you're right, Martin, I should get you across to Son Antoni soon. I can fill you in on the background to the symposium on the way. And I've got a few things to attend to over there myself. Then I can come back here to check my emails and change before the reception and dinner tonight.'

They drove away from the *possessió* by a different route through the green heart of the island. As he guided the Jaguar through the narrow lanes, Vasco passed on the latest gossip from the mathematical fraternity. It seemed there was bad feeling between Tako Natuke of Japan and the Mexican Ignatio da Silva. These two old rivals were proposing different theoretical approaches to create an empirical formula for the design of the perfect golf club.

'As we are having the symposium at a resort with two golf courses,' chuckled Vasco, 'that seemed like a happy coincidence.'

He went on to explain that a French professor, André Boulard, was due to read a paper demonstrating, mathematically, that it was possible to create an unbreakable encryption system. Several governments were sending delegates to attend that presentation. That old chestnut, Fermat's Last Theorem, was going to have yet another airing. There would be a controversial paper on a new approach to Chaos Theory by an obscure Peruvian delegate from the University of Lima. After more good natured insights from Vasco, they arrived at Son Antoni, the ultra modern Mansfield Vacation Club complex near Llucmajor. After he had parked, Vasco ushered his guest through the lofty and impressive lobby. Its furnishings included a cavernous sofa, chandeliers and large heraldic devices high up on the walls at either end. They continued through to the reception area, with a tantalising view through the bar to the terrace and swimming pool beyond. As Martin signed into the hotel, Vasco took his leave.

'I'll see you at the official reception later. Right now I must check on the sound system in the conference room. And I expect there will be a whole lot of other problems to sort out – there always are. Sometimes I wish I didn't enjoy these jamborees quite so much.'

He grinned, clapped Martin on the shoulder and was gone.

After unpacking his bag in his first floor room Martin was soon luxuriating in a hot shower. After changing into a pale blue shirt, navy slacks and a dark blue corduroy jacket, he sauntered to the symposium desk on the ground floor. An unsmiling young woman dressed in a severe grey trouser suit regarded him fiercely through steel-rimmed glasses as she handed him his bulky symposium pack.

'Kindly be on time for the official reception and dinner Mr Weston,' she snapped. 'You have been seated with some of the most distinguished guests at the special request of Professor Valseca.'

Martin grinned at her expressionless face as he took the folder. She almost smiled before turning away to take a phone call. Martin drifted off to join the group clustered around the tables where Son Antoni staff were serving tea and coffee. As he took a steaming mug from a tray, he was surprised to catch sight of an old acquaintance from his time at Birmingham University. As so often happens, they had lost contact after those carefree times at the Students' Union. Shaking hands warmly, they headed for the lobby bar. This was a much better option than the Delegates' Lounge for catching up on ten years or more of living.

Around the time that Martin was registering for the symposium, the Acappella brothers were on the telephone yet again, putting the finishing touches to their plans for the capture of Navegator.

Meanwhile, their client was at his desk in the huge office of Viktor Dankovitch Shipping, even though it was very late on a Saturday afternoon. This was quite normal for him, as he usually took the opportunity to escape from his wife Anya and her disagreeable sisters, who always seemed to find an excuse to invite themselves for lunch on Saturday and stay on for hours afterwards. Viktor pretended to be a passionate supporter of SKA, St Petersburg's ace ice hockey team, but his Saturday afternoons were not often spent at the Ice Palace Stadium. More frequently he would be participating in a very different sport on the enormous chaise-longue in his office, with the eager participation of his sultry secretary Irena. Today, though, he was actually working and taking great care with the briefing of his courier. Ygor Krasnov sat in an uncomfortable chair in front of the biggest desk in St Petersburg.

'You will do exactly, precisely, as you are told, Ygor. I am entrusting you with a task of the greatest importance and nothing, nothing at all, must be allowed to go wrong. Do you understand that?'

'Yes, Comrade Viktor, you can trust me absolutely.'

'I certainly hope so. If only he could be spared, I would send Kyril, but you did a good job the other night. Think of this as a reward, eh?'

Viktor reached into his desk for a bottle of vodka and a couple of glasses, then poured two generous shots.

'Let's drink to the success of your trip. *Na zdrov 'ye!*'

They downed their drinks at a single gulp. Viktor leaned across the vast expanse of his desk.

'You'll get your travel information and a cash advance from Irena. It's all very simple. You take an Aeroflot flight to Frankfurt via Moscow tomorrow and then on to Palma in Mallorca with another carrier. Once you are in the arrivals hall, go to the information desk and pick up an envelope addressed to you. Inside will be a set of keys, the location of the car and a ticket to get you out of the multi-storey car park at Palma airport. You'll find all the detailed information about the rendezvous in the glove box of the car. Then all you have to do is check into a hotel and wait around, you lucky dog. There's plenty of time for you to do a bit of sightseeing and check the location for the handover, which is set for somewhere outside Palma at precisely 11.00 a.m. next Wednesday. You must on no account be late. That's absolutely vital. Once you've made the pickup, you will come back here immediately by the same route. Is that clear?'

'Yes, Comrade Viktor. Absolutely.'

'Good. Then get going. I've just had news about a very talented Turkish chemist who could be useful to us. He can help us upgrade our production unit for counterfeit prescription drugs. I want to get him to work for us as soon as possible, so it's time to make a few phone calls.'

Viktor Dankovitch beamed, waved Ygor away and reached for the phone as his courier reverently left the palatial office. On his way out, Irena summoned him imperiously to her huge green marble desk, smiling coldly as she handed him a bulky envelope. Then she turned away and went back to burnishing the already flawless varnish on her deep crimson nails.

In another part of St Petersburg, on the west side of the city not far from Kirovsy Zavod metro station, Ygor Krasnov lived in a cramped apartment with his elderly mother, Anna. She had straggly grey hair and was vastly fat. The old woman wore a bulging floral print dress which badly needed laundering and carpet slippers which had once been blue. Anna was an ill-tempered alcoholic who reluctantly fed him and provided accommodation. In return, he helped with the rent, with rides to the coast nearby, with maintenance jobs and shopping expeditions. He hated the arrangement and the relationship was sour and difficult. As Ygor came into the room his mother was drinking strong black tea laced with brandy and watching a TV game show. She reacted angrily when he turned off the set.

'What the hell do you think you're doing, you bad-mannered lout? You know very well that's my favourite programme and I always watch it every Saturday. If only Vladimir could be here to take care of his poor mother. I don't know why he has to be away all the time, working for GazProm. He really cares about me, not like you. You're just a waster. I can't put up with you any longer.'

'Please don't start that again, Mama. I have something I must tell you about immediately. There's this job, a very urgent job I have to do at once and it means going away for a few days.'

'Holy Mary preserve me! Are you going to desert your old mother and leave her without anyone to help her? You're a heartless brute. I'm sorry I ever bore you.'

She took a long swig of her tea and brandy and belched behind a pudgy hand. Ygor shrugged, turned the TV set back on and went into his tiny bedroom. Pulling a scratched old suitcase and a cheap carry-on bag from under the bed, he began to pack it with clothes from the plywood cupboard in the corner. He had just returned from the bathroom with his shaving kit, when he heard a cry and a

136

crash. Ygor dropped his razor bag and ran back into the living room to find his mother face down on the floor, her tea spilt across the threadbare carpet. Kneeling down, he felt a faint pulse through the rolls of fat in her neck and he could just detect shallow breathing.

'Sweet Jesus!' he cried. 'What do I do now?'

Grinding his teeth with effort and frustration, he dragged his mother's inert body to the ancient couch and propped her up on the stained satin cushions. Grabbing the telephone, he dialled the emergency number for an ambulance, gave an operator the details and hung up. Then he dug out his pocketbook. After a frantic search he found the number for his married sister Natalia who was living at Ladogskaya, beyond the river on the far side of the city centre. After a few rings the phone was answered by his brother in law, Fedor. The two men were close friends. They had served together in the Red Army's disastrous campaign in Afghanistan and often had a night out together.

'Hi there, Fedor,' panted Ygor, 'we have a serious problem with Mama. Is Natalia there please?'

'Sorry, Ygor. She's gone to visit a friend on the north side, way out at Ozerky for a couple of days, but I expect her back on Monday evening and I'm stuck here looking after the kids till then. What's happened now?'

'Dear God!' Ygor groaned, 'I really don't know what to do. The old lady's just had a bad fall. She's still breathing and I don't think it's really serious, but she's unconscious and I've sent for an ambulance. You know what she's like, Fedor, as soon as she comes round, she'll start playing merry hell. It's going to get even worse because I've been ordered to travel overseas for my boss and I ought to leave immediately. You know how it is with my work – I just can't refuse. If only I could talk to Natalia, she might have an idea, then perhaps …'

'Calm down,' Fedor interrupted. 'It's not the end of the

world. If you've got to go away for a bit then that's just too bad. She'll just have to grin and bear it. But I can see your problem. She's a bitter, twisted old bitch, but after all she is your mother and you have to live with the old devil. Problem is, I don't see how I can do anything right now. Katrina is too young to be dragged across the city – and our babysitter's away for a week. But when Natalia gets back we can sort something out. We can take it in turns to visit the hospital and take the old lady those trashy magazines she likes. Young Alex can come along as well. The lad wants to be a doctor and likes hospitals. His grandma will be glad to see him too. Sorry, Ygor, but that's the best I can do. You'll just have to change your travel plans a bit – I'm sure your boss will understand.'

Ygor groaned inwardly. He couldn't possibly let Comrade Viktor find out that he wanted to delay travelling until Tuesday morning. But even then it should be OK. He would still arrive in Mallorca with just enough time in hand to get to the rendezvous on Wednesday. But he'd have to find a way to sort out the changes to the flights himself. Somehow he must find the time to do this in between visiting hours at the hospital. God, how he would hate that – sitting at his mother's bedside listening to her non-stop grumbling. And she wouldn't stop, even though he'd be bringing her favourite sugar plums from Kiev, where her family came from – and brandy, of course …

'Are you still there, Ygor?' Fedor cut into his reverie.

'Yes, just wondering if I can change my flights. But I guess it should be OK. Anyway, thanks, Fedor, I definitely owe you one. If you and Natalia can keep on visiting Mama until the end of the week, it'll be a great load off my mind. Thanks again, mate. I'll let you know which hospital Mama has been taken to as soon as I know myself.'

Ygor hung up. He checked that his mother was still breathing and stared out of the window, chewing his lip as he waited for the ambulance to show up. Then he checked his watch and turned away impatiently. There was no point in finishing his packing now. He turned the TV onto the sports channel and went over to the fridge for a bottle of Baltika beer.

He hadn't seen much of the soccer match before the bell rang. He opened the door to two burly ambulance men who hurried in. The senior orderly quickly examined the unconscious woman, nodded and loaded her onto a stretcher.

'We'll be taking her to Hospital Number 26 near the Moskovskaya Metro straight away, but I guess it's only concussion. If you want, you can come down to check on her in two or three hours. There's no point in getting there sooner. They'll still be doing the paperwork.'

He nodded again before Ygor could say anything, grunted as he and his partner hefted the stretcher and kicked the door shut as they left. Ygor reluctantly turned off the TV and took a pull at his bottle of beer. Getting out the bulky envelope containing his travel documents and a fat wad of pesetas, he opened it and found his airline tickets. Frowning, he sat at the table, picked up a scribbling pad and sat by the phone to dial the number for the Aeroflot office. He was in for a long, frustrating session. Changing his flights would take forever – and he had to reorganise his schedule with Air Berlin too. God, but he might not get through before the office closed for the day. That would mean starting all over again tomorrow. Ygor sighed again and drummed his fingers on the table as the phone rang and rang. Putting down the handset for a moment, he went to the fridge for another beer, and took a long swig. He sighed deeply, picked up the phone and gazed grimly out of the dirty window as he waited for someone, anyone, to answer the phone at Aeroflot.

9

At around nine o'clock on a bright sunny Sunday morning at Son Antoni, Martin Weston seemed wistful as he gazed through the window of his room towards the dramatic skyline created by the steep mountains a few miles away around the picturesque village of Randa. He was missing Isabel so much and would have liked nothing better than to have her here at his side to show him her island home. They had spoken briefly on the phone from his bedroom last night, but it hadn't been very good for either of them. Isabel was just about to take Gabriel and Rachel out for an early meal in Soho. Martin had had to admit that he'd left the charger for his mobile phone on the island unit in Isabel's kitchen – and now the battery was flat. In the end, they had laughed and agreed that it would be easier to save all the talking until Martin returned to London on Wednesday. They both blew kisses into the phone before hanging up.

He turned away, took his conference notes from the desk and went downstairs for breakfast. He chose a solitary table in a corner and opened the bulky folder. While reading the material he needed to get ready for the morning session, he sampled the amazing variety of food on offer at the buffet. Finally, he pushed his plate away, finished his coffee and stood up.

Weaving his way past the other diners, Martin made his way reluctantly towards the conference room where the symposium was due to reconvene at 9.45.

At about the same time, a few miles away in Palma, Paulo Acappella carried a coffee cup and a glass of freshly squeezed orange juice to the kitchen window of his apartment. The grey tracksuit he was wearing was proudly emblazoned with the crowned red and gold badge of his favourite soccer team, Real Club Deportivo Mallorca. He had just returned from his morning run and was panting a little. Gazing out over the rooftops towards the fairy-tale cathedral and the blue of the bay beyond, he started to plan his day.

First, he would have a workout in the room that doubled as his gymnasium and study. After that he would take a shower, shave and change into simple, elegant clothes for the day ahead. He would probably wear a pale-blue, open-necked shirt, his blue-grey suede jacket and some navy-blue slacks. Then, ready to face the day he would have a slice of toast and another cup of coffee. Next, another exchange of emails with his brother. This would take some time. His brother's plan was complicated, needing precise timing and co-ordination to succeed. His own role would involve using all of the talents he had developed during his time as a maître d'. Although that would be very rewarding in itself, one feature was disturbing and unpleasant. Paulo shrugged and finished his coffee. He would steel himself for that part of the operation. After all, he had done far, far worse things years ago on the docks in Genoa – and of course he had to think about his own reward and those wonderful stamps to be added to his collection. He carried his empty cup and glass over to the sink, washed them, and crossed to the door. Now it was time for the exercise routine, with the first few minutes on the rowing machine, perhaps.

Meanwhile, his brother Enrico, immaculate as always, had already taken the helicopter transfer shuttle from Monaco to Nice Airport. On arrival, he carried his soft leather overnight bag, laptop and Bottega Veneta briefcase to the

141

shuttle bus for the nearby Novotel. Normally, he would have chosen somewhere more elegant, but he would only be having a short stay. The important thing was that it was clean, modern and quite adequate; a perfect place to complete the details of his plan. It was also vital to have a base which was easy for members of his team to reach, so a location alongside the airport was ideal. He would need several people to visit him within the next forty-eight hours and the logistics would work well.

Once he had arrived in his room on the second floor, he opened his briefcase, which contained a mobile phone, large-scale maps of Mallorca, timetables and his personal organiser. This contained all of the vital phone numbers which were not already stored in his laptop. From his overnight bag Enrico produced a small printer which he positioned carefully on the built-in desk and connected it to the laptop. Both of these had their own power supplies which he set up. Finally, he plugged in the cable which would allow him to connect his computer to the phone line just as soon as he was ready to use the internet. Alongside, he set out A4 size paper, a scribbling pad, a spiral bound notebook and a silver-mounted travelling clock.

After switching on the laptop, he picked up the phone and ordered coffee and croissants from room service. Then, stretching himself to his full height, he yawned, flexed his fingers and sat down at the keyboard. There was a faint rumble, muffled by multiple glazing in his window, as an Air France flight took off from the airport, but he hardly noticed. Like an experienced general developing the tactics of a military campaign, Enrico Acappella was totally focused on the details of his plan.

First, he needed to make a call to Paulo to make absolutely sure that he had picked up the package of special stationery from the hotel near Son Vida Golf Club. Without this vital element for his complex scheme, nothing else would work. It didn't take long to get that reassurance: everything had gone like clockwork. Yesterday morning the golfing brother of the crooked lawyer in Barcelona had left a carefully wrapped parcel at the hotel's reception desk. Paulo had duly picked it up and the BCIB headed notepaper was now loaded into his printer in Palma.

Next, he opened the computer files where he had already created drafts of a preliminary legal agreement and a covering letter. He just wanted to review them one more time before emailing them to Ernesto Marquez for editing and advice. Within a couple of hours, the lawyer had returned the material to him. It didn't take long to forward the text to his brother in Palma. A little later another phone call established that Paulo had received everything without any problems and would print out the documents after lunch.

Lunch? Enrico had forgotten about food. His coffee was cold and he had hardly touched the croissants he had sent for earlier. The lawyer in Barcelona was now working on the next set of legal documents; he would need these on Tuesday, when they could be sent over to Mallorca with all of the other 'props' for his complicated plan. Now Paulo would be hard at work, printing off the special documents, while he, the mastermind, would take time off for a light gourmet meal. After checking his appearance in the mirror, he locked his room and went down to the lobby. Within a few minutes a taxi was whisking him away to an elegant seafood restaurant on the Boulevard des Anglais.

10

Although the Monday morning air was a little chilly, it was already clear and sunny, with a lovely day in store. Some of the delegates to the Mathematics Symposium had taken the opportunity to have a few holes of golf or a swim in the thermally heated spa pool before breakfast. There was the usual chatter and bustle in the dining room and Martin was enjoying the whole experience.

Meanwhile Vasco was on his way to Son Antoni, driving through the island's lanes from the *possessió*. He was frowning a little, having received an unexpected message on his answering machine the previous afternoon. The caller, a man who spoke Spanish with a cultured voice, only said that Professor Valseca should expect to receive a package containing important documents at Son Antoni on Monday morning. He was intrigued, especially as he had been unable to trace the source of the call. He advised the senior receptionist at the resort that he was expecting a special delivery and asked to be notified as soon as it arrived.

The Mathematics Symposium reconvened at 9.30, with the delegates being herded into the conference room by the fierce grey-suited woman with the steel-rimmed glasses. Vasco chaired the session – 'Further Insights into the Development of Chaos Theory' – featuring a paper by a professor from Montreal. As they broke for coffee at mid-morning, Vasco called back at the reception desk. He was just in time to catch a glimpse of a helmeted, leather-clad motorcyclist wearing a tabard with the DHL Logo. The rider left the lobby, mounted a powerful black machine which started immediately and accelerated away.

The receptionist called out: 'Professor Valseca, I've just signed for that special delivery you were expecting.'

Vasco turned and picked up the bulky envelope. He was surprised to see that it bore the imprint of the Barcelona Head Office of the Banco de Catalunya y des Illes Balears and the BCIB logo. In addition to his own name it had been endorsed, 'Strictly Private and Confidential: for the personal attention of the addressee only'.

Intrigued, Vasco found a small empty meeting room, pulled out a chair and sat down at a desk littered with empty coffee cups. He slit open the envelope and with a puzzled frown pulled out a second envelope with a lengthy covering letter clipped to it. The letterhead showed that it came from the office of the bank's Chief Executive Officer, Felipe Montserrat-Ribas. Like the envelope, it had also been marked, 'Strictly Private and Confidential: for the personal attention of the addressee only' and was dated Friday 8 March. Vasco could hardly believe his eyes as he started to read.

Dear Professor Valseca,

On behalf of our Board, please accept my apologies for this unusual and direct approach. As this letter will explain, extreme urgency and the need for total security have made it necessary to adopt this unusual method of making contact. I am writing to you personally on Friday evening under conditions of the greatest secrecy. This follows the late inclusion of a special item at the regular meeting of our directors on Friday afternoon. The matter under discussion was a report submitted to us by Ramón Vila, manager of our BCIB branch at Plaça d'Olivars, Palma, in which he gave a glowing endorsement of your Navegator program.

After a lengthy discussion I have been authorised, subject to a successful personal demonstration, to acquire the intellectual property rights to Navegator for BCIB on an exclusive basis. Naturally, given the opportunity which this affords to achieve a major step forward in the security of our bank, we are prepared to recognise the value of your innovative and unique program. You will be well aware I am sure that, quite apart from your own unfortunate experience at the hands of a hacker, our bank has been the target of many similar frauds. We must admit that some of these have been very costly indeed and, unless something can be done, there will inevitably be similar breaches of our security in the future. Naturally, we will be making restitution to you and to all of our other clients who have suffered in this way. We also intend to do everything in our power to bring these criminals to justice.

As to terms, I am already fully authorised to act on behalf of our Board and an initial lump sum payment of one million dollars is available if we are able to acquire the certified one and only copy of the Navegator software. Furthermore, I am empowered to increase this sum very significantly if we are also granted worldwide exclusivity to sub-license other reputable financial institutions with similar problems. We are prepared to agree that 50% of the income from such sub-licensing would also accrue to you.

You may now begin to appreciate the extreme urgency of this matter. It is also essential that the very existence of our approach to you is kept absolutely confidential. This is because knowledge of this development of yours – and of our involve-ment with it – could have a significant impact on the price of BCIB shares. It is evident that charges of insider dealing, even if totally untrue, could be damaging for our bank's image and reputation. This means that nobody at all, not even Professor Miquel Santiago or Ramón Vila, for example, can know anything of my approach at this stage.

It is my intention to fly to Mallorca and, hopefully, to conclude this matter within the next few days. Please do not

*try to contact me or my office, as I shall be travelling back from
a meeting in Zurich. Accordingly, I shall send a message to
the Information Desk at Palma Airport on Tuesday morning,
suggesting a location for a rendezvous late that same evening
at around 10.30pm. I sincerely hope that you will be able to
accommodate this imposition on your own time and the late
hour proposed for our meeting, but my diary is impossibly
crowded and it is imperative that I leave Palma on a very
early flight on Wednesday morning.*

*It is my earnest hope that you will be able to fall in with the
pressures imposed by my schedule and agree to our meeting on
Tuesday night. Might I suggest that you leave a confidential
reply for me at the Information Desk at Palma Airport? My
grateful thanks, in advance, for your understanding.*

*Attached are drafts of a Licence Agreement in favour of the
Banco de Catalunya y des Illes Balears for your consideration.
I must apologise for their bulk, but our legal department is
meticulous in these matters. I look forward to meeting you in
person on Tuesday night.*

The letter concluded with formal greetings and the
flamboyant signature of Felipe Montserrat-Ribas, Chief
Executive. Vasco was stunned. The BCIB had taken
Navegator very seriously indeed and he could scarcely
believe his good fortune. This was far and away beyond his
most optimistic imaginings, with the promise of such a huge
financial payment. This could be used for a campaign on
behalf of PIIB. What a political impact that would make!
And the approach seemed to be totally genuine. He read
the letter again and quickly scanned the draft legal documents. Everything appeared to be authentic, even to the
BCIB watermarks on the expensive paper.

His mind was in turmoil, but he suddenly slapped his
hand to his forehead and froze. There was a serious problem. Tuesday evening was already committed to the special

dinner for Martin Weston to meet Teresa at Samantha's. That couldn't possibly be changed. Then he brightened. Tuesdays were usually quiet at Samantha's and he had booked one of the elegant private dining rooms upstairs. They could eat early 'because Martin is flying back to London tomorrow'. This would allow them to say their goodbyes by 10 p.m., leaving him free to have his own meeting with Felipe Monserrat-Ribas later that night. No problem! Vasco crammed the bulky envelope into his briefcase and was whistling as he strode back towards the conference room.

It was approaching noon as Isabel guided her silver Peugeot towards Abbotswood, one of the older residential parts of Guildford, to the north-east of the town centre.

'There's my old school,' she cried, pointing for Rachel's benefit as they drove along London Road in the direction of the tree-lined avenue where Margo lived. Finally, she pulled up outside the imposing ivy-clad house. They were among the first to arrive, so there was still room to park – though several handsome cars, including a dark blue Bentley Continental and a metallic green Audi Quattro, had managed to get closer to the front door.

Rachel was visibly awestruck as she climbed out of the car and smoothed her skirt. She was wearing a slim-fitting, polo-necked cream jersey dress with an embroidered jacket on loan from Isabel. Gabriel had put on a tie for the occasion and hoped his informal clothes – dark chinos and a check shirt under rather crumpled jacket – wouldn't be out of place. His sister, as usual, was stunning in a stylish dark-green outfit from Basler – a beautifully tailored pinstriped trouser suit. She hitched the strap of a jade-coloured Prada bag onto her shoulder as Gabriel opened the hatch and retrieved a hold-all containing their aunt's birthday presents. Then the trio linked arms with Rachel in the middle and walked to the porch, where the double doors stood wide open. Once they were inside, a uniformed waitress from a local catering company stood ready with a tray of drinks to greet guests as they arrived.

They were just helping themselves to flutes of champagne when, with a whoop of delight, Margalida Ponseti, wearing a flame-coloured tunic, rushed towards them with outstretched arms.

Gabriel and Isabel shouted 'Happy Birthday!' and held out their presents.

'Thank you so much. I'll open these later Bel, my angel,' she cried in Mallorqin as she enveloped her in a bear-hug, 'you're lovelier than ever! And Biel, so handsome – it's been a long time.'

She kissed him enthusiastically.

'This must be your lovely girl, you sly dog. My God, she's absolutely gorgeous. But you never said she was black, you rascal! That will shake those old biddies in Palma.'

Turning to Rachel, she switched to English.

'Thank you so much for coming to see this old lady my dear. Please call me Margo. You're very lovely and very welcome.' She kissed an astonished Rachel on both cheeks. Rachel replied breathlessly:

'Thank you so much – and I hope you have a very happy birthday.'

'It's certainly started well,' said Margo, 'and now you must come and meet some people.'

She shepherded them through to an enormous sun-room overlooking a well- maintained garden, where a paved terrace had steps leading down to a beautifully tended lawn. On the far side, banks of rhododendrons, azaleas and a pair of magnolias stood behind an established herbaceous border.

'I'm sorry it's too cold to go outside today, but there's just enough room, I think. It's going to be a bit of a squash, but we'll manage.'

She steered them to a group beside the French doors.

'Hello everyone,' she shouted, 'this is my handsome nephew Gabriel – all the way from Washington USA, with his beautiful girlfriend Rachel. Some of you might remember Gabriel's twin sister, my lovely goddaughter Isabel. They've all come down from London for my party.'

A tall woman in a bronze kaftan stepped forward and held out her hand.

'Isabel! Yes, Isabel Valseca, of course I remember. You were my star pupil in maths. Once upon a time I used to be Monica Black, and you horrible girls used to call me Blackhead – but as you can see my hair's snow white now.'

She had a tinkling laugh.

'Marjorie Watkins would have been teaching biology during your time here too, come across and see her.'

Isabel looked over her shoulder and shrugged as she was dragged away to another group.

Margo squeezed Gabriel's arm and turned to Rachel.

'Sorry about all of this. You three hang on after the others have gone. Then we can catch up properly after a cup of tea … Oh, my God! Archie Benson's just arrived and he's going to make a disgracefully embarrassing speech unless I can talk him out of it. Please excuse me, my darlings.'

A flash of beautiful white teeth and she was gone. She moved quickly to the door to intercept a big florid man in a green tweed suit, sporting a spotted yellow bow tie. He kissed Margo enthusiastically and presented an enormous bouquet with a flourish.

Gabriel and Rachel stuck together through the chatter and half-heard introductions of the reception. Soon the room was overflowing into a library, the hallway and a snug, feminine television room. Occasionally they caught sight of Isabel, swallowed up by old friends of Margo's who remembered her as a young girl. Now they wanted to know all about her new life in London, having already heard that she had been swept away by a big romance. Now she was being seriously cross-examined but managed to deflect the most persistent questioners. Avoiding alcohol helped; in any case she had to keep a clear head for the drive back to London.

At last it was time for the meal, a relaxed but semi-formal affair with a seating plan. Rachel was glad to find that she was sitting next to Gabriel, but Isabel waved from a distant table where she had been surrounded by neighbours from the Avenue. Margo sat next to the flamboyant Archie Benson, former Sales Director of the Ponsetis' artificial pearl-exporting business, along with the widow of another associate, plus bridge partners and friends from a local artists' club. The meal passed in a blur for Rachel as she tried to understand the unwritten rules of the occasion – peculiarly English, even though it had a Mallorcan hostess.

The coffee appeared along with the birthday cake and then there was a speech – mercifully only one – by Archie Benson, who managed to be sentimental, sincere and funny without being too outrageous. Margo was toasted with champagne before making an emotional reply.

Suddenly it was all over. People started to consult their watches and drift towards the door. Isabel joined Margo as guests embraced her and took their leave, while Gabriel and Rachel waved their goodbyes from a distance as they hung back near the French doors to the terrace, surreptitiously nibbling abandoned pieces of birthday cake. When even Archie Benson had gone, Margo hugged them all in turn.

'Wasn't that a lovely party? I'm so lucky with my friends. And now, my dears, let's go into my little TV room. We can have a cup of tea, put our feet up and have a good old gossip.'

Soon they were enjoying the informal luxury of comfortable chintz armchairs and sipping Darjeeling tea from fine bone-china cups. Margo kept up a non-stop flow of chatter, questions and anecdotes, while skilfully drawing Rachel into the conversation. The American girl relaxed and was soon completely at ease with this formidable lady, but when Gabriel started to yawn and Rachel joined in, Isabel stood up suddenly.

'Margo my love,' she said, 'we really must be getting back. These two are still a bit jet-lagged and they were exhausted even before they got on the plane in Washington. So, I think it's time for me to see that they get some more rest. It's been the most wonderful party and thank you so much for being such a wonderful hostess. But we can talk lots on the phone and catch up – I'm sure you want to do that. Please forgive us if we go now, otherwise I'll have to carry them to the car!'

Margo smiled a little sadly and stood up too.

'Of course I understand my darlings. Off you go.'

Then she added in Mallorquin:

'I think Rachel is quite lovely. She's just perfect for you, Gabriel – but I imagine you want to tell Vasco about her yourself. I won't say a word until you're ready for me to speak. And if you have any trouble with your papa, don't worry. I'll take care of him. Teresa too, if necessary.'

Then, switching back to English, 'Sorry about that, Rachel. That was just a bit of family stuff. It has been really wonderful to meet you my dear. And I hope to see you again soon.'

She gave her an enormous hug and kissed her on both cheeks. Then there was a flurry of emotional goodbyes, but soon they were outside and Margo was helping them into the car.

'What a lovely lady and what a lovely party!' sighed Rachel drowsily as she leaned against Gabriel in the back of the Peugeot. Soon they were both sound asleep as Isabel drove as smoothly as she could back along the A3 towards London.

In Palma it was starting to get dark. Paulo carried a bag containing a delicious cheese, a jar of olives and a bottle of wine as he walked up to the door of the building next to his apartment in the old town. The owner was another widower, Jaime Torrens, a trader in second-hand washing machines and fridges. Paulo wanted his neighbour to do him a favour. He already rented a secure area in Jaime's small warehouse up the narrow street behind the building as a garage for his Ducati. Now he wanted to borrow his neighbour's Citroen C25 for the evening. Many of these unremarkable panel vans were in use on the island, so it would be anonymous – absolutely ideal for his secret mission.

The door opened a few moments after Paulo knocked and when he produced the gifts, Jaime's craggy face cracked into a broad grin. Within a couple of minutes they were sitting in Jaime's small dark kitchen and sampling the wine, a robust red from one of the newer vineyards around Benissalem. It didn't take long for the two widowers to agree a small fee for the loan of the van. No questions were asked and, with Jaime eager to finish the remaining two-thirds of the bottle, Paulo was soon on his way. There was just room for the Ducati in the Citroen. He tied down his precious motorbike securely and checked that it was anchored properly before easing the van out of the narrow street to begin his careful drive out of the city. Now he was on his way to hide the Ducati where he would need it, ready to carry out the final part of Enrico's masterplan. All he had to do was make sure that he returned the van undamaged before Jaime needed it in the morning.

11

The Mathematics Symposium had ended on Tuesday morning with a report-back presentation by syndicate leaders. Then, after the coffee break, there was a summing-up session. Vasco took the chair, thanking the eminent speakers for their penetrating insights and all of the delegates for their participation in the discussions and working groups.

Afterwards there was lunch in a banqueting suite, where representatives from visiting universities gave short speeches of thanks, praising the Universitat de les Illes Balears for the organisation and for the choice of location for the symposium. Finally, toasts were drunk and the crowded room became noisy with goodbyes as the chattering delegates started to drift out towards the lobby. All of them had checked out of their rooms earlier, so that individuals were able to pick up their own bags from the stack near to the entrance. Many climbed onto the coaches waiting to take them to the airport. A few small groups lingered near the reception desk, exchanging email details, phone numbers and addresses.

Like all the others, Martin had already vacated his room at Son Antoni and waited patiently for Vasco. He had already said goodbye to Vasco's UIB colleagues, including Miquel Santiago. His host had been ambushed by a group of academics who were reluctant to take their leave. At last he turned and, with a final wave of his hand to his guests, came over and clapped Martin on the shoulder.

'Well, that's over for another year, thank God. It's going to be the Brits' turn next time and they're hosting the symposium at my old university, Cambridge. That's one of the places where they're doing some interesting theoretical stuff in the field of fluid dynamics. That's become a rapidly evolving science that's going to be used more and more in aerodynamics.'

Vasco picked up Martin's bag and called over to his friend, Miquel Santiago, who was still trapped by a few stragglers.

'Thanks for all your help, Miquel. Just make sure you turn up for our dinner with Teresa at Samantha's tonight at 7.30 on the dot. You definitely count as family and Martin's going to need some moral support to help him cope with my sister. Don't be late and for God's sake, man, try to find a clean shirt!'

Miquel grinned, nodded, shook his fist and turned back to the animated group. Out in the car park, Vasco put Martin's bags into the rental car before shaking him by the hand.

'I brought forward our dinner to 7.30 tonight, Martin. I've got to make a very early start in the morning, so please excuse me if I don't come to the airport to see you off. There's so much tidying-up to be done after this jamboree and a whole lot of postgraduate students are wanting time with me too. I really don't know where to begin. Anyway I've jumped the gun and booked you into a hotel in the city tonight.'

He handed Martin an envelope.

'I've got you a room at the front the Gran Meliá Victoria right on the Passeig Maritim overlooking the yacht marina and the bay. It's quite close to the old town and not too far from our dinner venue, either. So, if you felt like it, you could take a stroll and look at the cathedral or do a bit

155

of shopping. You might have time for that this afternoon, or in the morning, perhaps. Is that OK for you?'

'That sounds really great. Thanks, Vasco. You really are the perfect host.'

'Think nothing of it. I'll pick you up around 7.15, but right now I've got a lot of calls to make. Ciao!'

Vasco waved and headed off across the car park to his Jaguar on the far side of the plot. Unlocking the boot, he stowed his jacket and briefcase inside before driving off towards Palma at a discreet distance behind Martin's Renault Clio. Vasco took the airport turn-off and, after parking, went into the main building, keeping a sharp look-out for any of the delegates from the symposium who might have been curious about his visit. He saw a research fellow from Stuttgart, but he was looking intently at an electronic display board showing flight departures and didn't spot Vasco. The attractive, dark-haired girl at the information desk smiled as she handed over an envelope. He tore it open impatiently and read:

Telephone Message
To: Professor Vasco Valseca
From: Felipe Montserrat-Ribas
   I sincerely hope that you will be able to meet me in the foyer of the Hotel Viña del Mar at 10.30 tonight. Please leave a message at this information desk to confirm agreement.

Vasco needed no time at all to consider the rendezvous – it couldn't be better. He had already promised to end the dinner party at around 10.00, and the short drive from Samantha's to the Viña del Mar would take no time at all. Actually, he would even have time to drop Martin off at the Gran Meliá Victoria too – but Teresa could easily do that instead. He, Vasco, had a perfect excuse because everyone thought he would be leaving the city in the opposite direction to head off towards the *possessió*. Brilliant!

Vasco glanced around. The man from Stuttgart had disappeared and he could see nobody else from the symposium. So, pulling out his notebook, he wrote a brief message agreeing to the time and place for the meeting and put it in an envelope provided by the pretty girl at the information desk.

He smiled as he wrote the impressive-sounding name: *'Personal – for collection by Sr. Felipe Montserrat-Ribas'* on the outside, sealed it carefully and gave it back to the girl. Soon he was whistling cheerfully as he drove out of the airport. He could have taken the Via Cintura bypass around the north side of the city, but it was a fine day and at this time traffic would be relatively light. So, instead, he took the scenic route along the Passeig Marítim alongside the spectacular cathedral and, a little further on, past the imposing front entrance of Martin's hotel, the Gran Meliá Victoria, before taking the turning for Samantha's at Genova. He would have plenty of time to check the menu, the table settings and the décor before going home to change.

Meanwhile, Enrico Acappella was just leaving his room at the Novotel at Nice Airport. He had several pieces of luggage – a suitcase, a laptop computer, his own briefcase and an overnight bag.

Since his arrival on Sunday morning only two days ago he had not had much sleep during the relentlessly hectic hours which followed. The first round of couriers had arrived quickly in response to his urgent telephone calls. Some of them had even made deliveries to him aboard *Angelina* the previous night. Other contacts had promised to supply vital information by telephone or email.

He had brought with him the heavyweight headed notepaper and blank continuation sheets stolen for him on the Spanish mainland and brought directly to the marina in

Fontvielle. But before he could use it Enrico needed to complete the painstaking job of sifting and editing the pages of legal text fed back to him electronically by his accomplice, the lawyer in Barcelona. At last he was satisfied with the complex documents he had created and printed everything onto the special paper. That task finished, he phoned Paulo in Palma and told his brother to collect his special delivery of equipment on Tuesday evening. He would need to go to Mallorca's original airport, now used only for private flights and freight, at Son Bonet on the northeast side of the city.

After a night spent working on his project, Enrico expected a few hours' lull before the activity started up again. So, around mid-morning on Monday after a refreshing shower, shave and a change of clothes, he took a taxi to the Hôtel Négresco for a late breakfast – eggs Benedict with pancetta, croissants and coffee. Then he sat for a while in the old-world luxury of the foyer, reading *Le Monde* and sipping more coffee before taking a taxi back to his own hotel.

Now he had time for a little rest. Enrico took off his jacket, folded it carefully and lay down on the bed to wait for the activity to start again. Soon he was fast asleep and it was five o'clock in the afternoon when he was roused by the phone. He took an urgent call from one of his forgers: the man in Paris couldn't get the item Enrico had specified until Wednesday, so what should he do? They agreed on an alternative with delivery to a man in Barcelona later that evening. There was just time to send for a tray of tea before the phone rang again, followed by a string of emails with attachments.

Enrico had continued to work non-stop with his computer and printer until the first part of his task was complete. He was just sorting the mass of papers into separate folders when his first visitor, an elegant young woman from Barcelona, arrived at 6.30 in the evening. For a moment, he was distracted but immediately realised that he had no time for flirtation. Returning her smile with unusual restraint, he gave concise instructions as he handed over one of the sets of documents. She glanced through them quickly, flashed him a dazzling smile and promised to return after breakfast next morning. So it continued through the night: visitors, messages, printing and urgent revisions. At last Enrico was satisfied and grabbed a few more hours of sleep around dawn.

A breakfast tray arrived punctually at 7.30 on Tuesday morning and he grabbed mouthfuls of croissants and strawberry jam, washed down with coffee, while showering, shaving and dressing. He took particular care with his preparations to face the day. After all, when his work was done, he could afford to have a little relaxation. But not at the Casino – gambling was a mug's game. Well groomed at last, he tidied his desk again and sent down for some serious coffee, a double espresso. He was savouring the aroma, looking out of the window and enjoying the caffeine rush when the phone rang. It was his Barcelona contact and the news was good. Enrico smiled broadly, and said 'Si' and 'Ciao' several times before putting down the phone.

Now was the time to get ready to assemble the kit which would be sent on its way to Paulo in Palma later in the day. Earlier, Enrico had given one of the porters a generous tip to buy him a lightweight suitcase from the nearest shopping centre. Now he took it from the wardrobe, and laid it on the bed alongside some of the elements of his complicated 'jigsaw' – the remaining pieces would not be available until later. There was a new laptop computer – after talking with his brother they had decided that his existing machine was not really adequate for the task to be performed in Palma. The first item to go into the case was an elegant and costly black lizard-skin briefcase, followed by the laptop, then a handsome leather-bound desk diary, personalised with gold embossed initials; an engraved gold pen with matching propelling pencil by Caran d'Ache and, the icing on the cake, a Sony dictation machine – the most expensive model, of course. The sets of specially prepared documents needed for the elaborate charade, conceived so meticulously for Paulo's virtuoso performance, would have to be collated and added at the last minute.

He was admiring his preparations when the phone rang. It was Paulo, telephoning from Palma after returning from his morning run. He listened for a short while and smiled at his own reflection in the mirror.

'Don't worry Paulo, everything's coming together nicely. I expect to have all the rest of the stuff soon and I'll be leaving here with it early this afternoon …Yes, I know there are a lot of bits and pieces, but it's important to get every last detail absolutely right. You know what Mama used to say – "If a job is worth doing, it's worth doing well." So, how's the weather? … That's good news for us. Let's hope it stays that way. We can check that you're happy with the consignment the moment I arrive. By then I should also have confirmation that the funds we are expecting have arrived in the Swiss bank … No, Paulo, I don't think the Russians will drag their feet on payment. Big Viktor has too much to lose if he doesn't pay up as promised. Ciao, Ciao.'

Enrico hung up just as his first visitor of the morning arrived. His eyes sparkled as he opened the door to the young woman from Barcelona who had called on him the previous evening. Her almond-shaped green eyes returned his gaze and for a moment he thought of the possibility of a quick, passionate encounter. But her manner was businesslike, aloof even, as she handed him the bulky envelope, sat in the chair near the window and crossed those elegant legs. Tearing himself away from his fantasies, Enrico cleared his throat and offered to send down for coffee – or something a little stronger. Declining politely, she invited him to check the papers so that she could catch the next flight back to Barcelona, where she had an important lunch engagement. Inwardly disappointed, but revealing nothing, Enrico murmured his thanks for her visit and started to check the contents of the package.

Everything was there. The parcel contained airline tickets, passport, handsome visiting cards embossed onto thick ivory board, three sets of reports and accounts from major international corporations and, naturally, a series of labelled, transparent folders containing an impressive array of financial statements and other business papers. Finally, as the icing on the cake, a disk in a sleeve labelled 'Suspicious BCIB accounts'. Enrico looked up from the desk to meet the enquiring look of the young woman.

'This is a seriously impressive achievement. All the things you've brought me have the very aroma of authenticity.'

'And so they should. Perhaps I should have told you that I am deputy to the company secretary of BCIB.'

She held out an elegant hand as she rose and walked to the door.

'Here's my card. Please do give me a call the next time you visit Barcelona. It would be good to meet again. But for now, I really do have to fly – no pun intended.'

Then with a smile showing a flash of dazzling white teeth she was gone, leaving Enrico standing open-mouthed as she closed the door. Pulling himself together, he started meticulously sifting and checking the rest of the papers. Although his preliminary examination had been reassuring, it was necessary to be absolutely certain that the wording was right and that there was nothing missing. The long, painstaking process took the whole of the morning, with a break for more coffee when a small package was delivered by a courier service. It contained an authentic-looking copy of a dark red BCIB tie in heavyweight silk, prepared by a craftsman in Verona, working from colour photographs provided by the Barcelona contact only two days ago. The tie, wrapped carefully in tissue paper, was added to the other items. His final task was to prepare two copies of a list of all the contents of the suitcase: one for Paulo, which he put into the case, the other for himself.

By this time it was close to midday and Enrico called Nice Airport and asked them to have the Beech Baron prepared for take-off. Enrico had already ordered a tray to be sent up to his room. While he ate a salad and sipped a glass of dry white wine, he spoke to the Swiss bank and was delighted to learn that the sum of $2.5 million promised by his Russian partner had been deposited in his account that morning. Enrico consulted his watch. The flight to Mallorca was likely to take something over two hours. So it would be possible to hand over the stuff to Paulo no later than 17.00 at San Bonet airfield. It was time to go. Before calling for a porter, Enrico had a last look round. Everything had been done and his plan was on schedule. He was delighted. Even a slight delay should leave Paulo plenty of time to complete his own preparations – and have a good dinner as well.

Earlier in the afternoon Martin had already taken Vasco's advice. After checking into his hotel room at the Gran Meliá Victoria, with its spectacular view of the bay, he had wandered into the city. There, he had joined the tourists gazing in awe at the cathedral and window shopping on the Born. Then it was time for a cup of tea at an outdoor table at the Bar Bosch while watching people strolling past in the spring sunshine. He checked his watch, paid the bill and returned to his hotel to take a shower and rest. Wrapping himself in a bathrobe, he lay on the bed, picked up the phone and set up a call for 6.15.

While Martin was dozing, Paulo Acappella was waiting

anxiously at Son Bonet airfield. Naturally, he was not able to use his Ducati for the rendezvous with Enrico; it was already safely hidden away far out of Palma, ready for use in a few hours' time. He had spoken to Jaime and persuaded him to extend the loan of his Citroen in return for an extra payment and the promise of a home-cooked meal on Wednesday night. He leaned against the roof of the van and peered into the sky, finally picking up the outline of the incoming Beech Baron. Soon the drone of its twin engines grew louder. Within a few minutes the sleek machine had made a perfect landing and was taxiing towards the main building. Paulo relaxed and folded his arms as Enrico jumped out and walked towards him to embrace his brother with the bag he had brought from Nice. The brothers chatted briefly as Paulo took the suitcase and put it in the back of the van. Then they stood side by side as the contents were checked against Enrico's list. Paulo clapped his brother on the back. 'That's really most impressive. Everything looks 100% genuine. There's an excellent little restaurant near here. Why don't I buy you a meal before you get back to Nice? I know you won't want to hang about here and you can be back in Monaco in time for a nightcap.'

'That's a great idea. Thanks a lot.' Enrico got into the van. 'We'll have a quick bite and then you can get on with your part of the scheme.'

Paulo started the engine. Enrico stretched luxuriously and massaged his cramped legs – still aching after the flight from Nice. After a convivial meal at a local charcoal grill, Paulo returned his brother to Son Bonet and wished him an uneventful return flight. Then he drove carefully through the early evening traffic towards his apartment. In theory there was no hurry, but he couldn't afford to make any mistakes in carrying out his role. He needed time to prepare for the part he was to play later tonight. First, he would shower and change. Then, after a final rehearsal he would be in the right state of mind for his task. He might even have time to have a final check on the special album he had got ready to receive those wonderful stamps he was going to add to his collection. His face shone with happy anticipation as he guided the van and its precious cargo towards the heart of Palma.

The call to Martin's room came through precisely on time. He had lapsed into a deep, dreamless sleep and it took a few moments for him to wake up fully. He stretched as he rose from the bed, took a long drink of water and dressed with care. Looking in the mirror he hoped he would do justice to his darling Isabel. He was wearing an immaculate grey pinstripe suit. Even so, when Martin went down in the lift to the lobby, he felt apprehensive about meeting Teresa Valseca in such a formal way. He fiddled nervously with his tie as he waited for Vasco to pick him up in the Jaguar. He tried to calm his nerves by reading a newspaper, but he couldn't concentrate. At last, it was the appointed time for his pick-up and he strolled outside the handsome entrance and watched anxiously as tourists came and went.

At last Vasco arrived. Bright-eyed and beaming, he leapt out of the Jaguar and clapped Martin on the back. He was wearing a smart lightweight suit and was evidently in high spirits.

'Everything's organised and we're going to have a wonderful evening – definitely one to remember. Don't look so nervous, Martin. Teresa's dying to meet you and, before you ask, she's secretly delighted. Isabel's been on the phone, telling her what a splendid chap you are.'

He opened the passenger door.

Martin climbed into the car uncertainly.

'I hope you're right, Vasco. Frankly, I'm a bit worried, especially after hearing all those tales about Teresa. She sounds like a very tough lady.'

'I promise you won't have a problem at all. She's really a pussycat at heart and you'll have her eating out of your hand in no time.'

On the way up the hill to the restaurant Vasco tried to put his guest at ease with family small talk, but Martin was quite unable to take it all in.

Arriving at Samantha's, Vasco turned into the gateway and parked the Jaguar carefully before ushering Martin through the handsome portico and across the marble-floored hallway, then up the curving staircase to a private dining room upstairs. It was just after 7.15 when a smartly uniformed young woman ushered them into a parquet-floored reception area. As she served cava in tall crystal flutes Martin admired the floral arrangement in the centre of of the immaculate place settings on the oval dining table in the adjoining room.

'Let's drink to a wonderful evening,' said Vasco as they touched glasses. 'And don't be too disappointed if Teresa or Miquel are a bit late. In Mallorca it's difficult to arrange for people to turn up when you want them, but tonight could be different. The British have a reputation for punctuality and Teresa's secretly very eager to meet you. I expect she'll make a special effort to be on time tonight.'

For a short while they admired the view of the Bay of Palma from the windows and then turned back to take canapés from the silver tray held out by the waitress. At that moment they heard a woman's voice and Teresa Valseca was ushered into the room. She wore a beautifully tailored cream outfit without any jewellery at all, but her gold lamé handbag must have cost a small fortune. Taking Martin's hand firmly in both of hers she looked directly into his eyes and nodded imperceptibly, before her face lit up with an enigmatic smile.

'How lovely to meet you Martin,' she said in a lilting accent, 'and welcome to our beautiful island.'

Before Martin could reply Miquel Santiago appeared at the door. He was surprisingly smart in a well-pressed, dark-blue blazer and he grabbed a glass of cava as he came over to give Martin a warm handshake. 'I've arrived just in time to rescue you from this interrogation.' He winked at Martin and clinked glasses with Teresa. 'Actually, this lady can be very charming and has a great sense of humour – though it doesn't always show.'

Vasco moved over to join them. 'Miquel, you really mustn't be so rude to my sister – though I'm sure she doesn't really mind. Come on now, let's chat over our meal. We just want Martin to relax and feel at home.'

They took their places and soon were enjoying succulent melon and wafer-thin slices of serrano ham. Vasco steered the conversation skilfully and Martin found his anxiety slip away as Teresa became less and less formal. He quickly realised that her severe manner was a veneer which concealed a warm and sensitive personality. The rest of the delicious meal seemed to pass all too quickly and by the time coffee was served Martin was feeling confident that he had passed the test.

There had been much good-humoured banter involving Miquel and many stories about the Valseca family. Martin also found himself being quizzed sympathetically about his own background. He had also been given strong advice to make the most of his time next morning, before catching his flight back to London. They all insisted that his visit to Mallorca would not be complete without a visit to one of the typical markets in a small town. He finally promised Teresa faithfully that he would visit the Wednesday morning market in Andraitx, a short drive to the west of Palma. He could easily find time to do that before his flight.

Vasco looked at his watch and tapped his wineglasss. 'I'm sorry to break up this party, but as we all know, Martin leaves tomorrow and I have a huge amount of work to do in the morning. So, sadly, it's time to say our farewells. We've all had a wonderful evening, I think. We really ought to find an excuse to do this sort of thing more often. I really want to thank Martin for giving us a reason – and a very happy one – for having this little dinner party. I can tell you that Teresa is as delighted as I am that you and Isabel want to be married. And her godfather Miquel too, of course. You certainly have our blessing, my dear fellow. Please carry our love and greetings back to your beautiful fiancée when you return to London tomorrow. And now, let us drink a toast to Martin and Isabella, with the hope that we shall see them here soon.'

Martin looked up shyly as they their glasses and drank. Now it was Martin's turn to speak and he cleared his throat nervously.

'I really must reply to Vasco and thank my future father in law – and both of you – for giving me such a wonderful welcome. I really didn't know what to expect, but you've been amazingly warm and generous. My only regret is my darling Isabel's absence – but we will certainly plan to come back together – and soon. As you know, I have strict orders to visit the market at Andraitx before I leave tomorrow. That means an early start for me to make sure that I get back to the airport in time for my flight home. And we know that Vasco has a huge pile of work to do after the symposium. So, with thanks again for an evening I shall never forget, let's all drink to Isabel – and to Gabriel, of course – before we say goodnight.'

They raised their glasses with murmurs of 'Isabel' and 'Gabriel' before Vasco, with one eye on the time, gently began to ease the other three downstairs. Finally, after bear hugs from Vasco and Miquel, Martin found himself a passenger in Teresa's Alfa Romeo for the short ride to the Gran Melia Victoria. Teresa got out of the car and kissed Martin warmly on both cheeks before he was allowed to enter the hotel. Then she slid back into the driving seat, slotting the Alfa skilfully back into the evening traffic on the Passeig Maritim as she headed back to her apartment at Cala Gamba.

After the last of his guests had gone, Vasco walked out into the car park and shivered a little in the cold night air.

Vasco smiled and checked his watch. He still had almost ten minutes before he was due at his rendezvous – and the Viña del Mar Palace was only a short distance away. He opened the boot of the Jaguar, took out the laptop in its padded bag, putting it on the passenger's seat beside him. Then he drove carefully down to the hotel, where he found that valet parking was available. Taking out his briefcase and computer, he was given a ticket by a young porter who smiled to show his approval of Vasco's car as he eased it smoothly away from the entrance.

As he entered the foyer, Vasco couldn't help being impressed by the sheer opulence of the place. Chandeliers sparkled above guests checking in at the reception desk. Most of them were dressed in expensive clothes, with only a few wearing casual jeans, tee shirts and trainers. Looking around him for a good vantage point to wait for his visitor from Barcelona, he noticed a rack of tourist information leaflets beside the desk where a smartly uniformed concierge was explaining something to a couple of elderly women. He had just reached the display and set down his briefcase, when his attention was caught by the arrival of a newcomer who walked purposefully into the open space as though he owned it. He was not particularly tall, but his conservatively tailored dark grey suit could not conceal the powerful muscles of his back and shoulders. A dark red tie secured with a pearl tiepin glowed against a cream shirt as he turned, looked straight at Vasco and walked purposefully towards him with his hand extended.

168

'You must be Professor Valseca,' he said, as he shook Vasco's hand firmly. 'My name is Felipe Montserrat-Ribas. I am so glad that you were able to join me this evening. It is very good of you to make the time to see me at such short notice.' His voice was deeply resonant, to match his charismatic bearing. As the two men greeted each other, the banker gestured towards the row of lifts. They spoke very little as they glided swiftly to the top floor, where his host opened the door for Vasco and ushered him into his large penthouse suite with a flourish.

'Please do take one of these seats, Professor Valseca.' He gestured to a comfortable easy chair near to a very large glass topped coffee table. 'Oh, I almost forgot. Have you eaten this evening?' he enquired in his deep baritone.

'Thank you, yes. I've just come from a family dinner party. It was quite close to this hotel. I must say it's most impressive here. They even have valet parking. The smart young porter who took away my Jaguar seemed to know exactly what he was doing. It really is very civilised indeed. But perhaps you need something to eat yourself, Senyor, after your flight from Geneva.'

'Well, yes. Actually I do need a snack – so I rang down a few minutes ago and they've already sent up some smoked salmon sandwiches. There are cheese and biscuits too. There's also an excellent cava and I hope you'll join me in a glass.'

'With pleasure,' said Vasco, setting down his laptop beside his chair and relaxing comfortably as he surveyed the spacious room, with its picture windows and modern paintings. They, the furnishings and an abstract sculpture on a console table near the door, all suggested tasteful luxury. The banker returned from the side table, handing his guest a crystal flute brimming with the bubbling golden nectar. They toasted each other and Vasco found himself opposite his host at the coffee table where a black crocodile leather briefcase stood open to reveal annual reports from major public companies, literature and folders bearing the BCIB logo, plus all the expensive paraphernalia of a top level banking executive; tape recorder, mobile phone, embossed ivory visiting cards and a passport. Beside it stood two thick BCIB files labelled 'NAVEGATOR' and a golden pen with the cap removed.

'We both know why we are here, so let's not waste valuable time. Professor, let's drink to a successful demonstration, a harmonious discussion and a mutually satisfactory agreement. And please do call me Felipe.'

'Of course, I'll drink to that. And of course you must call me Vasco.' The two men touched glasses and drank. Vasco cleared his throat, a little nervous now that so much depended on this demonstration. 'As you say, Felipe, time is important to both of us, so perhaps I should show you immediately what I have to offer BCIB.'

Setting his laptop on the table, Vasco switched on and booted it up. While he prepared for his demonstration, 'Felipe' strolled back to the side table and helped himself to a plate and some of the smoked salmon sandwiches. He took a bite and chewed appreciatively. 'Mmmm. These really are very good. Are you sure that I can't tempt you?'

'No thanks. I really couldn't eat a thing.' Vasco found that the palms of his hands were sweating. After a few anxious moments the familiar icon appeared – a caravel in full sail – then after a short delay following a double click on the caravel the system was ready to run. 'Now, perhaps you would care to let me have a few e-mail addresses so that I can give you a real-time demonstration.'

'That's fine with me. First, let's do something easy. Here's my business card. Perhaps you could show me how Navigator translates my e-mail address into the geographical location of my office.'

Vasco took the card and entered 'fm-r@bcib.es'. Within

seconds the geographical coordinates were displayed. A few more keystrokes and another window appeared, showing a general map of Barcelona and a larger scale street map version. Both indicated the location of the BCIB Head Office, marked by a red dot; a small box gave the street address. Vasco gave a sigh of relief. 'Unfortunately I didn't bring a printer with me, otherwise you could have had a hard copy.'

'That really isn't necessary, my friend. Those results are seriously impressive,' said the banker, refilling their glasses. 'Now, please try the website address too.'

Vasco typed in 'http://www.bcib.es' and then frowned when the coordinates appeared followed by the window showing the maps and address. 'There is something very strange here. The coordinates are totally different. And look, I'm getting a map of Madrid, for God's sake – and a street address near the city centre. I really don't understand this at all.' He turned to his host, who was smiling broadly.

'I'm even more impressed now,' said Felipe, 'That was actually a trick. You see, we've farmed out the hosting of our website to a specialist IT company in Madrid. In fact you've just come up with the address of WebCasa, so you've passed the second part of the test with flying colours.'

Vasco realised he had been holding his breath for a long time and exhaled gratefully. 'I'm very happy to demonstrate further; just give me some more e-mail addresses or any-thing that's been corrupted with a virus and I'll get to work on those. It won't take long.'

'Yes, that would be the acid test,' said the banker, who produced a data disk from his briefcase. 'See what you can make of this. And while you're doing that, I'll pour us a brandy to celebrate the success of your Navegator pro-gramme. After what we'd been told by Vila, our manager here in Palma, our board was confident that your demon-stration would be convincing. So, in anticipation of this moment, I brought along a bottle of Armagnac in my bag. It certainly seems to be justified by such a special occasion.' He disappeared into the bedroom and reappeared a few moments later with a handsome bottle. He took it over to the side table, where he poured generous measures into two crystal balloon glasses.

As Vasco concentrated on his laptop, he didn't notice that a small glass tube of liquid was being decanted into one of the glasses. He turned as his beaming host came towards him carrying the Armagnac, which glowed like amber in the large goblets. 'So, do we have proof positive? What have you got for me?'

'Yes, I really have got solid evidence for you. This disk is carrying some very interesting stuff. I think you'll find it rewarding. From my own selfish standpoint, it's given me the location of the hacker who got into the account of our small political party, the PIIB. The address is on the mainland, near to Santander. It's probably a Basque separatist group trying to raid our funds. Cheeky bastards – we can get the police onto them immediately, I imagine the authorities will be very happy. The other attempts to damage the bank's security are very interesting too. For instance, there are some people in Uruguay who've been getting into your system at head office. They also seem to have linked up with other addresses in Spain and around the world. I suppose these could be branches of your bank, but I haven't had time to check. Would you like me to do that?'

Felipe clapped his guest on the shoulder and held out a glass of Armagnac. 'My dear fellow, that won't be necessary now. There will be time for that in the morning. I'm completely convinced. Let's drink to a mutually satisfactory negotiation, now that your programme has shown exactly what it can do.'

Vasco got to his feet, took the brandy and touched his

glass to the banker's. 'To Navegator,' they said together and drank. There was an appreciative pause. 'That Armagnac is impressive,' said Vasco, 'I don't come across anything like it very often – the brandy we see here is from Mallorca or the mainland.'

His host waved a hand towards a comfortable settee facing the window with a panoramic view of the bay. 'Let's sit here my friend and talk about our proposal.' He walked over to the coffee table and returned with the two bulky folders. Sitting down alongside Vasco, he handed him one of them and opened his own.

'First, I must just clear up one small but crucial matter. Can you give me a positive assurance that this computer contains the one and only copy of the Navegator programme? Don't you have a backup copy?'

'Yes, it really is the only one,' replied Vasco. 'For one thing, I've been so preoccupied with the mathematics symposium and the visit of my future son-in-law that I didn't get around to it. And for another,' he grinned, tapping his temple, 'it's all in here and I could easily do it again if necessary. It would be a chore, but it wouldn't be difficult for me. Naturally, I would happily sign any undertaking which would bind me not to create it again for any third party.'

'That seems fair enough,' said the banker. 'And I don't think that the undertaking you mention will be necessary in the circumstances. Now, let's discuss the terms of our offer. The letter which I sent to you by courier on Monday has already given an outline. These legal documents are merely a formal expression of those terms. In fact, based on what you've just shown me, I'm authorised to increase our offer substantially. If we can shake hands now, I will alter the documents myself to incorporate those favourable adjustments. I can also assure you that there are no hidden traps.' The banker produced a copy of the original letter which

Vasco had received at Son Antoni. Lying next to it was a copy of the BCIB annual report and accounts with a photograph of Felipe on the cover. He gave a throaty chuckle as he noticed Vasco glance towards it. 'Isn't it terrible? It's almost as bad as my passport photograph. Now, let's talk about the improved terms I am suggesting for our agreement …' The deep voice droned on hypnotically with words and phrases registering dimly. The photograph of Felipe Monserrat-Ribas swam before Vasco's eyes and he heard the words 'two million dollars for exclusive rights' coming from a great distance. Then, finally, his leaden eyelids drooped and he slowly slid sideways onto the gold satin cushions of the settee.

The banker got to his feet, took a deep breath and stretched before relaxing into the identity of Paulo again. 'Though I say so myself,' he said aloud, 'that was a great performance.' He chuckled and checked the time. It was close to midnight now and there was much to do. First he checked Vasco's breathing and pulse. No problems there; the rohypnol had worked well and his victim was deeply unconscious. Then he booted up Vasco's laptop and the machine supplied by Enrico as part of the elaborate kit flown over from Nice.

After clicking on the caravel icon and making sure that the Navegator programme was intact, he linked the two laptops with a cable and began transferring the software to his own machine. This would take a little time and while the data was being moved he wolfed another smoked salmon sandwich. Then he wrapped a piece of cheese in a linen napkin and put it in his briefcase, along with all the rest of his props. He finished the cava in his glass and looked wistfully at the half empty bottle. He retrieved his lightweight carry-on bag from the bedroom. Along with the rest of his gear, it now contained the rest of the bottle of Armagnac – that was far too good to leave behind.

He checked on the progress of the data transfer and grunted when he found that it was not quite complete. Then he levered Vasco's unconscious body to an upright position. His victim had said that he had handed over his Jaguar to the valet parking service. Paulo needed the ticket and after a brief search found it in the side pocket of Vasco's jacket.

The Navegator programme had now transferred to his own computer. He made a careful check to ensure that the caravel icon and all the rest of the software package would run properly. Then he disconnected the linking cable and made a thorough search to ensure that all trace of Navegator had been removed from Vasco's laptop. When he was satisfied, Paolo shut down both computers, putting his own into its carrying case. Vasco's machine was closed but had no case; it would be slightly more awkward to carry, but there would be no danger of a mix-up.

Finally, he washed and dried the glasses carefully and wiped down all the surfaces his victim might have touched. He checked his watch, which showed that it was now 12.35 am. That was excellent. The front desk staff would have changed over at midnight and he would have a different porter to retrieve Vasco's car from the parking lot. This would make any investigation by the authorities just a little more difficult.

He rang down to the lobby and explained that he had a problem. His guest seemed to have had a lot too much to drink. He would take his visitor back to his home and explain the situation there. He would need to be very diplomatic, of course, but he knew the family well. Would a porter kindly bring the Jaguar round to the front entrance? He gave the number on the ticket and went on to ask for help with the briefcases and laptops. To avoid any problems if he, Felipe Monserrat-Ribas, was invited to stay at his friend's house it seemed like a good idea to settle his account now. The receptionist was sympathetic and helpful. A porter would arrive at the penthouse suite within a few moments; the car would be brought round and the senyor's account would be prepared immediately; it was a pleasure to be of service.

By the time the porter arrived, Paulo had the baggage ready and he was supporting Vasco, now semi-comatose, with his victim's arm across his shoulders. 'Sorry about this. I'm afraid my guest had rather too much brandy. Perhaps I can manage him if you look after the rest of the stuff.' Together they stumbled to the lift with the porter following. Arriving in the lobby, Vasco was half carried to the waiting Jaguar and the porter strapped him into the passenger's seat. While the porter put Paulo's briefcase, the bags and the laptops in the car, he went back to the front desk and paid his bill with a forged platinum BCIB VISA card, signing the account with a flourish. In his distinctive baritone he thanked the receptionist for her assistance, then strode to the car and handed the helpful porter a generous tip.

'Thank you very much indeed senyor. I hope your friend will feel better tomorrow.'

'I don't think he will be feeling any pain at all,' muttered Paulo grimly as he put on calfskin driving gloves before getting into the Jaguar. He smiled to himself; there would be no need to wipe down the car for fingerprints. He adjusted the driving seat and mirrors, blipped the throttle and drove off. Within minutes he was starting to leave the city lights behind. Vasco lolled semi-conscious beside him as he headed for the Tramontana mountains in the northwest of the island.

The roads started to become narrower. The car cruised silently through the narrow streets of a village where not a light showed. Then the country became less populated and the winding road grew steeper as it wound higher into the mountains. After forty minutes or so, Paulo slowed and peered into the darkness, finally turning onto a narrow track which snaked up the hillside. There was no hamlet nearby, not even a small finca, for this was barren country. After a few more minutes he turned off again. The surface was broken and bumpy now. The only people to penetrate this inhospitable area would be occasional tourists in high summer, serious walkers, shepherds or goatherds looking for stray animals. Finally, with the help of a glimmer of moonlight, Paulo saw his destination through the darkness. There was the cairn of stones he had been looking for, about two metres in height and close to a rocky outcrop and a clump of stunted bushes. He carefully brought the Jaguar to a halt and stepped out of the car to check his exact position. He would have to hurry. The jolting movement of the car for the last ten minutes or more had started to arouse Vasco from his stupor.

As his passenger stirred and mumbled beside him, Paulo got back into the car and eased it carefully forward down a slight incline until the front wheels were checked by a log he had positioned near the edge of a black void. He put the handbrake on, selected neutral, but decided to leave the engine running before getting out. After putting his own computer, bag and briefcase near the cairn, he checked that Vasco's laptop was on the back seat. Next came the really hard part; getting his victim from the passenger's seat into the driving seat. As he leaned across Vasco to release the seatbelt, he started up, shouting incoherently. Despite Paulo's prowess in the gym, it was only with the greatest difficulty that he was able to half carry, half drag, his protesting passenger around the car and put him behind the wheel. Fastening the seat belt was too difficult to try. Vasco was rapidly regaining consciousness and he was evidently fit and quite strong.

Now was the moment to act decisively, without a

moment's delay. Paulo stepped back from the car for a moment, then quickly yanked open the passenger's door and released the handbrake. Vasco was squirming, shouting and trying to get out of the car as he slammed the door, dragged away the log that was checking the front wheels and gave an almighty heave to the rear bumper. The Jaguar's wheels crunched on the stony surface as it slowly gathered speed. Then, with a sound of tearing metal, it ran ever faster over a few small boulders, the engine revving as Vasco's foot caught the accelerator before the car vanished out into the blackness. A few seconds later there were several rending crashes, then stillness. Paulo crossed himself. 'Poor bastard,' he muttered, 'he seemed like a really nice man. A pity he had to go that way. I hope he felt nothing – but then I do have these serious priorities of my own.' He thought of the rare stamps which would soon be in his priceless stamp collection. Perhaps he might even get the very latest Ducati. Suddenly there was a loud explosion and a fireball shot skywards as the Jaguar's fuel tank exploded.

Paulo ducked instinctively and crossed himself again as rocks and debris rained down for a few seconds. Then everything was quiet again, except for the call of a night creature on a distant mountainside or the occasional clank of metal as another piece of the stricken Jaguar plunged down to the very bottom of the precipitous gully. He watched, mesmerised, as the fire smouldered on for while, but soon the flames had died away and it was pitch dark except for the faint moonlight – as Paulo collected his gear and prepared to leave the scene.

Opening his bag to find a powerful torch, he located his motorcycle in the middle of the clump of bushes. This was the isolated spot where he had hidden the Ducati after bringing it here last night in Jaime's van. Now he dragged the powerful black machine out onto a piece of level ground beside the cairn, propped it on its stand and took his helmet and motorcycling kit from a collapsible tote bag from the same clump of shrubs. He shivered with the cold as he stripped off the banker's outfit, then quickly put on his leathers. 'Christ, but it's freezing up here,' he muttered as he stowed the suit, shirt and shoes carefully into the panniers of the bike along with the briefcase and the rest of his gear, except for his laptop in its carrying case. This, with the priceless Navegator programme installed, went into a small backpack which Paulo strapped on securely.

Before leaving, he swept the torch carefully over the whole area to make sure that he had left no obvious traces of his visit. Everything seemed to be undisturbed, except for some distinctive wheel tracks and a smear of oil from the underside of the car that showed where the Jaguar had taken its fatal plunge. He cursed under his breath. Nothing should be left to chance. Near the shrubs where he had hidden the motorcycle, he found a dead branch and used it as a broom to sweep away the telltale clues. Finally he was satisfied and threw the branch over the edge where the Jaguar had disappeared into the blackness below.

Paulo listened carefully. Everything was still except for the noises of the night. He checked the time and found it was just after 3am. This seemed like a good time to call his brother to confirm that the plan had gone like clockwork. He grinned mischievously and reached into his leather jacket for his mobile phone. Up here, though, there was no signal at all. He shrugged, zipped it back into his pocket, exchanged the calfskin gloves for the black leather motorcycling gauntlets and mounted the Ducati. My God, what a night! He would be lucky to be back in his apartment by 4.30 am. There wouldn't be much time for sleep, though. He had a lot more to do to be ready for the final act of the drama at Andratx, but perhaps setting the alarm for 8 o'clock would still give him plenty of time. Meanwhile, he promised himself a hot chocolate laced with some of that delicious Armagnac to round off a successful night's work. He looked forward to giving an update to Enrico during the morning. There might even be time for a chat with the stamp dealer too – but that would have to wait until later in the day.

He fired up the machine as quietly as he could and ghosted down the stony track towards the lane which would take him back to the road leading down towards the first distant cluster of houses and then on towards the faint glow in the sky where the lights of Palma were reflected from the night sky.

12

In his apartment among the rooftops of Palma's historic quarter, Paulo sat up in bed with a start. The phone on the bedside table was ringing insistently. Cursing furiously, he peered blearily at his wristwatch as he picked up the handset, then shouted:

'Enrico, you bastard, you've woken me up! Don't you know what time it is? I've had barely an hour's sleep. Don't you know I've had a bloody hard night of it – and there's still a hell of a lot to do here … It's all very well to say that you've been worried. What about me? … No, stop. Is this line really safe? Have you got secure encryption on your phone?'

At the other end of the line Enrico was evidently turning on the charm and after a while Paulo's fierce expression relaxed.

'OK then … Basta, Basta. Yes, everything went exactly to plan. By the way, Valseca seemed like a nice guy. It's a pity he had to go. But, Christ, he was heavy – it was almost impossible to manhandle him from one side of the car to the other. It's a good job I've been keeping in shape at the gym. I'll call you later, when I've completed the handover. Ciao, ciao.'

Paulo ended the call, stretched, yawned and scratched himself as he stumbled to the kitchen to make his first espresso of the day. He gulped it down as he glowered at the kitchen clock, which showed barely 6.15. Cursing under

181

his breath, he carried his second cup of coffee into the bathroom for a scalding shower. Emerging a little later in boxer shorts, he put on his running gear. Soon he was out on the street, empty at this hour except for the street cleaning team and one or two traders heading towards the nearby market. He headed down towards the sea front for his workout, a cycle of sprinting and jogging which took him along the lake by the cathedral and then back up the hill again into the old town.

By the time Paulo had trotted up the stairs to the attic apartment, his distinctive tracksuit with the logo of Real Deportivo Mallorca was black with sweat. After another shower and two more cups of strong coffee he felt ready to face the day. Soon he had changed into his normal clothes, a baggy pair of old tan trousers and a dark-green cardigan over a brown check shirt. There was still a chill in the air as he strolled along the narrow streets before emerging into the little square beside the market hall. He was greeted by many of the stallholders as he picked out beef, vegetables and fruit for the celebration meal he would prepare for his neighbour Jaime that evening. That was the reward promised to his friend for the loan of his van without asking any questions. There would be no problem about the wine: he had a fabulous Italian red to accompany the hearty casserole.

Just as he was nodding to old Carlos on his way out of the building Paulo stopped in his tracks and put his hand to his brow. 'My God, I've forgotten the herbs,' he muttered and turned back again to get the fresh rosemary and sage he needed to make the dish to the traditional recipe. A little later he had picked up his copy of *Ultima Hora* and was sitting at his usual table in l'Olivera Vella with another espresso and a basket of croissants.

The owner, Antonio, strolled over for a chat about the weather and the latest scandal about the butcher's wife until another customer called him over to put a shot of brandy in his coffee. Paulo lingered over his breakfast, but kept a careful check on the time. It was still early but he had an important job to do back at his apartment. With a sigh he folded up his paper, left some money on the table, and left the bar to return home. Once inside, he put away his purchases in the kitchen, then went over to the table, retrieved the 'banker's' laptop from its carrying case and booted it up. His eyes gleamed as he checked the Navegator software again. Everything was just fine. Within a few minutes, he had connected it to a separate disk writer and burned the program onto a blank. A final check confirmed that the transfer had gone without a glitch. Then he smiled as he slipped the disk into the specially prepared case supplied by Enrico. Although he was feeling some remorse for the events of last night, it was still possible to appreciate the lighter side of Paulo's scheme.

Paulo checked his watch. It was only a little after 8.30 and he still had time to relax for a while before changing into his motorcycling gear. He set the alarm to give himself an hour's rest and was stretched out in his favourite chair with his eyes closed when he had an idea. After he had done the handover at Andratx, the Ducati would easily get him back to the city, cleaned up and changed out of his leathers before one o'clock. Brilliant! He sat up abruptly. He would take the stamp dealer out for lunch – to the Yacht Club, perhaps. Maybe he could soften him up and get a better price for those wonderful Queen Isabella specimens. His eyes shone with anticipation as he reached for the phone.

Although this March morning on the island of Mallorca gave a promise of spring, Ygor Krasnov was not a happy man. The once-crisp olive green shirt clung to his back with dark patches of sweat as he pushed the baggage trolley holding his suitcase and carry-on bag, jogging up and down as he looked for the Fiat Uno he had been instructed to take from the car park building opposite the terminal at Palma Airport. He had originally hoped to arrive a day or two beforehand to enjoy a dose of early sunshine, relaxation and sex to set him up after the fierce winter which was still biting hard in St Petersburg. But his mother's fall and hospitalisation had put paid to that dream. After hours on the telephone he had eventually managed to book flights for the Tuesday, unknown to his boss.

Now the whole scheme was falling apart. The first leg, a midday flight from Pulkovo at St Petersburg to Moscow's Sheremetyevo Airport, was right on time, but his connecting flight for Frankfurt was seriously delayed. His aircraft had developed pressurisation problems and the Aeroflot engineers took over four hours to fix it. By the time he finally arrived at Frankfurt, all Tuesday's flights for Palma had gone. He was forced to spend the night at an airport hotel, needing a very early start on an Air Berlin flight to give him any chance at all of getting to his rendezvous on time. Unfortunately there was yet another delay caused by an air traffic controllers' dispute.

It was hardly surprising that his nerves were shredded. If he didn't get going immediately he would fail the giant of a man who had sent him to collect this apparently priceless package – whatever that might be. And just a few days ago Viktor Dankovitch had broken a man's arm, just before his own arrival at the party in the Senat Bar – and that was only for spilling a little vodka.

He was already running over an hour behind schedule. Ygor had been told repeatedly that exact timing for the rendezvous was absolutely critical, because the Italians were so paranoid about security. He had good reason to sweat with terror and frustration when he realised what his punishment would be for screwing up a mission of such importance.

At last he saw the car in a distant corner of the building. There it was, the yellow Fiat with a red sticker on the windscreen. Breathing a sigh of relief, Ygor took the keys and car park ticket out of the envelope he had picked up at the information desk in the terminal, unlocked the car, yanked open the door and heaved his luggage inside. When he opened the glove box the local people had done their stuff and there was the second envelope he had been told to expect. He tore it open and found a map and further details for the collection, relaxing a little when he found that they were in Russian. He even smiled when he saw that his contact would speak to him in English. That should be quite OK – he had done well in English conversation classes while he was in the army.

Then he swore angrily. The Italians had added some special security measures. As proof of his identity, they wanted Ygor to bring four specific items in a carrier bag, obtained from the market beside his rendezvous. He looked at the list. They wanted him to buy a fake Rolex wristwatch, a special stand for holding dried ham, some sort of cake thing called an *ensaimada* and a CD by some local folk singer called Tomeu Penya. Mother of Christ, this was absolutely unbelievable! Did they think he was a babushka to go shopping for God's sake – and how could he find the time to do that now? He checked his watch and saw it was 10.25. His meeting was due to take place in only thirty-five minutes' time! He ground his teeth with frustration. This would mean an extra delay. There was no time for these silly games.

He fumed while he paid to leave the car park; fortunately he had sufficient pesetas to cover the charges. Once more Ygor cursed long and loud as he looked at the marked map and the rendezvous instructions. He knew it would be impossible to reach his destination some distance outside the city and complete his shopping task in time. Ygor cursed loudly as he accelerated violently out of the airport complex. He was soon driving like a madman as he switched lanes, weaving his way through the traffic on the major arterial highway which runs around the north side of Palma.

Enraged by the difficulty of making headway through the traffic and with thoughts of Comrade Viktor never out of his mind, the Russian headed towards the southwest of the island. A few kilometres after leaving the bypass, the dual carriageway narrowed to the width of a normal main road. He approached a roundabout much too fast and took the wrong exit onto a minor road, heading towards the mountains. Ygor tore at the wheel and swerved into a gateway, intending to reverse out and return to the main road. There was a sickening crunch as one of the Fiat's wheels dropped into a ditch and a spur of rock punctured the car's sump, hot oil pouring onto the ground.

Purple with rage and frustration, he screamed a torrent of curses at Viktor, Viktor's mother, the unmarried parents of all Italians, the makers of Fiat cars and the island of Mallorca. When he was completely exhausted and out of breath, Ygor finally realised that his only chance of getting to the meeting place at all was to get back to the main road and hitch a lift.

Sweating more profusely than ever, the Russian grabbed his bags from the car. Then, clutching the envelope, he jogged back to the steady stream of traffic and stuck his thumb out. He cursed quietly and bitterly when he looked at his watch. Even if he got a lift soon, he would be at least forty minutes late when he reached the rendezvous.

Every Wednesday morning in Mallorca, many people in the south-west of the island head for the market at Andratx. This day was no exception, with a clear sky and a hint of warmth in the air to remind locals and tourists that winter was losing its grip and spring was not far away. Yellow buses from Palma, ancient cars from nearby villages and newer rental cars which marked out the visitors, nosed their way through the good-natured crowds. The market stalls spread over several side streets to the right of the main road from Palma. Farmers and their wives from nearby fincas were selling local produce, fruit and vegetables from the centre of the island, many types of olives, cheeses, fish, poultry, meat and chorizo sausages. And, inevitably, stalls laden with craft items, leather goods, rugs, folkloric cassettes and CDs, improbable lingerie in exotic colours, shoes, shapeless dresses, jeans, ironmongery, mobile phones, electrical equipment, kitchen utensils, pottery and garden plants.

Martin Weston had taken Teresa Valseca's advice to explore this Mallorcan institution on his last morning on the island before making his lunchtime departure for London. Around the time that Ygor Krasnov's delayed flight was touching down at Palma Airport, Martin was getting lucky – finding a parking space for his rented Renault Clio in a side street behind the Andratx market. He picked his way through the chattering crowd, intent on finding a few gifts for two special people. For Isabella of course, something typical of the island. He had missed her desperately while he was at the symposium. He smiled as he hurried on: he would be with her again soon. Of course he would have to find something for Gabriel too.

Martin's athletic stride took him quickly through the crowd, his sharply pressed cream slacks and striped blue polo shirt marking him out from the locals. Looking around him he was glad that he'd taken Teresa's advice. The glittering boutiques of Palma stocked little that was different from the expensive trinkets sold by the shops in Bond Street or the Faubourg St Honoré. So, the market at Andratx was an ideal place to find a few presents – not necessarily expensive, but different and somehow special.

A stall selling carved and polished olive wood products caught his eye. He saw a beautiful salad bowl and thought that Isabel might like it. Just in time though, he remembered that it was similar to one she already owned. Then he spotted a bewildering display of saucepans, paella pans and kitchen gadgets nearby. Amongst them he picked out something just right; an unusual piece of equipment with a local flavour, a *jamonero* – the special carving stand for holding the much-prized serrano ham from mainland Spain. Then, just as he was passing a stall selling vinyl records, old 78s, DVDs and CDs, he recognised the distinctive cover of one of Isabel's favourites – songs by the Mallorcan folk singer Tomeu Penya. She already had the identical disc, but had often said she would like another to play on the sound system in her car. He bought it quickly, plus a few more that she didn't have in London. Then he hurried on to buy a typical Mallorcan delicacy, *ensaimada*, the sweet sausage-shaped bread which is coiled like a catherine wheel, dusted with icing sugar and sold in a distinctive octagonal box.

He still needed to find something for Gabriel. Through a gap in the crowd he saw a stall selling imitation designer watches. It didn't take long for Martin to choose a very convincing copy of a top-of-the-range Rolex. He bought another – an imitation Breitling – for himself. Then he went a bit mad and bought some more Mallorcan delicacies, the bitter aperitif *palo* and the traditional biscuits, *galetes d'Inca*. He had already said his goodbyes to his host after their dinner with the Teresa and Miquel previous night. That had been the most wonderfully relaxed and happy occasion. Vasco had been a charming companion whenever pressures around the organisation of the symposium allowed him. Between the mathematical presentations at Son Antoni, Martin had managed to find time to arrange a rental car, so that he could take himself off for a few local excursions. Soon it would be time to use it for his drive to the airport. It really had been a marvellous trip. Though now that Martin thought about it, there had been times, even at last night's dinner for example, when his future father-in-law did seem very preoccupied. He checked his watch: quite soon he ought to be leaving Andratx. But before finding his car and heading back towards the city, he had enough time in hand for a drink.

Now, clutching his gifts in a large brightly coloured carrier bag, he noticed the Café Nacional on the corner of Avenida Juan Carlos I and Carrer Son Esteva. Martin was intrigued by the lettering carved on the honey coloured stone facade which proclaimed 'Teatro Argentino Ano 1912'. As a nearby church clock struck eleven he pushed open the aluminium and glass doors at the end of the building. Inside was a cool oasis where four men played cards at one of the yellow plastic tables. A leather-clad motorcyclist propped up the bar beside a brandy glass. A middle-aged woman with no teeth and wearing a shapeless pink dress served him with milky coffee and a glass of mineral water. Another woman of about thirty came in wearing a navy blue top and shabby red trousers. She ordered a beer and flicked her straggling hennaed hair away from her eyes as she flirted with a couple of young men delivering a fruit machine.

Martin drifted into a reverie as he relaxed with his drinks and checked his airline tickets. He really ought to think about getting to the airport, but before returning to his car a visit to the toilet seemed like a good idea. Leaving the carrier bag beside his table, he pushed through the double doors opposite the bar and found himself at the back of a semi-derelict cinema with faded posters for films of the eighties. He paused, looking into the auditorium, amazed at the sight of faded splendour: the cobwebbed gold eagle over the proscenium arch, the dusty blue plush seats, the balconies and the boxes. He turned to enter the primitive toilet and, emerging a few moments later, stood with his hands on his hips facing the torn screen, now faded to a shabby grey.

'So, you like this old movie theatre?' said a deep cultured voice behind him, in a slight accent which Martin couldn't quite place. He turned, coming face to face with the motor-cyclist from the bar standing six feet away. He held up Martin's carrier bag with one hand. Before Martin could do more than gasp with surprise, the man spoke again.

'Don't say anything. It really isn't necessary. You arrived exactly on time. Punctuality is a great virtue – I really like that. The four items on the list are all correct and here in the bag, so you've passed the test. And I see you have got some other things too. Well, you deserve a few extras for your trouble. You can tell Viktor all about Enrico's scheme when you get back – it was an interesting task wasn't it? Now you really ought to be getting back to the airport as fast as you can. Your people already know that everything is OK and we're happy about the money. So, off you go, my friend.'

Before Martin had a chance to recover from his surprise, the man thrust the bag into his arms, spun him round and shoved him into an alleyway through a fire exit. The door slammed shut and locked behind him. He checked the contents of the bag. It only took a moment to see that everything was there. His own wallet, passport and travel documents were secure in his jacket.

What a bizarre incident, he thought! Nothing the motor-cyclist had said made any sense, but there seemed to be no point in involving the police. Why would they be interested? And it would take ages to make a statement. Why run the risk of missing his flight to London? Shaking his head, Martin emerged from the narrow passage beside the old theatre and retraced his steps to the car. Soon he would be back in London with so much to tell Isabel about his wonderful trip. He was smiling again as he turned the ignition key.

About forty minutes later, the door of the Café Nacional burst open. The bar was busier now. Conversation stopped as Ygor Krasnov staggered in, sweating and dishevelled, panting with fatigue and shaking with suppressed fury. He looked wildly around him, but could see no sign of the motorcyclist he should have met at eleven o'clock. He was about to grab one of the card players and demand information when he noticed two smartly dressed officers of the Polícia Local having coffee at a table in the corner. Controlling himself with difficulty, he moved away, slumped into an empty chair and called for vodka. When the toothless woman in the pink dress produced his drink he downed it in a gulp and asked for another. Then he put his head in his hands as his shoulders began to heave uncontrollably.

One of the card players looked across at the policemen, winked, shrugged and started dealing again.

Miquel Santiago slumped forward onto his desk at the University, then sat up abruptly. Dear God, he'd been fast asleep. Then he remembered the party at Samantha's last night. For him, it had been a very late night indeed. After he had got back to his apartment at Illetas he had opened a bottle of brandy and smoked his pipe while watching TV. A man needed a little relaxation after an evening like that. But he'd fallen asleep, only to be roused by cramp in his shoulder. He had stumbled into bed around three in the morning. No wonder he felt terrible. He yawned and stretched sleepily, then looked at his watch. It was lunchtime. Where was Vasco? Last night he had said that he had urgent things to do this morning. Even so, it was strange that he hadn't found the time to put his head round the door. Miquel lumbered to his feet and walked along the corridor to Vasco's office, which was empty. Curious, he picked up the phone and called down to the front desk. The receptionist told him that Professor Valseca had not been in today. It would be appreciated if Professor Santiago would kindly let him know that there had been eleven messages and several more callers who said that they would ring again. Miquel frowned, put down the phone and went back to his own office, where he lit his pipe and tried to think.

Perhaps Vasco wasn't well, or had gone to the airport with Martin – but surely he would have sent a message? Well, there was one way to find out. He picked up the phone and dialled the number for C'an Valseca. His call was quickly answered by Antonia.

'Oh it's you, Professor Santiago. Have you any idea where Professor Valseca might be? There have been three phone calls for him here and I didn't know what to say. Perhaps he stayed in Palma after the dinner party?'

Miquel cut in quickly.

'I really don't know, Antonia. He isn't here in his office, but please don't worry. There's sure to be a simple explanation. I'll make some enquiries and call you again just as soon as I have some news.'

He hung up and sucked noisily on his pipe. This was completely out of character, so perhaps Vasco had had an accident? After a few phone calls he learned that there had been only one car crash anywhere near to Palma last night – on the main road to Inca between a Ford Escort and a heavy truck. The drunken driver of the Ford had been seriously injured, but the truck driver was unhurt. None of the hospitals had admitted any patient who might have been Vasco.

It was time to act. Miquel grabbed his car keys from the ashtray on his desk and trotted downstairs. He called 'Back tomorrow' to the startled receptionist and hurried out to the car park. After some hesitation, he remembered where he had left his car. Having overslept he had arrived at the university campus very late, there had been no parking spaces near to the Mathematics building. Finally he remembered where he had managed to squeeze it in beside a bush. There, on the far side of the crowded parking lot, he caught sight of the faded blue roof of his battered old Rover. Opening the creaking door he slid into the seat and smiled grimly when the engine reluctantly coughed into life. It didn't take long to reach the city, where he found a parking space not far from the Placa Espanya. He jogged to the BCIB office but drew another blank. Ramón Vilar had not seen Professor Valseca since their interesting meeting the previous Friday – and he was still waiting for head office in Barcelona to reply to his urgent report. He hoped that Professor Santiago would understand that these things took time to be properly considered in such a large organisation.

Miquel grunted and hurried out. His next stop was l'Olivera Vella, but Vasco hadn't been there either. What now? He swallowed hard and considered the options. Should he contact Teresa? Certainly she had a right to know that he seemed to be missing. He fished in his pocket for his mobile phone but it wasn't there. He slapped his forehead and swore softly. Now he remembered. He hadn't owned it for long and wasn't yet in the habit of carrying it with him. In his haste he had left it on his desk back at the university. He would have to use another way. He walked aimlessly for a while considering his options.

At last he came to a decision. Teresa must be told. Finding a tapas bar close to the spot where he had parked his car, he shouldered his way through the doorway into the cosy interior, ordered a coffee and asked to borrow their phone. He was lucky to find Teresa in her office at the Secretarial College and breathlessly told her about his search for Vasco. She was immediately sympathetic and seemed as worried as he was. Yes, she would ring round anyone she could think of but this would be a forlorn hope. The whole episode was completely out of character. There was nothing for it but to contact the authorities. Miquel agreed and said he would do that immediately.

The offices of the Polícia Nacional were within walking distance and one of his brighter students was the son of Chief Inspector José Diaz. He had met him at a function at the university and remembered him as a taciturn man, but intelligent and occasionally witty. Perhaps he could make an informal enquiry. Miquel trotted the few blocks to the Passeig de Mallorca and pushed open the doors of the Policia Nacional headquarters. He was out of breath and panting as he asked at the desk for Chief Inspector Diaz. The duty officer was unhelpful and demanded to know why the Chief Inspector should be disturbed. At last he accepted that it was a personal matter and grudgingly made a phone call. After a few minutes a smart young woman appeared and ushered him into the Chief Inspector's sparsely furnished office. C. I. José Diaz, immaculate in a crisply pressed dark grey suit, a dazzling white shirt and a burgundy silk tie striped with gold, rose to greet his visitor. His hair was black and sleek, complementing his neatly trimmed moustache. He was formal and polite, but not unfriendly.

'Please do sit down Professor Santiago. This is an un-expected pleasure. I hope there's no problem with my son.'

As he pushed a bulging folder labelled 'Personnel' to one side of his desk, two or three files spilled out.

'Absolutely not, Chief Inspector. Alessandro is a first-class student with an excellent mind and he's hardworking too. No, it's not about him at all. It's just that I'm seriously worried about my friend and colleague Vasco Valseca. He hasn't been seen since we had dinner with him last night. I've tried everywhere I can think of. Nobody has any idea – his home, friends, family, the hospitals. I didn't check the airport, because I haven't got the authority.'

He looked at his watch.

'It's 4.30 now and by tonight it will be a whole day since anybody has seen him. Of course I realise that a problem like this is probably not a matter for your organization, but we are all desperately worried and just wondered ...?'

His question hung in the air as José Diaz pursed his lips, placed his fingertips together and stared out of the window at the afternoon traffic. After a few moments he cleared his throat.

'Well, this wouldn't normally be a matter for us – not if it turned out to be a straightforward accident, for example. That would be dealt with by the Guardia Civil, who would have picked up news of an incident from the Policía Local or the ambulance service. However if, heaven forbid, some foul play seemed to be involved then it would be very different. In that event, we would be called in by the Guardia Civil. It's their job to make some preliminary enquiries – and Professor Valseca has not yet disappeared for a whole day. So, technically speaking, he is not even a missing person – not yet, anyway. However, there is a helpful factor. Unlike some less fortunate places, here in Mallorca the Policía Nacional and the Guardia Civil actually cooperate very closely. This is helped by the fact that I and my opposite number in the Guardia Civil are tennis partners and we encourage similar contacts between our respective colleagues. So, you may get rather more help here than elsewhere.'

By this time Miquel was fidgeting impatiently.

'I know that you are anxious to have your friend and colleague found as quickly as possible, Professor Santiago. Be assured that we will do everything we can. I have great respect for Professor Valseca's reputation. He is an eminent man and his family is part of this island's history.'

He allowed himself a sudden smile.

'And Alessandro tells me that you, Professor Santiago, can actually make mathematics entertaining. Now that really is a rare talent. So, I will make a few discreet phone calls and see if there is some news I can bring you within an hour or two.' He stood up and extended his hand. 'It was good to see you again, Professor Santiago. I'm only sorry that the reason was not a happy one. Please leave contact details with Margareta in the outer office. You may expect to hear something quite soon – even if there is nothing significant to report.'

Miquel murmured his thanks and the two men shook hands again as the Chief Inspector escorted his visitor to the door. He turned back to his desk, frowned as he consulted a small black notebook, then picked up the phone. He would get back to the personnel files later.

Earlier that afternoon Isabel and Gabriel were waving and shouting as they saw Martin's figure standing taller than most of the other passengers as they pushed through the crowded exit from the baggage reclaim and customs area of Terminal 1 at Heathrow airport. Soon they were embracing and all talking at once. It took a while to get to Isabel's Peugeot 206 in the multi-storey car park. The babble all around them, the rattle of the wheels of the baggage trolleys and the squeal of car tyres made it too difficult to carry on a conversation. All three of them were bursting to exchange their news, but they had to wait for the relative quiet inside the car. The chatter was in full swing as they negotiated the exit towards the M4 motorway, finally joining the afternoon traffic heading towards central London.

By the time they finally reached Isabel's apartment Martin had given them a very brief account of his stay in Mallorca: his delight with the *possessió*, his bonding with Vasco, his time at the symposium with Miquel and Vasco's intimate dinner party at Samantha's. It seemed he had even made a good impression with Teresa, who had been unexpectedly warm and friendly. Gabriel and Isabel had had a great time too.

Martin was soon put in the picture about events back in England; how they had managed to persuade Rachel to come over from Washington and that she had met Aunt Margalida at her birthday lunch in Guildford. When he heard about Gabriel's engagement to Rachel, Martin was delighted. He turned round from the front seat to shake hands.

'My God Gabriel, you sound nearly as lucky as me! What a pity I couldn't see her, but I guess she wanted to get back to tell her parents in person. Next time I won't miss out. And there's hardly any time at all before you have to get back to your top-secret project in Washington. You're leaving later today aren't you, Gabriel? What time's your flight?'

'I need to check in at around six o'clock. I've got my ticket and passport right here in my pocket.' He patted the front of his jacket. 'Anyway there's still time for a chat and a cup of tea before I have to go to back to Heathrow again.'

Martin looked puzzled.

'Aren't all transatlantic flights early in the day?'

'That's almost true. Nearly all of them are, but one or two are much later. You see, I thought it would be just great to hang on here in London as long as possible. I wanted to spend more time with Isabel – and I simply had to know every single detail of your encounter with Teresa in Mallorca. So, I'll be flying to New York tonight and staying at an airport hotel for a few hours before getting a connecting flight to Washington very early tomorrow. That way, I'll still be back just in time for the meeting of our team at ten o'clock in the morning.'

Isabel stopped the car right outside the apartment building.

'I got lucky for once,' she said as they climbed out of the Peugeot. 'In an hour or so, that parking slot would definitely have been taken.'

Martin took his bag of gifts and another of duty free purchases from the hatch and Gabriel carried his suitcase while Isabel locked the car and let them into the vestibule. As soon as they reached the spacious kitchen, he furtively got out his mobile phone and plugged it into the charger. Isabel raised an eyebrow, mimed a slap on the wrist, but said nothing. She put the kettle on and soon they were all sitting around the table with steaming mugs of coffee while they went on with their exchange of news. Martin had already met Margo and had been captivated by her vivacity and charm; now he wanted to hear more about her birthday party and her reaction to Gabriel's engagement to Rachel.

'And when are you going to pass on the news to Vasco?' he asked.

Gabriel laughed.

'Margo promised not to blow the whistle before I had a chance to phone and tell him myself. It's probably best to wait until just before I leave for my flight. That way, I can plead pressure of time and cut him short if he tries to make a big deal out of it. He's sure to complain that he hasn't had a chance to meet her himself.'

They all laughed together and Isabel turned to Martin, put her hand on his knee and gazed into his eyes.

'And you, my darling, how did you really get on? What about Teresa?'

'She wasn't a bit intimidating. Not after the first five minutes anyway. She's a lovely lady. I think she liked me and after a while she was really very warm. That reminds me – she told me I must visit the market at Andratx and I went there this morning. That's where I got some small gifts to bring back with me. Actually, I had a very strange encounter in a bar just after I bought them – but I'll tell you about that

198

later. Now just hang on while I get the bag.'

Martin came back from the hallway and started to bring out his souvenirs.

'Sorry I didn't have time to organise gift wrapping,' he said. 'There are a few for you two, but now this is for all of us.' Like a conjuror, he produced the octagonal carton. 'We really should eat this *ensaimada* while it's still fresh.'

Isabel clapped her hands with delight and tore open the box. Soon they all had a dusting of sugar on their fingers as they made short work of the light sweet pastry.

'We just can't get them like this in London, darling,' said Isabel as she planted a sugary kiss on Martin's cheek. 'So what's next?'

'Well,' said Martin, 'I do have these.' He lined up the other Mallorcan delicacies; the *palo* and the *galetes d'Inca*. Then he produced the *jamonero* with a flourish and Isabel immediately put it in pride of place on the worktop next to her shelf of precious cookery books.

'Thank you, sweetie, that's a lovely present. I'll get a proper serrano ham from Fortnum's tomorrow so that we can have a special treat.'

'Now it's Gabriel's turn. Not a very inspired present,' said Martin as he handed over the look-alike Rolex watch. 'I got myself an imitation Breitling too.'

Gabriel grinned broadly.

'Thanks a lot, Martin. I wasn't expecting anything at all – and maybe it's not quite the genuine article, but it's going to wow them back in Washington.'

'And for you, Bel my darling, a little musical reminder of Mallorca. I know you've already got this CD of Tomeu Penya, but you've often said that you'd like another copy so that you can listen to his songs in the car. And there are a few more as well.'

He handed over the case as she planted another kiss on his cheek.

199

'How clever of you – that's just wonderful. We'll listen to my favourite right away.'

She turned, opened the case, took out the disc and slotted it into the CD player audio system on the island unit. After a few moments they were all looking puzzled. Except for a faint background hum, no sound at all came from the speakers.

'There must be something wrong with my machine,' said Isabel, 'but we can listen to my favourite Mallorcan singer anyway.'

She rummaged in the stack of CDs beside the player, found her other copy of Tomeu Penya's songs and soon the folk music filled the kitchen.

'I'm afraid you were sold a bad copy, darling – probably pirated.'

'I can understand someone pirating a big selling disc from the pop charts,' said Martin, 'but I can't imagine anyone taking the trouble to make copies of a folk singer. Just let me look at the other disc for a moment.'

He took it from Isabel and held it to the light.

'Well, it's difficult to tell, but it's quite possible there's something recorded.' He frowned for a moment.

'It could be a data disk of some kind. Shall we run it on your machine, Bel, and see if we've got anything at all here?'

Isabel walked to the door.

'Follow me, gentlemen,' she said as she led them to the computer at the workstation in her bedroom and started to boot it up.

Gabriel looked at his watch.

'I hope this isn't going to take too long. There isn't much time before I need to think about getting to Heathrow – and I really ought to phone Papa about my engagement to Rachel.'

'Don't worry, Biel, there's plenty of time – and my PC is almost ready to go.'

She slotted the disk into the drive and within a few seconds they were looking at a home page headed 'NAVEGATOR' and with an icon in the shape of a caravel to gain entry to the site. At the bottom right hand corner were the words 'Site Design by Vasco Valseca'.

'What in heaven's name is this?' cried Martin. 'It can't even be a practical joke by your father – I promise you this really did come from a stall in the market at Andratx. There's only one possible explanation. Somehow that weird guy I met in the bar near the market must have dumped it on me.'

He told the twins about the stranger in the old cinema at Andratx while they stared in amazement.

'It's unbelievable!' said Gabriel 'But it's happened. Anyway let's have a look at what we've got in Papa's program. Probably some new navigation software he's developed. You know he's always been hooked on that, even though he doesn't sail any more because of what happened when we were born.'

He exchanged a mournful look with Isabel, who clicked on the caravel icon.

There was a stunned silence as the programme opened, with simple instructions about the method of pinpointing the source of any email or the origin of any activities involving hacking, computer viruses or out-and-out computer terrorism. Nobody said anything for a long time.

Finally Martin spoke.

'I just can't believe that this is some kind of hoax. Why don't we see if it works? Then at least we'll know what it is that we've got here.'

Isabel nodded.

'I would download this software into the computer, but I don't think there will be time for that before we have to take Gabriel to the airport. So let's work straight from the disk.'

201

She found a file and took out some papers. In a few moments she had entered the first of a series of email addresses. After ten minutes or so a dozen emails had been checked against the locations of the senders. Nobody spoke and they hardly dared look at each other.

'Now for the big test,' muttered Isabel as she produced a floppy disc from a drawer. 'This has some corrupted material we carefully extracted from one of the machines in the office. It has a really nasty virus with the potential to lock up every file on your computer. Let's hope we can keep it from doing any damage while we see if it can locate the source.'

They need not have worried. After loading the floppy disc the system defended itself successfully while the corrupted material quickly gave up the secret origin of the virus. This was revealed as a location in the Philippines, close to the centre of Manila.

Nobody spoke for several moments. Gabriel realised that he had been holding his breath and exhaled with a gasp.

'Wow!' he exclaimed, 'that was seriously awesome. But, you're not going to believe this ...'

He paused for a moment as the other two looked at him blankly.

'Well, I can't tell you any more, but it's imperative that I take away this disk carrying Papa's software. It's vital to the national security of the United States and I hope you'll both understand. This is absolutely not negotiable.'

Martin stepped back a pace. He looked as though he had been slapped in the face.

'Hang on a minute, Gabriel. This is my disk. I bought it and we're on British soil here. If there's any question of national security, then I can throw defence of the realm into the argument. Just remember, I used to work for British Intelligence. This disk belongs here. UK jurisdiction has priority over any other claim and that's final.'

There was a tense silence. Before the two others could move, Isabel suddenly reached over to the computer, took out the disk and slipped it into the case for the Tomeu Penya CD.

'Actually,' she said, 'at the moment it's mine because Martin gave it to me. And I don't have to remind you that although possession may be nine points of the law, this is actually stolen property. The rightful owner has to be someone called Vasco Valseca and I'm holding it for him and the Valseca family in trust. If there's any question of national security, then that should be a matter for the authorities in Mallorca.'

She folded her arms, clasping the Tomeu Penya case to her body. 'So, how about that, gentlemen?'

Both the men started shouting at once and Gabriel gripped Martin's arm.

'I couldn't tell you before – and I shouldn't be telling you now. But this secret project I've been working on, well, it was aiming to create software just like this ...'

'I don't give a monkey's about that!' roared Martin. 'There's an overriding British interest here. It would only take one phone call to my former colleagues at GCHQ to have a crack security team here inside two minutes. Just you watch me!'

Isabel flounced to the door, still clutching the precious disc.

'Have fun, boys,' she cried. 'I'm going for a stroll while you get hold of your tempers. When I come back I expect you both to have started to behave like adults and we'll talk about this like reasonable people. Ciao, my darlings.'

She blew them a kiss and was gone. Martin and Gabriel looked at each other blankly as they heard the front door slam. Isabel took a turn along the terrace and around the block. She thought long and hard as she hugged herself against the cold. How could she choose between her brother and her lover? She was between a rock and a hard place. Finally she came to a decision, compressed her lovely mouth into a thin line and headed back towards her apartment.

Shivering with the cold, she flung open the door and was horrified to find the two men wrestling in the kitchen. Martin was holding a rolling pin but Gabriel had got him in a headlock.

'Will you two stop this nonsense at once!' she screamed. 'You're no better than a couple of thugs.'

She stamped her foot angrily.

'This is my apartment and I won't have it!'

Reluctantly, they relaxed their grips and straightened up sheepishly as they moved apart. Neither of them could meet Isabel's furious gaze.

'Back off, both of you!' she yelled turning on Martin. 'If we're going to be married, I'm telling you right now – you've got to control your temper a damn sight better than that!'

She turned back to Gabriel and switched to Mallorquin. She was still shouting, but the words didn't match her tone of voice.

'Dear Biel, I've decided to take your side, but we'll have to trick Martin. I expect the Americans to pay Papa for this. You take the disk and use my car to get away and catch your plane. I'll hold up Martin somehow. Just knock him over when he doesn't expect it. Just do it. Yes, do it. Do it now!'

Martin had watched Isabel's apparent tirade with a puzzled expression. He was completely taken by surprise as Isabel smiled at him, so that he didn't see Gabriel's head-long charge which made him trip over a chair, before he fell in a heap in the corner, banging his head on the edge of the worktop as he fell. Isabel crouched down quickly beside Martin.

'He's OK, just knocked out for a moment, I think.' Here,

take the Peugeot, leave your bag and go – just go.'

As Martin started to stir, Gabriel gave his sister a quick embrace, grabbed the car keys and the precious disk and rushed out of the apartment.

'The bastard! Did you see what he did?'

Martin staggered to his feet. He swayed unsteadily and had to hold onto the back of a chair for support as he shook his head and rubbed his brow with his spare hand.

'He won't get far. I'll bloody well nail him before he gets to Heathrow, you can bet on that. And I'll deal with you later, you treacherous bitch!'

He swayed a little as he turned to hurry out of the apartment, holding onto the wall as he groped in his pocket for the keys of his BMW. As the door slammed, Isabel sank to her knees and put her head in her hands. She was weeping and kept saying over and over in Mallorquin,

'Please, please, dear God, forgive me for what I've just done!'

Outside, Martin stumbled as he reached his car, which was parked in Isabel's space in a small courtyard at the back of the apartment block. He could hear the sound of her Peugeot racing off along the roadway on the other side of the building as he struggled to get the key into the BMW's ignition. He swore aloud as he found that a carelessly parked Honda Civic forced him to make a three-point turn in the congested parking area. At last he was clear of the obstruction. He wrenched the steering wheel and accelerated hard into the early evening traffic, giving chase to the flying Peugeot. Gabriel knew that Martin would be close behind and drove Isabel's car at the limit as he carved his way through the congested streets on his way to Heathrow.

For a short distance, Gabriel was lucky. He had a good sense of direction and he had memorised much of the route from previous visits. Driving on the left was also fairly familiar – though he sometimes got confused at intersections. His first test was a misunderstanding with a London bus at Hyde Park Corner. The driver was furious as the Peugeot cut across in front of him, missing the bus by inches. The traffic seemed to be moving at a snail's pace. Gabriel earned some very dirty looks as he squeezed the silver car into tight spaces, changing lanes without warning and making illegal use of the bus lanes.

Behind him, Martin was frustrated. He couldn't make use of the BMW's power and acceleration because of the rush-hour traffic. Occasionally he would catch a tantalising glimpse of the Peugeot's tail lights. He nearly lost ground by diving down a side street in pursuit of an identical model, but realised his mistake just in time. In Cromwell Road he almost had a chance to catch up with Gabriel, but a taxi and a tour coach took up both lanes as they crawled towards some traffic lights which seemed to stay red for ever, while the Peugeot disappeared from sight. Eventually, as lighter traffic allowed Martin to use some of the BMW's speed, disaster struck. He was accelerating hard on the Hammersmith flyover when a red Mini Cooper driven by a fierce-looking blonde swooped onto the main carriageway from the slip road and cut straight in front of the BMW. Martin braked hard, but was unable to avoid contact. The Mini swerved as Martin's car clipped the rear bumper. Almost at once the Volvo behind him gave the nearside rear taillight of the BMW a heavy nudge. There was no serious damage to any of the cars and all the drivers were unhurt, but Martin's BMW spun through ninety degrees and finished up sideways on to the traffic, which trickled past at a snail's pace as a tailback started to build up, clogging the route back towards central London.

In front and behind the other two cars had stopped immediately, boxing in Martin's BMW. He gripped the steering wheel and put his head on his clenched hands as the other two drivers stormed up to him and the recriminations began. The Volvo driver wanted to blame Martin for the whole incident and started shouting when accused of tailgating. Meanwhile, the driver of the Mini Cooper was talking into her mobile phone with her fingers stuffed into her other ear. Martin realised that he had left his own mobile phone to recharge on the island unit in the kitchen at the apartment. But, in any case, what use would it be now? He pounded his hands on the steering wheel with impotent rage as the minutes dragged by.

It seemed to take for ever for tempers to cool, but finally details of insurance companies were being exchanged. While this was still going on the police arrived and took in the scene quickly – similar incidents were common. Their priority was to keep the other traffic moving while taking lengthy statements. They paid particular attention to Martin.

'In a big hurry to get to Heathrow, were we, Mister Weston? Trying to catch a plane, no doubt. Or perhaps we were meeting a lovely lady from overseas, were we sir?'

Martin ground his teeth with impotent rage. It would do no good to explain his chase to recapture the valuable computer program. They would laugh in his face or possibly take him to the police station. Either way further precious time would be lost. He swallowed hard and managed not to react with the fury he was feeling.

The senior traffic cop produced a breathalyser.

'Now, if you would be kind enough to breathe into this tube, Mister Weston. That's it, nice and steady, Sir, if you please. Well, that wasn't too bad, Sir, was it? I don't know what you think, Kevin, but I'd say Mister Weston can't have had more than two very small glasses of champagne. So that's not really enough to explain why he's blocked the A4 and given us all a lot of grief. ...'

He tutted again and closed his notebook.

'I daresay you'll be hearing something from the authorities shortly, sir. Careless driving, I shouldn't wonder – or driving without due care and attention if you're lucky. Don't you forget to have that rear lamp fixed immediately, sir – and do drive carefully on your way to the nearest garage.'

He turned on his heel and went off to help his colleague to get the traffic flowing again.

Martin got back into the BMW and slammed the door furiously. He looked at his watch. He simply could not afford this delay. It was now only thirty-five minutes before the scheduled takeoff time of Gabriel's flight – his chances of catching up with him were almost nil, but he just had to try. There was an agonising delay, while the Mini Cooper was manoeuvred clear. Then he chewed his nails during another long wait until other cars were held up so that he could drive away at last.

Once out of sight of the police, Martin put his foot down. To hell with the consequences – he just had to get to Heathrow in time to stop Gabriel. He ruthlessly carved up other drivers, provoking angry reactions. At last he reached the Heathrow exit from the M4 and soon he was speeding illegally through the tunnel. At last he was at Terminal 3. He abandoned his car in a 'No Parking' zone right outside the building. He noticed that a team from Security was checking Isabel's car where Gabriel had abandoned it. Soon it would be towed away.

'Serve the bitch right!' thought Martin bitterly as he ran into the building, shoving angry passengers aside.

Once inside he stopped in his tracks and looked at the departures board. The display showed 20.11 and indicated that the plane to New York had already departed on time. Now he had no chance at all to stop Gabriel. It was an American Airlines flight and after takeoff it became effectively US territory. Even if Gabriel could have been challenged, the magic words 'national security' would protect him in an American plane. Sinking to his knees,

Martin put his head in his hands, oblivious to the other people bumping into him as they struggled towards the check-in desks with their baggage trolleys.

After what seemed an age, he dragged himself to his feet and made for the nearest bar in the terminal. Three double scotches later he looked outside where the security staff were already hoisting his BMW onto a breakdown truck. It would cost him a fortune to retrieve it later. He shrugged and made his way to the taxi rank outside the exit from the arrivals hall.

Even then, his luck was out. There was a long queue and it took him another ten minutes before he could jump into a black cab, shouting 'Regents Park – and hurry!' as he slammed the door. Throughout the journey Martin slumped in the corner of the back seat. He didn't respond to attempts by the driver to talk about football, politics or anything else. Finally he drifted into a black reverie, full of thoughts of the confrontation awaiting him when he reached the end of his ride. He only came to his senses when the taxi pulled up with a jerk outside Isabel's apartment block, where the phone had been ringing – but with nobody to answer. It stopped a few moments before Martin climbed stiffly out of the taxi. He scowled as he paid the obscene amount demanded by the driver and stormed into the building.

Leaping up the stairs two at a time, he paused as he realised that the door to the apartment was ajar. He pushed it open shouting,

'Where are you, you bloody traitor? Don't you realise what you've done to our relationship? I've just spent the worst few hours …'

The words tailed away as he rushed from room to room, where everything was chaos. The lights were on everywhere. One of the mugs had overturned on the kitchen table and a thin stream of coffee was still dripping onto the floor. CDs had been knocked over from the stack beside the telephone base station on the island unit and littered the floor. A tea towel lay in the doorway beside the discarded telephone handset. In Isabel's bedroom it was even worse. The wardrobe stood open and clothes were strewn everywhere. An empty suitcase was lying open beside the bed; a bag of toiletries had been half emptied onto the dressing table. The computer was still powered up, with an infuriating animated cartoon screensaver dancing backwards and forwards across the screen.

Martin stopped in his tracks, panting with rage. Then his face contorted angrily as he stormed back to the kitchen, kicking at the CDs on the floor as he crossed to the notice board. He ripped at the year planner calendar and tore down invitations pinned to its cork surface. At the bottom right hand corner, next to a press cutting, was a small photograph of the two of them taken at a recent charity event. He froze, stared at it closely, took a deep breath and started to shout.

'So you couldn't face me after what you just did? Bitch, bitch, bitch! I suppose you've taken off to stay with one of your old school chums – or Margo, perhaps. Well, see if I care ...'

His face suddenly crumpled. Then, with an effort, he straightened up, flung open a cupboard and took out a bottle of Famous Grouse. Pulling out the cork with his teeth he took a long pull at the whisky, wiped his mouth with the back of his hand and slumped onto a kitchen stool. Dark thoughts overwhelmed him as he sagged forward and stared blankly at the floor between his legs. Soon he had finished the bottle. Presently shock and exhaustion kicked in and he slumped across the table with his head resting on his arms. Almost at once he was in a deep sleep and snoring loudly.

13

When Martin woke up early the next morning he jerked violently. He had been having a terrible nightmare. Isabel was running away from him towards a burning building and he was paralysed, unable to save her from the flames. Now, as he gradually came to his senses, he felt like death. His head was splitting and his tongue felt too big for his mouth. There was a crick in his neck and he had cramp in his shoulder. He staggered clumsily and groaned. As he got to his feet, he knocked over the empty whisky bottle. It rolled across the table and fell to the floor, collecting two coffee mugs on the way. They hit the ceramic tiled floor with a loud crash. Fragments of glass and china scattered amongst the CDs there already.

'Oh Christ,' he croaked, 'that's all I need.'

Stumbling to the bathroom, Martin rested his throbbing head on the cold marble wall tiles as he peed noisily. He had a king-sized headache from his hangover. The back of his skull was still hurting like hell where it had hit the worktop. He was still seething with anger about Gabriel's surprise attack in the kitchen at the apartment. After splashing his face with cold water he looked at his haggard face in the mirror.

'Now look here,' he said to his reflection, 'get a grip, man! It's time to pull yourself together. Let's think about all of this.'

The very idea of thinking made his pounding headache

even worse. He rummaged in the bathroom cabinet, took out a pack of paracetamol tablets and washed a couple down with a very long drink of water.

Returning to the kitchen, he looked at the mess of broken glass, china and CD cases littering the floor. He noticed one of the Tomeu Penya CDs with the guitarist's photo on the lid and stamped on it furiously.

'You're the cause of all the bloody trouble – and you don't even know it, you bastard,' he shouted.

Then, making an effort to control himself, he decided to have some strong coffee and switched on the electric kettle. While waiting for the water to boil he gazed moodily out of the window. Would he ever look out from here over Regents Park again? It seemed unlikely and his shoulders drooped as he surrendered to a feeling of total despair. At last, the thermostat on the kettle clicked. He poured water into the cafetière and, after a few moments, sat at the table with a comforting mug of fragrant black nectar. He added a lot of sugar and breathed in deeply. It was almost too hot to drink, but he took a quick sip and began to take stock.

It was now almost 9.15. Isabel was gone. There was no point in sitting around here waiting for her to contact him or return to the apartment. He thought about calling her mobile number and decided against it – for a day or two, anyway. He picked up his own mobile phone and charger from the island unit where he had left it, forgotten, when he chased Gabriel to Heathrow. He switched it off and slipped it into his pocket. He didn't want to talk to anyone, anyone at all – not now. Not for a very long time. It was important to have space and time to think. He would go back to his own apartment near Sloane Avenue and try to work this all out.

Martin gave a deep sigh, stood up and went to the bedroom to pack his own gear into the tote bag he'd brought over to Regents Park – how long ago? Within ten

212

minutes he had found a dustpan and brush to clear up the mess in the kitchen before leaving the apartment. Finally, he shut the door of the apartment, locked it and, with a gesture of despair, posted his own set of keys back through the letter box before trudging wearily down the stairs. His own car was impounded somewhere – and damaged too. He would just have to take a taxi. When he walked to the corner, he saw a black cab and flagged it down. As he climbed in, the driver was full of chat and wanted to talk about last night's soccer match. When his passenger didn't respond, the driver switched to politics. Martin groaned and closed his eyes as he sank back into the corner of the seat.

As Martin's taxi headed towards Marble Arch, the phone started to ring in Isabel's apartment. That was the second time there had been a call since she left. Once again there was nobody there to answer. Once again, it didn't stop ringing for a very long time.

A short time later, the phone rang in Martin's apartment; the answering machine had been turned off and the caller eventually gave up. Not long afterwards, the key turned in the lock and Martin shouldered his way in with the tote bag over his shoulder. He looked terrible, unshaven, with untidy hair and crumpled clothes. Kicking a pile of post out of the way as he pushed the door open, he slammed it shut after him and threw the bag down. Then he went into his austere bedroom, where he stood with his hands on his hips looking at his image in the mirror. He didn't like what he saw, and scowled; after a few moments his stern look started to crumple and he hurled himself face down on the bed.

Around the time that Martin's taxi was reaching his apartment west of Sloane Square, Gabriel woke with a start as an automatic wake-up call dragged him back to consciousness. It was still pitch dark and he had no idea where he was. He groped for the light. It was a hotel room, but it could be anywhere. Rubbing his eyes, he felt his way to the built-in desk, switched on the lamp and peered blearily at the headed notepaper. His memory flooded back with a rush. Of course, he was in the Howard Johnson Inn at Kennedy Airport. God, it was all coming back to him now! He had remembered to set his watch – the look-alike Rolex that Martin had given him – to New York time. It told him it was just 4.30 a.m: time to get going. A quick shower and a comb through his hair was the best that he could manage before walking out of his room. His clothes were creased and, without any baggage at all, he couldn't shave. At least he was clean, he thought, as he grabbed a cup of coffee and a roll in the breakfast bar.

A few minutes later he had paid his bill and was boarding the shuttle bus to the terminal for the 6 a.m. red-eye flight to Washington. Although his jacket was warm, he shivered in the cold morning air. If only he'd had time to grab his parka before running out of Isabel's apartment. But there was no time to worry about that now. With luck it would be warmer in the terminal. After checking in he found he had enough time to buy a disposable pack of toiletries from a drug store. He had just finished shaving in a rest room when his flight was called. Gabriel patted his pocket. The precious disk was still there. He couldn't wait to see the look on Hobnails' face when he showed him the incredible prize he'd brought from London.

The flight was crowded with a mixture of businessmen and women, politicians, government servants and tourists. He managed to get a window seat and dozed fitfully on the flight, fatigue mostly winning over excitement. He was seriously worried, though, about the terrible fight he'd had with Martin and the damage to his twin's relationship. But it was all too much to handle just now. His mind kept selfishly turning towards his reunion with Rachel in just a few more hours. He would have no chance to contact his lover until they would meet again at the Sniper Team's HQ at the Watergate complex. Thoughts about Martin and Isabel would just have to wait.

Although the flight had departed on time there was a delay in arriving at Washington's Dulles International Airport. As frequently happened, the runways were congested with so many aircraft taxiing for their take-off slots. Gabriel had walked off the plane, bypassed baggage claim and stood in line for a taxi. It was now coming up to 8 a.m. He should be able to catch Hobnails at his office in the Pentagon Building and give him a demonstration of the Navegator program before the Sniper Team's meeting in the Watergate complex started at 10 a.m. He got lucky. The cabs were plentiful this morning and by the time he had taken a ride to the Pentagon, cleared security and found his way to Charlene's office, he was congratulating himself. It was only 8.40 but Charlene was plainly agitated, though she was evidently pleased to see Gabriel.

'Why, Mr Valseca, we weren't expecting you here. Shouldn't you be over at Watergate getting ready for the meeting?'

She looked uncomfortable as the sound of angry voices came through the door to the inner office.

'I've got some incredibly valuable information for the Admiral, Charlene. It's like a miracle. I really must see him just as soon as possible – and it's just vital I do that before the meeting.'

'Well, I'll see what I can do, but he's in an unscheduled discussion right now with Mr Jorgensen from the CIA. Why don't you sit there a moment, while I find some extra papers for this morning's meeting and look at the morning mail.'

Gabriel looked very nervous at the news. He lowered himself slowly to the edge of a chair while Charlene opened filing drawers and collected up folders. The voices in the Admiral's office grew louder. Suddenly, the door flew open and a tall hatchet-faced man in a dark suit stormed out. When he saw Gabriel he stopped in his tracks and pointed an accusing finger. Gabriel got to his feet uncertainly.

'There you are, you bastard! I've had it up to here with you, agent Valseca. Admiral Hobring's protecting you right now, but God help you when you come crawling back to us at Langley! It will be a real pleasure to whip you back into line.'

He grinned maliciously, showing sharp, uneven teeth and marched out of Charlene's office, slamming the door.

As he stood gazing after his angry CIA boss, the Admiral called out to him.

'Is that you out there, Gabriel? You'd better get in here right away, son. We need to talk.'

Bracing his shoulders and smoothing his crumpled jacket, he walked into the office and stood in front of the desk.

'Sit down, Gabriel. You're making the place look untidy – and just look at yourself. Anyone would think you've been up all night. Incidentally, Ben Jorgensen is seriously pissed off. Seems like you've had a couple of emails from your twin sister in that strange dialect you use. Here are the printouts ...'

Hobnails waved a couple of pieces of paper.

'... and he wants to know what they say. Oh, and he reminded me that you've been expressly forbidden to use that secret language. And he's even more pissed off because you were given compassionate leave to go and see her after her accident. That's the imaginary accident you and I both know was just an excuse to let you see those two CIA guys in London.'

He held up a hand as Gabriel tried to stammer something.

'No, don't say a word. You don't get to see those emails until you tell me what's going on – and why you're in such a tearing hurry to see me in advance of the meeting.'

He cocked an inquisitive eyebrow.

'Well, come on Gabriel, out with it. What's on your mind?'

'It's a complicated story, Admiral, and it's almost impossible to get my mind round. But we haven't much time, so I'll cut to the chase.'

He produced the Tomeu Penya disk and laid it carefully on the desk.

'This looks like a Mallorcan folk singer's CD, sir, but in reality it's a data disk. It carries a program which does everything – absolutely everything – we've been trying to achieve with the Sniper Project. It literally fell into my hands and I still can hardly believe-'

'Hold it right there, son.'

Hobnails was sitting bolt upright now.

'Are you out of your mind? How can something like this just happen? I stopped believing in Santa Claus a very long time ago. This has got to be a bad joke, Gabriel, and I'm not falling for it. We've got no time for make believe. Now take this thing away… '

He flipped the disk back to Gabriel, who caught it clumsily.

'… and go smarten yourself up. Get back to Watergate pronto and make sure the team's ready for the meeting. And let's hope for some fresh ideas this morning after everyone's had a break.'

'But Admiral Hobring sir, won't you please let me give you a quick demonstration? It'll take but a minute.'

There was a long pause while the old man massaged his leg and looked into the middle distance.

'What have I got to lose?' he murmured, as though talking to himself, then, aloud:

'OK, Gabriel. But this had better be good. My computer's already up and running, so come around here to my side table and make it snappy.'

Hobnails drummed his fingers impatiently on the desk while Gabriel stood beside the old man and inserted the disk into the drive. Then, suddenly, the computer's built-in speakers filled the office with the strains of a guitar and Tomeu Penya's baritone voice. Gabriel froze as thoughts raced through his mind – was it just an accident that he'd brought the wrong disk? Had his twin done this on purpose? That was unimaginable. He jerked into action and shut off the sound. Then he stole a glance at the Admiral. His boss jerked as though he had been struck, his face white with fury as he struggled to his feet, clutching his leg as a cramp seized him.

'You pathetic moron!' he shouted. 'I put a lot of faith in you, Valseca, and this is how you repay me. Get out of my sight! You'll be back at Langley within hours. Jorgensen can feed you to the lions for all I care.'

He slumped back in his chair.

'And that reminds me. I already told you that your CIA boss is seriously unhappy with those emails from your sister.'

He waved the printouts in Gabriel's anguished face.

'Just out of interest, you'd better tell me if there's anything in there I should know. It might even begin to explain this crazy fiasco.'

Gabriel took the first email and scanned it. Startled, his face went white and his eyes widened as he read it again. He just couldn't believe it. This couldn't be happening. He looked up. The Admiral was staring at him with eyes like daggers.

'Well, what's it say? It doesn't look good from where I'm sitting.'

'Well, Admiral, there's some terrible family news. It seems my father's on a life-support machine in a hospital in

Mallorca. He's been attacked, he's in very bad shape and the family has been sent for.'

The old man's features softened for a moment and he seemed to be about to speak, but Gabriel stammered,

'This time the accident isn't a trick, sir. It really was a very serious attack – and there's more that you have to hear. I'll try to make it brief, but it's hard to explain.'

Admiral Hobring's jaw clenched as Gabriel hurried on.

'It's all in this second email. I guess it was sent just a few moments before the other one with the news about my father's accident. You see, Admiral, Martin – that's my sister's fiancé – brought back a CD from Mallorca with songs by a local folk singer. But when we played it at her apartment, it turned out to be a data disk instead. It carried a program – and this is even more incredible, sir. It seems that my own father actually created it for his own reasons and called it Navegator. It must have been stolen from him and planted on Martin – by mistake, probably. My father must have been attacked during the robbery. It's almost unbelievable, I know, but my father's program actually does absolutely everything we wanted from the Sniper Project. Everything, sir, I swear it, just as I told you before. We ran a real-time demonstration at my sister's place and it really worked. It really, really worked, I promise. It passed all of the tests we threw at it. Of course, none of us knew anything about the attack on my father just then – I've only heard this very moment, sir.'

Hobnails was glaring at his blotting pad, his face a livid mask.

'Anyway, Martin and I had a big fight because he wanted to hand the program over to the Brits because he used to work at GCHQ. Now it seems my sister Isabel had other ideas, because she must have switched the disks. I ended up escaping with the wrong one and that's why I've just made this terrible mistake.'

He paused for breath and Hobnails cut in.

'Hold it right there, son. Believe me, I do sympathise with you over this terrible attack on your father. And I will try to get you released to go see him in hospital – once we get proper confirmation.'

He took a deep breath.

'Right now, though, we've got to deal with a situation involving national security. I have to be tough and real about this. There are bigger issues at stake than either one of us. Let's get back to your father's software, Navegator, or whatever. It seems you're trying to tell me that your sister betrayed you and now those GCHQ bastards have gotten their hands on this disk? This is unbelievable! Even if I don't have your balls for this, then you can bet your boots that Jorgensen will.'

He slammed an angry hand on the desk. Gabriel dropped his eyes, unable to meet the Hobnails' furious glare.

'It's even worse than that, Admiral. It seems she tricked Martin as well. You see, Admiral, he really believed I had the genuine disc – so he came chasing after me when I made a dash for Heathrow airport. Then, while he was trying to catch me, Isabel started to make several copies of the Navegator program so that she could mail them out to a clutch of computer magazines, software companies and the press. She just doesn't know what's at stake here. My sister doesn't understand the security issues at all. She's simply dead set on finding a way to get back at the crooks who got hold of my father's program. She evidently planned to make their stolen prize worthless. Within a day or so anybody, absolutely anybody, will be able to have a copy of that disk.'

He sighed deeply and his shoulders drooped.

'I just don't know what to say, sir. I'm so very sorry I let you and the team down, Admiral. But thank you for your sympathy for my father's serious condition. I guess I'll keep in touch with Charlene to see when it might be possible for me to be released to fly to Mallorca. And, of course, I'll get some proper confirmation about his condition just as soon as I can. Goodbye, sir, and thank you again.'

Gabriel got to his feet wearily, took the CD out of the computer, and started for the door. As he turned to leave, he glanced back to take a last look at Admiral Hobring. The old man was staring straight ahead, but his shoulders were shaking. Gabriel suddenly realised that he was trying to suppress an explosion of laughter, which suddenly burst out. Between loud guffaws the Admiral was spluttering and holding his aching sides.

'Gabriel Valseca, you get back in here,' he gasped. 'I don't think you're going to believe this, but you've just made my day.'

He paused to get control of himself.

'You see, son, this is how it all plays out. Because of what you're telling me, I can inform the President that we actually don't need the Sniper Project at all. Somebody else has done our job for us. No sweat. It just happens to mean that the USA doesn't have sole and exclusive rights to pinpoint computer terrorists. And there'll be quite a splash when that news breaks, I can tell you. I know how the President's mind works. When I put him in the picture I'll bet my life he won't allow anyone to spend one more dime – not a single one – on this project. That just wouldn't be right, would it? Congress would have him for breakfast …'

He broke off in another gale of laughter, slammed his hand on the desk and wiped his eyes.

'Oh boy, oh boy! I'm really looking forward to seeing the look on his face. This project will have to terminate right now and I'll get to retire immediately. That's just wonderful! Come over here and give me your hand, son.'

He leaned forward and took Gabriel's hand.

'I want you to know that I wish your father a full recovery and right now, I'm going to join you while we drink his health.'

He pressed the button on the intercom.

'Charlene, hon, get in here right away. The hell with the coffee, you can forget about that. Just bring the rum – and three glasses.'

14

After Gabriel and Martin had rushed out of her apartment, Isabel's sobbing gradually subsided. She wiped the tears from her face and ran her fingers though her hair, sweeping it back from her face. Her eyes were red and swollen. She stumbled to her feet and went over to the sink for a glass of water. Groping for a tissue she wiped her running nose. The kitchen clock said almost 7.15. There was a lot to be done and she would have to be quick.

Squaring her shoulders, Isabel took a deep breath and went to the phone. She needed to talk to her father at once. He had a right to be told what was happening – and why. Allowing for the time difference from London, it would now be an hour later in Mallorca. The offices at the University would be closed by this time, so she called the number for the *possessió*. After several rings, the answering machine intercepted the call. She hung up with a frown. Even if Papa wasn't home, then Antonia or Guillem should have heard the phone ring. Consulting her personal organiser, she found Miquel Santiago's number and called his apartment. Once again, there was no answer; she could get no reply from Teresa either. This was all very strange, but she couldn't worry about it now. With or without her father's blessing, she had a job to do. The decision had already been made after she flounced out of the argument between Martin and Gabriel. In a way, their bitter row had helped her make up her mind as she walked around the square. There had been no time to consult him before she had made her judgement and decided to act on it; he would surely have approved.

The logic was simple enough. Somebody had stolen Papa's Navegator program. The way this had been done hardly mattered now, but it was obviously extremely valuable. Worth millions, perhaps. She had seen for herself that governments would want it very badly – and probably other people too. Papa must have lost control of the disk before it reached Martin. So the program on it could already have been copied and offered to a whole lot of buyers. That meant it had no value to the Valseca family any more. The important thing was to prevent the crooks from gaining anything at all from their crime. That was simple. All it took was to publish multiple copies of the program before they had a chance to negotiate a big deal. Then their valuable prize would be worthless. Now she had to move fast. There was no time to lose.

First, she must send an email to Gabriel; he wouldn't be able to pick it up until he got back to Washington, but writing it was a bitter task to be faced. Isabel went into the bedroom, sat at the workstation and booted up her computer. Soon her fingers were flying over the keys, composing a message. She knew it would send her twin crazy. At first he would see it as a betrayal; one day she hoped he would see it differently.

The text was in Mallorquin and the message was stark and simple. She was devastated at having to make a choice between her twin and her fiancé, so she had decided to treat them equally – equally badly. Martin thought she had given Gabriel the chance to escape with the Navegator program; Gabriel thought he was the one with the precious software disk in his pocket. Both were seriously wrong. She had switched the data disk and the CD. Gabriel had taken the Tomeu Penya CD and she still had Papa's software. In a few moments she would start to create several disks carrying copies of the Navegator program. They would be posted to computer magazines, software houses and the media. Her message to Gabriel spelled out the consequences, though that was hardly necessary. The crooks who had taken the disk from Papa would quickly find that the program they had copied from the stolen disk was worthless. She ended with endearments and heartfelt wishes that Gabriel would understand.

Isabel pressed the 'Send' button and, as soon as the email was on its way, went back to the kitchen to retrieve the fake Tomeu Penya disk which carried the precious program. She had just picked it up with the pile of other CDs from the island unit when the phone rang. She answered, listened for a moment and then froze. As she pressed the phone to her ear with her eyes closed, the colour drained from her face and the CDs crashed to the floor. Her voice shook as she answered, asked a few brief questions and then, her voice trembling, said:

'No, Gabriel left here some time ago, about forty minutes or more. He may even have checked in for his flight already.'

After listening a while longer she said loudly:

'I'll be on the next flight.'

She slammed down the phone and ran to her bedroom. Within moments, wardrobe doors were pulled open, drawers tipped onto the bed and toiletries collected from the bathroom. Less than ten minutes after taking the phone call, Isabel had packed a suitcase and was just starting to run out of the room when she stopped dead. She had to find a moment to give Gabriel the terrible news about Papa. She had left her computer running after sending the first message, so it would only take a moment. Dropping her case, she stood at the keyboard as her fingers flew over the keys. As soon as it was done, she sent the message and switched off the machine.

Her feet hardly touched the floor as she rushed headlong out of the apartment to search for a taxi.

A few hours earlier, in the offices of the Polícia Nacional, the heating system seemed to be playing up again. It was uncomfortably warm and the heat made Chief Inspector Diaz feel drowsy. He yawned as he picked up another folder from the stack of personnel files. The annual review was due shortly and this was another boring administrative task to be tackled before he could get back to something more interesting. Suddenly, the intercom buzzed.

'It's Sergeant Ferrer, Chief Inspector. He'd like a word and he says it may be urgent.'

'Thanks, Margareta. Please ask him to come in.'

The sergeant knocked and came into the room. He was plainly agitated but stood to attention in front of his superior's desk. When asked to sit down, he perched on the edge of the chair indicated by his boss.

'What is it, Ferrer? Margareta said it might be urgent.'

'It may be nothing, sir, but the Polícia Local in Bunyola had a report of a burnt-out car at the bottom of a steep cliff in the mountains a few kilometres to the northwest. The car was described as 'unusual' – whatever that means. They passed the word along to the Guardia Civil and in view of your own personal interest, they're keeping us informed. It looks like a very recent incident and could be an accident. On the other hand it might be something deliberate. At the moment they don't know one way or the other. I'm trying to get more information, but it could connect to that enquiry you had earlier.'

'Thanks, Ferrer. As you say, there may be a connection, though I can't imagine what Professor Valseca would have been doing in that area – and at that time of night. Hmm. I think we should take this seriously. Please let me have an update every half hour or so.'

'Yessir.'

The sergeant got up and marched smartly to the door, closing it carefully behind him. Chief Inspector Diaz pulled thoughtfully at his lower lip. He lit a cigarette and stared out of the window. It was far too early to tell Professor Santiago about this report. It might all come to nothing. He got out a map of Mallorca and spread it on his desk. The mountainous area between Bunyola and Orient was wild and difficult to access. It was too early to speculate, of course, but if the unfortunate Professor Valseca had been injured in this incident, then getting him out of that rugged terrain would almost certainly be a job for the helicopter. He reached for the phone and issued instructions for the air ambulance team to be put on standby. Now, there was nothing he could do except wait.

He picked up one of the personnel files, then threw it down again. He couldn't be bothered with this stuff when there was the possibility of a major investigation. Over time you got a nose for these things – and Chief Inspector José Diaz thought he detected a whiff of homicide. He could be wrong, of course, but his taste for administrative work had completely evaporated. There was only one thing to do – get out of the office.

He left the building, strolled down the Passeig de Mallorca in the direction of the bay and crossed over at the traffic lights to the newsstand. He hadn't had an opportunity to look at today's paper, so he bought a copy of *Ultima Hora*. Then he continued across the road to a café near to the Jaime III Hotel for coffee and a sticky cake, surrounded by the chatter of some of Palma's fashionable matrons. Though he couldn't really concentrate on the words he was reading, he tried to take an interest in the gossip pages and the sports columns. Eventually, he couldn't stand it any more. He had to get back to his desk. With any luck there would be more news about the wrecked car in the north-west of the island.

He left money on the table and attempted to stroll casually back to his office. But this was just a charade and it was difficult to prevent himself from hurrying. When he finally reached his office, Ferrer was standing outside the door, waiting to report.

'Come on in, Sergeant. Don't make the place look untidy.'

Diaz waved him to a chair and tried to appear nonchalant.

'Have you some news for me?'

Sergeant Ferrer was obviously excited, but managed to maintain a professional detachment.

'Early this afternoon a shepherd's dog alerted his master to something unusual in a steep gully. It was at the bottom of a sheer drop beside a stony track in the mountains, around three kilometres off the road between Bunyola and Orient. He saw a burnt-out car down below and the wreck was still smoking. When he scrambled down to have a look, he found a man lying unconscious face down about ten metres away. He seemed to be very seriously hurt, with multiple injuries. Apart from checking that he was still alive, the shepherd didn't examine the man, so we don't yet know his identity. He knows nothing about cars, but he said it looked expensive, was quite old and he'd never seen one like it before. He got to the nearest *finca* as fast as he could, and phoned the Policía Local in Bunyola from there. They called the Guardia Civil, who've sent a couple of men to investigate. An ambulance has been despatched, but it sounds as though it's going to be very difficult to retrieve the injured man. We should get another report' – he checked his watch – 'in about ten minutes. Do you think we should alert the helicopter ambulance, sir?'

'I've already done that, Sergeant. But it might be a good idea to warn the Urgencias unit at Son Dureta Hospital that there could be a casualty coming in by helicopter within the next hour or so.'

'I'll do that right away, sir.'

The Sergeant sprang to his feet and walked purposefully out of the office. Diaz walked restlessly round his room like a caged animal, picking up a small trophy from a side table; peering at a wall calendar; fiddling with a cluster of paper clips on a magnetic desk tidy. It was no good – he just had to have another cigarette. He shook one from the packet, lit it and stared moodily out of the window. Just as he was thinking that he couldn't stand the suspense any longer, the Sergeant knocked at his door and came in quickly. The Chief Inspector pointed his cigarette at the chair in front of his desk, then stubbed it out in the ashtray. He laced his fingers together to conceal his excitement. Ferrer took the chair quickly and sat bolt upright as he gave his report.

'The accident definitely seems to involve the individual you were asking about, Chief Inspector. Documents in his pockets confirm that it's Professor Vasco Valseca. He's deeply unconscious and very badly hurt. I said that you'd already alerted the helicopter ambulance, so it should be on its way to bring him in by now. The Urgencias Department at Son Dureta is on standby too.'

Ferrer consulted his notes.

'There are a few other details, sir. The Guardia Civil officer I spoke to thinks that the injured man was probably thrown clear of the car when the driver's door burst open on first impact. The car was very distinctive too – a Jaguar from the eighties – and in addition to physical damage it was totally incinerated. There was nothing of interest in the wreckage except a laptop computer – also incinerated, of course. It's not possible to estimate when the incident took place, but it seems likely that it was shortly after midnight, in the very early hours of this morning. There's no indication of foul play at the moment, but their people have already sealed off the site in case a forensic team needs to go in along with a vehicle recovery crew. Would you like me to arrange that?'

He looked up expectantly.

'Thank you, Sergeant. Your initiative is commendable.'

He stole a glance towards the personnel files.

'Yes, please continue to liase with the Guardia Civil about the logistics. We'll need to go on working closely with them – I don't need to remind you that in the unlikely event that it does turn out to be a homicide attempt, then we'll be taking the lead on this anyway. And now I think it's my unpleasant task to inform Professor Valseca's family and friends.'

As Sergeant Ferrer marched out of his office, Chief Inspector Diaz sighed, lit another cigarette and reached for the phone.

Miquel Santiago was dozing in front of the television in his apartment in Illetas when the insistent ringing of the telephone woke him with a jerk. He was still half asleep, but after he had put the phone to his ear for a moment, jumped to his feet as he began to understand what José Diaz was saying.

'My God, that's terrible! Are you absolutely sure it's him? … At least he is alive, but how badly is he hurt? Where? … I can't believe it. What would he be doing up there? How did it happen? … Yes, yes, of course, Chief Inspector. That's understood. I'll let the family know – and the university, of course. Thank you for what you are doing. We'll be in touch with the hospital very soon. Goodbye and thank you again.'

He frowned as he hung up, then sighed deeply and turned off the TV. He got out his pipe and lit it with shaking hands. He could not imagine how his oldest friend could have suffered such a terrible accident, but the reality had to be faced. He must immediately tell the family, the university – and Guillem and Antonia, of course. He got up to find his diary to check on the phone numbers. While he got ready to make the calls, he poured himself half a tumbler of whisky to steady his nerves. First, he tried to ring Teresa, but her line was busy. Next he spoke to the *possessió*; Antonia was distraught when he told her about Vasco's accident, but eventually calmed sufficiently to understand the situation. She insisted that she needed to find out the senyor's condition for herself. She would have Guillem drive her to Son Dureta; they would both wait for news there. Miquel ended the call and shook his head; the university could wait until morning. His second attempt to call Teresa was successful; she took the news in silence and then, after a long pause, started to ask a lot of searching, measured, questions. Miquel could only answer a few of them. After talking for a long time about Vasco's mysterious accident they decided to meet at Son Dureta. They also agreed not to inform any other family members until they knew more about the extent of his injuries.

At Son Dureta, Guillem and Antonia had been sitting anxiously in the waiting area for nearly ten minutes when Miquel arrived by taxi, followed by Teresa a few moments later. The nursing staff at the reception desk at the Urgencias Department were sympathetic but could tell them nothing. Professor Valseca was undergoing emergency surgery and they would be given information just as soon as the surgeons had stabilised his condition.

Teresa sat on the edge of her chair, her face set in stone. She stared at a fixed point on the wall and spoke to nobody. Guillem had his arm round Antonia's shoulder as she wiped her eyes with an embroidered lace handkerchief. Miquel paced restlessly up and down, wishing he could smoke his pipe. The hours dragged past. Further enquiries produced no information, just another shake of the head. Just as

231

Miquel felt that he couldn't stand it any longer, a young doctor appeared. A label on his coat gave his name as Fernando Vargas. He shook hands politely and asked them to come with him to a small private room. They sat nervously around a rectangular plastic topped table in the bare, featureless cubicle. He cleared his throat and spoke in a low, gentle voice.

'I am sorry to tell you that Professor Valseca's injuries are very serious indeed. Even now, he will be in danger for some days and he has been moved to the intensive care unit. There is no easy way to tell you the rest. He is on a life-support system and his situation is precarious. At the moment he can have no visitors as medical interventions are needed almost constantly to maintain his vital functions. There has been much loss of blood. It was necessary to operate to relieve the pressure on the brain from a severe skull fracture. His right leg has sustained a compound fracture of the tibia. He also has three broken ribs from contact with the steering wheel – the result of not wearing a seat belt. Paradoxically, in an accident of this type, that may just have saved his life. Otherwise he would certainly have perished in the fire which totally destroyed the car. He also has a broken collar bone and a ruptured spleen.'

There was a pause, broken only by the sound of Antonia sobbing quietly. Teresa had her hands tightly clasped, her knuckles white, but she was the first to speak, sitting upright and composed.

'We understand, of course, that it is not possible to give a prognosis at this early stage. But, Doctor Vargas, should we be preparing ourselves for bad news? Should we ask close family to come to Mallorca in case his condition becomes even worse?'

'Senyora Valseca, I cannot make a prediction, but as I have just explained, the Professor's condition is very grave. It could deteriorate at any time, given the nature and extent of his injuries. Naturally we will do everything in our power to save his life, but even in the best case I must warn you that a total recovery is unlikely. In your place, I would be asking next of kin to be close at hand. We may know more in the morning, but I suggest you all go home and get some rest. We have your contact details and you will be called at once if there is any need for that. Now, if you will excuse me, I must get back to the medical team.'

He got up quickly and slipped out of the room before anyone could speak again. Teresa immediately took control of the situation.

'This has been a terrible, terrible shock to all of us and we must be brave. We must all pray for Vasco's life and for his recovery. Now – dear, dear Guillem, please take Antonia back to the *possessió* and help her to be calm. The house and estate still have to be looked after and that is the best way for you both to help Vasco. I promise that we will tell you at once if there is any change in his condition.'

She turned to Miquel.

'You and I will have to deal with the other problems, old friend. It seems best if I take on the job of informing the family, starting with Isabel and Margalida in England. I'm not sure how to get in touch with Gabriel, but Isabel is sure to know. I'll inform the others too. And I'll also make it my responsibility to maintain regular contact with the hospital and tell you all what's happening.'

Miquel stood up, frowning.

'I have just made a decision. Vasco often complained when I smoked that old pipe of mine. So, until he is fit and well again, it will stay locked in my drawer. Apart from that, what else can I do?'

'It's important that you deal with the university, please, Miquel. And the police. And the press – they're sure to smell a story. Can you please keep them and the other media off our backs? From what you were saying earlier, it sounds as though Chief Inspector Diaz may be able to help restrain intrusive journalists, but there will only be so much that he can do.'

She paused.

'Now I'm going to the front desk to arrange a couple of taxis for myself and Professor Santiago. And you, Guillem, do you feel able to drive Antonia home, or would you prefer to leave the car here and take a taxi too?'

Guillem put his arm round Antonia's shoulder and gently helped her to her feet.

'We'll manage all right, thank you, senyora. I don't mind the drive back to the *possessió*. It will give me something to do. I'll look after Antonia when we get back and she will be stronger in the morning.'

They murmured their goodbyes as he helped his wife out into the corridor. Miquel turned back to Teresa.

'As I told you on the phone, Chief Inspector Diaz hasn't ruled out the possibility that Vasco was attacked, though there's no evidence to suggest that. Not yet, anyway. But I just can't imagine who would wish him any harm. The police will have to ask us all a lot of questions, but I'll do my best to keep the investigation away from the family. And I'll try to hold off the media too – though that may not be easy. Now I'll find us some coffee while you call for our taxis.'

He held the door for Teresa and together they walked wearily back to the reception area.

Later, when she got back to her beautifully furnished apartment overlooking the sea near Cala Gamba, Teresa went into the open-plan living room and kitchen. She laid down her neat, expensive handbag and stood like a statue, looking at the flower arrangement in the pale blue vase beside it.

'Vasco gave me that beautiful vase for my birthday,' she said aloud, 'and now he may be dying – or may never speak again.'

Her hands gripped the back of a chair and a few tears ran down her cheeks. Grabbing the handbag, she pulled out a small handkerchief and dabbed her eyes.

'Pull yourself together, woman,' she muttered. 'There's work to be done.'

As she crossed to the desk, she paused to collect a glass and a bottle of Pellegrino from the fridge. She took a long drink, and found a pen, a note pad and her telephone address book in a drawer. With a sigh, she sat down to make a list of essential phone calls to be made. The first must be to Isabel; Martin would have arrived back in London just a few hours ago. She checked the time. It was just before 8.30 in the evening in Mallorca, so it was coming up to 7.30 in London. Isabel and Martin would be exchanging news – at her apartment, probably. She checked her list and called the number.

After a few moments, Isabel answered breathlessly. It was obvious that she was agitated, but Teresa had no time for a subtle approach. Bad news must be dealt with like bitter medicine. In a few short sentences, she told Bel about the Vasco's terrible accident, the extent of his injuries and the doctor's advice that the family should come at once. Teresa heard a loud crash from the other end of the line.

'What's happened? Are you OK?' … Yes, please come immediately – tonight if you can – and get a taxi straight to my apartment at Cala Gamba. I can easily put you up here. … No, don't hang up. I need to talk to Gabriel too. How can I reach him? … Oh, I see, so he'll be boarding his flight at any moment. Then we'll just have to wait until we can find a way to contact him. Perhaps we can send an email from here in the morning … Yes, yes. Let's do that. I'm so very sorry, my darling.'

Just as Isabel was saying that she would be on the next flight, Teresa tried to interrupt. She wanted to add '– and give my love to Martin', but the line went dead before she could speak.

Immediately after Teresa had ended her call, she tried to reach her sister Margalida in Guildford. After several rings, though, an answering machine cut in. Margo was evidently out for the evening – playing bridge, probably. Teresa just couldn't leave a detailed message about Vasco's accident. All she could do was ask for an urgent call back – and that might not be until the morning, or even later. Margo was notorious for ignoring the flashing light on her answering machine – and although she owned a mobile phone, she would only use it for outgoing calls. Teresa sighed; it would have been so much better if Bel and Margo could have travelled together. Now she must get on with the rest of the phone calls. She took another long drink of Pellegrino and pulled the notepad towards her.

Isabel was still distraught and kept having sudden, uncontrollable bouts of weeping as she sat in the departure lounge at Gatwick Airport. She had gone directly there by taxi. The cost was enormous, but she didn't care. The only thing that mattered now was to be on the very next flight. And she had guessed that there would be more flights to Palma from that airport, rather than Heathrow. She was lucky – check in for a flight with one of the low-cost airlines was due to close in five minutes just as she reached the desk. The young woman who handed over her boarding card gave her a sympathetic look. It was hardly surprising; she was still terribly distressed and her eyes were red and swollen. It was all made so much worse by the terrible row she'd had with Martin. She couldn't wait a moment longer to explain.

She had already tried calling Martin's mobile number from the taxi on the way to Gatwick, but there was no answer. Then she remembered that when he had chased off after Gabriel he had left it behind. It was recharging on the island unit at her apartment. Perhaps he had come back and forgotten to switch it on again – and he hadn't tried to call her. Even if he was still furiously angry, surely he would have wanted to speak to her, if only to shout and scream down the phone. She couldn't guess what had happened after he left her apartment. Had he caught up with Biel? Probably not – her brother must have had at least five minutes start. So, the disk was almost certainly on its way to America – and Martin would be in a smouldering rage.

In desperation, she tried to call her own apartment. The phone rang for a very long time, but there was no answer. As she put her mobile phone away, she realised that they were making the final call for her flight to Palma. She sniffed back a tear and wiped her face as she got unsteadily to her feet; she would just have to wait until tomorrow before trying to call Martin again. By that time there might be more news about Papa's injuries.

15

Teresa was out of bed early after a terrible night. In between long periods when she couldn't sleep at all, her dreams had been full of frightening images – demons and witches were trying to catch her in a haunted forest. Wrapping herself in a bronze and gold satin housecoat, she padded barefoot to the kitchen. She made herself a cup of camomile tea and sat by the window of her apartment, looking at the sea, the colour of pewter in the tentative light of dawn. The events of the last few hours had affected her deeply, though she would never let her emotions show. Her composure must not be allowed to crack under the strain. That was not her way – Valseca women were always strong. But her heart bled for Isabel. She could be forgiven for breaking down.

That poor child; she had arrived very late last night in a taxi, weeping, totally exhausted and at her wits' end. Not only was her father on a life-support system, but her relationships with Martin and her twin brother were in ruins. Between sobs, she had explained what had happened. She told her aunt how she had tricked both of the other two men she loved for her father's sake. Now he was desperately clinging to life – and her own might as just as well be over. She didn't even know whether Biel or Martin would ever speak to her again. Teresa had comforted her as best she could, then put her to bed with a couple of herbal sleeping pills and hot milk with brandy to wash them down. She had left the door ajar and listened awhile. Eventually, after a long vigil, she had heard sounds of deep rhythmic breathing and had tiptoed to her own room.

Now, as the morning light gradually increased, Teresa finished her camomile tea and went to shower and dress for the day ahead. She emerged, refreshed and elegant, wearing her business clothes – a pencil-slim skirt and tailored jacket in the finest navy pinstripe worsted, with a cream coloured silk blouse. Her slim feet were flattered by navy and cream Gucci pumps. There was no way, though, she could find time for the secretarial college today. She would call in later and explain the situation. Her deputy was perfectly capable of running things in her absence.

She moved stealthily towards Isabel's room and listened at the door; she was still breathing deeply. Teresa checked her watch. It was just after eight; so, not too early to ring the hospital – thank God there had been no emergency call from them during the night! But it was important not to wake her sleeping guest. She took her mobile phone into the bathroom, and, out of earshot, rang Son Dureta.

After waiting for an eternity she finally got through to the senior nurse on duty in the intensive care unit. The information was sympathetic, but impersonal: unfortunately there had been no improvement in Professor Valseca's condition overnight, but there had been no deterioration either. It might be a day or two before there was any change, meanwhile the medical team was with him constantly; it was out of the question for him to receive visitors. … Teresa didn't really hear the rest; she forced herself to keep her composure, spoke some meaningless words of thanks and ended the call.

She thought she should tell Miquel that there was really nothing to report, but they ought to be grateful – no news was good news. He answered at the second ring. It was obvious that he had had a bad night too and responded with a grunt to the 'no change' bulletin on Vasco's condition. He was more animated when Teresa told him that Isabel was now staying with her at Cala Gamba – and the bizarre chain of events that had played out in London, including the way she had tricked Gabriel and Martin.

'That poor girl,' he said. 'She may be amazingly clever, but she's still only a child. Tell her, please, that Uncle Miquel sends his love. But there's a lot more you should know, Teresa. I had the police on the phone half an hour ago. The media have got hold of the story. People around Bunyola spotted the helicopter ambulance and the story about the burnt out car in the mountains is common knowledge too. Chief Inspector Diaz is saying as little as possible, but the press are camped outside his office. Vasco's disappearance has also been picked up and they're asking if there's a connection. It's only a matter of an hour or two before they track you down at Cala Gamba – and I'll warn Guillem and Antonia too; they'll need to lock the main gates at the *possessió*. The main thing is not to answer any questions at all. These people are just trying to get a story, so be very careful. I'll do what I can to keep them at bay and warn the university too.'

Miquel hurried on.

'There's one more thing and it's very strange. It seems that Vasco was seen with another man at the Viña del Mar Hotel late last night after the party. He had claimed to be the top man of the BCIB and seemed genuine enough. He was elegant, immaculately dressed. On top of that, his name matched that of their CEO – and he had all the trappings of a top executive, including impressive documentation. Even his faxed hotel reservation – for the best suite in the place – appeared to have come from the bank's head office in Barcelona. But now it seems that the man has been an impostor; BCIB's Chief Executive has been in Frankfurt for talks at the headquarters of Deutsche Bank for the last three days – and he's still there. So, Diaz is convinced that this impostor is involved in Vasco's accident and it's looking like a homicide attempt.'

Miquel paused and cleared his throat.

'I don't quite know how to tell you this, but the police now think that there is a possible connection between the attempt on Vasco's life and a computer program that he'd been working on. I do know something about that because both of us were involved in trying to get the bank interested – but you don't want to hear all this. I'll call you later if there is any more news. I've got the number of your mobile. And if you get anything more from the hospital do, please, call me at once.'

'Yes, of course I will, Miquel. But I am worried about the media. What can we do to get them to leave us alone?'

'I'm afraid you'll just have to act dumb and try to go in and out as if they aren't there. It's difficult, I know, but you can do it. The only good news is that the police aren't saying anything about the mystery man at the Viña del Mar. At the moment they're almost sure it was a premeditated attack, but they have to wait for some feedback from the forensic team.'

'My God! The whole situation's so terrible. Unbelievable. How could anybody do this to poor Vasco?' Teresa's voice shook almost imperceptibly and Miquel sensed her deep distress.

'Keep your faith, my dear. I'm sure he'll pull through. All you Valsecas are made of pretty tough material. Now I really must cut and run. Somehow I've got to sort things out here at the university and help them to cope with the fallout from all this. It's not going to be easy trying to cover for Vasco.'

'Yes, of course you must, Miquel. And thank you for all that you are doing for us.'

She rang off, then stood for a moment before moving

quietly back to the living room. She went over to the window and stood there like a statue, her hands clasped together, looking out over the sea. Her home, this place that she loved, seemed very bleak today.

It was a very long time before the sound of a barking dog brought her out of her miserable reverie. The clock on the wall showed that it was just before 9.30. She decided that she should give Isabel a little pampering and was just starting to prepare a breakfast tray when her niece appeared in the doorway, stretching and rubbing the sleep from her eyes. She looked frail, miserable and dishevelled in a crumpled floral nightshirt. Teresa felt a rush of maternal feeling, gathering the young woman into her arms in a comforting embrace.

'Darling Bel, you poor girl, you must try to be brave now for your dear papa's sake. I already checked with Son Dureta this morning and there's no change in his condition. So, that's good news isn't it?'

There was no response. She led Isabel to a chair and sat her down gently while she boiled some water for the waiting cafetière.

Teresa tried to make conversation, trying to interest Isabel with her impressions about her first meeting with Martin at the party just two days ago. But Isabel didn't respond, except to look down dejectedly at her hands, their fingers laced together, clenched on her lap. When she had poured two cups of strong black coffee, Teresa handed one to Isabel, who took it without a word, then sat facing her.

'Listen, Bel darling. I've a lot to do and I need you to help me. But first you really must find the strength to face the day. Why don't you go and have a lovely relaxing shower and get yourself dressed while I go out for a short time. I need to go to the shops round the corner for a few things. Then we'll have food here to last us for a while – and you won't have to see anybody or go anywhere if you don't want to. I'm off now and I'll be back soon to make us breakfast. We'll talk more then.'

Teresa stood, drained her coffee, smoothed her skirt, picked up a shopping bag and her handbag. With a last look back at her niece, she quietly opened the door of the apartment and closed it carefully behind her.

When she returned half an hour later, she was relieved to find that the media had not yet found their way to the apartment. As she went in carrying a couple of bulging bags, she could hear the shower running. She gave the ghost of a smile, then started to make fresh coffee as she laid the table and put the groceries away.

She picked up the morning paper and was still reading the front page when Isabel came in. She had pulled her hair back from her face and had dressed in a smart trouser suit. She smiled bravely as she embraced her aunt.

'I'm so sorry I've been such a pain,' she said, 'You've been so kind and I really will try to behave like a grownup now.'

Teresa smiled back, squeezing her niece's hand as she waved her towards the other chair and went across to fetch croissants and coffee, butter and jam from the marble worktop beside the cooker. While they ate, Teresa passed on Miquel's news. As her niece's face crumpled, she stroked her dark hair.

'Please try to be strong for your papa, Bel, darling. We'll get through this together.'

Isabel managed a weak smile. A little later she wiped the crumbs from her mouth, pushed her plate away and drank the last of her coffee.

'Thank you so much, that was just what I needed. I know there's a lot to be done and I'll help all I can, but first please can I try once again to contact Martin? I can't think of anything else properly until things are straightened out between us.'

She looked miserable, blinked hard and gulped once or twice. She looked at her watch.

'Almost half past ten. It'll be around 9.30 in London now, so I'll try to get him at my apartment.'

'Of course, darling. Just use this phone for as long as you like.'

Teresa carried the plates over to the sink and returned with the handset. Isabel tried the number for her own apartment but, just like last night when she had tried to call from the taxi on the way to Gatwick, it seemed to ring for an eternity. There was still no answer. The same thing happened when she tried to phone Martin's apartment. In desperation she tried his mobile phone again, but it was still switched off. She thought about ringing the office, but decided against it; in any case, Martin didn't really work there any more – and neither did she. Defeated at last, she put her head in her hands and sobbed soundlessly. Teresa laid a comforting hand on her shoulder.

'I'm sure you'll hear from Martin eventually, darling. But if you really want to get your story across to him, why don't you send him an email. That way, you'll have got a lot of the difficult part out in the open. I always think that the phone is not very good when you've got personal problems to sort out. And, believe me, I really do know what I'm talking about.'

She paused and looked out at the sea for a moment as her eyes clouded with an unhappy memory. Then she turned back to Isabel.

'So, what do you think, my dear?'

'I suppose you're right,' sniffed Isabel between sobs. 'If I can borrow your computer I'll do it right away.'

Teresa smiled.

'Of course, Bel dear. Just help yourself. At least you were able to send an email to Gabriel from your apartment before you dashed out to the airport. He must be horrified by the news about the attack on Vasco – surely his bosses will give him compassionate leave to be with his father. But he'll be in very deep trouble when they find out he's brought them a CD of songs by a Mallorcan guitarist, instead of that special program they really wanted. You're going to need the phone line for the computer, so I'll give you some peace and quiet; I can use my mobile phone from the bedroom. I've still got a lot of calls to make myself – and when they're done it will be time to phone Son Dureta again.'

She cleared a space next to the monitor on her desk, booted up the computer and typed in her password. Then Teresa found the list she'd made earlier, gave a second notepad to Isabel and planted a gentle kiss on the top of her head. She gently closed the kitchen door after her and went to her bedroom. Sitting in the pretty Victorian chair beside the dressing table, she picked up her mobile phone and consulted her list. Top priority was making contact with Margo in Guildford, then several other family members.

This time her attempt to reach Margo was successful. True to form, she hadn't checked her answering machine and was just going out to shop, then on to visit her hairdresser. Before Teresa could start to tell her sister about Vasco's desperate condition, Margo had launched into a torrent of chatter about her birthday party and the lovely black girl, Rachel, who seemed to be Gabriel's true love. She had made a wonderful impression and had captivated everybody. Eventually, she had to stop to draw breath and Teresa cut in quickly.

'You must let me speak, Margo. I have terrible news about Vasco.'

There was a gasp from the other end of the line and her sister listened patiently while she heard the news about Vasco's accident. When Teresa finished, Margo spoke in a quiet voice.

245

'I'm so sorry, Teresa – and not just for poor Vasco. It's terrible that you are carrying this burden on your own. I'm a silly, selfish woman and I feel so guilty that I wasn't here to answer the phone earlier when you needed me. I'm going to pack at once and catch the next plane to Palma. Poor, poor Vasco – he needs all of us around him to bring him through this. And please give my fond love to that darling girl Isabel – and keep strong, Teresa, my dear. I'll be with you before you know it.'

The line went dead. Just as she was getting ready to make another call the phone rang. She answered at once, afraid that it might be bad news from Son Dureta. Instead, she heard the familiar voice of Miquel Santiago.

'I couldn't reach you on the land line, so I tried your mobile number. As you didn't call me, I'm assuming that there's no more news on Vasco since we spoke earlier.'

Teresa was about to speak, but he cut in.

'No, don't apologise, I wasn't expecting to hear again quickly – and I know you've got a lot on your mind. But you need to know that the police have just been on the phone again, asking a lot of questions about Vasco's contacts. They've grilled me pretty thoroughly and now they know that Isabel's here in Mallorca. They think that she may be able to give them some leads, so they've asked for her to come round to see Chief Inspector Diaz at the Policía Nacional HQ – otherwise he'll come and see her at your place. He's quite a good guy, but he's persistent and they want an answer straight away. So, how is the poor girl bearing up? Tell her that Uncle Miquel's thinking of her. It's terrible for her, I know, to have the police asking questions at a time like this. But they have a job to do and all of us want them to nail the bastard who attacked Vasco. They are wondering if it might be the Basque separatists – after all they could have been responsible for raiding the PIIB bank account. But it's clear they are still in the dark. Still, they're treating it as attempted murder. And there's no getting out of an interview – so what should I tell Diaz?'

'Well, Isabel seems to have got through the night OK, but right now she's busy. Give me half an hour or so and I'll call you back.'

'That should be fine, Teresa. I'll tell him I can't reach her just yet, but perhaps I can tell him he will definitely be able to see her this morning. That should satisfy him for now. Anyway, he's not in his office at the moment. He phoned me from the Viña del Mar. Apparently there's a forensic team going over the room where the mystery man was staying. While he's waiting for results from them, he's interviewing any of the hotel staff who may have seen him. And there's one intriguing thing they've discovered. The hotel reservation was made by a telephone call and confirmed by fax. As I told you, the fax was on a genuine BCIB letterhead but, interestingly, it was sent from the same location as the original phone call – a small, two-star hotel in the centre of Barcelona. Nobody can remember who sent it. The whole thing sounds as though it was premeditated. Puzzling, isn't it?'

'Thanks a lot for keeping me in the picture, Miquel. And you're right about Vasco. There's been no more news from the hospital – I'm going to phone them again just as soon as I've made two or three more calls. I'll let you know immediately if there's any change. Isabel's still very distressed and right now she's sending an email to Martin to tell him about Vasco – and to try to explain why she deceived him. She's already had to send a similar message to Gabriel, so it's not surprising that she's almost out of her mind'

'Hang on just a minute,' said Miquel, 'there's a bit more news and it will help you both to cope. The press tailed Diaz and his team to the Viña del Mar Hotel and they've got hold of the story about Vasco's mystery attacker. I expect they'll be following that lead now – it will make much better headlines – so with any luck they won't be bothering you and Isabel any more.'

'That's quite a relief. Thanks again, Miquel. And I'd be grateful if you could give that message to Guillem and Antonia too.'

Teresa ended the call, consulted her list and, after a while, finally managed to contact all of the family who needed to know about Vasco. Her last call was to Son Dureta, where the nurse on duty told her that there was still no change – and there was little point in calling again until the evening. Visitors were still out of the question – and the police were waiting to interview Professor Valseca just as soon as he was able to talk. Teresa thanked the nurse, sighed deeply and rang off. She went back into the kitchen where she found Isabel sitting staring at the computer screen.

'There's no point in sitting there waiting for an answer to your message, Bel, darling. And anyway, I have to tell you that the police want to ask you a few questions. They think it's possible you may be able to tell them something that would help to find the man who tried to kill Vasco. They could come here, but now you're up and about you might prefer to go to them – that way you could get a bit of fresh air. It's a lovely bright morning. I can keep you company – and we could look at the shops too. Come on, my dear, it would do us both good to get out of here. Just waiting for that phone to ring isn't doing either of us any good.'

Isabel sighed.

'I suppose you're right.' She managed a bleak smile. 'I'll just get my handbag and a jacket.'

While she waited for her niece to return, Teresa phoned the Chief Inspector's office and arranged to bring Isabel to meet him at 12.30. Leaving the apartment, Teresa was pleased to see a young woman driving away in a small SEAT displaying the *Ultima Hora* logo, probably headed for the Viña del Mar. Soon, the two women were in Teresa's Alfa Romeo, heading for the centre of the city. Isabel had brightened just a little at the prospect of a stroll along the Avinguda de Jaume III. Window shopping was fine, but she just might consider buying some shoes.

Later, around lunch time, Martin was leaving his apartment near Sloane Avenue. He was in a foul mood, a tote bag slung over one shoulder and a computer case in his free hand. After recovering from his anguished attack of self-pity, he had dragged himself up from the bed, showered, changed and had some more coffee. Then he spent the rest of the morning with everything shut down; no phone calls, no emails, no human contact of any kind. He needed a complete break with time to think, to put his life together again. Now he had a plan to achieve just that. His mouth was set sternly as he made his way through the crisp early morning sunshine towards the shops clustered near to the tube station at South Kensington. A travel agent's window caught Martin's eye. There were posters offering last minute reductions on short cruises; within a few moments he had used a credit card to buy a ticket for a 'taster' voyage on the cruise ship 'Excalibur'. He needed to be at Tilbury in less than two hours, but that should be no problem.

Martin looked a little more relaxed as he pushed his way out of the travel agency and walked the few yards to South Kensington tube station to take the short ride to Victoria. Tonight he would leave England behind. He would be on a ship and nobody could find him; no phones, no emails. When he returned, he might have decided what to do with his life.

On her way to the city centre with Teresa, Isabel decided to have her interview with Inspector Diaz before doing anything else. In any case, the traffic had been heavy and, after her aunt had parked the car, she wouldn't have more than a few minutes to spare before her appointment at the headquarters of the Polícia Nacional at 12.30. Then, after her interview with Chief Inspector Diaz, her time would be her own – and she would be free to go out to Son Dureta just as soon as her father was allowed visitors. Teresa agreed to wait for her niece in the Jaime III Hotel; when she returned from her interview, they would decide what to do next.

Isabel's interrogation by the policeman did not last long. He quickly established that she knew even less than Miquel Santiago about Vasco's business contacts – or the possibility of someone bearing him a grudge. But he was seriously interested in her account of the mysterious appearance of the Navegator program disk, the fight between Gabriel and Martin, her own switching of the disks and her plan to publish her father's software to the world. He asked a few questions and took rapid notes. Finally, though, he looked her straight in the eye.

'So, Isabel, how many copies of the program did you make and where did you send them?'

Isobel gasped and put her hand to her mouth.

'Actually, I didn't make any. I had no time to do any of that at all,' she said in a faint voice. 'Just as I was getting ready to make the copies, Aunt Teresa phoned to tell me about Papa's accident. So, I quite literally dropped everything and dashed out to the airport.' She froze and put a hand to her mouth.

'Oh, sweet mother of God – I've already sent emails to Gabriel and Martin to explain what happened. Mostly I was desperate to tell them about the attack on Papa. So, I completely forgot to tell them that I didn't actually have the time to carry out my threat to publish the Navegator software. Oh, my God! That could be very important couldn't it?'

'Yes it could. Very important indeed. And the disk is still at your apartment in London? And Martin could have returned and found it?'

'Yes, I suppose so. But I haven't been able to reach him anywhere. I haven't really thought about anything else except my father ...'

Her voice tailed away.

'Yes, of course, that's understandable. But I think we need to find out if that disk is still there. It could be vital evidence and there are bad people somewhere who would commit a serious crime to get their hands on it. I must look into this urgently while you and your aunt wait for news of Professor Valseca. And please, if you think of anything – or if you hear anything more from London, please let me know immediately.'

Chief Inspector Diaz stood up, gave a sympathetic smile and extended his hand.

'Thank you for coming to see me.'

He ushered Isabel to the door, closed it after her and darted back to his desk, grabbing the phone. Within a few minutes he was speaking to his brother Alfredo, who lived in Madrid and had a job with the Spanish Foreign Ministry. The fact that he often travelled abroad and would never tell him anything at all about his job clearly showed that he was involved in high-level security work, probably with CESID, the Spanish intelligence service. After a few moments Alfredo had grasped every detail of the situation.

'So, José, you are telling me that there is a very valuable piece of software, a disk – intellectual property, shall we say – which has been stolen violently from a Spanish citizen, here in Spain. It is disguised as a CD of songs by a guitarist, Tomeu Penya. This software could have major security implications at a national or international level and it is believed to be in the kitchen of an apartment in London. You have given me the address and you're asking me to see if it can be retrieved. Is that it?'

'Yes, precisely. I just thought you might know some-one …?'

Alfredo was a man of few words.

'This is highly irregular, as you must realise. Still, you are my brother and blood is thicker than water.'

He paused for a moment.

'Give me two hours or so and I'll call you back.'

They hung up together and José scratched his chin thoughtfully. He would have to find something to stop his mind from going round in circles while he waited for Alfredo's reply. He frowned. There was nothing for it, he would have to have another go at those bloody personnel files. He sighed deeply, lit a cigarette and reached across his desk for the bulky folder.

Over coffee in the Hotel Jaime III, Isabel told Teresa about her interview with Chief Inspector Diaz. After paying the bill they strolled out arm in arm and around the corner. Within a few minutes they were looking at some lovely Ferragamo sandals in a shop opposite El Corte Inglés department store. Just as Isabel was trying on a pair with improbably high heels, Teresa's mobile phone trilled insistently from her handbag. She tore it out of the side pocket and frowned, speaking rapidly and gesturing with her free hand. Ending the call, she turned to Isabel with a smile.

'That was the hospital. Earlier, they told me not to call again till this evening, but the news about Vasco is better. He's still in intensive care, but now he's more or less stable. The medical team don't expect to make any more emergency interventions. So, although he's still deeply unconscious, we can at least go and hold his hand. Let's get the car and go straight to Son Dureta – I'll phone Miquel and everybody else just as soon as we've seen Vasco for ourselves. Shoes and lunch will have to wait.'

Thrusting the lovely shoes back into the hands of the disappointed shop assistant, the two women almost ran out of the door and headed for the car park.

In fact, it was nearer to three hours before Chief Inspector Diaz got a call back from his brother in Madrid. His impatience had grown every minute while he waited, with only two personnel appraisals completed before he could stand no more. He had been for a walk round the block. He had shouted down the phone at the leader of the forensics team, demanding results – and sulked when he was told that there was still very little to go on. He had drunk six cups of coffee, eaten a dried up sandwich and a sticky bun from the canteen and smoked nine cigarettes. His mouth tasted disgusting and his head throbbed. Pacing the room like a caged tiger, he was on the point of going to the main office to find someone to criticise, when the phone finally rang. He dashed to the desk and snatched up the handset for the direct outside line.

'Thank God it's you, Alfredo, I've been going out of my mind waiting for news from you!'

'As you know only too well, José, these things take time. Also, I am in a meeting so I must be brief and speak with discretion. There is news, but it won't be very helpful I'm afraid. A team of ...,' he paused and cleared his throat, '... electrical contractors visited a certain apartment and conducted a very careful and thorough survey. Unfortunately, however, they were unable to find any evidence of the serious problem which you reported. Sorry we couldn't be more helpful. Now, I really must ring off. Ciao.'

Alfredo ended the call immediately, but just before the line went dead, José heard someone – the head of counter-terrorism, probably, shouting, 'Come on, Alfredo, what about those Algerian bastards ...?'

Chief Inspector Diaz said something extremely obscene

and banged the receiver back into its cradle. So, assuming that Isabel was telling the truth, where exactly was that bloody disk now? The only people who might be able to shed further light on this were Martin Weston and Gabriel Valseca – and how the hell could he reach them? He would have to get in touch with those Valseca women again. He tried the mobile phone numbers for Teresa and Isabel, but could get no answer. Perhaps they were at Professor Valseca's bedside at Son Dureta? Naturally, in the hospital, their phones would have to be turned off.

He rang the hospital, gave his name and rank and asked for the Urgencias Unit. Within a few moments he was speaking to a senior nurse, who confirmed that Professor Valseca was in intensive care and still deeply unconscious. However, close relatives were now being allowed to visit and, yes, Teresa and Isabel Valseca were with him now. Diaz asked the nurse to tell them that he had important news. Would they please stay at the hospital until he could speak to them personally. He expected to be there in fifteen minutes or so. He put his head round the door of the main office, shouted to Sergeant Ferrer that he was going to Son Dureta and dashed down to the transport pool. Grabbing a set of keys from the officer on duty, he jumped into the nearest car and was soon on his way to the hospital.

As Chief Inspector Diaz was driving towards the hospital, the members of the Sniper Team were about to start their ten o'clock meeting at Watergate. Only half an hour earlier Gabriel had said an affectionate goodbye to Admiral Hobring as the old veteran set off for the Oval Office to explain the situation and to ask for his long-delayed retirement to begin immediately. He was confident that an exasperated President would be glad to see the back of him. As his personal assistant, it was Gabriel's job to advise the team of the new situation and tell them all to sit tight pending further instructions. As soon as that task was complete, he was banking on getting compassionate leave to visit his stricken father.

Gabriel reached Watergate with only ten minutes to spare and handed over his cell phone at the security point. He managed to find Rachel and they spent a few precious moments embracing passionately in a quiet corner. Their romance was common knowledge amongst their colleagues, who strolled past grinning like idiots. With an effort, Gabriel broke free.

'Rachel, my darling, I'm so sorry I didn't call you. I left London in such a hurry, there was no time to bring a bag – or to call you, even.'

She stared at him in disbelief as he raced on.

'There's a mountain of stuff to tell you – but it's all to do with Sniper. Sorry, sweetheart, but you'll have to get most of the story at the same time as the rest of the team. I've had some really terrible family news too, but I don't even know the whole story myself. I'll tell you all I know later. Right now we really do have to go.'

Looking hurt and confused, Rachel turned away, picked up her papers and walked towards the conference room with quick, angry steps. Gabriel followed, his shoulders slumped with dismay as he joined the rest of the group around the table. When the clock on the wall showed ten o'clock, Gabriel stood up next to the vacant chair where Admiral Hobring should have been sitting. The loud babble of conversation continued for a while: 'Say, where did you get to on your days off, Benny?' ... 'I managed to get some skiing at Whistler, how about you?' The chatter went on and on, but finally died away as Gabriel pounded on the table with a heavy paperweight.

'There's an important announcement I have to make, so please let me have your attention. Admiral Hobring has decided that this is the moment for him to seek leave to retire with immediate effect. He is making those arrangements with the President right now.'

There was a stunned silence, followed by subdued murmurs of disbelief which quietened down as Gabriel held up his hand.

'He has asked me to thank you all for your efforts in attempting to carry through this difficult project, but the situation has changed dramatically. The facts, which must remain absolutely confidential within this team, are simple but almost unbelievable. It seems that software has already been developed elsewhere which does precisely – precisely – what our Sniper Project was intended to achieve. This program will be published to the world within a few hours. This means that anybody, anybody at all, will be able to pinpoint the origin of hostile internet activity. There is therefore not a chance for the United States to have exclusive ownership of this strategic capability. It follows that the need for the Sniper Project has totally disappeared. Pending a decision as to the future direction of this team, I am instructed to ask you all to remain here in our dedicated facility until we have new instructions. Has anyone got any questions?'

There was immediate uproar, with people calling out.

'So what happened exactly?'

'When can we expect to get back to our homes again?'

'This is bullshit!'

Eventually it was possible for Gabriel to make himself heard above the clamour.

'I'm as much in the dark as anybody here, but I guess they'll be telling us something in two or three hours or so. Till then I suggest we disperse to chat, play a game of cards, read or whatever. Rachel and I will send out a call to everybody just as soon as there's anything to report.'

There was a buzz of conversation as everyone got up, collected their papers and headed for the door. Gabriel caught Rachel's hand and pulled her towards him.

'Please don't be mad at me, darling,' he whispered, 'I've got so much to tell you that I can't share with the others. You're going to find it hard to believe what's happened since we were together in London. Let's go to the commissary for a coffee and I'll explain what's been going on – and I haven't forgotten that you've been meeting up with your folks, so I want you to tell me all about that too.'

Rachel's solemn expression relaxed and she gave Gabriel a shy smile.

'It's OK honey, I guess I had no idea what was coming when you made that bombshell of an announcement. Let's go and have that coffee.'

Chief Inspector Diaz soon found Teresa and Isabel holding each other's hands at Vasco's bedside. He was in a special high-dependency unit, connected to an array of monitors, cables and tubes. He was not a pretty sight and the policeman could see that both women had been weeping. Vasco's bandaged head was propped up on pillows, his bruised face almost hidden behind an oxygen mask. He had his left arm in a sling and his right leg in traction.

As gently as he could, the police chief asked Isabel for a few minutes of her time in a private room. Reluctantly, with a backward look at her father, she followed him down the corridor, round a corner to a small empty office near the reception area and sat on the plastic chair he pulled out for her. Isabel spoke before he could open his notebook.

'Chief Inspector, I want you to find the animal who did this terrible thing to my father. I'll help you as much as I can, but I've already told you everything I know.'

'Yes, of course – but now I need to speak to your brother and to Martin Weston too.'

He coughed discreetly.

'It seems that the disk you abandoned at your apartment

can't be found now.'

Isabel frowned, wondering how he could know a thing like that, but before she could ask an embarrassing question, he hurried on.

'One of them may be able to help us find that vital piece of evidence – and you're the only one who can help me to reach them. So, Isabel, how can I contact Gabriel and Martin?'

'My brother's very difficult to reach. I have no idea whether he'll have any information about Papa. He and the group he's been working with are all held incommunicado in Washington. But after what's just happened, I suppose that team may be disbanded at any time. In that case I suppose he would get his mobile phone back again. But you could also try to reach him by email. That way a message would definitely get through, but it would be intercepted by the CIA first. Anyway, I can let you have those contact details.'

Diaz handed over his notebook and Isabel wrote down the information.

'I suppose,' she choked back a sob, 'you'll be needing contact details for Martin too. You see, he just might be the one who has the Navegator disk now. That's assuming he did go back to my place after he tried to hunt down Gabriel when my brother made his dash for Heathrow.'

She sniffed and wiped her nose.

'I've tried to reach Martin myself, but I can't find him anywhere. The only thing I can do is give you his address, phone number, mobile phone number and email address and hope that you have more success than I did.'

She went on writing, trying to control her emotion.

'As I told you already, Chief Inspector, I couldn't contact him any other way, so I sent an email to explain what happened the other night at my apartment – but I've no idea whether he ever got it.'

She handed back the notebook, wiped her eyes with a tissue and stood up.

'Now, if you'll excuse me Chief Inspector, I must get back to my father's bedside.'

She stood up and hurried out into the corridor.

Less than half an hour later Chief Inspector Diaz was on the phone in his office, consulting the information Isabel had given him as he tried unsuccessfully to reach Gabriel and Martin. Frustrated, he banged down the handset, threw himself into the swivel chair at his computer and fired off emails to both of them, requesting immediate contact. He sat with his head in his hands. Surely there was something else he could do.

Coming to a decision, he shrugged and reluctantly reached for the phone again. Soon he was speaking to his brother in Madrid.

'Alfredo, you know how I hate to trouble you, but this investigation is driving me crazy so I was wondering if you could possibly help me again ... Yes, I know just how busy you are, but this is absolutely crucial and going through the proper channels is going to take for ever ... Well no, it shouldn't be too difficult – not with your ...,' he coughed discreetly, '... special skills and facilities ... No, there's no surveillance involved, I promise. All I need is a trace on any phone calls or credit card transactions for an individual in the UK – or overseas, just in case he's gone off somewhere ... No, it's only for a very short period – from the early hours of this morning. And if you could possibly keep it going until there's a result, that would be brilliant. Oh, and I'm particularly interested in any calls or transactions suggesting travel – buying airline tickets, or anything like that ... Well, obviously it's going to be after midnight tonight at the earliest before anything shows up electronically – and of course it could be even later than that ... Yes, I know it's a lot to ask, but I'm desperate Alfredo, and

I really need your help right now ... You will? Good man, I definitely owe you one. Yes, I'll email you all the details for our target, a man called Martin Weston ... Yes, I will – and give my love to Angela and the kids ... You too, Alfredo.'

José Diaz ended the call, rubbed his hands, muttered 'pompous bastard' under his breath and grabbed the pack of Dunhills. Now he must send Martin Weston's contact details to Alfredo – and then wait as patiently as possible for a result. He lit up and inhaled deeply, blowing a cloud of smoke towards the ceiling. God, he just couldn't stand this continual waiting! Looking down again, he glared at the personnel folder with something like hatred as he opened his notebook and peered at the contact details for Gabriel and Martin. Then he took another drag at his cigarette and started to type an email to Alfredo.

Gabriel and Rachel were still sitting in the commissary waiting for instructions. Earlier they had their heads close together and had exchanged news about events in their lives since they had been in London together. Gabriel wanted to hear from Rachel first; she told him about her happy meeting with her parents when their cruise ship called in at Baltimore. They had been having a great time. They were sorry to have missed meeting Gabriel, but were delighted that she had found herself a 'lovely man', as her mom had put it. Then Rachel listened open-mouthed as Gabriel described the amazing discovery of his own father's Navegator program, the near-fatal attack on Vasco and the big fight in Isabel's flat. Then he told her about the big row in Hobnails' office caused by his sister's emails, sent in Mallorquin from Palma, and the way the disks had been switched.

'So this was the cause of all the trouble,' she had said, as Gabriel pulled the Tomeu Penya CD from his pocket. 'It hardly seems possible. But what about your dad's injuries?

Surely they'll let you go to him – and what's the latest news
on his condition?'

'I just don't know. There's been no time to check on that.
I can hardly wait to call Isabel or Teresa in Mallorca to find
out what's happening at the hospital. Come to think of it,
though, I'm so sore with Isabel right now, I don't know if I
can trust myself to speak with her after she pulled that trick
on me.'

He frowned, then gave a reluctant grin.

'But, as it's all turned out, maybe her mad scheme wasn't
so stupid after all. I always said she was crazy like a fox.'

He sighed deeply and put his head in his hands.

'I just wish I could get out of here and take you with me
on the next flight to Mallorca.'

That's when Rachel had leaned forward and laid her
hand on Gabriel's shoulder.

'Don't worry darling, I'm sure it won't be long before
they'll release us from quarantine. Meanwhile, couldn't you
use the phone near Security to make a call? Didn't you do
that once before?'

'Yes, but that was when there was no one else here. We'd
all been given a few days' leave, remember? I can't use
that phone right now – not while it's about to bring us
instructions from our bosses. I guess I'll just have to wait
until they've put us out of our misery – then afterwards
perhaps I can make those calls.'

'So, how shall we pass the time till then, Gabriel? It's so
difficult to put my mind to anything right now.'

He leaned forward and whispered in her ear. She put her
hand to her mouth, smiled shyly and slapped his wrist.

'Why, Mister Valseca, I do declare you're a very wicked
man – very wicked indeed. You just wait till I can give you
the punishment you deserve.'

She arched an eyebrow.

'It's such a pity we have to wait here for that phone call.'

Just then a scientist from NASA strolled past and offered them a plate of doughnuts. It was a very obvious excuse to try and get inside information, but Gabriel was not about to say anything more. They both smiled mute thanks as they took the plate. Gabriel realised he was desperately hungry. Soon they were licking sugar from their fingers and drinking more coffee as they settled down for a long wait.

Time passed slowly and all the doughnuts had gone when one of the security guards came into the commissary and beckoned to Gabriel, miming a phone call.

'That was quicker than I expected,' he said to Rachel.

He hurried to take the phone by the checkpoint. But when he put the handset to his ear, he was surprised to hear Joe Karlsen on the line from the American Embassy in London. That was nothing compared to his astonishment when Joe read out the text of the note he'd found on the windshield of his car, offering to sell the Americans a program that did the same job as Sniper.

'And, you bastard,' he went on, 'where the hell have you been? I've been camping here in my office at Grosvenor Square since Saturday and phoning this special number every four hours. I'm pretty pissed off, I can tell you.'

Gabriel could hardly believe what he was hearing. Quickly, he told Joe how the Sniper team's office space had been shut down for days, about the amazing chain of events in Mallorca and London – and that the Navegator program was being published to the world. Now it was Joe's turn to be amazed, but eventually he sounded convinced. Gabriel decided to push his luck.

'Say, Joe, I hate to give you another job right now – just when you've been stuck in the Embassy for days. But there's one more thing we'd be grateful for your help with.'

A loud snort came from the other end of the line. He hurried on.

'Could you please check around the IT community – the computer magazines in London and so on – and ask discreetly whether they've heard about any unusual new software in the past few hours? We do need to confirm that Isabel really did carry out her threat – though knowing my sister the way I do, I'm sure she's sent copies of the Navegator disk to everyone.'

Karlsen sighed deeply.

'OK, Gabriel, just for you, old buddy. At least I can leave this bloody office for a few hours. There are a few guys I know who may open up over a beer or two. Meanwhile, should I phone the number in this note? These guys who claim to have a program that replicates Sniper are trying to sell us something that is worthless now. So, should I tell them – whoever they are – to take a hike? It's your call.'

Gabriel thought for a moment.

'Let me think about that, Joe. Perhaps we should do nothing until your contacts confirm that the Navegator software really has been sent to the IT community.'

'OK Gabriel, I'll call you later – and this time you'd better be sure there's someone around to answer that phone.'

It was now early evening in Palma. Teresa and Isabel had returned to the apartment at Cala Gamba. They were both emotionally drained by their vigil at Vasco's bedside and had only left reluctantly when Miquel Santiago arrived to sit with his old friend.

They had only been back for a few minutes and were sitting in the kitchen over mugs of coffee when the doorbell rang. It was Margo, newly arrived in Palma. She flew into the apartment and embraced them both.

'Oh, my darlings, what a terrible business. I'm so sorry to have got here so late. What's the latest news of poor Vasco?'

When Teresa told Margo the extent of their brother's

injuries, Margo sank into a chair and dabbed her eyes with a small handkerchief.

'I know that Miquel is with him now, but I would like to sit with him as soon as I can and give all of you a break. And I won't be any trouble to anybody – I've already checked into the Portixol Hotel just down the road, so I'll be nearby whenever you need me. And I've parked my rental car just outside – so if you want me to do any running around I'd be happy to do that.'

The three women sat together, united by anxiety. Margo got to hear Isabel's saga of misfortune for the first time and gathered her niece to her like a mother hen. They drank more coffee and talked quietly about the sudden way that misfortune had rained down on the Valseca family.

Gabriel and Rachel had been waiting around the communal areas for almost five hours and everyone was getting restless. Just before four o'clock, as Gabriel was finishing another diet cola in the commissary and thinking about going to his room for a book, a different guard from the security area called out from the doorway.

'Is Gabriel Valseca here? There's a phone call.'

He jerked his thumb in the direction of the checkpoint as Gabriel stood up to follow him. When he reached the end of the corridor he took the handset from one of the other members of the security team. As soon as he had identified himself a familiar contralto voice answered at once.

'Don't be too surprised, Gabriel. Yes, its Lynne Kowalski here. We've both been around the block a few times since I recruited you three years ago. So, young man, what have you been up to – playing games with this Navegator software? I've heard blow-by-blow details of the story from the Admiral himself and I couldn't have imagined it in my wildest dreams.'

Gabriel tried to speak but she went on quickly.

'Let's get on with it, shall we? Hobnails has retired with immediate effect. He's already cleared his desk and left the building – he's going on that well-earned vacation right now. His wife Andrea's going to be delighted, I guess. On the other hand, Charlene's pretty cut up, but I'm taking her under my wing, so I guess she'll get over it.'

'Well, I'm very happy to talk to you again, Ma'am. What do you want me to tell the team?'

'I understand you've got a conference room over there at Watergate. I can be there quite soon, so assemble all the Sniper people. I'll make an announcement to all of them at four fifteen – meanwhile, say nothing. It shouldn't take long to wrap this up. Oh, and while you're arranging that, get someone to install a direct outside phone line in a private office – one with a desk and a few chairs. And I'll need a computer with outside access too. Fix it for me, will you, Gabriel?'

The line went dead before Gabriel could reply. He hung up and hurried off to tell Rachel the news, so that she could help him to round up everyone for their meeting with Lynne Kowalski.

Soon there was a buzz of expectant speculation and chatter in the conference room. Exactly on time, Lynne Kowalski swept into the room. She was a tall, fair-haired woman, who moved like an athlete. A tailored black suit emphasised her slim build. Her age could have been anything between forty-five and sixty; the piercing blue eyes in the strong aquiline face swept the room. Her commanding presence produced an immediate hush.

'Please sit down everyone.'

There was a scramble for places and an expectant silence fell.

'As you already know, Admiral Hobring has retired with immediate effect after a lifetime of service to this country. I'm sure we all wish him well. However, it's time to move on. I'm authorised to confirm the report given to you by Gabriel Valseca here. Yes, we've just learned that a program now exists with the same capability as Sniper. What does this mean for you people? Well, it's imperative that spending on unproductive defence projects is eliminated so that funds can be diverted elsewhere. Clearly, Sniper is now redundant. So, as of now, this project is terminated and you'll all be returning to your own units. You've all worked hard and your efforts are appreciated. Unfortunately, though, someone else got to the finish line first. So, please pack up your gear and vacate this facility as soon as you can. I expect you all to be out of here within an hour from now. In case you were wondering, a team will come in tomorrow to remove the computers and the equipment at the checkpoint. I shall arrange with the security people to shut down this whole area tonight. That's it. Thank you again and goodbye.'

There was a sudden outburst of chatter as everyone got up, gathered papers and brief cases and started to move away from the conference table with farewells, backslapping and handshakes as they all made their way to the door. Gabriel hung back for a final word with Lynne.

'You asked for a phone and a computer set up in one of the offices. We've given you the phone from Security and there's a computer too. They're ready for you in room 11 – that's just along the corridor to your left. Goodbye, Ma'am.'

He turned to leave, but she called him back.

'Not so fast, Agent Valseca, you're not quite done here yet. I need a couple of people to help me clear up a few loose ends. Now, a certain Admiral took quite a shine to you. I can only imagine he must be a romantic at heart. So, he said that you and Rachel Jefferson made quite a team and I'd be well advised to keep the pair of you around for a day or two to finish up here – oh, and he winked when he said that. Now why was that, do you suppose? You go find Rachel and come back to see me in room 11 just as soon as you can.'

Gabriel coloured. He stammered 'Yes, Ma'am', and rushed off to find Rachel.

When they reached room 11, breathless and confused, they found their new boss seated at the desk, peering at a computer screen through horn-rimmed glasses. She waved Gabriel and Rachel to a couple of chairs, took off the glasses and banged them down on top of her briefcase beside the keyboard.

'I hate these damned things!' she said, 'They make me look a hundred years old.'

Lynne turned to face them.

'Thanks for coming along to help with the wind-down of operations here. We've got some serious talking to do and things to fix. You, Gabriel, will be doing whatever is necessary to tidy up any loose ends. You might care to know that I asked for you to be assigned to me and that's been cleared with Langley. That may be just as well because your old boss Ben Jorgensen was looking forward to giving you a really hard time. But it so happens he's packing to go to the Gulf right now. They're sending him out there to beef up our intelligence operations in the region.'

Gabriel allowed himself a secret smile.

'Rachel, I've also cleared it with your Air Force bosses that you can go on working with me. Your job is to take notes of all that goes on and maintain files of our activities. But none of us can go on living here. You'll have to make your own arrangements for overnight accommodation. That shouldn't be any problem for you, Gabriel, as I just happen to know you have an apartment not too far away – no doubt Rachel can find somewhere to sleep too.'

The older woman looked away discreetly as she reached for a notepad. Rachel exchanged a shy glance with Gabriel. Outside in the corridor they could hear the sounds of their former colleagues leaving the building to return to their own agencies.

'Look here, Gabriel,' Lynne consulted her notes. 'We need to get a few things straight and, as we're going to be working closely together, just call me Lynne. I'm going to be upfront with you. For me, this job represents therapy right now. I was involved in an operation in southeast Asia that went badly wrong and we lost some good people. There was a lot of trauma and I sustained severe burns – mostly on my shoulders and back where it doesn't show, fortunately. Anyway, I'm on light duties for a while. But I've been given authority to do whatever's necessary to close this operation down in the best way possible. So, I'm going to start by taking stock. You've been at the heart of this from the beginning, so remind me of everything that's happened from day one – including those bizarre events in London. And I'm so very sorry to hear about your father. I'll release you to travel to see him just as soon as we've covered all the bases – but it's difficult to say how long that's going to take.'

She held up a hand as Gabriel began to speak.

'Let's just get this over with. Rachel, please feel free to cut in with an additional comment or correction at any time.'

Rachel looked up from her own notepad and nodded as Gabriel began the story, including the surprise phone call from Joe Karlsen.

It was a full half hour before he had finished. Lynne closed her eyes and rubbed her hands across her brow.

'So, let's be clear about all of this. At the moment, we've shut down Sniper entirely on your say-so, Gabriel. My God, Hobnails must have put a lot of trust in you. But I'm paid to be cynical. Where's the independent verification that Navegator actually works? Who's actually seen the program perform?'

'Two others that I know of,' Gabriel answered, 'My sister Isabel and her fiancé Martin Weston.'

'Fine, so let's get them on the phone and find out what they saw.'

268

'Well yes, but I hope I can raise her. It's around 11 p.m. in Mallorca right now.'

'That's too bad. I'm sorry if it's going to wake her, but I need you to try the number right now. So, please do it anyway.'

Lynne was passing over the phone when it began to ring. They all jumped and Gabriel took the call. He put his hand over the mouthpiece.

'It's Joe Karlsen, calling back from London,' he muttered. Then:

'Yes, Joe, I hear you, but I'm in a meeting and there's no time to chat. What's the word on the street? ... Really? Nothing at all? That's very strange. I'll have to find out what happened from Isabel – I was just about to call her anyway ... Yes, and many thanks for that. I suggest you don't do anything about the note you found on your windshield. Not for the moment, anyway ... Bye.'

He ended the call and looked up at Lynne.

'I think you know what that was about. It seems that there's no news in the London IT community about an amazing new program for pinpointing hackers. Unless there's anything else, I'll call Isabel immediately to find out exactly what she did to publish that software – may I?'

'You go right ahead, Gabriel. But before you do, tell me again about the note on the windshield of Karlsen's car.'

She listened, frowning, as Gabriel told her the story. Then she bent her head for a moment. Finally she looked stonily at Gabriel and rasped.

'Well, for once I agree with you. Let's wait a while on that one. Now you call that sister of yours. And the news had better be good, otherwise you're going to be counting yaks in Outer Mongolia for the next few years. And to make sure I'm really getting the full picture, I'm switching on the speakers, OK?'

Gabriel gritted his teeth, nodded and dialled the number for Isabel's cell phone. To his surprise, she answered sleepily after the third ring.

'Biel, thank God you've called. I was just trying to get some sleep,' she began in Mallorquin.

Gabriel quickly cut her short, replying in English.

'Bel, my darling, I'm sorry to disturb you when you must be exhausted, but it's very important. And we have to speak in English. I'm still on duty and this call is being monitored on loudspeakers, so I hope you understand. Before you ask, I do understand about the trick you played on me, so let's not talk about that.'

There was a pause, then:

'Yes, of course. That's not a problem. But first I must tell you that Papa is still dangerously ill and in a high-dependency unit at Son Dureta. The police are hunting the bastard who tried to kill him to get Navegator. All the relations have been told and Margo's flown in from England to be with him. She's just arrived and we saw her briefly – but she's on the way to take over from Miquel Santiago at the hospital right now'.

'OK, I understand – and I hope to be able to get out to Palma soon. But there's a higher priority here. So there are some questions I need to ask, Bel, and it's important that my colleagues can hear your answers. First off, can you confirm that we did a thorough test of the Navegator software, you witnessed that test and the program successfully pinpointed the source of a number of emails and viruses?'

'Well, yes I definitely can – and so could Martin, if only I knew where to find him. He seems to have completely disappeared. I think he must be totally furious because I tricked him too. I guess our future plans are definitely off …' Her voice tailed away.

'Please, Bel, don't be upset. It will all be sorted out

270

eventually, trust me. Please try to calm down. Now, just as soon as we end this call, can you please email me with all of Martin's contact details. We'll trace him one way or another. And think hard. Is there anyone else at all who might have seen the program in action?'

There was a short pause.

'Why yes, of course. Miquel Santiago was telling me how amazing it was – and that Papa had demonstrated it to the manager of the local branch of the bank. The BCIB, I think. But I'm not sure of his name and contact details – should I ask Miquel?'

'Yes, please do that – and email that manager's details, plus I need a phone number for Miquel too. I'll need to speak to him as soon as I can. Now, Bel, there's one more thing. Did you carry out your plan to send copies of Navegator to computer magazines, software houses and the rest?'

There was a long pause. Lynne looked sharply at Gabriel and raised an eyebrow.

'Well, no, Biel. I just didn't have time. I was about to make those copies when Teresa rang with the news about Papa. I literally dropped everything. I only had a few seconds to send you the email about Papa's accident before rushing to Gatwick to get the next flight to Mallorca.'

Lynne's face was like thunder. Gabriel saw her furious expression and swallowed hard.

'So, Bel, you're telling me that the original Navegator disk could still be in your apartment? Where's Martin? Did he go back to your place? He certainly didn't catch up to me on the way out to Heathrow, though I thought I saw him in my mirrors a few times.'

'That's the same question the police were asking me here. But I just don't know how to answer – I've tried and tried to contact him, but he seems to have vanished off the face of the earth.'

'Now listen, Bel. This is very important. You remember

271

that Martin threatened to take the disk to his former associates at GCHQ. Do you think it's possible he might have
taken it from your apartment and given it to those guys at
Cheltenham? Please think hard.'

There was a long pause.

'I just don't know how to answer. I only know that my life
is in ruins ...'

Gabriel cut in quickly.

'Please get a grip, Bel. It will be OK in the end. Trust me.
Now I really do have to go. Send my love to everyone.'

He ended the call before Isabel could reply.

Gabriel and Rachel jumped as Lynne slammed her fist on
the desk.

'Shit! That's exactly what I don't need. I was suspicious
after that call-back from Karlsen. But we now know for sure
that Isabel didn't get that software out to the IT community.
So, where is it now? That's the sixty-four-thousand dollar
question. There are only two realistic possibilities. Either
that disk is still sitting in Isabel's apartment, or Martin's
taken it someplace – possibly to those computer geeks at
GCHQ.'

She glared at Gabriel.

'You realise what this means don't you? If that program is
not in the public domain after all, then somebody else –
friend or enemy – now has exclusive use of it, instead of us.
Let's just think what that means: nobody may have spelled
this out, but if it had been successful, this Sniper project
would have been able to do more than pinpoint the
location of hackers. The origins of any internet traffic by
a hostile power could be identified too. So it would be easy
to get precise locations for significant military command
centres right to the top of the tree. But now we've shut
down our own project, it follows that the United States is
now on the back foot. And even if we wanted to, we no
longer have the capability to restart our own activity – not

without a significant delay anyway – because the Sniper team's been disbanded. And all because of your report. How does that make you feel, Gabriel?'

Before he could answer, Rachel looked up from her notes, her eyes blazing.

'You may be Gabriel's boss, Ma'am, and you certainly outrank me by a mile, but I have to remind you that hindsight has twenty-twenty vision. Surely you can't blame him for not making the right call after he'd just heard that his father had been attacked and was critically injured. The family's been called to his bedside and Gabriel is still tied up here. Surely you must agree that everyone, including Admiral Hobring, did the best they could with the information they had at the time.'

There was an icy silence, but gradually Lynne's expression softened and her mouth relaxed a little. Eventually, she smiled and leaned across the desk to lay a hand on Rachel's arm.

'Well, you certainly know how to stand by your man. Perhaps I was being too tough on Gabriel.'

She turned her smile on him.

'So, let's move on, shall we? The priority right now is to act on those additional contact details – just as soon as we have them from Isabel. Meanwhile, try and contact Joe Karlsen again, please Gabriel. I'd like to speak to him myself. We've got our own resources in place in London and an urgent search of Isabel's flat is top priority. There shouldn't be any problem about setting that up. As a senior CIA officer I've got full authority to have our people go through it with a toothcomb. We need to know whether that software disk is still where she dropped it. If not, then we need to find Martin Weston – and fast. So, Gabriel, would you please try to get Joe Karlsen right now? And Rachel, could you please keep an eye on the computer here and print out those contact details just as soon as Isabel sends them through. Meanwhile, I'll go find us some coffee – I think we're going to need it.'

She swept out of the room and Gabriel turned to Rachel and squeezed her hand.

'Thanks for sticking up for me, darling, but actually her bark's worse than her bite.'

He opened his personal organiser, checked the index and picked up the phone. He had just finished punching in Joe Karlsen's number when Lynne returned with the coffee.

It was answered at the fourth ring. Joe was just leaving his office and was not happy to get another call from Gabriel, but his tone of voice changed as soon as he heard that Lynne Kowalski had an important mission for him. Taking over the phone, she briefed him in a few terse sentences. Joe agreed to put together a crew immediately to have Isabel's apartment searched for the false Tomeu Penya disk, promising to get a report back within three hours. He certainly wasn't about to complain to his superior officer that he was being asked to send out a search team so late at night.

When the call had ended, Gabriel was just taking back the handset from Lynne when he felt a wave of nausea and dizziness wash over him. As his vision quickly blacked out, he slumped forward onto the floor and Rachel jumped forward to cradle him in her arms.

'Oh my God. He's totally exhausted. Please can't you let him have just a few hours' sleep? Gabriel's got jet-lag, his father's in intensive care, he's had the biggest fight of his life with his twin sister and he's hardly slept properly for days. Surely he's due a little rest now.'

He stirred and started to get up.

'I'm fine really. All I need is to lie down for a while.'

As he struggled to his feet, Lynne gently guided him to a chair.

'You just take it easy for a few minutes, Gabriel. Rachel

and I will make a few calls – then we'll be all through here for the night.'

While Gabriel sat with his eyes closed, they checked the computer. Sure enough, Isabel had sent through the contact details they'd asked for. Quickly, they tried all of the numbers, but without success. Martin Weston was still not answering his phone. It seemed pointless and confusing to send him another email, when he obviously hadn't opened the one Isabel had sent earlier. Miquel Santiago's phone was switched off too – and until they were able to speak to him, they couldn't get contact details for the bank manager either. Disappointed, Lynne threw down the phone.

'I guess everyone over in Europe's asleep right now. We'll just have to wait until morning. Rachel, why don't you get that young man away from here and make sure you're both properly rested before tomorrow. I'm going to stay here until Joe Karlsen calls back. While I'm waiting there'll be time for some quiet strategic thinking. So, cut along now, pick up your stuff and go down to the front entrance while I call you a cab. Just make sure you're both back here at 8.30 tomorrow morning.'

'Yes Lynne, I'll do that.'

Rachel helped Gabriel to his feet. He was like a dead man walking as she guided him to the corridor and called back to say goodnight. Behind them, Lynne Kowalski rubbed her eyes before phoning for a cab for Gabriel and Rachel. Then she thought for a moment. It ought to be possible to get a trace on Martin Weston through credit card transactions, but the timing wasn't helpful. It was now the small hours of Friday morning in Europe. Allowing for the time zone differences, she wouldn't have any sort of answers until after the weekend. Damn, she thought! It would just have to wait – but she made a phone call anyway to initiate the search. Then wearily she opened her briefcase, put on her horn-rimmed glasses and began to read from a bulky dossier.

Settling as comfortably as she could into the plastic chair she put her feet up on another. It could be a long wait.

It was almost three hours later when the phone rang and Joe Karlsen was on the line.

'Well, Ma'am, the news is not good. Our team went through that apartment inch by inch and there's no trace of that Tomeu Penya disk you are looking for. There were quite a few other normal CDs, but somebody had obviously left the place in a great hurry. I was there myself. But here's something else. It looked very much as though another team had been over the place before we arrived. If so, they were professionals – the Brits or some other people. It was hard to tell. Maybe they found what we were looking for – or perhaps they were disappointed too.'

'Shit! That's just what I didn't want to hear. Damn, damn, damn! But you're off the hook, Joe. I'm sure your guys did their best. Now I have to decide our next moves. Thanks again and goodnight.'

She hung up the phone and shrugged on a coat before gathering her briefcase and turning out the lights as she walked out of Room 11 towards the elevator.

16

Victor Dankovitch was in a foul mood. He had tossed and turned all night. It was now Friday morning and there had been no news about the collection in Mallorca. He couldn't stand the waiting any longer. He had heard nothing from Ygor Krasnov or from that mad Englishman, Foxtrot. He sent for the car, then showered and dressed hurriedly.

It was not yet 7.30 when his driver Sergei Bulgakov, a powerfully built ex-wrestler from Pulkovo, helped him out of the big BMW at the warehouse near St Petersburg docks. It was a dark murky morning, the air was desperately cold and Viktor was glad to reach the warmth of the offices. There was nobody else around yet, so he helped himself to a glass of black tea from the samovar in the main office. Then he pushed open the heavy door into his own palatial suite, set down the tea and threw himself into his massive, black-leather swivel chair.

He switched on the computer and drummed his fingers impatiently on the leather bound blotter while he waited for it to boot up. At last the screen came to life. Viktor took a gulp of the hot black tea, then reached into a cupboard behind him for a bottle and murmured 'Ah, my vodichka' as he added a large slug of vodka to the steaming glass. He checked his emails impatiently and his face darkened with rage as he saw that there was nothing from Krasnov or Foxtrot. Quickly he composed a furious email to Foxtrot asking what had happened when he approached the

Americans about the possible purchase of Navegator. In his experience no news was often bad news and the silence made his blood boil. He stood up and downed the rest of the hot vodka-laced tea, then carried the glass back into the main office, where some of the staff were arriving.

His driver was standing beside the samovar.

'Ah, Sergei. I might have a little assignment for you. When you see that good-for-nothing son of mine Kyril, bring him to me will you? I may have a job for both of you – just make sure you've got your passport in your pocket. I need to find that filthy rat Ygor Krasnov. He was on a mission to Mallorca. He should have completed it on Wednesday morning. That's two days ago and there hasn't been a word from him. If necessary are you ready to find him wherever he's hiding and drag his treacherous arse back here?'

'Yes, of course, comrade Viktor. I could be ready to leave at a moment's notice. I always keep a small travel bag in the car and my passport is right here.' He patted his pocket.

'Good man. There's almost nobody else around here I can rely on.'

He clapped Sergei on the shoulder before helping himself to another glass of tea and went back into his own office, slamming the door behind him.

During the night, Vasco's friends and family had attended his bedside in turn, staying two or three hours at a stretch. There had been no change in his condition and even taking an optimistic view the doctors expected to see no improvement for another few days. Margo had sat with her brother for much of the night. She had been relieved by Guillem and Antonia who arrived at Son Dureta from the *possessió* early in the morning. After her tiring plane journey and overnight watch by Vasco's side, Margo was now resting and trying to sleep at the Hotel Portixol. Teresa was embraced warmly by Guillem and his tearful wife when she took over from them at around ten o'clock. At around two o'clock one of the nurses told her that they would be taking Vasco to X-ray for further checks on the progress of his injuries. There was no cause for alarm, but there was no point in waiting. The tests could take some time and the hospital would call as soon as visiting could resume. Teresa was quite relieved to be given some respite. She hurried back to her car and drove straight home to Cala Gamba. When she opened the door of her apartment she heard voices and found Miquel Santiago sitting at the table opposite Isabel drinking coffee and chatting quietly.

Isabel turned sharply.

'How's Papa – is there any news?'

'Nothing more yet, I'm afraid, but he seems to be holding his own and we must be grateful for that. They have just taken Vasco for some more tests - but there's no cause for alarm - we'll get a call when we can go back to sit with him. Then you might want to visit again for a couple of hours, darling. I really don't feel like any lunch and it's a bit late anyway, so if you've both eaten let's just relax for a few minutes while I join you in a coffee – and perhaps a little *ensaimada*. I'll bring it over so that you can have some too.'

'Not for me, thanks,' said Miquel. He looked desperately tired and worried. 'I really should get back to the university. Things are a bit disorganised at the moment and I have work to do before –'

At that moment his mobile phone rang and he snatched it out of his pocket.

'Oh it's you, Biel. What a terrible business this is … Yes, I see … OK, I'll speak in English. That's not a problem. Actually, I'm drinking coffee with Bel in Teresa's apartment. And she's just joined us after a visit to Vasco. He's not out of danger yet, I'm afraid and still unconscious – but it seems he's holding his own … Yes, yes of course. I understand.

Isabel told me you'd been asking her about the Navegator demonstration ... Well, yes, I was there when Vasco showed its paces to the bank manager, Ramón Vilar. There was another man from the bank, a young IT guy and he saw the trial run too. They asked for the system to be tried out thoroughly. Vasco put it through a lot of tests and it passed them all with flying colours ... Yes, I realise you must be very tied up right now ... You don't have time to speak to Bel or Teresa? That's terrible. Not even a moment? ... Well, yes, I think I understand. We all hope to see you here soon, dear boy – and I'll send contact details by email for Ramón Vilar's office at the bank as soon as I get back to my own place. I don't have them with me ... Yes, yes. I will. 'Bye.

'I think you know what that was all about. Gabriel is still tied up in Washington and his bosses are looking for extra confirmation that Navegator really worked. He sends his love and hopes to be in Palma soon. But now I really must be on my way. Please don't get up, either of you. I'll see myself out.'

He got wearily to his feet. There were murmured goodbyes as he kissed Teresa and Isabel lightly on their cheeks and left the apartment.

'Well, I guess that's further confirmation about Navegator.'

Gabriel checked his watch.

'It's twenty after eight now and it will be another hour at least before Miquel calls back with contact details for the bank manager. What should we do now, Lynne?'

'From where I'm sitting, it seems we're pretty much screwed. Unless we get a very different story from that guy Vilar, we have to face the fact that this amazing piece of software really does work and it's out there somewhere. And there are some very bad people who want it just as badly as we do. According to Karlsen, somebody – but we don't know who – tried to contact him with a note on his car windshield. That somebody wanted to sell us a system which sounds just like Navegator. Or perhaps it was a trick – or was it really Navegator? It seems there are too many things we don't know.'

'Yes, I can see that, Lynne. But we can't find the one individual who may hold the key to all of this – Martin Weston. When we tried all of his contact numbers just before calling Miquel Santiago, there was still no answer, just like last night. I've got a team trying to trace him. But where the hell can he be?'

Chief Inspector Diaz was feeling virtuous. He had just eaten a frugal lunch at his desk while attacking the last few files in the personnel folder. It had been sitting on his desk for days now. He was heartily sick of the sight of it. But after another hour or so of concentration he had completed the last of the appraisals. He was enjoying a celebratory cigarette when the phone rang. It was his brother Alfredo on the line from Madrid. He sat bolt upright and gripped the phone tightly as he prepared to take notes.

'Alfredo! It's good to hear from you. Do you have any news at all? … Really? Well done! That's very interesting indeed. Ah, so our man used a credit card at a travel agency in London? … On Thursday morning? Excellent! Is there any information about what he paid for? … Oh, you antici-pated that question too? Good man. What's the answer? … A cruise? No wonder he hasn't been answering his phone … Well done. Let me repeat that. He's on a ship belonging to the Camelot Line, *Excalibur*. It sailed from Tilbury yester-day night for a four-day cruise to Hamburg and Amsterdam. Do you have the ship's phone contact details? … This gets better and better. I'm just writing that down. I can't tell you how much I appreciate this, Alfredo. I really do owe you one …Yes, I'll keep you in the picture about the investiga-tion. This information will help it along enormously … Yes, you too – and thanks again.'

He hung up and rubbed his hands. His English was a bit rusty, but he'd done pretty well when he went to London on secondment to the Metropolitan Police five years ago. Now it was time to see if he could still make himself understood. After a few failed attempts, he finally managed to telephone *Excalibur*. Initially, his call was picked up at the reception desk on the main deck. First he asked to be put through to Martin Weston, but there was no answer from his cabin. Then he explained to the receptionist that he was making enquiries in connection with an attempted homicide and the call was quickly transferred to the Officer of the Watch. The Captain was off duty at that time, but after his credentials had been checked, Chief Inspector Diaz found himself speaking to the Communications Officer.

'It is very important that I speak with one of your passengers, Martin Weston, who may have vital information connected with a savage attack on his future father in law, here in Mallorca ... No, Mr Weston is not a suspect, but I should like to ask him some questions on the telephone – and I understand that he is not in his cabin. So, is it possible that he could be paged? ... Thank you very much. I will call back later. Oh – and are passengers able to receive emails on board *Excalibur*? ... Good, that's very helpful. So, would you please ask Mr Weston to check his emails? It's very important that he reads an email sent to him by his fiancée, Isabel Valseca, before I speak to him ... Of course ... Yes, I appreciate that it may take a long time to locate him. So, perhaps I should wait at least one hour before I phone again ... Yes, I will. Thank you very much for your help. Goodbye.'

After he hung up, the policeman reached for his cigarettes, only to find that the pack was empty. He frowned, then decided to have a walk around the block, buy some more Dunhills, pick up a paper, have a coffee in a bar – do anything at all to curb his impatience and keep his blood pressure under control while he killed time until he could make another attempt to call Martin Weston.

Just after five o'clock the hospital phoned as promised to say that Vasco's tests had shown satisfactory progress. It was now possible for limited visiting to resume. Isabel left Cala Gamba at once, driving Teresa's Alfa Romeo with considerable panache en route to Son Dureta. She intended to call at Chief Inspector Diaz' office on the way there, to find out if he had been able to find Martin. The policeman might even have been able to speak to him. She bit her lip with frustration as the Friday afternoon rush-hour traffic built up along the Passeig Maritim.

Luckily, she had little trouble in finding a space in the underground car park on the Passeig de Mallorca and walked the short distance to the sombre building on the other side of the roadway.

Isabel walked into the reception area, where an unsmiling officer at the desk asked her name and business, then spoke briefly on the phone. Within a few moments Chief Inspector Diaz appeared and escorted her to his office. After shaking hands and offering her a chair, he sat at his desk and picked up his note pad.

Isabel looked at him expectantly.

'Please tell me if there's any news about Martin. I haven't been able to sleep wondering what's happened.'

'Yes, we've found him and I've just finished speaking to him on the phone.'

He held up his hand as Isabel half rose from her seat.

'Please be patient. There's a lot to tell you. First of all, he has only just seen your email and he now understands what a terrible decision you had to make. He said I should tell you that he still loves you deeply.'

Chief Inspector Diaz paused for a moment and looked away tactfully as Isabel closed her eyes and bent her head.

'When he was so angry and confused he had no idea what to do, so he decided to go away for a while to think about things. Right now he's on a short cruise and the ship reaches Hamburg in a couple of hours. He's already packing his bag and he'll disembark as soon as they dock. He said I should tell you that he'll be on the first available flight to Palma. He hopes to be here some time tomorrow.'

Isabel's eyes were shining.

'How can I speak to him?'

Diaz passed her a slip of paper.

'You won't be able to connect with his mobile phone until they reach port, but here's the ship's phone number – and his cabin number's there too.'

'Thank you so much, Chief Inspector. I'm so grateful. That's wonderful news. I'll try to call him as soon as I've left your office.' She stood up. 'And I have to go now anyway – I'm just off to Son Dureta to sit with my father for a while.'

'Not so fast, Miss Valseca. There's more I have to tell you – and you may not like this. Martin tells me that he went a bit crazy and made quite a mess in the kitchen of your apartment. He cleaned it up before he left yesterday morning. There was quite a lot of broken glass and some CDs he'd stamped on, including one by Tomeu Penya. Anyway, he swept the whole lot into a pile and put everything down the rubbish chute. Now, that particular disk may lead us to your father's attackers – so what happens to the rubbish in your apartment building after it goes down the chute?'

Isabel put her hand to her mouth.

'Oh, my God! It goes straight into a skip in the basement. It's collected every morning by contractors and taken away – to a landfill site, I think. Or it might be incinerated, I'm not sure. So it will definitely have gone – either yesterday or today.'

'You must realise what this means, Miss Valseca. Sooner

or later, those people who know about Navegator and want it so badly will realise that the disk has gone. This means that the one and only place where that valuable information is stored is in your father's head. Those people may stop at nothing to get what they want. I'm going to post one of my men at the hospital for his safety until we know more. Please keep me informed. Martin may remember something else, so I'd like to see him as soon as possible after he arrives. Now, I must make those security arrangements at Son Dureta and keep the pressure on our forensic team – and all the others who are working on this case.'

He held out his hand.

'Good luck. I hope that Professor Valseca's condition improves very soon.'

He pressed a button on the intercom.

'Margareta, kindly show Miss Valseca out – and please ask Sergeant Ferrer to come in here right away.'

When Isabel reached the street she dashed into the nearest café and ordered an espresso. She got out her mobile phone. Soon she had reached the *Excalibur* and was put straight through to Martin's cabin. He answered at once and the next few minutes were spent in mending their relationship and catching up with the news. Both were desperate to be together again. Martin told Isabel he would phone with his flight details as soon as he could. Isabel promised to be waiting for him at the airport. Her coffee was almost cold, but she drank it anyway and ordered another.

While she waited for it to arrive she phoned the number Gabriel had used last night when he called from Washington. It was quickly answered by Rachel, who was delighted to speak with Isabel again. But there was no time for small talk. Lynne Kowalski had taken over the phone and was firing questions.

'Hi, Isabel. Is there any news from your end? Oh, and

how's your father getting along now? I'd put Gabriel on, but it's his turn to get us some coffee – why, here he is now. OK, I'll hand you over to him while we listen on the speakers.'

'Biel, I'll be quick. I'm on my way to sit at Papa's bedside. There's no change yet, by the way, but they've just done some tests which seem to show he's making some progress. I guess that's the best we can hope for at the moment. But there's important news. The police here have located Martin. He's on a cruise ship, *Excalibur*, due in Hamburg tonight. I'll give you the contact information, but you should be able to reach his mobile phone after the ship reaches port in about two hours.'

Lynne looked thoughtfully at Gabriel as Rachel wrote down the details. Her face grew grim and pensive as she heard how Martin had gone berserk in Isabel's apartment – and the Navegator software disk had gone for good. She snapped her fingers impatiently and signalled to Gabriel to end the call. He hung up reluctantly, promising to phone again as soon as he could.

'Damn! Damn! Damn! It's time to take stock. Listen, both of you. This is how it looks to me – just cut in if my reasoning's adrift here. One, the Navegator software works; we had further confirmation of that when we spoke to the banker, Vilar, just now. Two, it's valuable – perhaps priceless – and we aren't the only people who know about it and want it very badly. Three, we've just learned that the original has been destroyed or lost – and there are no copies. Four, the only person who can reconstruct that program, Gabriel, is your father. And right now he's unconscious and in a critical condition. Are you with me so far?'

'Sure,' said Rachel, 'but if someone out there knows that Navegator exists – and the program works – what's to stop that somebody from creating something similar from scratch?'

'That's a fair point. True, it's happened before with other

technical breakthroughs. But the owner of Navegator would have a head start and that could prove strategically priceless. Anyone trying to play catch-up might take a year or longer to come up to speed.'

Gabriel had been listening intently and turned his head to face Lynne.

'Are you saying that the United States still wants to get hold of this program and use it?'

'Of course. The Sniper exercise demonstrated that trying to write this piece of software is extraordinarily difficult. But there's no way anyone will authorise a new initiative when everything we need is out there already.'

'In that case, it's only right I should speak for my father, as he's in no position to speak for himself. He created that piece of intellectual property and it still belongs to him. I can't believe that the American authorities would actually steal it.'

'No, of course not. But there are others who wouldn't hesitate – as we already know. And I think your father would sell his software to us, Gabriel. While we've all been waiting around here for the phone to ring, you've told me a lot about his background and I read him like this: he's got no interest at all in making Navegator available to the Spanish authorities. He actually sees them as hostile to his ambitions to get greater autonomy for Mallorca. Remember, we believe his principal motive for offering his software to the bank was to get money for his small political group. Sure, he wanted to get even with those hackers, but his real reason was more independence for the Balearic islands. Yes, I'm convinced he would sell to us.'

Gabriel looked thoughtful.

'I think you're right. But we have to nurse him back to health first – so when do I get to see him?'

Lynne rubbed her temples for a moment, closed her eyes, then suddenly snapped her fingers.

'I've got it! This is absolutely perfect. This ticks all the boxes. Here's how it goes. We all know that it could be some time before your father's well enough to talk to anybody. But we need to be sure that whenever that is, we are right there beside him to have that conversation. We also know that he's probably still in danger from the bad guys – OK, so the police in Palma are providing some cover and they want to talk to him about the attempt on his life. But is that good enough, I wonder? No, definitely not. So, here's my suggestion. We arrange round-the-clock cover. Someone will be at the bedside of Vasco Valseca and this will be arranged 24/7 for as long as it takes. That needs a team of four – and they need to be people we can trust absolutely. My suggestion is that they should be Gabriel Valseca, Rachel Jefferson, Teresa Valseca and Miquel Santiago. So, what do you think of that?'

Gabriel and Rachel sat open-mouthed as Lynne nodded and went on.

'There's no need to maintain any staff at all at this end. The costs would be minimal and well within my discretionary budget. All I would need from you is a weekly email report to my office at Langley. But obviously you would call me immediately if anything really important crops up. Then, Gabriel, as soon as your father recovers consciousness we can take it from there. Can you see any problem with that?'

'Lynne, I think that's brilliant. I'm one hundred per cent sure that Teresa and Miquel will agree to join in – but there's just one problem. Isn't a team of four too thin for the task? It would be much better if we could make it five.'

'Let me think about that.'

She paused and pursed her lips for a moment.

'I think you're right. A team of five would give better cover. But that's no problem, Gabriel. Joe Karlsen's under my control. He's sick and tired of his desk job at the

Embassy in London. That little task we gave him a few hours ago was a welcome diversion, but he'll only get something like that once in a blue moon. He's utterly reliable and he knows the background to the Sniper project – you've already put him in the picture on that. Plus, he was with you at Langley. He'd jump at the chance of a change of scene and some different golf courses. I'll fix that right now while you two go and get ready to leave. See you back in here in ten minutes – then I think we're all done.'

Gabriel and Rachel rushed out of room 11, hugged briefly then, as the door banged shut behind them, they went to collect their own stuff. Soon they were back, shaking hands with Lynne Kowalski as they said their goodbyes.

'Off you go! You should get a flight to Madrid tonight and then you'll be in Palma tomorrow. Have a great time and don't forget the weekly reports. And you can send me a postcard too.'

She shooed them out of the room and they got lucky, finding a cab almost at once. Soon they were at Gabriel's apartment to pick up their clothes and pack. Isabel would now be visiting their father in the intensive care unit at Son Dureta, where cell phones were forbidden, so he sent her an email to tell her they were on their way. Meanwhile Rachel called her parents with the news. She spoke to her dad, who was home marking some exam papers while her mom was out getting groceries. He laughed a lot when she told him her plans and said he would have to think about another cruise. They might do it during the summer vacation, in the Mediterranean this time – with a stop at Palma. She blew kisses down the phone, then hung up and turned her radiant face to Gabriel.

'My folks seem to be really happy for us – so what are we waiting for? Let's catch that plane!'

17

There was much excitement as welcome parties thronged the arrivals area at Palma airport on a busy Saturday morning. Isabel and Teresa were in the crowd too, standing hand in hand as they waited for Martin and for Gabriel and Rachel. They constantly scanned the information display showing the expected times of arrival for the incoming flights. Martin's Air Berlin flight from Hamburg arrived first. When he appeared at the exit from baggage claim there was an emotional reunion between the lovers as a tearful Isabel threw herself into his arms. They spent an hour talking incessantly, with explanations and apologies punctuated by frequent embraces. Teresa hung back discreetly, drinking coffee at a nearby counter while she looked into the distance, thinking about her brother's terrible injuries.

Groups of families on holiday kept arriving. There were business travellers too, technicians on special assignments and local residents returning from holidays on the mainland or from visits to their families. Teresa, Isabel and Martin watched the new arrivals anxiously. Then, at last, came another surge of European passengers disembarking from their relatively short flight along with a few others who had transferred from long haul routes. Among them were Gabriel and Rachel, weary from their overnight flight from Washington. Gabriel pushed a heavily laden baggage trolley, while Rachel carried both their cabin bags.

As soon as she spotted them, Teresa took charge. She pushed forward and spoke directly to the new arrivals.

'You must excuse me for getting involved here, but there's one thing we have to sort out, even before the introductions. It's not acceptable that you two' – she indicated Gabriel and Martin – 'bear each other a grudge over that fight in Isabel's apartment. It's time to make up and be friends again. Come on, now.'

The two men looked sheepish for a moment, then grinned awkwardly and shook hands. Isabel hugged them both before breaking off to embrace Rachel. Then there were more hugs and introductions.

As the excited group exchanged more embraces, Teresa took control again.

'Just listen a moment. The important news for all of us, Gabriel, is that Vasco is still holding his own – but there's still no definite improvement either. Meanwhile we all hope and pray. For the rest of the things we want to talk about, we'll have all the time in the world. But right now we need to get beds and a tidy up for our visitors. There's an easy way to do this. First let's all go to my place. We'll get Margo round too.'

She checked her watch.

'She should be free now, as Miquel's sitting with my brother at Son Dureta for the next two and a half hours. We'll have a drink and Isabel can help me put together a big bowl of pasta – or something else simple. While that's going on, you can all have a shower and freshen up.'

'That's wonderful,' said Gabriel, 'but you said something abut beds. We really are dead tired. Do we have someplace to stay?'

'That won't be a problem. I've already thought of that. All of you can stay at C'an Valseca. It will give Antonia and Guillem something to do and they'll be delighted to look after you. And another thing: you just explained how you've got a plan for us all to take it in turns to sit with my brother at the hospital. Well, Martin and Rachel may not realise that Son Dureta is so close to the edge of the city, alongside the Via Cintura – that's the bypass that skirts the north side of Palma. And that means it's quite easy to get there from the *possessió*.'

Gabriel looked up and smiled at his aunt.

'That's brilliant, Teresa. And I should explain that my old buddy Joe Karlsen will be joining us within a day or two to help out with the bedside watch on Papa. He can stay with us too – there's plenty of room.'

'That's a wonderful idea, Gabriel! Now let's get away from here.' said Teresa, I'm afraid you won't all be able to get in my car, so why don't Isabel and Martin find a taxi, while I take Gabriel and Rachel. Come on, we'll all meet up at Cala Gamba.'

She turned and strode towards the door. The others followed close behind, still chattering away like excited schoolchildren.

Two days later Joe Karlsen flew in from London. He had arranged for some of his stuff to follow on, anticipating a long stay. Gabriel met him at the airport and they drove straight to C'an Valseca where Guillem helped him with his bags while Joe lovingly carried his handsome bag of golf clubs from the car.

Soon the new arrival had met the rest of the group who had been taking turns to keep watch at Vasco's bedside. They all got on well together and within a day or two a routine had been established, with some time off for relaxation – riding horses around the local countryside or walking in the woods with Glove and Mitten, the two friendly Labradors. Joe took the opportunity to play a lot of golf. Until the jet-lagged arrivals had recovered – and they waited for Joe Karlsen to join the team – Margo was needed to help out with the roster. However, she had left a problem behind in Guildford. Just a day before she left for Palma her house had developed a major structural problem. It was the result of subsidence and had to be dealt with as a matter of urgency. But there was no way Margo was going to leave Palma until she could be sure that Vasco was on the road to recovery. However, Teresa, Gabriel and Isabel convinced her that the worst was over and she could return home with a clear conscience. For the rest of the group there was a dawning realisation that their vigil might go on for a long time.

Shortly before Joe Karlsen arrived in Palma, Viktor Dankovitch was sitting in his palatial office. It was early in the day and he had just read an email that Kyril had brought to him – but he was furious with the messenger as well as the message.

'Is everybody useless? Why am I cursed with this useless bunch of no-hopers? Is it really so difficult to make a simple contact with an American? This stupid idiot, Foxtrot, has the nerve to tell me that the man he was supposed to negotiate with, Joe Karlsen, completely ignored his approach. But he did nothing by way of a follow-up. Now, to crown everything, Karlsen's just packed up and left London. And nobody knows where he's gone. That's just bloody marvellous!'

He smashed his fist on the desk. A silver-mounted photograph of St Petersburg's SKA ice hockey team fell over with a crash. Kyril winced.

'And as for you, you useless layabout, why haven't you started looking for Ygor Krasnov yet? Won't you do anything unless I tell you? Why are you still here? I want you and Sergei Bulgakov to be in Mallorca within thirty-six hours or I'll personally chuck you in the Neva. Do you understand me? I've had Sergei on standby since Saturday, hoping against hope that there would be some encouraging news. But the message from that English cretin is the last straw.'

He scowled at his son as he stabbed viciously at his desk blotter with a lethal-looking paper knife.

'And you know the worst thing? I've already paid that Italian crook Enrico Acappella an obscene amount of money.'

He was talking to himself now, gazing through the window towards the forest of cranes at the nearby docks.

'But I don't even know whether Ygor collected that program or not. I can hardly phone Acappella and ask the bastard. For sure that slimy spaghetti-eater would have set him some tricky task – and perhaps he failed it. Or perhaps he did make the collection but then took off on his own to try to find a buyer for himself. Ha! He'll be lucky! And he must know that I'd have him hunted down anywhere if he tried to double-cross Viktor Dankovitch.'

He swung round to the cupboard behind him and grabbed the vodka. He appeared to have forgotten all about Kyril as he took a quick swig from the bottle and wandered aimlessly round the room.

'No, he's got no chance,' he muttered. 'Even with my contacts I don't have a buyer at the moment. That reminds me. I must put out some more feelers – with the Chinese, or the Iranians perhaps. And where the hell is that disk anyway? Not knowing is driving me bloody mad and the only way to find out what's really happened is to get hold of that imbecile, Ygor.'

He banged the vodka bottle on the desk so hard that Kyril jumped. Surprised, his father whipped round.

'Why are you still hanging around, you blockhead? I want you on the next plane out of here. Get moving for God's sake! Take Sergei with you and don't you dare show your face again until you bring me Ygor Krasnov. And I want a daily report by email. When you've found the rat, drag him back here from wherever he's hiding. I'm looking forward to asking him some questions myself.'

His face contorted with barely suppressed rage.

'Yes, I'll really enjoy that. What are you waiting for? Get out of my sight right now or I'll kick you out myself!'

Kyril fled, pausing only to pick up a bundle of currency from Irena before collecting Sergei from the outer office. Within five minutes they were driving furiously towards St Petersburg's Pulkovo airport.

Chief Inspector Diaz arrived at his desk early. He was getting more impatient by the day. The forensic people had come up with nothing useful. Not yet, anyway. The burnt-out car had yielded no results at all. They had found some traces of oil and the faintest imprint of a motorcycle tyre at the crash scene, but these were inconclusive. The only potentially useful evidence came from fingerprints and some DNA in the suite at the Hotel Viña del Mar. But these were of no use because they couldn't be matched to any previous records on the central database. And the team of investigators had found nothing either. Nobody recognised the photofit picture of the mystery 'banker' and the grainy pictures from the surveillance cameras were no use either.

It was so frustrating. The bulletins from the hospital were the same every day. *'The patient's condition remains critical but stable.'* There was no knowing when, if ever, he would regain consciousness. Nobody could say when he might be able to respond to questions about the attack which so nearly killed him. The policeman stared gloomily at his in-tray. There were reports to be read covering crime statistics, travelling expenses, budgets for expenditure, public-awareness campaigns and many more mind-numbing topics. It was enough to make a man wish he'd gone into a different profession. He sighed with feeling, shook a Dunhill out of the pack, lit it and inhaled deeply. Only then did he feel able to drag one of the bulky folders from the top of the pile.

Irena heard the shouting through the thick door of Viktor Dankovitch's office. It was mid-afternoon and she had been about to take him a glass of black tea. But a few minutes ago she had put through a phone call from Enrico Acappella and they seemed to be having a furious row. Now the roars of rage had grown even louder. She realised that this was not a good moment to interrupt, left the tea on the end of her desk and went back to polishing her nails.

A few seconds later there was a crash from the inner office and the intercom on Irena's desk buzzed insistently. She smoothed her skirt, picked up the tea and opened the door. Viktor was sitting sideways, his face a livid mask. The wrecked telephone lay on the floor just below a ruined picture of Venice, a present from Enrico Acappella, which had been the target for his wrath.

'Come in and sit down, girl,' he growled. 'There's nobody else in the building I can talk to. Misha's gone to Kiev, Pyotr is dealing with a problem in Murmansk and you're the only one I can tell about this bloody mess.'

Irena sat across the desk from her boss as he reached into his cupboard for the vodka, poured a generous slug into his steaming tea and another shot into a tumbler for his glamorous PA. She clinked her glass against his and sipped daintily. He took a noisy gulp and turned to face her. With his fists clenched, shoulders slumped and staring out of the window towards the river, Viktor didn't look so big and powerful any more.

He had a miserable story to tell. Enrico Acappella had phoned to ask if the Navegator software had demonstrated the results he had promised. And if it was OK, then just how soon could he have the balance of two million dollars? At that point Viktor had become emotional, asking what sort of trick the Italian was playing, because he had not seen any software at all. Acappella reacted angrily; Viktor's representative had duly taken delivery last Wednesday morning exactly as planned. During further angry exchanges, Enrico had explained the 'shopping list' task. Viktor denounced this as bloody stupid. The Italian retaliated by asking why he objected, when Viktor's man had completed the assignment successfully. After that, Viktor had rather lost track of the shouted accusations of bad faith – treachery, even. The call ended after the Russian roared that all Italians were pimps and homosexuals. Enrico screamed that his former partner was a cheat and a liar. This was the moment when the Russian had finally snapped and thrown the telephone at the Venetian picture on the wall.

'Don't you worry about that horrible Italian, dear Vitya,' purred Irena, as she slipped around the desk and settled herself comfortably on her Viktor's lap. 'Your little Ira will soon make all your troubles go away.'

As she started to loosen his collar he closed his eyes and started to relax. There would be time enough later to worry about that total catastrophe in Mallorca. For now, though, it seemed better to enjoy the ministrations of Irena's beautifully manicured fingers.

Aboard his ketch *Angelina*, Enrico Acappella was still white with fury. He was swearing under his breath, muttering a string of the foul curses he used to use during his gangland days in the docks at Genoa. He poured a violent torrent of abuse on Viktor Dankovitch, his parents and all Russians as he beat his fists on the desk with impotent rage. Paulo had handed over the Navegator disk to Viktor's man, but now that bastard in St Petersburg wouldn't pay the balance of two million dollars. It was an insult, not to be tolerated. There should be revenge. As he struggled to think of a way to get even, the phone rang. It was Paulo, phoning from Palma in a jaunty mood.

He was bubbling with excitement as he told his speech-less brother that he had already spent most of his share of the first payment for the Navegator software. Those gorgeous Queen Isabella stamps were now a part of his collection and he was over the moon. It was a beautiful morning in Mallorca and he felt like going out on the Ducati. What a wonderful machine that was, but the new model was even better and he felt like trading up – so when were the rest of the funds coming through?

Enrico cut across his brother's happy monologue and told him angrily that the Russian was saying that his man had not returned with the program. So, Viktor Dankovitch was refusing to pay up. Hearing the news, Paulo was just as furious as his brother. He had done absolutely everything and carried out every detail of the assignment exactly as Enrico had planned it. If there was a problem, it was certainly not his fault. He was entitled to his share of the second payment and he wanted it now. There were some bitter words, but eventually Enrico promised to pay Paulo his full share of the money, no matter what the outcome was. But first he wanted to hear every detail of the handover at Andratx. He listened carefully to Paulo's account.

Viktor's man had entered the Café Nacional at precisely eleven o'clock on the Wednesday morning. He was carrying a large carrier bag, sat alone at a table and ordered coffee and a glass of mineral water. When he went out of the back of the café into the disused movie theatre to use the toilet, Paulo had checked the contents of the carrier bag. Every-thing in it was an exact match for every item on Enrico's shopping list. There were a few more purchases as well. At the same time he had switched the disks, so that the Tomeu Penya case now contained the Navegator software. Then he had taken the bag through to the old cinema behind the bar, handed it over to Viktor's man and let him out through the side door into the alleyway.

'Did he say anything at all when you gave him the bag?' asked Enrico.

'No. I just told him the money was OK and everything was there. What else should I have done?'

'Nothing, nothing ... mm ... what did this man look like?'

'Fairly tall, fair, slim build and about thirty-five years old. You didn't give me any description. The shopping list was supposed to be enough, wasn't it?'

'Yes, yes,' said Enrico, grinding his teeth with suppressed rage. 'It's sure to be OK in the end – and I've already agreed that you'll be getting your full share anyway, so you have nothing more to worry about.'

'That's fine with me. I'm going to pay a visit to the Ducati dealer later. He might even buy me lunch.'

Paulo was warm and friendly as he ended the call. Enrico forced himself to be pleasant in return, but it was a super-human effort. Every instinct told him that something had gone wrong. It was just not possible that there could have been a flaw in his meticulous plan. He pounded his fore-head with his fist. It was crystal clear: that devious bastard Viktor Dankovitch had made a fool of him. This was not to be tolerated. One day soon he would find a way to get his revenge for the deadly insult. Meanwhile he just had to relax somehow. Wearily, he called for Bruno to bring him strong coffee and a bottle of his favourite grappa. Then he switched on the HiFi system, selected the Callas CD of *Traviata*, leaned back in the luxurious leather swivel chair and closed his eyes.

18

Two weeks or so after he had been attacked, Vasco's team of sitters had settled into a rota. Margo had returned to Guildford, so the major burden of keeping watch at his bedside was now the responsibility of the 'professionals', Gabriel, Rachel and Joe Karlsen. Martin, Miquel and Teresa did their share too – and there was always a police officer waiting in the corridor outside. When off duty they all enjoyed the tranquillity of the *possessió*. If the weather was not so good they read or played cards. On sunny days they went riding or walked the dogs. Once or twice Joe managed to persuade Martin to come along for a game of golf.

One or two cameramen and reporters had stationed themselves at the gates of C'an Valseca. It was a great relief when they finally gave up their surveillance about a week after the story first broke. They contented themselves with occasional approaches to Chief Inspector Diaz, but eventually that scent would also go cold. Meanwhile Antonia and Guillem kept the place running like clockwork and they made no secret of their pleasure at having the old house full of voices and activity.

Then, one day in the middle of the morning, Gabriel was visiting Son Dureta. He had just taken over from Joe Karlsen and was settling down beside his father's bed with a fresh cup of coffee and a motoring magazine when he heard a small sound. He looked across to see that Vasco's eyes were half open and he was struggling to speak. A nurse came hurrying in only a few seconds after Gabriel had pressed the call button. She took one look at her patient, then shooed Gabriel out of the room and summoned a colleague. Sitting next to the waiting policeman, Gabriel tried to make sense of what was going on as members of the medical team came and went. At last Fernando Vargas, the doctor who had originally examined Vasco, appeared and introduced himself.

'I'm pleased to tell you that your father's condition has begun to show a marked improvement. He is slipping in and out of consciousness and he may be able to talk within a day or two if the progress continues, but he requires much more rest and any form of excitement is to be avoided. I must therefore insist that your visits remain as calm as possible. Do not, on any account attempt to ask him questions – or answer any, if he should ask. His neurological condition remains extremely fragile and I must insist that you respect these conditions.'

He turned to the police officer.

'And please ask Chief Inspector Diaz not to attempt any interrogation until I give approval. Is that understood?'

The policeman nodded agreement as Gabriel stammered a reply.

'Yes, yes, of course. Thank you, Doctor Vargas. It's good to know that he may have turned the corner. We'll all make sure that he is not excited in any way.'

When Gabriel returned to the C'an Valseca there was relief, laughter and a small celebration after he brought the news. In his office, Chief Inspector Diaz was delighted when Ferrer told him about the call from their man at Son Dureta. Within a day or two he would be able to get away from this damned paperwork and have a chance to talk to the victim of this attempted homicide. That would be much more to his taste. He lit another Dunhill to celebrate before opening yet another of those bloody folders – but now it was with a lighter heart.

The days became weeks, with little further improvement in Vasco's condition. Then, on the morning of Good Friday, the ninth of April, Chief Inspector Diaz took the long-awaited phone call from Doctor Vargas. As arranged, he presented himself at Son Dureta at ten o'clock. Naturally, he was impatient to interview Vasco Valseca, but first had to submit to a briefing by the doctor.

'The patient is still very weak. His wounds, both physical and mental, will take a long time to heal. He has serious neurological damage too. Of course, I understand that you have a job to do, Chief Inspector, but I beg you to go carefully and try not to tire him too much. On this first visit you should spend no more than two or three minutes questioning him.'

'Yes, of course. I do understand. I'll be very gentle, I assure you – and my thanks to you and your team for their efforts.'

They shook hands and the policeman came to Vasco's bedside where Teresa had been keeping watch. She had been soothing him with memories and old stories from their childhood, calling for little or no response from her injured brother. She submitted without protest when Diaz asked her to leave while he carried out his interrogation. He sat at Vasco's bedside and leaned forward, speaking quietly, as if to a sick child.

'Professor Valseca, permit me to introduce myself. I am Chief Inspector Diaz and I need to ask you a few questions. We are making great efforts to find the man who carried out this terrible attack on you. Can you tell us anything at all about him?'

Vasco's voice was hoarse and hesitant.

'I'm sorry Chief Inspector, but I can remember very little.

302

It was at night and I was feeling very happy.' He paused and closed his eyes for a moment. 'But I don't know why I was happy. Perhaps there was a reason. Then I remember being in a big hotel, in the foyer. And I met a man there, a stranger. He seemed very pleasant.' He frowned and winced with pain. 'Sorry, I can't remember much about him. But he seemed quite big and powerful. I don't remember what we talked about or anything else. I'm sorry Chief Inspector.'

He closed his eyes. The policeman leaned a little closer.

'Does the word "Navegator" mean anything to you, Professor Valseca?'

There was a long pause. Vasco opened his eyes and looked puzzled. He replied weakly:

'I had an ancestor, Gabriel Valseca, who was a navigator. Is that what you mean?'

He closed his eyes and appeared to drift into semi-consciousness again. Diaz stood up and was about to leave as a nurse hurried in.

'Your time is up, Chief Inspector. Doctor Vargas asked me to remind you that the patient is still very weak.'

'It's all right nurse, thank you, I was just leaving. It's a pity Professor Valseca seems to remember nothing about the attempt on his life. I'll just have to wait until he's stronger before trying to question him again.'

He nodded goodbye before walking out and along the corridor, shaking his head with disappointment. Perhaps he would have more success next time.

By the time evening came, the team of 'sitters' had gathered at Ca'n Valseca. The only one missing was Joe. He was due to stay with Vasco until midnight, when it would be Miquel's turn. They were all delighted with the big improvement in Vasco's condition. Everyone was feeling more cheerful and they were nibbling olives and salted almonds along with drinks before their evening meal.

Gabriel had just returned from the study after emailing his report to Lynne Kowalski. He wondered how she would react to the news that his father had just regained consciousness. He didn't have long to wait. He was sitting on the arm of Rachel's chair and had just taken a sip of wine when the phone rang. They all looked at each other.

Teresa reacted anxiously.

'Do you think that could be bad news from the hospital?'

'No,' said Gabriel, 'don't worry. It won't be anything like that. I'll bet it's Lynne calling from Washington. She'll want to know more, now she's seen my email. I'll take it in the study.'

He left the room as the others relaxed and returned to their conversations. Gabriel returned in less than five minutes looking flushed but confident. He smiled as he returned to his perch on the arm of Rachel's chair.

'There's bad news and good news. The bad news is that Lynne's putting pressure on me to get information about Navegator out of Vasco "by any means". She doesn't care that he's only just come out of a coma. The good news is that Washington is more desperate than ever to get a system which locates computer terrorists. It seems there have been a few more very bad incidents. So they really do want the Navegator software – and they want it yesterday. Anyway, the upshot is that we are to continue our watching and protection role indefinitely. That means they're giving us all the time we need to help my father get his memory back.'

Rachel looked up at Gabriel and smiled.

'That's wonderful news, darling! This Easter weekend we'll give special thanks for your father's improvement. And I think we should be grateful that we can all be together a while longer – even though it's the result of this terrible thing that's happened to him. I'm so looking forward to getting to know him properly when he's feeling stronger.'

Miquel was just going to speak when Antonia came into

the room and announced that the evening meal was ready. It took a few moments for the six of them to gather up their glasses. Then, still smiling at Gabriel's news, they continued their conversations as they headed for the dining room.

Kyril Dankovitch hoped that his father's anger would be calmed by the news that Ygor Krasnov had been found. He had sent Viktor an email, but not waited for a reply. Now, he and Sergei were delivering their victim to Viktor's dacha near St Petersburg for punishment.

Kyril had tracked Ygor down by hacking into the airlines' computer systems. It hadn't taken long to discover that their man had travelled with Aeroflot to Frankfurt, then with Air Berlin to Palma. He had also flown back to Frankfurt with Air Berlin. After that – no trace. So, assuming that their man was still in Frankfurt, they had bought a second-hand Mercedes and driven there from Moscow. It took almost two weeks to find him, but they got lucky. The obvious area for a fugitive to hide out was the red-light district across from the main railway station. They spent many hours every day and night trawling the area. Then, late one night in the streets between Elbestrasse and Moselstrasse they spotted him. Ygor seemed to be working as a bouncer at a strip club, so they sat at a window table in a bar across the street. From that vantage point they could keep watch on him unobserved.

At five in the morning, Ygor finished work, but he didn't get far. He almost collapsed with shock when Sergei and Kyril fell into step on each side of him. He was so traumatised that he put up only token resistance when they handcuffed him. Then he was frogmarched two blocks to the Mercedes, bundled aboard and driven away. They made a brief stop to pay the bill at their seedy hotel and pick up their bags. Then they frisked their captive and found that he was carrying his passport. That meant he could 'disappear' from his job and they could leave immediately. Soon they were driving out of the city towards Berlin. Their plan was simple. Avoid people; keep Ygor sedated most of the time, especially when crossing borders; be sure to make those border crossings in the small hours, when a comatose passenger would arouse no suspicion from sleepy frontier guards.

It took time and patience, but there was no hurry. When Ygor was conscious Kyril questioned him in detail. They left the motorway several kilometres before the Polish border and found a motel. Ygor was escorted to the bathroom, then shackled to a bed. He whimpered with terror until Sergei slapped him hard and told him to shut up and answer some questions. At first he would say nothing, but after a serious beating he finally broke down. He admitted that he had changed the travel plans to suit himself, so that he was late for the rendezvous at the small town near to Palma. But that didn't stop him complaining about the complicated task he had been set. Sergei sneered and hit him across the face with the edge of his hand. Ygor collapsed face down on his bed and blubbered into the pillow.

After watching television for a while Kyril went out and returned with coffee, beer and some takeaway food. They ate in silence, then drifted into an uneasy sleep. About two hours after midnight they left and crossed into Poland without a problem. They followed the same routine, travelling during the 'graveyard hours' across national boundaries into Belarus, Lithuania, Latvia and, finally, the Russian Federation. At last, more than eight hours after leaving Latvia, they pulled up outside Viktor's dacha south of Volkhov.

A few hours earlier their boss had risen early and driven the BMW out of St Petersburg to meet them. After breakfast at a roadside café busy with truck drivers he had pressed on to the dacha and arrived well before the others. Soon he had got the wood-burning stove pumping out some welcome warmth. He had just made tea when he heard the Mercedes approaching and was waiting outside when Kyril and Sergei arrived. It was not yet mid-morning and the slanting sunlight shone on the ice cold waters of the lake in front of the house. A rowing boat moored to the jetty bobbed in a light breeze. They dragged Ygor from the car and through the house into a freezing lean-to at the back of the dacha where his left leg was secured to an iron bed with a length of chain. They left him shivering with cold and terror while Viktor took them into the front room. There, sitting beside the stove sipping from glasses of tea laced with vodka, they told him about their hunt and its successful outcome.

'It's all been a very bad business,' complained Viktor, 'but I suppose you two have done your job OK. So, that idiot Ygor was late for the rendezvous, eh? Well, I'll deal with that piece of garbage later. Oh yes, he'll really pay for his mistake. We can't treat ourselves to a celebration, but we have to eat, so let's go to Volkhov. We can have lunch at the Hotel Zvanka. Afterwards I'll book a room there so that you two can relax after your long journey. While you're resting, I'll come back here to punish Ygor for his failure. Come on, I'm feeling quite generous. I'll drive the BMW and talk to Kyril on the way. Sergei, you take the Merc.'

He strode out of the house. The other two walked behind, Kyril joining his father in the BMW with Sergei following them in the Mercedes. Ygor Krasnov heard the cars drive off and shuddered. He was chilled to the bone and whimpered aloud as he buried his tear-stained face in the filthy mattress.

Some hours later Kyril and Sergei dragged a tin trunk along the jetty. With a final heave they manhandled it over the end and into the water with a loud splash. The force of

307

the wave rocked the rowing boat violently so that it banged against its wooden mooring piles. Then they went back into the house to tell Kyril's father that Ygor was now with the fishes along with a heavy load of stones to keep him in his place. Viktor was sitting moodily by the stove clutching a glass and a bottle of vodka. He had been disappointed; no chance to work out his frustrations on the helpless victim. What did he find when he got back to the dacha? That slippery bastard had cheated him again; Ygor had managed to drag the bed across the room and then use his own belt to hang himself from a roof truss. He belched loudly, threw his empty glass against the stove and got to his feet, swaying slightly.

'So that's it then. Ygor didn't make the collection and we have absolutely no idea who's got the Navegator software now. And those pasta-munching crooks say they haven't a clue either. So, I guess we'll never know what really happened.'

He sighed deeply.

'It's not really about the money. It's just that all of the fun has gone out of these battles of wits. I'm fed up with those Italian bastards. I won't be dealing with them again – ever. Except for some very creative revenge. And one day I will have that revenge – I swear it on my mother's grave.'

His face contorted with suppressed fury. After a few moments, he relaxed a little.

'I'm fed up with this bloody place, too. Sergei, get the BMW ready and drive me back to St Petersburg. Kyril, bring the Merc this time, will you? Let's go and find some women. I need cheering up.'

19

Vasco made amazing progress, once he had regained consciousness. He chafed at his enforced inactivity in Son Dureta and was soon badgering the medical team to get him mobile. After several confrontations with the cautious Dr Vargas he was finally allowed to start a strictly monitored regime of exercise and physiotherapy.

Despite a superhuman effort, Vasco failed to meet his objective to secure his release from hospital before the twins' birthday on 15 June – and the dedicated team at the *possessió* felt just as disappointed as he did. So, to give the day some significance, they all eagerly agreed to Gabriel and Isabel's suggestion that they should visit the regular Tuesday market at Santa Margalida. Rachel turned to Gabriel.

'Margo should be here today for your birthday,' she said. 'It's a pity she can't come with us to the market which shares her name.'

The outing was a great success, with some craft shopping in the market followed by a memorable birthday lunch, with succulent food from the charcoal grill in the cloistered ambiance of the Es Convent restaurant at Santa Maria. Afterwards, they were well on their way back to Palma, where they went to Son Dureta and gathered around Vasco – now allowed out of bed for an hour or two – for birthday tea with Teresa, his current 'sitter'. Miquel had also turned up and they invited the police officer on duty to join them for a slice of the twins' birthday cake.

Finally, on Tuesday 22 June, exactly thirteen weeks after he was attacked, Vasco was allowed to leave Son Dureta in the afternoon, after Doctor Vargas had pronounced satisfaction with his progress. He would be allowed to go home, but it would take weeks of convalescence, physiotherapy and supervised exercise to restore him to health.

They had shaken hands, then Teresa and Miquel helped him to the car. Vasco had needed to use a walking frame to get to the Volvo, but his determination was obvious. They talked and pointed out the local landmarks as Teresa drove. When she finally turned into the driveway to C'an Valseca, Vasco smiled as he looked across the sunlit pasture towards the house. When the car pulled up at the door, everyone came out to greet him and the Labradors joined in the happy homecoming. There were hugs and a few tears as they helped him up the steps into his home. Antonia and Guillem had prepared a special welcome for the Senyor's return. There were flowers everywhere and coffee was served on the terrace along with Vasco's favourite, Antonia's special cake made with honey and almonds.

After a while, they all relaxed and started to play cards, but Vasco said he would like to see the mail which had built up during his time in hospital. Gabriel helped Vasco to his study and volunteered to help him sort it out. There was the usual mess of unsolicited junk, plus bills, invitations, thank-you letters from delegates to the symposium and bulky packets from the university. Finally, in the smallest pile, there were personal letters with handwritten envelopes. Vasco forced himself to open one or two of those; news from an old friend in Canada; a request from a former colleague to make a speech at a dinner; a letter of congratulation from a fellow panellist who had shared the platform with Vasco at the Royal Society. He tossed them aside and turned to Gabriel.

'Biel, my dear boy. I really can't deal with any of this just now. It's not so much that I'm physically tired, more that there seems to be a gap in my brain. You've all been telling me about this Navegator program and that policeman has been asking me questions too. But I can't recall a thing. After the dinner at Samantha's I remember nothing at all about the attack on me. It's all a complete blank – apart from a very vague impression of the man I met. I certainly wouldn't recognise him. So, Chief Inspector Diaz seems to have scaled down the investigation. His forensic people don't seem to have got anywhere. And without any witness statements – from me or anyone else – he and his people can't really do any more.'

He sighed and went on.

'As for the program I'm supposed to have written, that means nothing to me either. You all say that I developed it all by myself and that its performance is amazing. The Americans, your people, will pay a fortune to get their hands on it. Well, that's a very handsome offer. I really would like to help and, if I ever do get my memory back, I'm ready to negotiate. The problem is that I remember absolutely nothing about it. All of my IT knowledge seems to have completely evaporated. All of it. It's totally unbelievable I know, but I couldn't even write the simplest program if I tried.'

'Look, Papa, nobody's trying to force you to remember anything. There's no pressure. We just want to be around if and when you do get your memory back. And we also want to be sure that the bad guys, if they're still interested, don't get a chance to grab you. Thank God you can be kept safe here! We'll all make sure of that. Now let's get back to the others.'

Gabriel stood up and gently helped his father to his feet.

Together, arm in arm, they made their way out of the study, one painful step at a time.

During the weeks that followed Vasco's return from hospital the days flew by in an agreeable routine. Miquel decided to give up his pipe for good. The devoted team of minders talked to Vasco constantly. He kept in touch with the outside world by email and telephone. Fortunately, he was able to carry out a lot of his university duties this way and his own pupils travelled to tutorials at C'an Valseca. Some had their own transport, but Teresa and Miquel also helped out, providing a taxi service whenever it was needed.

Meanwhile, Lynne Kowalski was growing impatient. Her emails showed her exasperation with the lack of any improvement in Vasco's recall of the Navegator program. She insisted that because they no longer needed to watch over him in hospital, the team of 'sitters' could be reduced in number. Joe Karlsen was ordered back to Washington immediately for reassignment. There was a rather sombre farewell meal around the big dining table in the old house. Then, next morning, Joe said his farewells including a big bear hug for Gabriel, his old roommate. They all felt a little flat as his large frame, rugged personality and precious golf clubs disappeared down the driveway.

The doctors were pleased with Vasco's convalescence, which had gone miraculously well. Thanks to his physique, discipline and long dedication to the outdoor life, his body healed remarkably quickly. Within a very short time after leaving Son Dureta, he was able to walk with only the aid of a walking stick, though his leg was still in splints. His head bandages had come off too, and his hair was starting to grow again. His broken ribs and collarbone had also mended well, so that he no longer needed a sling. Determination, fitness and a disciplined physiotherapy regime had worked wonders. That, coupled with a gradual increase in his daily exercise schedule was accelerating his recovery.

Mentally, though, Vasco was still in limbo. Every day he had two sessions of at least half an hour with one or other of his support team. Each in their own way encouraged him to reach back into his memory for the keys to his knowledge of computer science. But nothing at all seemed to be able to penetrate that veil, so that his knowledge of Navegator remained buried as deeply as ever. Neurological specialists were unable to explain it – especially as his capability in pure mathematics was quickly restored completely. His skills in the field of astronomical science were also recovering fast. Gabriel sent his weekly reports of 'no progress' back to Lynne Kowalski, but despite her impatience she still seemed to be prepared to wait indefinitely for a positive result.

Meanwhile, they had been on the lookout for possible intruders. There had been an alarm at dusk one evening when Guillem saw four men in dark clothes and carrying guns enter the driveway on foot. He took his own rifle and alerted Gabriel, who brought his CIA-issue Glock automatic. Martin came, too, with Vasco's Purdy shotgun. They shadowed the trespassers for several minutes as they made a detour around the house. Eventually there was a confrontation near some outbuildings followed by a tense stand-off. During a few angry exchanges in rapid Mallorquin, Guillem discovered that they were poachers, tracking game across the *possessió*. There were a few tricky moments when it seemed that there might be trouble, but in the end there was no incident. At last the intruders melted away into the gathering darkness.

Once a week Chief Inspector Diaz called at C'an Valseca for a cup of coffee and a chat. He always hoped to draw out some memory, no matter how trivial, which would give him a hint about Vasco's attacker. At each visit he was forced to admit complete frustration that Vasco could still remember nothing significant about the events that followed the dinner at Samantha's. The police experts had concluded that the

psychological trauma of the attack had shut out all mem-ories
– including any knowledge of the inner workings of the Navegator program. Meanwhile his forensic team had still failed
to link their findings to any suspect at all. There was plenty of
material to examine – but it couldn't be connected to any
individual, let alone known criminals. Even Interpol could
give no help. Towards the middle of July he finally admitted
that he could do nothing more unless Vasco could recall
something significant. Reluctantly, he would have to wind
down the investigation 'for the time being'. The policeman
shook hands with Vasco, said goodbye to the rest of the team
and drove off in a cloud of dust.

It was on the third Sunday in July that Gabriel, Rachel,
Martin and Isabel ambushed Vasco in his study after lunch.
They walked in quickly and shut the door behind them. He
was sitting in a comfortable chair near the window and
looked up from a book as he registered polite surprise.

'What's this then – a delegation come to complain about
the food?'

'I think you know better than that,' said Martin, smiling
as he laid a hand on Vasco's shoulder. 'We're all here to say
how pleased we are that you're making such a remarkable
recovery. But there is something else. You see, the four of us
have come to make a formal request. Will you please host
our double wedding here in Mallorca in September? Surely,
the idea can't be coming to you as a complete surprise.
Please say that you'll agree. It would mean so much to
Isabel and Gabriel – and to Rachel and me, of course.'

There was a long pause. Vasco laid down the book on the
table beside his chair and smiled.

'Well, well, well … No, I can't say I'm surprised. My love
and blessings to all of you.'

He levered himself out of the chair and embraced all of
them in turn.

'Yes, it's marvellous news. I'm absolutely delighted. And I

always need a project to get my teeth into. Organising this wonderful occasion will be great therapy for me. It's going to be my privilege – and fun – to make all the arrangements. It will be one form of therapy that I'll really enjoy. Now, let's go and tell the others.'

Weeks of frantic preparation for the big day followed the meeting in Vasco's study. First, there had been an all too brief visit by Rachel's parents, Dexter and Miriam Jefferson. They had been able to carry out their intention to visit their daughter while on a Mediterranean cruise. The ship was only staying in Palma for one night, but Rachel found time to take Gabriel to meet them at the port. After some warm and emotional introductions he was able to persuade them to come to the *possessió*. He phoned ahead to ask the rest of the group to be around to meet the Jeffersons for lunch. Antonia was delighted to hear the news and hurried to the kitchen to get busy with her preparations. The meal was a great success and afterwards Miriam made a beeline for the kitchen, accompanied by Rachel. She wanted to have some of Antonia's Mallorcan cookery secrets, so Isabel came along to act as interpreter. There was a lot of laughter and the women traded recipes, with Antonia promising to try Miriam's personal formula for Key Lime Pie.

Meanwhile Dexter and Gabriel were finding a common interest in the history of the American Civil War. Vasco was fascinated to hear them having a good natured argument about the tactics of the Confederate and Union generals.

All too soon it was time for the Jeffersons to return to their ship. Rachel and Gabriel drove them back to Palma after they had promised to return for the wedding. And the date was agreed too. They planned to hold the double celebration on Saturday, 18 September.

Martin moved swiftly into action; he had no family in Europe, but he had already warned his brother Harry in Hong Kong and also his parents, who were now living in New Zealand, close to Auckland. His father was too fragile to travel, but his mother was determined to come to Palma for the wedding. She planned a relatively short flight to join Harry and his wife Elaine so that she could have them with her on the long haul from Hong Kong to Palma via London's Heathrow.

When Gabriel's weekly 'no change' report added that he and Rachel were to be married on the first Saturday in September alongside Martin and Isabel, there was a rapid response from Langley. The phone rang within a few minutes. Gabriel took the call in the study while Vasco was out enjoying his afternoon walk with Glove and Mitten. Rachel followed Gabriel into the den and perched on the edge of the desk while he took the call. Lynne Kowalski was in a rage. She shouted furiously at Gabriel, so that he had to hold the phone well away from his ear.

'See here, Gabriel. This is absolutely impossible. The team looking after Vasco is just six people, now that Karlsen's been given an assignment in Lebanon. Only four of you are real professionals and if you all go and get yourselves married, I guess you'll be wanting a honeymoon. For two weeks, I guess. So that means that the team's down to two people – and they're both amateurs. What the hell am I supposed to do, just sit here on my ass and let you lovebirds go off and have fun? If it wasn't for the pressure from the Oval Office I'd be really angry – and that's not a pretty sight.'

Gabriel started to defend himself, but she cut him short – but in a softer tone.

'Look here, Romeo, you're in luck. I've just had an idea and it might possibly get you off the hook. I came into this thing in March and your wedding day's in September. That's six months give or take. So it's now within my authority to make an on-the-spot assessment myself. It's high time I met your father. He's an important asset and I should personally weigh up his potential. And I'm due some vacation too, so I guess I could add a day or two on to my stay. Then I could beef up Vasco's support team – for part of your honeymoon anyway.'

'That's wonderful, Lynne! You could come to the wedding too.'

'Dear God, Gabriel, I thought you'd never ask! Just give me the dates again. Do it officially and I'll come back to you with a formal acceptance and some travel plans.'

Gabriel started to reply, but Lynne had already ended the call. He turned to Rachel with a huge smile on his face.

'You'll never guess, my darling, but Lynne Kowalski's coming to the wedding too.'

They embraced for a moment, but Gabriel tore himself away.

'We can celebrate later, sweetheart, but right now I think we should go and tell the others.'

There was a lot of laughter when Gabriel told Martin and Isabel the news.

'That's absolutely wonderful, Biel. Wait till I tell Papa – he'll be delighted too. And she can have Joe Karlsen's old room, so accommodation won't be a problem.'

'That's a great idea, darling,' said Martin. 'I can hardly wait for Vasco. He'll be amazed when he gets back from his walk. He certainly thrives on problems and I want to see how he deals with the tricky protocol issues surrounding Lynne. She's Gabriel and Rachel's boss and also Vasco's chief interrogator. That's going to be an interesting challenge when it comes to placing her on the seating plan.'

The days passed. Vasco was sparing no expense to make this wedding an outstanding occasion. For weeks now, he had thought of little else. While maintaining his exercise regime and the routine sessions to try to unlock his memory, he had spent hours planning every last detail.

Printed invitations on gold-edged ivory board had been sent far and wide. The church of Santa Creu in Palma's old town had been reserved for a three o'clock ceremony. The Order of Service for a double wedding had to be discussed with the church authorities – and more printing arranged after everything had been agreed. The reception venue was booked; caterers were found, the numbers and the menu agreed; with the enthusiastic help of Miquel, wines were chosen and ordered; transport was organised in a fleet of identical Mercedes, plus two white Rolls-Royce limousines; accommodation was booked for the many guests due to arrive by air.

Gabriel and Isobel had been amazed by their father's daily improvement in energy. Nothing seemed to escape his razor-sharp mind as he juggled correspondence, emails and lengthy phone conversations. Antonia went round shaking her head, worried that the Senyor would burn himself out before the big day. For Vasco, though, it was like a new lease of life and he relished the new challenges which continually cropped up. But unknown to the rest of the group, he had begun to get occasional stabs of pain in his right temple. He had been completely free of symptoms when he left hospital, so told himself that there was nothing to worry about. All the same, he promised himself he would see Doctor Vargas after the wedding was over. Meanwhile he took painkillers and said nothing to anyone as he got on with the arrangements. During the final days an unnatural calm descended. As he poured out drinks before dinner, just three days before the wedding, he turned to the group and beamed at them all.

'Well, this wonderful happening has been the best imaginable therapy for me. Thank you all for making it possible. I actually feel better than I've done for years. If it wasn't for this bloody limp, I'd be absolutely one hundred per cent now. I'm just so sorry that I haven't been able to help out with Navegator.' He looked pensive for a moment. 'But recently there has been a fleeting moment – it's happened twice now – when I almost got a feel for what I'd been doing before I was attacked. It was something like the dream you can't quite recall, but there's a ghostly memory you can't focus on. It goes poof! Just like that – and then it's gone.'

He rubbed his temple with his free hand.

'That's quite enough for now. Let's go through and eat. Lynne Kowalski arrives tomorrow. If what Gabriel and Rachel tell me is only half true she'll be worrying at me like a terrier, trying to wake up my little grey cells.'

He threw back his head and laughed before signalling to Gabriel to lead them in to dinner.

Just after eleven o'clock next morning Vasco was called by Gabriel who confirmed that he had just met Lynne from her incoming flight. She had slept well and was looking forward to meeting Vasco.

'Fine,' he said, 'I'll get Guillem to put out the red carpet. It's going to be quite an experience meeting this lady.' He ended the call, muttering to himself, 'I just hope she won't make too many waves.'

It wasn't long before she arrived, jumped out of the Volvo and trotted up the steps to the front door. Guillem hurried to bring her case and a smart suit bag from the back of the car. By that time she was already into the house as Gabriel and Rachel got ready to make the introductions. But Lynne was not waiting for any of that. She strode forward to Vasco with her hand outstretched.

'You must be Professor Valseca. I'm Lynne Kowalski and it's a great pleasure to meet you at last. Thank you so much for letting me stay here in your beautiful home. And I'm simply amazed by your remarkable recovery from your terrible injuries. But I see you've had a great team to look after you here.'

Vasco took her hand in both of his.

'Perhaps I should be thanking you. After all, you've made it possible for me to spend a lot of time with Gabriel and Isabel these last weeks. And that's not happened for years. Now, let me introduce you to the others and then perhaps you'd like to see your room and freshen up after your long flight.'

There was a brief round of handshakes and greetings before Lynne followed Antonia and Guillem to her room. A few minutes later she reappeared wearing a simple cotton print dress in grey and peacock blue. It was caught at the waist by a leather belt with an enormous buckle; a slim golden purse matched her open toed sandals. She beamed at Vasco.

'The view from my room is so beautiful – across the woods to the mountains. I can understand why Gabriel loves this place so much. No wonder he's always talking about it. And as for you, Vasco, you seem to be fighting fit now. So, whatever it is you're on, can you please get some for me?'

She broke off with a laugh and turned to Isabel.

'I can see now that you two are quite a team. Having a twin must be something very special. Sadly for me, I was an only child, but that's another story.'

At that moment Antonia came in to announce that drinks would be served on the terrace before lunch and they all filed out into the sunshine. Clutching a glass of cava, Lynne worked the group like a seasoned partygoer, spending time chatting for a while with every one of them.

A few hours later, after a siesta, Lynne cornered Vasco and asked for a little time to review his recall of the Navegator program. She was apologetic but firm, explaining gently that she had a job to do. Vasco frowned a little – he had intended to make adjustments to the seating plan for the wedding reception – but agreed to have a one-to-one discussion in his study. An hour later they emerged with disappointment showing plainly on Lynne's face, while Vasco looked strained. Nobody noticed how his face twitched as he made for the stairs. A few moments later he was rubbing his right temple in the bathroom and searching for his pain relief tablets. Then he went to lie on his bed for a while. With luck nobody would notice his absence and he would be ready to face them all again in an hour or so.

20

The morning was warm and sunny. Frantic preparations were in progress for Palma's wedding of the year. Florists had toiled for hours to fill the magnificent church of Santa Creu with banks of lilies, sweet scented stocks and freesias. At C'an Valseca, hairdressers had been brought in for Isabella and Rachel. Bouquets of white and apricot roses arrived for the brides and bridesmaids; more boxes held corsages for the matrons of honour. Buttonholes for the bridegrooms, for each best man, for the two fathers of the brides and for the six ushers were to be delivered directly to the church. A light lunch was brought to Isabel and Rachel on trays, but they were so excited that they could hardly eat anything, despite stern looks from Antonia. Afterwards, the girls were helped into their dresses, created by Teresa's friend Ursula, Palma's top couturier. Isabel had chosen ivory silk brocade, while Rachel was encased in a confection of palest lavender chiffon. As buttons were being fastened and a needle and thread used to adjust a minor fitting problem, a make-up specialist put finishing touches to two radiant faces.

Meanwhile, Teresa and Margo, the two matrons of honour, resplendent in matching peach silk damask, were fussing over the bridesmaids. Rachel had chosen two of her cousins, Emily and Cecile, sisters aged ten and seven. Their mother, Rachel's aunt, Candice Mason, had flown in with them from Seattle along with her husband Howard, a senior designer at Boeing Aircraft. She tried to calm the excited girls as Teresa helped them with their dresses – fluffy clouds of lavender tulle. Isabel's bridesmaids were the younger sisters of her best friend, newly married Catherine Forster. These two, Carmen and Rosie, were older than the others at fifteen and twelve. They were enchanted with their ivory organza dresses as Margo and Catherine adjusted hemlines and bodices.

Later, in the splendour of the deep red and gold interior of the baroque church of Santa Creu, the two fathers, Vasco Valseca and Dexter Jefferson, stood nervously checking their watches. Alongside them were two equally nervous bridegrooms, Martin and Gabriel. Each of them was flanked by his best man – Martin's friend Stephen Blackwood and Gabriel's old roommate, Joe Karlsen, happily paying a return visit to Mallorca. They all wore double-breasted pearl grey suits. Lynne Kowalski and Miquel Santiago sat alongside Rachel's mother, Miriam Jefferson. Chief Inspector Diaz was there too with his stylishly dressed wife. Guillem and Antonia sat proudly alongside a beaming Miquel Santiago and members of the Valseca family.

Apart from those who lived on the island, other relations had come from the United States, Argentina, the Spanish mainland and England. Many of Rachel's close family had flown over from the United States including a sprinkling of cousins and family friends. Martin's brother Harry and his wife had just arrived from Hong Kong, escorting Martin's mother and there were also a whole lot of friends and ex-colleagues from his old company Viacon-Weston. Distinguished guests from the island included many of Vasco's academic friends from the university.

The church was packed. The invited guests had dressed up for the occasion and there were some memorable hats. In addition there was a flock of curious local well-wishers, a few tourists – and the press. Banks of flowers were stacked against the massive columns and spilled from every niche. Their perfume filled the whole of the lofty interior as it echoed to the organ's delicate rendering of Handel's *Water Music*. Then, after a pause the organist launched into the stirring strains of Stanley's *Trumpet Tune*. More than two hundred pairs of eyes turned towards the western door of the church. There was an audible gasp as both brides entered along with their matrons of honour and brides-maids.

The ceremony was moving in its passionate simplicity. The two couples exchanged their vows as female relatives dabbed at their eyes with dainty handkerchiefs. The priest, a neatly bearded man with twinkling eyes behind gold-rimmed glasses delivered a brief but inspiring address. The choir sang anthems by Bach and Mozart – *Jesu Joy of Man's Desiring* and *Ave Verum* – as the register was signed. Young women in traditional dress performed a stately dance in the central aisle during the offertory. Then suddenly it was over and, as the organ thundered out Widor's triumphant *Toccata*, the two bridal couples led the way out into the sunshine of the square in front of the church. Two photographers, one for each couple, hurried to complete their assignments while guests jostled to take photos of their own.

When Vasco judged that enough time had passed for the camera professionals to complete their task, he gave a signal. Musicians in Mallorcan costumes appeared as if by magic and led an animated procession, headed by the newlyweds, along the narrow streets of the old town. Onlookers pressed themselves into doorways to let them pass. Flowers rained down from the upper floors of the houses along the way. A large group, including a number of tourists, cheered them as they passed through Placa Drassana. After a few more minutes they arrived at the massive oak portal of Cobaco, the historic location chosen by Vasco for the reception.

As they entered, the guests were overwhelmed by the building's lavish interior. Taking flutes of champagne offered by white-jacketed waiters, they gazed with amazement at the pictures, the antique hangings and priceless ceramics which adorned the enormous room with its lofty ceiling. At the head of the receiving line, Gabriel and Rachel stood side by side with Martin and Isabel. After embracing their guests they passed them on to another group of waiters who offered silver dishes laden with canapés. A large horseshoe-shaped table gleamed with a snow-white tablecloth, fine porcelain, crystal glasses and silverware.

In the middle of the open end of the table a gigantic column supported the ceiling beams; from chest height downwards it was covered with a dazzling display of fruit like a cascade, creating an exotic carpet around its base.

At the back of the room, under the wrought iron balustrade of the sweeping staircase, a string quartet struggled to be heard above the excited chatter. After a while all the guests found their seats, grace was said by the priest and the meal began. For the two happy couples the delicious food and fine wines might not have existed as they basked in their surroundings, revelling in the romantic atmosphere of the occasion. They were completely mesmerised by the warm tide of love and happiness which pervaded the lovely room.

There were traditional toasts and more speeches than usual – but under strict instructions from Vasco these were mercifully short. At last it was possible for everyone to get up, to move around and socialise, while the staff cleared away the large table and rearranged the room. They finished remarkably quickly, setting up a scattering of small tables and chairs around an open space for dancing. While this was going on many of the guests explored the rest of the remarkable building. Climbing the handsome staircase they found upper floors where there were salons whose balconies looked down onto the small open courtyard to one side of the main room. In that open space, the few smokers among them lit up with relief alongside the statue and water feature as they fed titbits to the birds in the aviary.

By this time the string quartet had been replaced by a five-piece dance combo. As soon as the music started Gabriel and Rachel took the floor along with Martin and Isabel. The guests clapped them as they danced, before they changed partners and, finally, dragged Vasco onto the floor to take part in an impromptu chorus line. Despite his limp, he managed remarkably well but finally had to give up amid thunderous applause.

The dancing went on and on. Waiters shuttled back and forth with trays of drinks and sweetmeats. After an hour or so the band took a break and two identical wedding cakes were presented to the newlyweds. There was much laughter as Isabel and Rachel finally managed to synchronise the first cut of both cakes, to tumultuous cheering. The dancing continued with a surprisingly spirited performance from Miquel Santiago, who whirled Margo around the floor in an energetic quickstep. Many others tried to emulate their style and there was some unexpected talent. Chief Inspector Diaz almost swept Rachel off her feet in a sensational tango. Despite the crush on the dance floor, Martin and Teresa produced a graceful and stylish waltz. Then the music stepped up a gear and the younger element took to the floor for some seriously energetic disco dancing.

While the party was in full swing, the newlyweds slipped away to a nearby boutique hotel to change. Both couples had to leave early for their honeymoons. Gabriel and Rachel were embarking on a Mediterranean cruise, sailing out of Palma that night. Martin and Isabel were flying to Frankfurt that evening, then staying at an airport hotel before their Lufthansa flight to Buenos Aires next morning. They all returned in their travelling clothes. Martin and Gabriel were similarly dressed with chinos and casual shirts, but the two girls were stylishly turned out. Rachel wore a chic pale yellow trouser suit; Isabel had chosen royal blue culottes and a fitted azure jacket. The guests applauded and made way for them as the brides had farewell dances with their fathers; Martin took the floor with his mother while Gabriel was partnered by Teresa.

Soon it was time to go. The street outside was packed with guests and passing well-wishers as the happy four embraced their families and climbed into the two Rolls-Royce limousines. The brides threw their bouquets in the air, to have them caught by two of the giggling bridesmaids. Then, under a barrage of flowers, the gleaming white cars inched carefully through the narrow streets and away into the evening twilight.

Back inside Cobaco the waiters were serving a light buffet supper of tapas at the long bar. Jugs of sangria were also placed on tables around the room to satisfy the thirsty dancers. It was going to be a long night. Vasco was beginning to feel the strain. The adrenalin which had kept him going for the last few weeks had peaked today and he was now experiencing the after-effects. Wearily he climbed to the top of the stairs where he found a dark-red salon which was empty except for abandoned wine glasses, some bottles of mineral water and a few small plates with crumbs of wedding cake. He slumped in a comfortable armchair, relishing the opportunity for a little piece and quiet – except for the distant beat of the music filtering up from the dance floor. His head was hurting again. As he massaged his right temple he had a momentary flicker of recall; he almost began to visualise some elements of his IT knowledge. Was his memory coming back, perhaps triggered by the dramatic events of recent days? Before he could focus his thoughts, the fleeting insight had evaporated like a dissolving mirage. Vasco sighed deeply, closed his eyes and laid his head back. Within seconds he had slipped into a dreamless sleep.

It was over twenty minutes later that the door was opened quietly. Lynne Kowalski, seeing Vasco asleep, tiptoed into the room. She glanced behind her for a moment before closing the door carefully. Looking down at his face, she realised that Vasco was showing all the classic signs of battle fatigue. As she gently touched his shoulder he opened his eyes immediately, one hand flying instinctively to his throbbing temple.

'We were all wondering where our host had gone,' she said, 'but I found you first. Vasco, I have to tell you that this is the most wonderful, inspirational occasion. Everyone wants to congratulate you. Nobody else could have dreamed up a fairy-tale wedding like this one.'

She paused and took a deep breath before he could reply.

'Well now, I was hoping that the drama of today's events might have kick started something in your memory. Have you had any more insights? I guess this is bad timing, but I have to take any chance I can.'

Vasco sat up.

'No, no, it's OK to talk. You have a job to do and I know you have only a short while here.' He rubbed his eyes and climbed clumsily to his feet.

'I'll walk around a bit if you don't mind. My leg stiffens up when I sit in an awkward position.'

He paused, leaning against an antique oak sideboard.

'I'll try to give you a straight answer. In a way you're right. These exciting events do seem to have stimulated something in my brain. Just a few minutes ago I had another of those unexpected memory flashes right here in this room. It was deeper and more detailed, but otherwise not much different from the others I've had before. Partial or total recall could suddenly come back next week, next month, next year – or perhaps never. I just can't say. Maybe I need another major shock to make it happen. I'll go and see the medical people next week.'

Lynne smiled thinly.

'I guess that's an honest assessment. Now I have to decide on what I and my team must do from here on in. Let me think about that for a while.'

Vasco had drifted across to the balcony overlooking the courtyard and stood there breathing the night air. Looking down he could see that the space below him was almost deserted. Most of the guests were obviously making the most of the opportunity to dance. Suddenly he stiffened and his knuckles turned white as he gripped the handrail. He turned his head.

'Come here quickly,' he hissed, 'I can hardly believe what I'm seeing.'

He pointed to a dark area in the far corner as Lynne joined him. She drew in her breath sharply. There could be no mistake. Miquel Santiago and Teresa Valseca were leaning their heads together and looking deeply into each other's eyes. As they watched from above, the two figures in the courtyard moved closer together and clung to each other in a passionate embrace.

Vasco stumbled back into the room and sat again, holding his right temple.

'If I hadn't seen that myself I would never have believed it. God, but my head hurts. I'll take another couple of pain-killers.'

As he reached to his pocket, his hand froze in midair.

'This is amazing – I've just seen another of those fleeting images. I don't know what it means, but it's an icon looking like an old ship – a caravel, if you know what that is … There, it's gone again.'

329

He swallowed the capsules, taking a drink from a bottle of mineral water on a side table.

'You just rest there a bit while I think about this.'

Lynne sat stock still, immediately understanding the importance of what he was saying. She remembered that Gabriel had told her about the caravel. On a computer desktop, it was the icon which gave immediate access to the Navegator program. So, was Vasco's memory coming back quickly after that shock or was this a false dawn? She needed to make a decision and she had to make it right now, immediately. She glanced over at Vasco, who had closed his eyes again.

There were three possible outcomes; one, Vasco would remember the Navegator program quickly; two, he would never remember it at all. The first of these would be the big prize. The second would also be OK for the USA. But a third outcome could put her country on the back foot. There was the appalling prospect that he might remember everything much later on, at a time when surveillance was slack. It might even have been withdrawn. Then, who knows, Vasco might be picked up by some very bad people and hypnotised or given mind-altering drugs to make him reveal everything.

Was that a risk she could afford to take? No way; that could give a hostile group a crucial advantage. So, how could that risk be avoided? If Vasco was unable to talk at all, then she would have achieved the second outcome. That would be a satisfactory result, even if it wasn't the best one. And national security had to come first. Despite her feelings for Vasco and his family, he might have to be silenced. An accident could be arranged here and now. He could appear to stumble on that long staircase with the marble floor at the bottom. That would surely do it, but was it justified? And there was always the possibility that he might remember everything tomorrow. It was a horrible dilemma …

Her thoughts were interrupted as Vasco opened his eyes and climbed to his feet.

'I feel a whole lot better now. Let's go and confront those lovebirds. I can hardly wait to see their faces. Perhaps you'd care to dance? Anyway I'm thirsty, so what about a glass of sangria? And my brain suddenly feels a bit clearer. It's quite possible I may remember some more stuff tomorrow. But then again, maybe not. Well, perhaps next year, even. Who knows? Come on, let's go down now.'

'Yes, indeed, Vasco, you're right. Who knows? You go ahead. I'm right behind you.'

Under the pretence of turning back to collect her purse she allowed Vasco to lead the way out of the salon. Still thinking furiously, she emerged and closed the door carefully behind her. Lynne Kowalski paused, frowned and lifted her chin. After another momentary hesitation she bit her lip and followed him to the top of the staircase.